WESTERN

Rugged men looking for love...

Depending On The Cowboy
Jill Kemerer

Rescuing Her Ranch
Lisa Jordan

MILLS & BOON

DEPENDING ON THE COWBOY
© 2023 by Ripple Effect Press, LLC
Philippine Copyright 2023
Australian Copyright 2023
New Zealand Copyright 2023

First Published 2023
First Australian Paperback Edition 2023
ISBN 978 1 867 27162 8

RESCUING HER RANCH
© 2023 by Lisa Jordan
Philippine Copyright 2023
Australian Copyright 2023
New Zealand Copyright 2023

First Published 2023
First Australian Paperback Edition 2023
ISBN 978 1 867 27162 8

MIX
Paper | Supporting
responsible forestry
FSC® C001695

Published by
Harlequin Mills & Boon
An imprint of Harlequin Enterprises (Australia) Pty Limited
(ABN 47 001 180 918), a subsidiary of HarperCollins
Publishers Australia Pty Limited
(ABN 36 009 913 517)
Level 13, 201 Elizabeth Street
SYDNEY NSW 2000 AUSTRALIA

Cover art used by arrangement with Harlequin Books S.A.. All rights reserved.

Printed and bound in Australia by McPherson's Printing Group

Depending On The Cowboy
Jill Kemerer

MILLS & BOON

Jill Kemerer writes novels with love, humour and faith. Besides spoiling her mini dachshund and keeping up with her busy kids, Jill reads stacks of books, lives for her morning coffee and gushes over fluffy animals. She resides in Ohio with her husband and two children. Jill loves connecting with readers, so please visit her website, jillkemerer.com, or contact her at PO Box 2802, Whitehouse, OH 43571.

Remember ye not the former things,
neither consider the things of old. Behold,
I will do a new thing; now it shall spring forth;
shall ye not know it? I will even make a way
in the wilderness, and rivers in the desert.
—*Isaiah* 43:18–19

DEDICATION

To my good friend Kristina Knight, whom I can always count on to ooh and aah over texts of puppies and baby goats. Love you, Kristi!

CHAPTER ONE

WOMEN MADE HIM NERVOUS. Pregnant women? Well, they terrified him.

Blaine Mayer gave the kitchen counter one last swipe, then straightened the pillows on the couch in the three-bedroom log cabin down the lane from his ranch house. The former foreman's home had been collecting dust for over a year. And that wouldn't do for when Sienna arrived.

Sienna Norden—Sienna Powell now. Blaine had good memories of being her lab partner in high school biology and hanging out with her and their friends on the weekends until she moved to Casper, Wyoming, right before junior year. She'd been one of the only women he'd ever considered easy to talk to, aside from his sisters, and they didn't count.

It had been jarring last fall when his sister Erica, now married and living in Casper, had announced she'd run in to Sienna. Since then, the two women had become good friends. When Mom had informed him a week ago that Sienna—pregnant and recently divorced—was bringing her niece and nephew to Mayer Canyon Ranch for the next two months, Blaine hadn't put up a fight.

It wasn't like he had a say in it, anyhow. Erica, too, was having a baby, and Blaine knew better than to argue with her. It would only cause tears or a battle. No thank you. Honestly, he didn't mind Sienna and her crew staying here for most of the summer. It had been lonelier than he'd expected when he'd moved to his half of the sprawling family ranch in Sunrise Bend, Wyoming, last year.

He gave the place a quick once-over. Yep, the cabin was ready. All morning he and his mother had disinfected and deodorized it. Mom had brought over new bedspreads for the guest rooms, and she'd made sure there were plenty of fluffy towels. To say she was tickled pink to be getting Sienna as a part-time helper for the candle shop *and* two teens to spoil for all of June and July would be the understatement of the century.

Blaine just hoped having them a mere hop,

skip and jump away wouldn't affect his plans for the ranch. He'd been riding out every afternoon to what he and Jet, his big brother and owner of the other half of the ranch, jokingly referred to as the dead pasture on Grandpa's land—Blaine's land now.

Blaine was convinced it could be a good source of additional hay. Last fall, he'd killed the weeds. This spring, he'd reseeded the entire pasture with drought-resistant wheatgrass.

It had been expensive. And risky.

With the dry conditions this year, he might have been better off keeping the pasture free for the cattle to graze. Now that it had been reseeded, it couldn't be grazed for two entire growing seasons. Jet, naturally, thought he was making a mistake and had told him so on more than one occasion. Maybe his brother was right.

What if the cattle ran out of grazing land this winter? What if the pasture didn't produce the hay he anticipated?

How would he feed his herd?

His phone rang, and he reluctantly took the call, stepping onto the front porch and closing the door behind him. "Blaine speaking."

"Oh, good." A woman with a no-nonsense

voice sighed. "I'm glad I caught you. It's Laura Cane. Ralph's daughter."

"Hi, Laura." Blaine had spent plenty of time on the Canes' farm as a teen. Ralph was an expert at breeding and training Australian shepherds as working dogs. Ten years ago, the man had moved an hour south to spend more time with his daughter. Blaine missed helping out with all those dog litters. "How's your dad doing?"

She hesitated, and he got a funny feeling he was about to hear bad news. "Actually, that's why I'm calling. Dad passed away two days ago. Frank and I are planning the funeral, and I don't know how to ask this, but…well, Tiara is due to have her pups within the week. I can't take off work to raise the puppies, and Dad would want Tiara and Ollie to go to someone with experience. You're the only one I could think of who could raise her pups. Dad promised two locals first dibs, so you'd have to find homes for the others if she has more. I know it's a lot to ask."

"I'm sorry about your dad." Blaine swallowed the regret that was lodged in his throat. He wished he had taken the time to drive down there and visit Ralph. Had thought about it several times over the past couple of years, but he'd never acted on it. And now, it was too late. "I didn't realize he was having health problems."

"He died in his sleep. It was unexpected, but he was eighty-two. We were blessed to have him as long as we did. The funeral's the day after tomorrow. I can text you the details if you'd like."

"Would you? My folks will want to come, too." Blaine figured she had a lot of arrangements to make, so he'd better get back to the reason for her call. He descended the porch steps and headed toward the gravel drive. "I take it both dogs are Australian shepherds…?" Blaine couldn't imagine Ralph breeding any other kind.

"Yes, Tiara is Lady Di's grandpup. Dad bought Ollie three years ago from a breeder in Montana. Beautiful dog. Those two are like an old married couple. I won't separate them, and they're too special to stop breeding. Would you be willing to consider adopting them both?"

He'd been there when Lady Di had her final litter. "I'll take Tiara and Ollie for now and raise this litter, but I'm going to have to think about continuing to breed them. It's a big commitment. Why don't I give you a call in a few months after the puppies are weaned? We can figure out where to go from there."

"I was hoping you'd say that. Thank you, Blaine. I'll bring them over this afternoon."

This afternoon? He opened his mouth to speak, but she'd already hung up. He pocketed the phone, his mind reeling with everything he'd need to do to prepare for a pregnant dog due any minute.

The rumble of tires alerted him that Sienna had arrived. Hopefully, her niece and nephew liked dogs, because he was going to need a lot of help when Tiara had her pups.

The silver crossover SUV came to a stop near where Blaine was standing. Both front doors opened, and one of the back doors, too. A tall, lanky teen unfolded his legs from the passenger seat. He had shaggy, dark brown hair, and he was wearing loose-fitting jeans, a black T-shirt and athletic shoes. The girl from the back seat stretched her arms over her head and smiled. Her hazel eyes widened and sparkled as she looked around. She had on light gray jogging pants and a pink T-shirt that said Be Happy. Long, unruly light brown hair trailed down her back.

Sienna stepped out of the driver's seat, letting out an *oof* as she placed a hand on her round belly.

Blaine inhaled sharply. She was still a stunner. Her wavy, dark red hair was a few inches shorter than he remembered, but he noticed her dimples hadn't changed a bit as she tossed him a smile. Took him right back to fifteen, stuttering pulse and all.

Enough of that. This was a platonic arrangement. Nothing more.

"Hope you had a good trip." He tipped his cowboy hat to her in greeting.

"It was good. Uneventful." Sienna slowly walked his way.

He braced himself. Should he hug her? Thrust out his hand? Back up and nod?

The decision was made for him as she held out her arms. He gave her an awkward hug with two quick pats on the back. Flames of embarrassment licked his neck, and he was pretty sure his face resembled a tomato.

"This is my nephew, Connor, and my niece, Lily." Sienna stretched out her arm to indicate the two teens and angled her neck to the side as they approached. They both said hi. "We're all excited to spend the summer here. It was kind of you to offer to put us up."

Well, technically Erica had offered, and Mom had been the one to volunteer his cabin for the three of them since it was the largest guesthouse on either side of the ranch. But Sienna didn't need to know all that.

"Glad to have you," Blaine said. "Want to tour the cabin before unloading?"

"Sure." Sienna beamed as she put her arm around Lily's shoulders and ambled toward the porch. Connor followed behind them, looking like he felt out of place. Blaine knew the feeling well. He'd spent a good portion of his life trailing two steps behind everyone else, especially his big brother.

He loped ahead and held open the front door for the trio, and when they were inside, he pointed out the bedrooms, bathroom and the large mudroom/laundry room off the kitchen.

"Wow, Aunt Sienna, this is amazing." Lily spun in a circle in the living room, looking up at the vaulted ceilings. "It's like a mountain getaway."

"Without the mountains," Blaine added cheerfully. "At least you can see them in the distance."

"Isn't this great, Connor?" Lily asked.

"Yeah, it is, Lil." His expression was hard to read, but his tone was pleasant enough.

The kids disappeared to claim their bedrooms, leaving Blaine and Sienna alone. His tongue must have tied itself into a knot, because he had no idea what to say.

"I really appreciate this, Blaine." Her big green eyes looked suspiciously watery. His gut clenched. The last time Erica was home, he'd asked her how she was doing, and she'd burst into tears and then jogged to the bathroom to throw up.

He was not making that mistake again.

"It's no problem," he said. "I lived in this cabin last year for a few months while I remodeled Grandpa's place. If you need me for anything, I'm in the big house down the lane."

"I saw it." She nodded. "You've done well for yourself. I figured this was what you'd be doing. Ranching always fit you like a glove."

She thought he'd done well for himself? Pride rushed through him, only to be dampened. Blaine was still feeling his way on making big decisions.

Their father had always been in charge until Blaine's youngest brother, Cody, had died a few years ago. Jet had taken over their father's duties while the man grieved. Then Dad retired, insisting Jet and Blaine divide the ranch between them, since their sisters weren't interested in raising cattle. The past year of being his own boss had been an eye-opener. And stressful.

"I hear you're still living in Casper," Blaine said.

"I am. I work for the community college. I'm the coordinator for special projects compliance. Basically, I help find and oversee grants. I'm thankful to have the summer off." A cloud crossed her face. "I needed this summer off."

"Yeah, I can see… Um, congratulations…" He gestured toward her baby bump.

"Thanks." Her dimples flashed again as she cradled her stomach. "I'm due in late August. Your sister helped me through a tough time. I can't wait until she has her baby, too."

"Yeah, uh…" He rubbed the back of his neck. All this pregnancy talk had him way out of his element. "Why don't I go get your luggage?" Before waiting for her reply, he pivoted and strode out the front door.

Idiot. This was Sienna, not some stranger. He couldn't even hold a conversation for two minutes? No wonder he was single.

Not that he wanted to change his status.

He marched to the back of the SUV, opened the hatch and started grabbing suitcases.

Connor jogged up next to him. "Here, I'll help."

"Okay." Blaine gave the kid a brief glance. "I'm assuming your aunt wants all this inside, so take whatever you can carry."

Connor hefted a large bin into his arms before falling in step next to Blaine. "Aunt Sienna said Lily and I will be helping out around here."

Blaine's mom had mentioned Sienna working part-time at the candle shop, but she hadn't said what Lily and Connor would be doing. Hopefully, enjoying their summer vacation.

"Can I help around the ranch? I don't want to hurt my aunt's feelings, but making candles just sounds…" He curled his lips in a sour expression.

Blaine chuckled. "I hear you, man. I'm not one to be stuck inside. You can ride out with me—that is, do you know how to ride?"

"I do. My buddy Jonah has horses. Been riding since I was six."

"Good. I can use a strong ranch hand like you. I'll introduce you to my part-timer, Bryce. He just graduated from high school. You'll meet Jim, my full-time cowboy, too. You can help us while your aunt is at the candle shop. I'll pay you, of course."

"Really? You don't have to. It's enough to be here…" Connor's voice faded as he frowned. Then he walked taller as he continued carrying the bin. "Thank you, sir."

"Call me Blaine."

A hint of a smile crossed Connor's face, and Blaine was glad to ease the kid's mind. The two of them continued unloading the back of the vehicle in silence, and when everything was inside, Blaine approached Sienna in the kitchen.

"I'll take you over to the candle shop whenever you're ready. If you'd prefer to unpack and relax, we can go there tomorrow. I have to warn you, though—Mom, Reagan and Holly are practically busting at the seams to see you."

"That's so sweet of them." Her eyes lit up. "Why don't we go over there now?"

Lily bounced over and gave Sienna a side hug. "Can we? I think a candle shop is the coolest thing in the world. I can't wait to see it."

Sienna kissed the side of Lily's head. Blaine wasn't sure what he'd expected from her and the kids, but their obvious closeness wasn't it. They made him want to linger, let some of their bond soak into him, too.

"I'll bring my truck over." Blaine rapped his knuckles on the counter and headed out the door.

The sun warmed his face as he took long strides down the lane. While he wasn't blind-sided by the fact that he was still attracted to Sienna, he was surprised to be drawn to her niece and nephew as well. It wasn't as if he lacked family or friends.

Family and friends were fine. They were safe.

He had a brother, two sisters, his mom, dad and four good buddies—plenty of bonding all around. The only person missing was Cody, and Blaine would do about anything to have his little brother back.

Back at his ranch house, Blaine climbed into the driver's seat of the truck and fired up the engine. Sienna's pretty smile plastered itself in his mind as he drove the short distance to the cabin. He was glad she'd be working with his mom and sister. They knew how to support women, unlike him.

Give him a horse, wide-open pastures and the big sky above him. He had cattle to raise, hay to bale, fences to fix and two dogs arriving soon. And that left no time for high school crushes. No time at all.

SHE'D DONE THE right thing by bringing the kids here for the summer. They needed a break from the chaos at home.

Sienna fought a yawn. After meeting all the Mayer ladies, she and the kids had been given a tour of the candle shop. Blaine's mom, Julie, and his sister, Reagan, made the candles, while his sister-in-law, Holly, managed the business and handled the marketing.

Lily was already enamored with Holly's eighteen-month-old, Clara. Sienna had a feeling her niece would want to babysit the cutie rather than help with candles. Fine by her. After meeting the Mayer clan, she had no doubt they'd welcome Lily's help in watching the child.

Connor, naturally, had hung back with Blaine. Her nephew was on the quiet side, very close to his sister and inclined to outdoor activities. He'd already mentioned he'd talked to Blaine about helping out on the ranch. She wasn't surprised her nephew would prefer ranch work, even mucking stalls, to being around half a dozen women every day.

"You must all be hungry," Julie said. "Kevin's got a big batch of sloppy joes slow-cooking for us. Why don't we head into the house and have some lunch?" She shooed everyone in the direction of the entrance. The group happily chatted all the way to the door.

Sienna fought an overwhelming wave of exhaustion. It had been a long day. A long week. A long year.

This summer getaway was an answer to a prayer. She just hoped God would answer the other prayers heavy on her heart.

The big one concerned her sister, Becca—Connor and Lily's mother. After Aaron, their father, announced he wanted a divorce and proceeded to move out four months ago, Becca had spiraled into a combination of anger, anxiety and bitterness, and it was affecting the kids. No matter how many times Sienna listened to her complain about how unfair the situation was, it wasn't enough. Becca would then unload it all on Connor, too.

Sienna sincerely hoped now that Aaron was ready to reconcile, her sister would stop burdening Connor with her tears and spiteful words about his dad. It wasn't right for her to put that on him.

Julie approached and tilted her head as she asked, "Are you okay?"

Sienna looked around and realized everyone was already outside. She forced her feet forward. "Me? Oh, yes. I'm a bit tired."

"I'm sure. We need to get you off your feet." Julie gave her a warm smile. Blaine's mom was so nice. "We're glad you decided to come spend the summer with us. When Erica mentioned you bringing Connor and Lily, I told her it was exactly what this ranch needs—a couple of teenagers to liven it up. And I don't want you thinking you have to work all the time. We want you to have a nice break before your little one arrives. Do you know what you're having?"

"No, I want it to be a surprise," she replied as they emerged into the sunshine.

"Another thing to look forward to." Julie patted her arm. "How's Erica? I talk to her every day, but it's not the same as seeing her, you know? It's about killing me not being around for her first pregnancy."

"She's good. We had a coffee date last week. Jamie's as busy as ever, and you know your daughter—full of energy." A dart of sadness pierced her heart. She wished she had a mother who wanted to be around for her pregnancy. Her own parents hadn't been in her life for years.

After her brother drowned as a child, their dad left them, and their mom became a shell of her former self. Sienna had been in eighth grade when her mother walked out of her life for good. That's why she'd moved to Sunrise Bend, to live with her grandmother.

Becca, seven years her senior, was living in Germany, where Aaron was stationed. After Grammy died before Sienna's junior year, Becca, Aaron and little Connor returned to Wyoming, and Sienna lived with them until she graduated from high school.

She and Becca were close, and they usually got along great. Her sister had always been prone to anxiety, though, and Sienna was no stranger to helping her through emotional rough patches.

"Erica does have a lot of energy." Julie strolled past potted red petunias and opened the back door of the big house down the lane from the candle shop. "I tell her to rest, but she doesn't listen to me. I'm glad you girls connected. She thinks the world of you."

"I think the world of her, too."

If it wasn't for Erica, Sienna wouldn't have had the chance to get the kids away from their home drama for a few months. She'd shared with her how uncomfortable Becca was making life for Connor. Erica also knew what a drain Sienna's own divorce had been. The offer to stay on the ranch had been a tremendous blessing.

Julie continued through the mudroom to the kitchen, leaving Sienna alone to gather her thoughts, which kept circling back to Blaine.

He was one of a kind. On the quiet side. Easygoing. And kind. So very kind.

She'd been nervous on the way here. What if he'd changed? What if he resented her and the kids staying in his guesthouse? But the instant she'd stepped out of her vehicle, she'd known. Blaine hadn't changed. If anything, he'd gotten better.

And she was a hot mess. Trying to keep everything together while her crumbling life refused to cooperate.

Sienna forced herself to join everyone in the kitchen. Conversation filled the air, along with the tangy aroma of sloppy joes. Connor and Lily both held plates overflowing with food, and her own tummy growled. She fell in line and began filling a plate.

"You and the kids can join us for supper on weeknights." Kevin, a wiry, gray-haired man with twinkling brown eyes, wiped his hands on a kitchen towel. "I cook for a crowd every Monday through Thursday. I'd cook on Friday, too, but Julie here says we have to have date night."

Date night. She loved the thought of them still dating after all these years. "Thank you, Mr. Mayer. We'd love to have supper with you if it's not too much trouble."

"No trouble at all." He beamed. "I'd be offended if you didn't eat with us."

Julie came up next to him. "I'd have asked him to retire years ago if I'd known he was going to whip up feasts all week."

"I didn't know I liked cooking until I retired." He chuckled, then pointed to the counter. "I think we need more napkins, hon."

Turning away, Sienna searched for an empty seat at the long table and set down her plate at the nearest one. After sitting, she took a bite and tried to relax.

She'd always wanted her own big happy family like this one, but it wasn't going to happen. Her ex-husband wouldn't even acknowledge his unborn child. The last time they'd spoken, Troy had informed her he was signing away all parental rights. She didn't even know if he could legally do that. She just hoped he wouldn't do anything drastic, but knowing her ex, she wouldn't be surprised if he did.

She munched on a potato chip. Would she have married him if she'd known him better?

Over the past two years, she'd done a lot of research to figure out what was causing his erratic behavior. She was ninety-nine-percent certain he had a personality disorder, not that he'd ever go to a doctor to get diagnosed.

Honestly, at this point, she couldn't even remember why she'd married him. And he must have felt the same, since he'd moved in with his much older girlfriend the day after she told him about the baby. Sienna hadn't realized he'd been cheating on her. But she couldn't say she was surprised.

"Sienna?" Blaine asked.

She blinked. "What? I'm sorry. I didn't hear you."

"Do you want me to drive you guys back after we eat? I'm sure you want to get settled."

"Yes, I do. Thank you."

She and the kids would unpack, then she was putting her feet up on the couch and resting for a good hour or two. Later, she'd take the kids into town for supplies.

One thing she was sure of—Connor and Lily were going to love Sunrise Bend as much as she did. In fact, she was going to give them the best summer ever. Becca and Aaron could work things out back in Casper. Connor and Lily could take their minds off their parents' problems. And she could rest easy knowing she'd done all she could to help them. This was the place to do it.

CHAPTER TWO

As Blaine drove Sienna and the kids back to the cabin after lunch, he toyed with the idea of riding out to the reseeded pasture and checking the new growth. If all went well, he'd be able to cut and bale hay in three weeks. But if the dry conditions continued, he'd have to harvest it sooner.

He wouldn't think about that scenario now. He had enough on his mind.

After he parked the truck, a large SUV kicked up a cloud of dust in the distance. It continued down the long drive before stopping in front of his house.

Tiara and Ollie. Forget checking the pasture. The dogs had arrived.

Laura stepped out. In a faded T-shirt and jeans, she was tall with short gray hair. Blaine loped down the lane to greet her, then gave her his condolences once more.

"Thanks, Blaine. I don't like making Tiara adjust to a new home this late in the pregnancy, but I'm at my wit's end on what else I could do."

"She'll be fine. In fact, she'll feel right at home here in no time." Blaine glanced over his shoulder. Sienna and the kids had followed him. "Do you guys like dogs?"

"Yeah!" Lily shouted. Connor nodded.

"Well, I'm going to need some help with these two." Blaine hitched his thumb to where Laura was letting the dogs out of the back seat. "Tiara's due to have her puppies this week."

"She's having puppies?" Lily clasped her hands beneath her chin as the beautiful and very pregnant blue-merle Aussie stepped down from the SUV. Laura handed Blaine the leash.

"She sure is." He bent to let Tiara smell the back of his hand, then he stroked the fur on her back and scratched behind her ears. She had a white forehead, chest and front paws. Her back and ears were light gray with black patches, and her blue eyes were surrounded by tan fur. She sure was a beauty.

"Look, Connor, she has blue eyes." Lily pointed to the dog. "How many puppies will she have?"

"The vet thinks at least three." Laura held a

leash for Ollie, a gorgeous black tri. The dog was mostly black with white paws, a white chest and tan around his eyes, cheeks and hind legs. Two brown eyes looked up at Blaine as if to say "pet me, too."

"He's a looker, isn't he?" Blaine took his leash.

"Yes, their previous litter was colorful." Laura gave the dogs a bittersweet smile. "It will be interesting to see the variety of pups in this one."

Anticipation rushed through him as it all came back—gathering supplies, checking her temperature and, when she was ready to deliver, the wonder of watching each tiny pup come into the world.

"Is there any way you can keep Ollie away from her for a few weeks after she gives birth? I don't want him bothering her. They get along great, but she'll have enough on her mind without his energetic self. I can take him back with me if need be."

"We can keep Ollie with us." Lily, all bright-eyed and hopeful, was petting him, and the dog lapped up the attention. "If it's alright with you, Aunt Sienna."

Blaine straightened. She seemed fine with the idea. "We'd love to have him."

"Ollie should stay with Tiara until she's ready to deliver," Laura said. "Dad trained both to herd, so don't be afraid to use him around the ranch."

Blaine gestured to the kids. "After Tiara has the puppies, Ollie can sleep in the cabin with you guys. In the meantime, he'll stay with me."

"That would be great." Connor crouched down and ruffled the fur on Ollie's head.

"Won't she miss him after she has the puppies?" Lily chewed her lower lip.

"She'll have too much on her mind to worry about Ollie during the first week or two after having her puppies." Laura gestured for Lily to come around the rear of the vehicle, where she lifted the back hatch. "We're going to set up a whelping box for her in one of Blaine's rooms. I brought everything Tiara will need. Why don't you help me get this stuff inside?"

"Do you mind holding them for a minute?" Blaine handed the leashes to Sienna. Their hands touched, and the feel of her soft skin whispered sensations up his arm. How could a simple touch be so disorienting?

"I don't mind at all." She met his gaze, and he was transported back to being sixteen, hanging on her every word but too shy to do anything about it.

"That's a lot of stuff." Lily poked around the boxes.

"Tell me about it." Laura grabbed a stack of folders and waved them to Blaine. "Here are their papers, vet records and the breeding book Dad used."

Blaine sprang into action, stacking the folders onto one of the bins and hauling it out of her vehicle. It didn't take long to move everything into his house. Once the back was unloaded, he told Laura he'd see her at the funeral. She gave Tiara and Ollie a final goodbye, swallowed hard and drove away.

"Well, guys," Sienna said, handing the leashes back to Blaine. "I'm getting pretty tired. Why don't we unpack and then go into town for supplies?"

Connor and Lily exchanged a glance.

"Go ahead and take a nap, Aunt Sienna," Connor said. "We're going to help get the dogs settled."

"You can see them later." She arched her eyebrows. "You need to unpack."

"Okay. We'll unpack." Lily sighed grudgingly before turning to Blaine. "Mr. Mayer, do you want us to help get Tiara's things organized once we're done?"

"You can call me Blaine, Lily." He was enjoying the teens. "And, yes, I could use some help."

He didn't really need help. He remembered exactly how Ralph's room had been set up for deliveries. But Lily seemed so eager and happy, it made him want to keep her eager and happy.

"Yay! We'll unpack our stuff and come over, right, Connor?"

"Can Ollie come to the cabin with us?" Connor's eyes met Blaine's.

"Why don't you let me give him a tour of my house with Tiara first? This is going to be a new experience for both of them, and it will be easier for them to be together right now." Then he turned to Tiara. "Are you ready, girl? Let's get you inside. You can check out your new home."

"Okay." Connor gave Ollie one more longing look. "We'll be over as soon as we unpack."

Blaine glanced at Sienna. "If you need anything, call or text me." He'd given her his number at lunch.

"I will." The three of them turned and headed back to the cabin, leaving him, Ollie and Tiara standing in his driveway.

"Come on, you two. We'd better get the

whelping box set up. We don't want those pups of yours arriving without everything prepared." Blaine led the dogs up the walkway to his house. Both were alert, sniffing the grass as they went along. Inside, he unhooked their leashes and let them roam around. He watched Tiara carefully. She was heavy with puppies, but she didn't seem uncomfortable or out of sorts. In fact, her curiosity kept her moving at a rapid pace.

He followed them from room to room, mentally deciding where he would set up the dog nursery. The spare bedroom next to his was the best option. It had a comfortable bed where he could sleep those first nights after she had the pups, and it had plenty of space for him to set up her supplies.

Blaine put together the whelping box and lined it with some of the soft blankets Laura had provided. He was glad to see Ralph had upgraded to a box with a pig rail—a protector rail—to keep the newborns from accidentally being smothered by their mom. To his surprise, Tiara walked right into it, circled twice, lied down and fell asleep. It wasn't easy being a pregnant dog, evidently.

Ollie stayed close to Blaine as he hauled the

rest of the bins into the room, stacked towels next to the dresser, put piles of soft blankets in one of the drawers and arranged all the necessary supplies on top of the dresser. He flipped through the breeding journal, noting the details of her pregnancy.

A knock at the front door had him clamoring to his feet and hurrying down the hall. On his doorstep, Connor and Lily were grinning.

"Where is she?" Lily asked. "Did she have the puppies yet?"

Connor rolled his eyes but didn't say anything.

"Not yet. According to Ralph's breeding journal, it should be toward the end of the week."

Ollie zoomed straight to Connor, then sat at his feet and looked up at him. The shimmer in Connor's eyes as he petted the dog told Blaine everything he needed to know. The kid already loved Ollie.

Blaine didn't blame him. He loved dogs, too. The ranch always had an array of working canines on it, and Jim's border collie, Ringo, rode out with them every day. It would be good to have another dog helping herd the cattle.

"Come on, I'll take you to Tiara's room." Blaine gestured for them to follow him. "Is your aunt doing alright?"

"Yeah, she fell asleep on the couch." Lily skipped over. Ollie ran ahead and Connor joined them.

Blaine took them past the living room and kitchen, then down the hall to the spare room where Tiara was now sitting up, tail wagging, as Ollie sniffed her ear.

"Aww, look, they love each other," Lily said.

"Do you think he'll be okay with us in the cabin?" Connor asked Blaine. "I mean, after she has the puppies? He's always lived with her, and he'll have to get used to sleeping in a strange place by himself."

Connor would have to get used to sleeping in a strange place, too, and Blaine wondered if the kid missed home, if he was nervous about staying at the ranch for weeks on end.

"I think he'll be okay. But maybe he could sleep in your room if you're worried."

Lily's face fell, and Blaine realized his mistake. "Or you two could take turns."

He didn't see how that would work, but he didn't know what else to say. This was why he tried not to get involved in other people's business.

"It's okay." She lifted her chin. "Once the puppies are born, I'm going to have to spend a lot of time with them, so Ollie can stay in your room, Connor."

Blaine hadn't expected that. "Do you want to be here when she gives birth?"

"I'm not sure." Lily's nose scrunched. "I mean, yeah, it would be cool to be there, but I don't know. Will it be bloody?"

"There are a few drops here and there. Mostly, Tiara will be shaking and panting between puppies."

"What's all this stuff for?" Lily drifted over to the dresser, noting the thermometer and all the other supplies.

Blaine explained what everything was used for, and she nodded eagerly throughout, asking lots of questions.

"Here's the breeding book I mentioned." Blaine pointed to the folders. "You might want to check it out."

"Yoo-hoo, I'm coming in." Sienna's voice carried from the front hall.

Lily raced out of the room and yelled, "Aunt Sienna, you have to see this!"

Blaine hitched his chin at Connor. "It might be weird staying here for the first couple of nights. I'm sure you miss your house and parents and friends."

He swallowed nervously. "Yeah, but it's fine. Like Aunt Sienna said, it's an adventure."

"You've got a good attitude." Blaine clapped his hand on Connor's shoulder. "If you want to loaf around for a few days—enjoy some summer vacation—I don't mind."

"No." He shook his head rapidly. "I want to help."

"Okay. Ollie will come with us. A good herding dog is worth his weight in gold on a ranch."

"How do you train a dog to herd?" Connor seemed to have a whole new appreciation for Ollie, who was snooping around the box in the corner.

Before he could answer, Lily dragged Sienna by the hand into the room. "See? It's Tiara's own pregnancy ward. Doesn't she look happy?"

"She does. What a great place for her to have her babies." Sienna's skin was flushed and her hair less tidy than before. She glanced at Blaine. "I hate to break up the party, but we really need to get some groceries."

"No problem." His voice was as gravelly as the driveway.

"I don't want to leave Ollie." Connor looked concerned. "It's his first day here."

"And Blaine's going to let me look at the breeding book." Lily's eyes pleaded with her aunt.

"They can stay here while you shop," Blaine said. "I don't mind."

"If that's what you guys want…" She gave them all a smile that didn't quite reach her eyes. "I'll just run into town and grab a few things. I'll be back before you know it."

"Okay," Connor said. "Hey, would you mind getting some beef jerky?"

"And gummy bears," Lily added.

"Got it." She took out her phone and made a note to herself before looking up. "Anything else?"

Connor and Lily walked her to the front door, telling her their requests, and then she opened it and waved to them both. Blaine stood behind the kids and watched her as she climbed into her vehicle. He continued staring as the kids turned their attention back to the dogs.

All that familiar red hair and those flashing dimples brought up questions. Like why was she divorced? And how could a man let a woman like her walk away?

Blaine had purposely *not* asked his mother or Erica any questions about Sienna. Figured it would be better that way. The less he probed, the easier it would be to remain detached. But now he wondered…

He closed the door and turned to Lily. "Let me get you that breeding book."

DITCHED BY HER own kin. Sienna drove down Main Street and, on a whim, went right on by Big Buck Supermarket to see if downtown Sunrise Bend had changed much in the years she'd been gone. How many times had she longed to drive back? To see her old friends? To soak in the town where she'd felt so at home during a terrible time in her life?

But she'd never gotten the nerve to come back. She'd lost contact with her high school friends years ago, and part of her had always worried that her memories were sugarcoated, better than the real thing. The reality of Sunrise Bend in the present might spoil her sweet view of the past.

She slowed her vehicle as she reached downtown. The candy shop was still there. A few new stores had opened, and one of them caught her attention. Brewed Awakening?

Coffee? *Yes, please!*

Sienna eased the compact SUV into one of

the angled parking spots in front of the coffee shop. If this place made decaf blended iced coffees, she'd be the happiest woman alive.

The baby kicked as Sienna stepped onto the pavement. Probably could sense the coffee coming soon. Smart child. She rubbed her belly affectionately.

Her life was messy at the moment, but this baby was the best thing she could ever imagine. She just wished it would have a father in its life. There was still a chance Troy wouldn't be rash and give up his parental rights. But even if he didn't, she had no illusions about him being a steady presence in their child's life. He was too erratic. She didn't see that changing.

She went inside and waited in line behind two older women. The interior was not the rustic affair she'd expected in a town like this. It was bright, modern and comfortable. She could see herself coming here often. In fact, a slideshow of future snapshots that were never going to happen rolled through her brain. Her carrying her baby inside at Christmastime for a coffee break. Sipping an iced brew while holding the toddler's hand in the summer. Getting a hot chocolate together after school in the fall.

"May I help you?" A striking brunette wiped

her hands down her denim apron. She was wearing a form-fitting black T-shirt and a necklace with a bird charm.

"Do you sell decaf blended iced coffee?"

"Yes, we do. What flavor can I get you?"

"Salted caramel, please."

"Coming right up." The woman turned away to make the drink, and Sienna scolded herself. Maybe her penchant for living in fantasyland was why she hadn't ever made the trip back to Sunrise Bend. One second in this coffee shop had been all it took to picture a rosy future for her and her baby here.

But she didn't have a future here. And she couldn't let herself forget it.

Two months. Then she'd be driving back to Casper, praying Becca and Aaron had worked things out, and resuming her normal life, albeit alone.

A bell above the door chimed. "Hey, Bridget."

Sienna turned to see who was speaking. A woman holding a small boy's hand came up to the register. Sienna scooted down to the end of the counter to give them space. She couldn't help peeking at the boy, likely three or four, with dark hair, brown eyes and a big toothy grin. He was adorable.

"Oh, hey, guys." The woman behind the counter—Bridget, obviously—looked over her shoulder from where she was making the drink. "And how is Tucker today?"

"Mama's taking me to the candle store. I have to be gentle with Cwara." His lisp was the cutest thing ever.

The candle store. They must be headed to Mayer Canyon Candles. The thought of working there, even part-time, filled her with cheer. The ladies all seemed fun and professional. She was really looking forward to spending time with them and doing something creative for a change.

"That sounds fun." Bridget injected excitement in her voice. "I know you'll be very gentle with Clara." He nodded solemnly. She turned her attention to his mother. "How's your dad doing, Tess?"

"Not good…"

Tess… Sienna drew her eyebrows together. She vaguely remembered a girl named Tess a few years younger than her. The two women finished their conversation, and Bridget handed Sienna her drink.

"Wait, are you Sienna?" Tess's jaw dropped and her brown eyes began to sparkle. "I'd recognize that gorgeous red hair anywhere. You probably don't remember me. I moved here not long before you moved away, and I was a few grades behind you."

"I do remember you." Sienna tucked away the compliment and pushed a straw into the lid. She didn't always love her red hair, and to hear it described as gorgeous was nice indeed. "It looks like you've been busy. Is this your little boy?"

"This is Tucker. He's three." Tess lovingly smoothed his hair. "And I have another one on the way. I see you've been busy, too." She grinned, pointing to Sienna's baby bump.

"How wonderful. Yes, I'm due at the end of August."

"It's baby season." Bridget, busy with Tess's order, gave them a backward glance. "I guarantee Holly gets pregnant soon."

"They've only been married for two months." Tess shook her head.

"So? There are babies in the air around here lately."

"I can't argue with you about that," Tess said. Then she turned to Sienna. "By the way, this is Bridget Renna, soon to be Bridget Tolbert. Do you remember Mac? They're engaged." Tess's eyebrows soared as if it was the best news ever.

"How exciting!" Sienna added just enough enthusiasm into her tone. She did remember Mac. Cute, rich, nice. He'd never been her type, though, and she was absolutely sure she'd never been his, either. Looking at Tess and Bridget, she couldn't help feeling they had their lives together, while hers had fallen apart. "Congratulations."

"Thank you." A smile brightened Bridget's face. "It's hard to believe how much my life has changed in the past six months."

"I hear you," Sienna said almost under her breath.

"So what brings you back?" Tess asked Sienna.

"I'm working part-time at Mayer Canyon Candles until the end of July. My nephew, Connor—he's sixteen—and my niece, Lily, who is thirteen, are with me. Erica offered to let us spend the next two months in one of the empty cabins."

"And your husband's okay with that?" Tess teased.

"We're no longer together." Sienna pushed

away the bitterness those words brought up. "We got divorced."

Tess's face fell as she exchanged a glance with Bridget. "I'm so sorry—I had no idea. What a dumb thing to say."

"It's okay."

Bridget faced Sienna then. "Are you staying on Jet's property or Blaine's?"

"Blaine's." Sienna could have hugged her for changing the subject.

"Oh, good," Tess said with enthusiasm.

Why was that good?

"You'll have to join us the next time we have a Friday night get-together." Bridget handed Tess the two to-go cups. "You can bring your niece and nephew. I'm sure Kaylee would love to meet them."

"Kaylee?" Sienna asked.

"Sorry, I've gotten so used to everyone knowing everyone around here—Kaylee is Mac's sister. She's sixteen."

"Oh, yeah, that would be great." She'd worried about Connor and Lily being isolated at the ranch. "I'm sure they would love to meet her. Although, they're both currently obsessed with Blaine's new dogs."

"New dogs?" Tess took a sip.

"Yeah, they arrived a couple hours ago. Both Australian shepherds. The female is pregnant. I think he took them in as a favor. A woman dropped them off while we were there."

"I'm heading to the candle shop now to discuss their invoicing system," Tess said. "I'll find out the scoop on the dogs."

"Oh, do you work there, too?" Sienna asked.

"I own a bookkeeping service. They're one of my clients. I love it because it gives me an excuse to hang out with them whenever I need a break from everything."

"The candle shop is amazing."

"That it is."

"Well, I'd better get going. I'm sure I'll be seeing you around." Sienna gave them both a smile, waved to Tucker and headed to the door. She hadn't expected everyone to be so friendly. And in the years that she'd been away, she'd forgotten how towns this small worked. Everyone seemed to know everyone else. Along with everything about them.

Which meant it was only a matter of time before the entire town knew she was divorced and about to be a single mom.

Sighing, she got back into her car and set the iced coffee, which was delicious, into the cup holder. People knowing her business didn't bother her. It wasn't as if she could change anything. But Connor and Lily... She didn't want anyone gossiping about them. Especially not about Connor. Her nephew often grew quiet and withdrawn after talking to his mom. If Becca would just stop dumping her problems on him...

Being away would help. Sienna wanted him to have a carefree summer.

After starting the vehicle, she let it idle and sipped her drink. She'd be there for Lily and Connor, the way she always had. She'd promised herself long ago that she'd be their rock. And nothing would change that.

HE HADN'T THOUGHT this through. He needed to get a plan in place for the Tiara situation.

The following morning, Blaine helped Tiara and Ollie into the back seat of his truck. The day was warm, without a lick of moisture in the air. He kept praying for rain, but it never showed up.

He drove the truck down the long driveway leading out to the main road. Earlier he'd taken Tiara's temperature—100.4 degrees, which was good since it meant she wasn't approaching labor. But when she did go into labor, he was going to have to drop everything to help her deliver the puppies. He would also need to watch her and the newborns closely the first week, which meant someone else would need to take care of the cattle.

His full-timer, Jim, was capable of handling the ranch duties during the day, and his part-timer, Bryce, worked every morning. Blaine planned on speaking to them both later about taking on extra duties once the puppies arrived. In the meantime, he couldn't leave Tiara alone when she was this close to giving birth.

His mom would know what to do.

Blaine turned onto the road leading to the other side of the ranch. The pastures spread out for miles. He passed Jet and Holly's new house, then his parents' house, and parked in front of the pole barn, where the candle business was housed.

He held open the door for the dogs to exit out of the back seat, then led them both into the showroom, where Holly and Reagan were standing in the kitchen area, laughing and sipping from mugs. Little Clara was pulling on Holly's pant leg. Mom was nowhere to be seen.

Although this was his family, he avoided

coming into the candle shop as much as possible. The gang of Mayer women always asked him questions he didn't know how to answer. None of the questions were about things he actually wanted to discuss, like the new calves or how the reseeded pasture was growing. No, they asked things like had he noticed Janelle wasn't sitting next to Richie in church? And then they'd suggest Blaine should call her. Blech.

Janelle was not his type.

Red hair and dimples were.

Stop thinking about Sienna. It's a dead end.

"Blaine!" Reagan face lit up. His sister was five years younger than him. A dreamer and very creative, she had a big heart. "I heard you're having puppies."

"Well, not me personally." He grinned as she crouched to pet Tiara, then Ollie. "This one here is, though."

"Can I get a ride with you to the funeral tomorrow?" Reagan asked, straightening.

"Yeah. Are Mom and Dad coming, too?"

She nodded. "But they want to go to the outfitter shop after, and I cannot stand around for an hour while Dad touches every saddle. I have my limits."

He chuckled. "Point taken."

Holly, carrying Clara, approached and pointed to the dogs. "See the doggies?"

"Woof, woof," Clara said, twisting in her arms and clapping.

"You know she's going to adore them." Holly lowered her to the floor, keeping her arms circled around the child. The dogs sniffed Clara, causing her to giggle. Holly sighed. "I am *not* ready for a puppy yet."

"Don't worry. You have plenty of time for a dog or two when she's older." Blaine doted on his niece. After handing the leashes to Reagan, he scooped up Clara into his arms and tweaked her nose. "You like the dogs?"

"Woof, woof." She beamed at him, placing her chubby palms on both his cheeks.

"You're getting pretty smart, little lady."

She smooshed his cheeks together. He couldn't help but laugh.

His mom came through the workshop door and made a beeline to him. "My, my, Tiara looks ready to pop, doesn't she?" She gently stroked the dog's fur, and Tiara's tail wagged.

"Yeah, about that. I'm in a bit of a bind." He handed Clara back to Holly. "I can't keep an eye on Tiara while I'm checking cattle."

"Oh, don't worry." Mom waved off his concerns. "Your dad will pick her up first thing in the morning and bring her to our house. He'll be glad to watch her for you. If he thinks she's close to going into labor, he'll give you a call."

Blaine was taken aback. Of course. Problem solved.

Why hadn't he thought of asking his dad? The man was retired and had time on his hands. Probably because after Cody died, Dad had withdrawn in his grief, and Blaine had been uncomfortable around him. He'd gotten in the habit of not asking for his father's help, but it was time to change that.

"Should I go over there now and ask him?" Blaine jerked his thumb to the door.

"It wouldn't hurt. Take the dogs, too. Then Tiara will be able to nose around the house and get used to being there." Mom pivoted toward the kitchen area. "Have time for a cup of coffee first?"

He debated escaping. He'd made it this long without any hints about getting a girlfriend. Why push it?

Mom's eager eyes did him in, though. She loved it when he stopped over, and he hated letting her down.

"Sure." He followed her and dragged out a

stool from under the counter to sit on. The dogs had their noses down and were smelling around the space with Reagan patiently holding their leashes. Holly took Clara over to her desk, where there was an adjacent play area.

"How is Sienna settling in, poor thing?" Behind the counter, Mom poured him a cup and slid the mug his way.

"Why do you say 'poor thing'?"

"Well, it can't be easy on her." She eyed him over the rim of her mug.

"Coming here for the summer with her niece and nephew?" He wasn't sure what Mom was getting at.

"No, Blaine, I'm talking about being pregnant and divorced. It's scary. But, yes, I give her a lot of credit for taking her niece and nephew for the summer. That isn't easy, either."

Sienna made it look easy. She made it look like she'd been a mother figure to both kids all their lives. They loved her, and she loved them. It was obvious.

"Just be extra gentle with her." Mom gave him *the look*. He wanted to roll his eyes like a sixth grader and give her a snotty *okay*.

"I will." To be honest, he didn't plan on spending much time with Sienna. He was busy with the ranch. She'd be working here, and when she wasn't, she'd be with Connor and Lily. There really wasn't much reason for them to interact.

"I mean it. Look out for her. She's got too much on her plate right now. We need to support her."

"Got it." But did he? How much support was he supposed to give? He wasn't even sure what his mother meant. He didn't want to know, either.

At least they were in agreement about Sienna deserving to be treated gently. He had no problem with that. But he still didn't plan on spending any more time with her than was necessary. His attraction to her hadn't faded, and she wasn't in any condition for a relationship. Why put himself through the pain of wanting something he couldn't have? He knew better than to get too close to a fire.

CHAPTER THREE

IT WAS TIME to give up on her hopes that her sister would stop calling Connor to cry and complain about Aaron. Didn't Becca understand Connor was her son and not her therapist? He shouldn't have to hear bad things about his dad. It wasn't right.

No matter how many times Sienna had gently asked Becca to stop dumping her problems on Connor, her sister wouldn't listen.

So much for her great plan of out of sight, out of mind.

Sienna slipped out of the cabin and quietly shut the front door behind her Thursday morning. So far, staying at the ranch had been great. In the three days they'd been here, Connor was smiling more often and playing with Ollie. He acted like any other sixteen-year-old boy would. But last night Sienna had overheard him talking to his mom, and he'd returned to serious mode again.

It infuriated her when Becca did this.

Maybe she should talk to her sister again about boundaries. Sienna was the one Becca usually turned to for emotional support. She no longer allowed her to cry or repeat the same complaints for hours anymore. It was too draining. And she didn't want Connor dealing with it, either.

Trying to shake off her nerves, she headed to the lane leading to the stables. The kids were sleeping in, and she'd been watching the comings and goings of the ranch enough since arriving to know Blaine would be riding back to the stables soon. She didn't have a clue as to what he did all day, but she did know the first hours of his mornings were spent on horseback.

The sun cast a glow on the sparse grass, flaxen in color due to the lack of rain. Normally, she'd soak in the view of the prairie and cattle grazing, but she had a lot on her mind.

Was it wise to tell Blaine what was going on with Connor? She kept her private life... private. And this was Connor's life, not hers. At this point, though, she felt it was necessary. Blaine spent hours with her nephew every afternoon, and he needed to know what Connor was going through, the pressure he was under. That way he wouldn't inadvertently make her nephew's problems worse.

Plus, she didn't want him misconstruing Connor's silence as defiance or rudeness.

The pounding of hooves made her pause. Right on time. Her breath caught at seeing Blaine on the large quarter horse with white forelegs. Ollie trotted alongside him.

What a cowboy.

He was handsome and rugged and everything she found attractive in a man, especially wearing that cowboy hat, a short-sleeved shirt, jeans, chaps and cowboy boots. Those blue eyes and dark blond hair were heart-stopping enough. His tanned arms were corded with muscles he'd earned working on the ranch. He was a sight that would brighten any woman's day.

Too bad she had no business looking. Had it slipped her mind that she was fresh off a divorce and pregnant? Maybe he had a pair of blinders in the stables she could borrow. The last thing she should be doing was checking out Blaine Mayer.

Her attraction was a dead end. She belonged in Casper, near Connor and Lily and Becca.

Blaine slowed the horse, dismounted and,

with the reins in his hand, strode over to her. Ollie joined them, and she petted the dog.

"Is something wrong?" He frowned, wiping his forehead right below his hat. "Are you feeling okay?"

"Nothing's wrong." It was so kind of him to ask how she was feeling. His mom, Holly and Reagan asked her often, too. She appreciated their concern. "I was hoping you'd have a minute. I wanted to discuss something with you."

His frown deepened. "Of course. Let me deal with Boots and I'll be right back."

She waited while he led the horse through the stables. He called out, "Bryce, would you come here a minute?"

The baby chose that moment to kick, and a shot of joy eased her worries. The rest of her life might be complicated, but having this child wasn't.

"Okay, I'm all yours." His face grew red. "I mean, I'm ready to talk. Or listen." His jaw shifted. "Let's go to the backyard. There's a bench swing. It'll be more comfortable than standing."

"Sure." The simple act of strolling next to him brought back a batch of memories and impressions. "Do you remember when we all went to the rodeo? Allie, Luke and Morgan ditched us, and you and I spent an hour combing the place for them."

He glanced at her, grinning. "Yeah, and we finally gave up and bought French fries and iced lemonades."

"They were delicious. And we actually watched the rodeo."

"They acted surprised when they caught up with us later."

"Did they really think we hadn't noticed they'd been gone half the day?" She laughed. "It was a good thing they took their time. I was so mad when we were trying to find them. I probably would have given them a piece of my mind and regretted it later. You were the one who said we should grab something to eat and not let them ruin our day."

"I did?"

"Yes, and I've never forgotten it."

His steps faltered. Sienna glanced his way, then mentally shrugged as he fell back into his easy stride. His backyard came into view, and he gestured to the wooden bench swing. The frame had been mounted on a concrete slab almost flush with the lawn.

"Have a seat," he said.

She did, although none too gracefully. Ollie sprawled out on the lawn, and Blaine leaned his forearm on the frame, watching her. It made her cheeks feel warm, so she patted the seat. "Why don't you sit down, too?" And not stare at her. She couldn't take the scrutiny.

"Nah, I'm good." Was that fear in his eyes? Couldn't be. Not this big, strong cowboy.

"I wanted to talk to you about Connor." She wrapped her arms under her stomach, clasping her hands lightly. A breeze tickled the hair around her face. She loved the warmth of summer after long, harsh Wyoming winters.

"Something wrong?"

"No." She shook her head. "He's, well… He can be…" Why did confiding in Blaine feel like she was inviting him to either criticize her or get close to her? She wanted to have an easy friendship with him—like when they were younger—but letting him in on the realities of her life and Connor's felt intimate. Too intimate.

A deep wrinkle formed in his forehead. "Is there something I should be worried about?"

"Yes. Well, not worried, exactly." She blew out a breath. "He's on the quiet side, and I don't want you to get the wrong impression."

"So he doesn't talk much." Blaine shrugged. "No big deal. I'm older, technically his boss and he doesn't really know me."

"I have a feeling he'll be quiet today, and he can come across as sullen, but he isn't. He just has a lot to deal with."

"Like what?"

She hesitated a moment. "One of the reasons I brought him and Lily here was so he could have some separation from what's going on at home. Their mom—Becca—is my sister. I love her dearly, and I don't want you to think I'm bad-mouthing her, but Aaron, their father, left about four months ago, saying he wanted a divorce."

"I'm sorry to hear that." His blue eyes shimmered with sympathy.

"It shocked her. He wasn't having an affair or anything. I don't know exactly what happened. All I know is my sister didn't handle it well and started confiding in Connor, often crying or complaining about Aaron."

He winced.

"No matter how many times I tell her—as gently as possible, of course—that she's putting her son in a difficult position and it's not fair for him to be in the middle, she doesn't stop."

"Does he ever see his dad?"

"They always had a decent relationship before Aaron left, but they haven't spent any time together since the breakup. And I'm hoping… Well, Aaron is in Casper now with my sister. They're trying to work things out."

"Ahh." A look of understanding crossed his face. "You're giving them space. That's why you're here."

His response was why it was dangerous to get close to him. He was perceptive and understanding, which tempted her to lean on him. But every man she'd ever leaned on had let her down. Walked away. As if she'd meant nothing to them.

She couldn't face that kind of rejection again.

"Yes, but it's more." She forced herself back to the issue at hand. "I brought Lily and Connor here so they could be normal teens for a few months, away from the drama of their home life. The thing about my sister, though, is she's either hot or cold. When she's happy, everyone's happy. When she's miserable, she repeats her troubles to anyone who will listen, including her son. And she can't always see clearly."

"That must be frustrating."

It was. In fact, it upset her and made her

sad. She'd spent hour after hour listening to her sister spewing about what a jerk Aaron was and crying about being left to fend for herself. Sienna had held Becca's hand, hugged her and brought takeout to eat with her night after night. For months she'd been wound tight with worry thinking about Lily and Connor dealing with the divorce. And this had been when she'd been dealing with her own divorce. It had been a rough year.

No matter how much emotional support Sienna gave, Becca needed more. From everyone. And she was so self-involved when things were bad, she couldn't see how it affected the loved ones around her.

"Yeah, well, it's hard to keep up with her," Sienna said. "One day Aaron is the biggest jerk who ever lived, and the next day she's ecstatic because he reached out and held her hand on their way to couples' therapy. It's like being the passenger on an emotional roller coaster. But you can never get off. I don't want Connor dealing with it."

Blaine rubbed his chin, his gaze off in the distance.

She'd said way more than she should have. Way more than she'd intended.

"You don't want me to talk to him about it." The way he said it was a declaration, not a question, and it was a relief that he understood without her having to spell it out.

"No, I don't," she said. "I just don't want you to be surprised if Connor seems down. He's not being surly or disrespectful, I can promise you that. These conversations with his mom tend to throw him in a funk."

A breeze waved between them. The scents of earth and fresh air tickled her nose. Blaine appeared to be lost in thought.

"I guess we'll have to help him." He faced her, adjusting the rim of his cowboy hat.

"Oh, no." She shook her head. "This isn't your problem."

"What were we doing in the summer when we were sixteen?" His eyes seemed to drink her in, and she blushed, uncertain where the conversation was headed.

"Getting pizza, riding horses, hopping on four-wheelers, going to the rodeo and any other local attraction that pulled into town." She had fond memories of those days. They'd been the most carefree ones she'd ever experienced.

"Then let's make sure Connor and Lily have the same thing."

There he went again, using the word *we*.

"I appreciate what you're saying, Blaine, but I've imposed too much already." She didn't want him to think she was ungrateful, but Connor and Lily were her responsibility, not his. "You don't have to do anything. I just thought it was important for you to know what's going on. That's it."

She couldn't have asked for a better response from Blaine, but it was dangerous accepting his help. Sixteen was a lifetime ago, and reliving it with Blaine, Lily and Connor might make her want more.

She'd been blessed to enjoy it once. Happiness like that didn't come around twice.

BLAINE GROUND THE heel of his boot into the dirt. He'd read that situation wrong. As usual.

He shouldn't have suggested getting involved.

Staring at Sienna's profile as she gently moved the swing back and forth with one sandal-clad foot, he had the odd sensation of having done this before. Not watching Sienna swing—no, having someone he cared about confide in him, then refuse to let him get involved.

Cody.

A flare of unexpected sadness hit him hard.

Blaine had tucked this particular memory deep down, tried to smother it until it disappeared, but it was still there, oozing guilt out of the seams of a patchwork pocket where he'd buried it.

His brother had been about Connor's age when he'd bragged to Blaine about drinking with older kids out at the flats. Blaine could still see the excitement in Cody's eyes. He'd told him not to hang out with those guys, that they were bad news. Cody had laughed it off, told him to lighten up, that if he wanted a lecture he'd have told Dad or Jet.

Those were the words that had stopped Blaine from doing the right thing. He'd liked the fact Cody had confided in him and not Jet. Everyone always went to Jet first.

But not that time.

And because of it, he'd kept Cody's secret.

If Blaine had done the right thing and told his parents, they would have kept Cody from hanging out with those guys. Then his brother wouldn't have wasted the next years of his life high and drunk, ultimately leaving the ranch in a whirlwind of anger.

And Blaine would have been able to tell him

how much he meant to him before the car accident that took his life.

Sienna stopped swinging, gripped the armrest and heaved herself to a standing position.

"Thanks for listening." She smiled. "I'd better get back."

"Wait." He wished he had time to think this through, to talk himself out of what he was about to suggest, but if he waited, he'd make the wrong choice. Just like he had with Cody all those years ago. "I know we can't change what's going on in Connor's life. His mom's going to call him, and he's going to talk to her. It's what parents and kids do. But maybe if he had things to look forward to all summer, it would help take his mind off the problems back home."

Her pretty green eyes gleamed as she digested what he was saying.

He said a silent prayer. *God, I know it's dicey getting involved with Sienna, considering we're not in a position to have a relationship, but my gut is telling me not to slink into the shadows on this one.*

"What kinds of things?"

She was actually open to his suggestion? He was surprised.

"The same things you mentioned." He

rubbed the back of his neck. "Riding horses and four-wheelers, getting pizza, going to the rodeo. There's a big Fourth of July festival every year."

"Hmm…but we were hanging out with our friends. He only has Lily."

"He has you, too." Blaine tilted his head. He belatedly remembered how packed the next eight weeks would be. He'd be cutting and baling hay sometime in June, putting the bulls out to pasture with the cows soon after…and then there were the puppies.

Promising to give Connor and Lily a fun summer with Sienna might be tougher than he thought.

"Mac's sister, Kaylee, would probably introduce him to some of the teens." He shifted his weight from one foot to the other.

"Even if she does, I don't know if he'd feel comfortable with new people so quickly." She tapped her chin. "I think you're right, though. I've been trying to get Becca to stop calling him with her problems, and she's clearly not going to. Maybe having some distractions would help. When's the next rodeo?"

"There's one every Friday if you don't mind driving half an hour to it." Excitement sprouted as he thought about spending more time with Sienna and the kids.

He should *not* be getting excited. Couldn't be, really.

She was only here for the summer.

She was having a baby.

Moving back to Casper.

And he'd still be here, trying to bring new life to a dead pasture and growing his herd. But he couldn't turn his back on Connor. He had to follow his instincts. He'd ignored them all those years ago out of pride. He wasn't ignoring them now.

His phone buzzed. He took it out of his pocket—Dad was calling.

"What's up?" he asked.

"Tiara's temperature dropped."

"I'll be right there." He ended the call and turned to Sienna. "I've got to pick up Tiara."

Her grin spread, looking as radiant as the sunrise. "Does this mean…?"

"Yep. It looks like we're having puppies tonight." Whether he was ready for them or not.

It was her phone's turn to buzz. She checked it and grimaced.

"What's wrong?"

"Nothing." The way her lips puckered told

him it wasn't nothing. She rubbed her forearms as they made their way to the front yard. Then she hitched her chin in the direction of the cabin. "I'll let the kids know today's the day."

"Are you sure everything's alright?"

"It's fine," she said curtly. "It's nothing. My ex. That's all."

Her ex.

He watched her walk to the cabin until she was halfway there.

She hadn't been divorced for long. And she was carrying the guy's child.

Did her ex want to get back together? Did she?

All the more reason for him to guard his heart. Getting close to her wouldn't be fair to either of them. He'd keep his focus where it belonged—on the ranch, the puppies and giving the teens a summer to remember. Good or bad, he had a feeling he'd be remembering it for years to come.

CHAPTER FOUR

"WHY HASN'T SHE had them yet?" Lily asked Blaine later that afternoon. He'd been in the spare room with her and Tiara for hours. Sienna and Connor had grown tired of waiting and had taken Ollie outside to play. Every so often they'd pop in to ask how it was going, and his answer was always the same. *Nothing yet.*

"Just be patient." If he had a dollar for every time he'd said those words today…

"Do you think something's wrong?" She was kneeling on the floor next to the whelping box, where Tiara was panting heavily.

"No. This is just how nature works. When the first pup is ready, it will come out. And then she'll have the remaining puppies every fifteen to thirty minutes until they're all born."

Blaine had to hand it to Lily; she was adamant about being here no matter what. Whenever Sienna checked on them, she asked Lily if she wanted to take a break, and the girl always shook her head. It reminded Blaine of his first go-round helping Ralph deliver puppies. Nothing could have dragged him away.

He checked his phone again. Jim had called earlier to let him know the herd was fine, but a section of fence needed to be repaired in one of the far pastures. The wheatgrass wasn't ready to be cut yet, so Tiara giving birth today was the best timing he could have asked for.

"Are you sure nothing's wrong?" Lily sat back and hugged her knees to her chest. "Why is she doing that?"

He studied the dog more carefully. Tiara was licking herself, and he could see her belly contracting.

"You know what? I think she's about ready." He pointed to the dog's stomach. "See how it's moving?"

Lily scrambled to her knees. "Oh, yes, I see it." Her voice trembled with excitement. "What do we do now?"

"Go ahead and put on your gloves." Blaine pulled on a pair of latex gloves while Lily did the same. "Look, she's starting to stand."

"Should we make her lie down?"

"No, she knows what to do."

He held his breath as he watched for signs of a puppy…and there it was. The first little dog came out.

"It's a blue merle," he said. "Just like his mama."

Lily's eyes glistened with wonder as she brought her hands into the prayer position beneath her chin. "Wow, she did it. What do we do now?"

"We let her and the puppy bond and then we'll move the little guy to the side. Can you make sure the heating pad is warm underneath the blanket?"

Lily placed her palm in the corner of the whelping box. "It's on."

"Good. Do you want to give Tiara some water while I log the puppy in the book? Or do you want to log it?"

"I'll log it." She stood and found the book and pen.

The puppy showed no signs of distress and was bonding with its mama. One down. Who knew how many more to go? Blaine smiled to himself. He hoped there would be plenty more.

Voices from the front hall drew his attention. Lily raced to the doorway and turned back to Blaine. "I'm going to tell them the first puppy is here." She shut the door gently behind her.

Smart girl. She'd remembered all of the instructions he'd been giving her about keeping the room warm and quiet.

Blaine stroked Tiara's head. Her tongue hung out as she lifted clear blue eyes up to Blaine while the puppy nursed. He offered her a drink of water from a cup, and she lapped it up before turning away.

The door opened a fraction. Sienna and Lily entered, followed by his dad.

"The first one arrived, huh?" His dad crouched near Tiara and nodded with a satisfied grin to Blaine. "Looks like I picked the right time to drop supper off. The puppy's cute."

"Yeah, a boy. Pretty colors, don't you think?" Blaine's chest swelled with pride.

"Sure is. It'll be fun to see what the rest will look like." Dad straightened. "Food's on the counter when you're ready. I'll let your mother know the puppies are finally coming."

"You don't want to stay?" Blaine remained kneeling, keeping an eye on Tiara.

"Nah, you've got plenty of help here." His father's eyes twinkled as he turned to Sienna and winked. "Don't you get any ideas, missy."

Sienna chuckled and rubbed her belly. "No worries there. I've got plenty of time before this one is due." Dad exited the room, and Sienna claimed his spot. "He is cute, isn't he? So tiny."

"Where's Connor?" Blaine peered back. "Doesn't he want to see the puppy?"

"He said he'll keep Ollie in the living room." Lily scooted around Sienna to kneel once more. "I think it grosses him out."

Blaine's lips twitched but he kept a lid on his laugh out of respect for the kid. Tiara's ears flattened backward as she began to pant.

"Lily, would you lift the puppy and move him to the corner like we talked about? I think Tiara's getting close to delivering another pup."

"Me? I can move him?"

Blaine nodded. Using both hands, she lifted the puppy to her chest for the tenderest of hugs, then placed it on top of the soft blanket, where the heating pad was located.

"I'm going to check on Connor." Sienna waved to the door.

"If you wait a few minutes, you'll get to see puppy number two arrive." Blaine watched as she turned the door handle.

"Uh, that's alright."

"Aunt Sienna, be sure to close the door quietly on your way out. We have to keep it warm in here for Tiara, and a loud noise might freak her out." Lily sounded serious.

"Got it."

Blaine glanced back as she left. He was surprised she didn't want to stay.

After a quick knock, the door opened slightly and Sienna's face popped back in. "Do you guys want me to fix you plates of food? Connor and I are going to eat."

"I'm not hungry," Lily said. "I need to take care of the puppies."

"I'll grab a bite later." Blaine kept his gaze on Tiara. "If you and Connor want to watch television, the remote's on the coffee table. I have a bunch of DVDs in the media cabinet, too. Help yourselves."

"Thanks, Blaine."

"I think another one's coming." Lily craned her neck to see.

"What do you think she'll have this time?"

"It had better be a girl." Her voice was dead serious. Blaine chuckled.

In no time, another puppy appeared. He and Lily repeated their routine.

"You got your wish, Lily. It's a girl. A black tri, like her daddy."

"Yay, a girl." She was careful not to raise her

voice, but the triumph rang through clearly. "Look at the little white cross on her forehead. She's so cute."

Blaine returned the dog to her mama, and Tiara licked her as lovingly as she had the boy. Lily logged the data and rushed out to tell Connor and Sienna about the new addition.

Over the next two hours, five more puppies were born. Dusk fell, and Blaine urged Lily to take a break to eat some supper, but she told him she couldn't leave the puppies. He knew the feeling. He wouldn't eat until they were all delivered.

"Do you think she's done?" Lily asked half an hour later.

"I don't think so." He had a gut feeling she had at least one more in her.

"How do you know?"

"She's still panting."

"Should I give her some more vanilla ice cream?"

"No, she's okay for now." They'd tried to give Tiara a calcium supplement after puppy number four, but the dog had turned her head away, so they'd given her a small scoop of vanilla ice cream to lick. She hadn't turned her head away from ice cream. Who would?

Lily continued to keep watch over the puppies in the corner of the box, and Blaine took the opportunity to stand up and stretch. It had been a long day, and he'd be staying in here to check on Tiara and the pups all night.

The door opened slightly. "Is it safe to come in?"

"Yes."

Sienna tiptoed over to check out the puppies. Lily gave her the breakdown of the litter—four boys, three girls. Of them, three were black tris and four were blue merles.

"Oh, look, Aunt Sienna, she's going to have another!" Lily pointed to the dog, whose ears had flattened.

"I'll leave you both to it." Sienna put her palms up as she backed away.

"Don't you want to stay and watch?" Lily sounded incredulous.

"That's okay. Come out and let me know what she has." The door closed again.

Sienna, skittish? The thought made him grin. Blaine had never pegged her as the squeamish type.

"How about you help her out this time?" Blaine said to Lily.

"Me?" Lily pointed to her chest. "Really?

What if something goes wrong, though? I don't want to hurt her or the puppy."

"If something's wrong, I'll take over."

She inhaled deeply and nodded. "Okay."

Five minutes later, another boy was in Lily's hands. Tears glistened in her eyes as she set the puppy in front of Tiara. He made sure the new pup—the runt of the litter—was nursing, then looked at Lily. "You did great."

"Thanks, Blaine. Thank you for letting me be here." She paused to swallow, clearly choked up. "This has been the best day of my life."

It ranked up there for him, too.

"You're going to have even better days than this one. I'm glad you were here to help. I couldn't have done it without you."

The words were true. Yes, he could have delivered the puppies and logged their stats, but having Lily here had taken a big load off his shoulders. He'd have to keep that in mind when making decisions about continuing to breed Tiara and Ollie. Could he do it on his own after Sienna and the kids left?

Did he want to?

He didn't need to decide tonight. But he'd have to figure it out before summer ended.

ALL OF THIS puppy birthing had exhausted her, and she hadn't even been in the room. Around ten o'clock that night, Sienna stifled a yawn from where she was sitting on the bed in the spare room with a good view of the whelping box. The eight puppies were so little and squirmy and cute.

After all of them were born, Connor had brought in Ollie to see Tiara for a few minutes. Her nephew had petted the pups while Ollie licked Tiara's ear, then Sienna had taken the dog so Connor could stay and enjoy the puppies for a while.

Now that Lily and Blaine had eaten supper and Tiara was enjoying some well-deserved sleep, Sienna was ready to take the kids back to the cabin and get some sleep herself.

"Well, guys, I hate to break up the party, but it's getting late."

"Aww, no fair." Lily's face couldn't have drooped any lower. "I want to stay here. What if something happens to the puppies?"

"Nothing will happen to them." Sienna had complete confidence in Blaine.

"I'll be right here all night." Blaine gestured to the bed, confirming her faith in him.

"But the tiny one can barely find room to

nurse. Look, all the other dogs are pushing him out of the way." Lily pointed to the smallest black tri, the one she'd delivered, whose little cries woke Tiara and had her nosing the pup back into the huddle of warm bodies.

"Her mama is taking care of it." Sienna put her hand on Lily's shoulder. She didn't want to rip the girl from the excitement, but they all needed to rest.

Talking to Blaine this morning about Connor felt like a lifetime ago. And then Troy had chosen that moment to text her when she hadn't heard from him in weeks. His text still had her stomach unsettled.

I miss you. I'm coming over to talk.

He missed her? Now? After all the awful things he'd said? After moving in with a woman old enough to be his mother? After telling her he never wanted to see the baby? That he didn't even want to know if it was a boy or a girl?

She didn't think so.

She'd texted him back that they could schedule a telephone call if he wanted. He hadn't responded.

"I won't be able to sleep." Lily trailed her finger down the tiny puppy's back. "I'll worry. I want to be here."

Blaine rubbed his chin. The bags under his eyes reminded her it had been a long day for him, too. He'd been so patient with her niece, so calm as the puppies were born—he had the kind of inner strength she admired in a man.

And Sienna couldn't help thinking how reassuring it would be to have a caring husband by her side when she had her own baby. That's why she'd passed on the opportunity to watch Tiara have her pups. Maybe it made it all too real—a reminder she wouldn't have a husband on hand to help with her child's birth.

She really did need to get some sleep.

"You guys can stay here if you want." Blaine's blue eyes shimmered as they met hers. "If we push the ottoman against the sectional, the kids can crash on it. And I have another guest room you could take."

Lily's face brightened with hope, and Sienna could sense the *please, please, please* about to erupt from her.

"I think we should head back to the cabin."

"I understand." Blaine stood, stretching his arms behind his back.

Sienna stared a beat too long at the chest

muscles straining under his T-shirt, then pivoted and left the room, hurrying down the hall to the living room.

"We'd better go back, Connor." She noted how comfortable he looked with his ankles crossed on the chaise and Ollie's head on his lap.

"Can I finish the movie?" Connor asked. "I want to find out what happens."

Her nephew rarely asked for anything. Lily, on the other hand, wasn't afraid to speak up about something important to her.

Blaine entered the living room with a grin. "Come on, he's got to finish the movie."

Connor blinked a hopeful glance her way. She twisted her lips as she considered. As tired as she was, she was willing to compromise.

"Okay. But as soon as it's finished, we're heading back."

"Yes." Connor pumped his fist.

"Thanks, Aunt Sienna!" Lily called from the spare room.

"You okay in there for a little while, Lily?" Blaine asked.

"Yeah!"

"Holler if you need me. I'm going to relax out here for a minute."

"I will."

Blaine pushed the enormous ottoman against the sectional and sprawled out, letting his head fall back against the cushions. Sienna sat on an oversize chair adjacent to him. It, too, had an ottoman, and the instant her legs were propped up, she felt better.

"What happens now that the puppies are born?" she asked.

Blaine lifted his head. "I'll be here with them constantly for the next couple of days. Next week, Dad offered to puppysit in the mornings so I can get some work done. I'll be on puppy duty in the afternoons. Jim, Bryce and Connor, here, offered to deal with the bulk of the chores."

The way he said it made her think he'd prefer to be out on the ranch rather than here with the dogs.

"These puppies are cramping your style, aren't they?" she teased.

"Nah." His lips curved up. "The first week is the hardest. It's just… I have a lot of stuff going on with one of my pastures."

Connor glanced at them as he continued to stroke Ollie's back. "We've been checking it every day to figure out when to cut it for hay."

She was glad her nephew was contributing

to the conversation. He seemed excited about checking a pasture. Go figure.

"Yeah, I really wanted to get out there." Blaine's face fell. "It will be a few days before I can check it again."

"Won't one of the cowboys check it for you?" she asked.

"He's got to see if it's growing right." Connor had resumed watching the movie and kept his gaze glued to the television.

"Can it grow wrong?" she asked.

"It's not growing at all." Blaine looked every bit as exhausted as she felt. "Well, that's not true. It's just the lack of rain. I'd hoped the grain would be taller and the pasture thicker by now. And time's running out."

"Oh, I see." She had no clue what pastures were supposed to look like. She did understand rain, though, and it had been weeks since they'd had any. "If it rains soon, will that help?"

He sighed, shrugging. "I want it to, but this late in the game? I have a feeling the pasture is as full as it's going to get this year. I can only hope it, along with the other pastures I cut for hay, will be enough to help feed the cattle all winter."

Another thing Sienna knew next to nothing about. "Is that all they eat? Hay?"

"I have a lot of acreage for them to graze. We move them around all winter, but the forage isn't enough, especially when it comes time for calving. So I feed them hay, too."

"The ranch keeps you busy." And here she thought her life was jam-packed.

"You don't know the half of it, Aunt Sienna," Connor said. "He takes care of the steers and rides out to make sure none of the cattle are sick. Yesterday, Jim roped a cow and gave him a shot of medicine because its hoof had something wrong with it. It was cool."

Blaine shot her a surprised look that said *a rotten hoof is cool?* She suppressed a laugh.

Connor glanced at Blaine, then Sienna. "We should take Lily around on the four-wheelers so she can see the cows and the new pasture."

Sienna blinked, realizing Blaine was right. Getting on a four-wheeler to ride out under a summer sky was Connor's idea of fun, just like it had been Blaine's and hers at that age.

Blaine held her gaze, and something stirred in her—the feeling of being young and free again.

She turned her attention to her hands resting on her lap. "You'd have to drag your sister away from the puppies first."

"No problem." Connor grinned. "We'll be here for weeks."

That they would. But would she be able to squash these feelings for Blaine?

Stay focused on the kids. It was what she did best.

CHAPTER FIVE

DRY AS A BONE. Just as he'd feared.

Blaine crouched on a bare patch in the dead pasture Monday morning. This was the first time he'd been able to get away from the puppies to check on the land. On Saturday, he'd taken them and Tiara to the veterinarian, and they'd all been deemed to be fine. By last night, he'd been exhausted from making sure Tiara had enough to eat and that all of the pups were still nursing properly and gaining weight. Even with Lily's help, the past few days had been a lot of work.

He was thankful to have a break from the puppies, even though they sure were cute. They were in capable hands with Lily and Dad. When Blaine mentioned needing to find them homes once they were weaned, Lily hadn't liked the idea at all. That's how life worked, though.

Sometimes siblings went their separate ways, and there was nothing you could do to change it.

Blaine rose, twirling a long stalk of wheat-grass between his thumb and finger. It wasn't brittle…yet. He'd have to keep a close eye on the pasture. If he waited too long, it would become brittle and difficult to cut and bale. If he cut it too early, the nutrients in the grass might be stunted.

The stalk bent between his fingers. It still had too much give in it, but it wouldn't for long. If the weather got hot and the moisture stayed low, he'd have to consider cutting the wheatgrass earlier than he'd originally planned.

Boots was nibbling on the grass, and Blaine took a moment to stroke the horse's neck before hoisting himself back in the saddle. He wasn't in a rush to return to real life. Four days of being cooped up inside without the sky above him had taken their toll.

His mental to-do list started ticking through his brain. Jim had fixed the damaged fence. The bulls were getting rowdier, a sure sign that mating season would be here soon. He'd kept several steers last fall, and they'd been behaving themselves for the time being. He doubted the good behavior would last, though.

He signaled for Boots to head toward the ridge farther out. The gully beyond it tended to hold a few inches of water even in the driest conditions. He hoped it still did.

As the ridge came into view, he added planning something fun for the kids to his list. There hadn't been time for him and Sienna to work out anything since they'd discussed it.

His phone rang, and he slipped it out of his pocket, answering the call without looking at it.

"Hello?" He hoped nothing was wrong with the puppies.

"We're getting together Friday night. It's been way too long." His best friend, Randy Watkins, was on the line, and Blaine grinned.

"Agreed. What are we looking at?" He kept an eye out for the gulley as Boots picked his way across the rockier terrain.

"Hannah's calling the girls. I offered up my grill and the backyard, but she said we're all heading to Mac's for barbecue and a bonfire."

His good mood faltered. Up until recently, when one of the guys called to get together it meant just the guys. No women. But his friends had all been pairing up, getting engaged, getting married, even starting families.

It was enough to make a single guy like him want to hurl.

"What should I bring?" He knew he sounded

like he'd been sentenced to prison rather than invited on a fun outing, but he couldn't help it.

"Bring Sienna and the kids. Bridget and Tess insist."

Another thing that annoyed him—everyone seemed to know what was going on way before he did.

"I'll ask them." But they might not want to come. Hanging out with a bunch of adults wouldn't be fun for a couple of teenagers.

"I guess Kaylee's having a few friends over, too, so they'll get to meet some other teens."

Had every argument he hadn't even mentioned been taken care of?

The women were behind this.

And it wasn't only Mac's fiancée, Bridget—who, he admitted, wasn't really the meddling type. It was the wives. Tess, who *was* the meddling type and married to his friend Sawyer Roth. And Holly, Jet's wife, who made no secret she was in matchmaking mode. Not to mention Hannah, Randy's fiancé, who taught elementary school in town and had weddings on her mind, since she and Randy had set the date for the first week in August. Mac and Bridget were getting married in September.

Which left him and Austin Watkins, Randy's brother, to hold the line and stay single. Although, now that Austin had a one-year-old son, Blaine wasn't sure how long he'd last as a bachelor, either.

"You still there?" Randy asked.

"Yeah, I'm here."

"Alright. I'll see you Friday at Mac's. Six thirty."

"Got it." He ended the call as the gully came into view. After dismounting, he bent to study the water level.

It couldn't be more than an inch deep.

This wasn't good. They needed rain more than ever.

Maybe a Friday night barbecue at Mac's would be a good thing after all. He could pick the guys' brains about the water levels at their ranches. Find out when they planned on cutting hay.

And if Sienna did come, his friends would be a much-needed buffer. Every time he got near her, he'd catch a trace of her tropical perfume or start staring at all that luxurious hair.

He'd forget she was leaving.

He'd forget she was pregnant.

He'd forget she was off-limits.

He needed to remember all of the above before he got hurt.

"THE PUPPIES WILL be in good hands, I promise." Sienna checked her makeup in the cabin's bathroom Friday while Lily continued insisting she didn't want to go to some stranger's house. "Kevin and Julie will keep them out of trouble."

"Will they even notice if little Sushi gets a chance to eat? Those other puppies bully him."

Sienna swiped on lip gloss and puckered her lips, blowing herself a kiss in the mirror. She'd had the same argument with Lily for five days running. The girl didn't want to go to Mac's. She wanted to stay here with the puppies.

But she'd spent almost every waking hour with them already. Sienna had practically dragged her to the candle shop every afternoon, and only when Lily would see Clara toddle up to her with her chubby arms in the air would she snap out of her puppy obsession.

What on earth was Sienna going to do at the end of July, when Lily would have to leave the puppies permanently? A shiver rippled down her back. She wouldn't think about it now.

"Sushi is gaining weight like the rest of them. He'll be as big as Otto soon."

"None of them will ever be as big as Otto."

Lily had given each puppy a nickname, and it had been fun watching them get bigger, al-

though none of them were able to do much beyond eating, sleeping and letting out little cries
when they'd strayed a few inches from their
mama at this point.

Sienna exited the bathroom as Connor
brushed past her to check his hair. She smiled
to herself. He looked cute and a little nervous.
He'd been told by Bryce that there would be
girls his age at Mac's place. She hoped he'd hit
it off with the other teenagers.

"Come on, Lily, get ready. Blaine's picking us
up soon." Sienna paused in the doorway to her
room. Her hair needed combing, but the shorts
and pink T-shirt were fine for the evening.

She could hear Connor's voice coming from
the bathroom, so Sienna leaned back. Was he
calling her? She kept her ears open.

And wished she hadn't.

"I can't talk now, Mom… I know, I'm sorry
you're upset…"

She clenched her jaw.

Becca would not ruin this night for him.

She strode briskly to him. "Let me talk to
your mother." She held out her hand.

He gave her a guilty look, and that bothered
her, too. He had no reason to feel guilty.

"Aunt Sienna wants to talk to you."

She could hear Becca's sniffles as he passed her his phone. She flashed him an understanding smile and took the phone to the living room.

"We're headed to a barbecue," Sienna said. "What's going on?"

"I miss the kids. Put Connor back on." The sound of her blowing her nose made her sigh.

"Is it Aaron?"

"You know it is." There was an edge to her voice.

"Why don't you tell me about it?"

"I don't want to bother you. Put Connor back on."

"He's busy." She held her breath, waiting for the outburst.

"Too busy to talk to his mother?" Becca's voice rose.

Sienna counted to three. "Yes, we're leaving soon. Listen, why don't you get out tonight? It's beautiful weather. It's the weekend. Call Aaron. Invite him over."

"He wouldn't want to come…" Her voice faded.

"How do you know?"

"He's been distant. Couples' therapy didn't go well yesterday."

In that case, Sienna was surprised Becca had waited this long to call Connor.

"I'm sorry, Bec. I am. I know you guys are trying. Just hang in there."

"Yeah, well, it's hard. He knows he's abandoning me. And he doesn't care."

The knock on the front door could only be Blaine. Sienna had to wrap this up. "I've got to go. Want me to call you when I get home?"

Lily trudged to the door and ushered Blaine inside. Sienna held up her index finger to him, indicating she was almost finished.

"Don't bother. I'll be fine..." Becca's voice trailed off to prove she would *not* be fine.

"I'll call you later."

"Whatever."

Sienna ended the call as Connor emerged from the bathroom.

"Is everything alright?" Blaine frowned at her. She handed Connor his phone back.

"Yes. Give Lily a minute to brush her hair, and we'll be ready."

Lily glared at her and practically stomped to the bathroom.

"What's wrong with her?" Blaine asked.

"She doesn't want to leave the puppies," Connor replied.

Sienna picked up the plate of lemon bars she'd baked this morning. The less she talked right now, the better. A minute later, with her hair tamed, Lily marched past the three of them and stormed out the front door.

"Shall we?" Sienna gave Blaine a tight smile.

What was supposed to be a fun night out was turning out to be stressful and tense. *Lord, can't anything just be easy for once?* She could only hope the night would get better. Friday nights were supposed to be fun.

BLAINE WATCHED SIENNA laughing at something Bridget said, and his heart felt funny. Reagan would probably call it the pitter-patter of his heartbeat, but she was girlie like that. Whatever it was, he was positive it had everything to do with his attraction to Sienna and nothing to do with a possible arrhythmia.

Why couldn't he tear his eyes away from her? Pretty sundress, lightly tanned arms, big smile, sparkling green eyes—yep, she was the whole package. The ladies had insisted on having her sit in one of the Adirondack chairs while he and Mac got the fire going. From the pastel peaches and lavenders spreading out across the sky, he'd give it half an hour before the sun headed home for the night. The snap and crackle of dry logs burning mingled with the conversations.

The teens were all still in Mac's fancy pole barn, playing their version of *Would You Rather*. Blaine was glad he didn't have to take part in it. Kaylee had introduced Connor and Lily to the handful of friends—a mix of boys and girls— she'd invited. Connor seemed to be fitting in well, as much as he could tell. All in all, a successful evening as far as Sienna and the kids were concerned.

But for him?

He should have just skipped the whole thing.

He didn't need all these reminders that everyone's lives were moving on while his stayed the same. At least the food had been good.

Austin dropped into the seat next to him with a grunt. "Hey, man, sorry we got interrupted earlier. Sidney's babysitting and wasn't sure if AJ could have Jell-O. Where she got Jell-O from, I have no clue. I don't buy the stuff." He shook his head. "So what's going on?"

Finally. Normal talk. Guy talk. Ranch talk.

Blaine shifted to face him. "Earlier I was out checking a gully in one of the pastures. I've never seen it this low before. If it had an inch of water in it, I'd be surprised."

"I know." Austin shook his head, blowing out a loud exhalation. "This dry spell has me worried. I know nobody wants to say the word *drought*, but..."

Blaine nodded as all the implications came back to him. "I'm getting nervous."

"The new pasture not taking? You planted wheatgrass, right? Having trouble with it?"

"It's not taking as well as I'd hoped."

"It is drought-resistant."

"Yeah, but it has to get established first. The pasture looks patchy."

Jet strolled their way, and Blaine clamped his mouth shut. He did not need any of his brother's I-told-you-so's right now.

Austin cracked his knuckles. "If it helps, I'm worried, too. Last year I debated if I should try to grow more hay as protection for the coming winter or just let the cattle graze the acres I was considering reseeding. Honestly, I'm trying to get a few more years out of my current equipment, so I opted for grazing. But there's barely anything for them to graze."

"The cold snap in May didn't help."

"The winds didn't, either." Austin stared at the fire. "I guess we can be thankful we didn't get hail. It could be worse."

"You should have told me about the equipment." Jet stood in front of them, his back to the flames. "You could have borrowed ours."

"I know, but I didn't want to," Austin said. "If anything breaks down on my watch...well, I don't want to be responsible."

"The offer stands. Anytime." Jet grabbed one of the camping chairs to sit next to them. "You're better off letting the cattle graze, anyhow. Blaine spent a big chunk of change on reseeding the dead pasture, and he couldn't have picked a worse time to do it."

Blaine stiffened as he gritted his teeth. His brother might as well announce to everyone that he was just a stupid bum who didn't have a clue how to run a ranch.

"It's hard to predict a drought." Austin shrugged. Blaine relaxed slightly. At least Austin got it. Jet acted like he had the inside scoop on everything to do with ranching and would never make a mistake.

Admittedly, his brother rarely made mistakes. But still.

Sawyer came over and sat next to Austin, angling his chair toward them.

"I thought I heard the word *drought*." Sawyer's lips drew together in a tight line. "We could really use rain."

Randy strolled over with Ned, the service dog for his heart condition, and sat, too. Mac wasn't far behind.

"I don't think I'll be able to cut even three quarters of the hay I put up last year." Mac toyed with a soda can in his hand.

"The creek behind my house is low." Randy puffed his cheeks. "The fishing is getting bad. Higher temps. Less oxygen. More predators picking them off. I don't like it."

All six of them stayed silent as ripples of female laughter on the other side of the fire reached them.

"Are you guys at a funeral or what?" Tess yelled, getting to her feet. "Mac, why don't you put some music on. This is a bonfire, not a wake."

"That's my lady." Sawyer rolled his eyes, grinning.

"What are you in the mood for?" Mac called back, rising out of his chair.

"Something lively."

"I'll help." Randy got up, joining Mac as he headed inside the pole barn, where a sound system had been installed. Speakers were mounted near the concrete patio area and strings of bare bulbs dangled overhead. They were attached to a pergola full of climbing flowers.

Holly drifted over to stand next to Jet. He wrapped his arm around her waist and drew her onto his lap. Blaine was used to their affection, but it was still hard to take sometimes. He glanced Sienna's way. She was nodding at something Bridget said.

"I've been a little worried about Reagan lately," Holly said. Blaine peered her way, thinking she was talking to Jet, but she was addressing him. "I think she misses Erica."

"She should go visit her," Blaine said. "Stay a week or two."

"Your mom and I have mentioned it, but she blows us off."

"Want me to talk to her?" Jet asked.

"No." She gave Jet a tender smile then turned to Blaine. "Actually, I was hoping, Blaine, that you'd convince her to go to the rodeo next Friday. Mac and Bridget are taking Kaylee. They invited Sienna and Connor and Lily. If they're all going, maybe you could bring Reagan. She needs to get out."

Mac and Bridget had asked Sienna to the

rodeo? He'd thought *he* was going to take her and the kids.

Holly was staring at him with her big blue eyes, the ones that saw too much. Admittedly, if they saw too much with him, they likely saw too much with his sister, too.

Holly was right. For the past year, Reagan had been going out less—and she'd never been one to get out much even before Erica got married.

"I'll take her to the rodeo." His mind flipped through to check if he'd missed more warning signs with Reagan. He couldn't think of anything offhand. "Do you think there's more to it?"

"What do you mean?" Holly asked.

"With Reagan."

"I don't know. I hope not. I wish she'd put herself out there a little. Go on a few dates."

Blaine couldn't think of anyone Reagan would want to date. Frankly, he couldn't think of anyone *he'd* want to date his little sister.

"I'll get her to the rodeo." Blaine threw up his hands. "As for dating, that's on you. I'm not rustling up a cowboy for her."

"I'm not, either." Jet shared a knowing look

with him, then frowned at Holly. "Reagan doesn't need a guy to make her happy."

"Yeah, she's got the candles." Blaine gave a firm nod. "She loves making them."

"No one said she doesn't enjoy making the candles." Holly stood again. "But she deserves to have someone to love, too."

He supposed he should be happy Holly wasn't trying to set *him* up with anyone. His gaze strayed to Sienna. Her head tilted as their eyes met. A rush of heat warmed his body. Only a fool would get attached to a pregnant woman who'd be leaving soon.

Unlike his friends, he'd never fallen in love. But the woman staring back at him had sure grabbed his attention.

CHAPTER SIX

"It can't wait any longer." The following Tuesday morning, Blaine slid open the barn door where he kept the farm equipment. "We've got to start cutting the hay today."

Jim smoothed his mustache and headed straight to the tractor. "The extra blades arrived if one of them breaks."

He and Jim had spent time over the weekend greasing and tightening bolts on all the equipment. They'd both agreed if the weather stayed dry and warm, they'd best get the prairie grass cut soon, even if it was a week earlier than they'd hoped.

"*If* one of them breaks?" Blaine tossed Jim the keys to the all-purpose tractor. "I'd be shocked if we don't have to replace at least three when it's all said and done."

"I reckon you're right." He adjusted his cowboy hat as he chuckled. "While you're cutting,

I'll brief Bryce and Connor on the cattle grazing the southeast pasture. They can check the cows on my radar out there. I'll take care of the rest of the herd. I'll hook up the rake now, and when I'm finished checking cattle, I'll start combing the windrows together so you can get to baling."

"Good plan. It will give me a chance to get a head start on cutting. With the grass so sparse this year, we might have to combine two or three windrows together."

"I was thinking the same. It'll be too hard to bale if we don't. It's a shame."

It really was a shame. Blaine wished they'd gotten rain in May when they'd needed it. Early June still would have made a difference. But they hadn't had a drop since late April. He supposed he should take Austin's lead and be thankful hail hadn't destroyed the pastures. Grasshoppers could do a number on them, too.

Lord, forgive me for not seeing the blessings even in the troubles. This could be worse.

He and Jim discussed the order of the fields they planned on cutting, and then Blaine climbed into the swather and drove it into the sunshine.

Connor and Bryce had both offered to help

out more while he and Jim were haying, and Blaine was thankful to have two hardworking ranch hands available. It saved him time and allowed him to concentrate solely on getting the hay in.

As he drove the swather down the dirt lane, his mind wandered here and there, stopping on Sienna. As usual.

Friday night on the way back home from Mac's, Connor and Lily had seemed excited when Sienna mentioned the rodeo. They'd had a good time meeting Kaylee and her friends. Blaine had asked Sienna if she and the kids wanted to ride with him, and she'd laughed and said, "Of course," which had eased his mind about Mac and Bridget setting up the rodeo excursion.

He'd even gotten Reagan on board. On Saturday afternoon, he'd taken his sister to Bridget's coffee shop and asked her to come to the rodeo with them. At first, she'd declined, but he'd told her he really wanted her to come. She'd finally nodded and agreed. They'd chatted a bit, and he'd been surprised when she admitted how much she missed Erica and how making the candles wasn't the same without her around.

Holly was obviously on to something there, but he had no clue how to fix it. He'd just listened and nodded. He wished he'd had some advice to give, but he didn't, so he'd let her talk. Jet surely would have known the right thing to say.

Oh, well. Blaine couldn't change his personality.

The grass on either side of the lane swayed in the wind. It was still flexible, ripe for cutting. He'd be mowing those fields later this week. For now, he was starting at the one farthest away—Grandpa's dead pasture. An eagle flew overhead in the distance, reminding him how blessed he was to own this peaceful, quiet land.

As he neared the dead pasture, his chest tightened. How many hay bales would they end up with from it? How many would they get out of the other fields?

There wasn't anything he could do to control the situation, so he forced his mind elsewhere. The puppies were doing well. Lily had begged Sienna to stay with them in the afternoons instead of watching Clara at the candle shop, and they'd compromised. She could stay with the puppies in the mornings while his dad was there, but she had to go to the candle shop with Sienna after lunch.

Blaine had to give it to his father—the man not only offered to puppysit so Blaine could continue working, but he also showed up every morning with sacks of groceries so he could make the big suppers everyone on the ranch enjoyed. He'd put a video baby monitor in the spare room to keep an eye on the pups while he cooked. Pretty smart.

When the pasture came into view, Blaine turned the swather toward the far end. His nerves sizzled and frayed.

Lord, this is all I've got. I'm not a take-charge guy, like Jet. I don't have Reagan's creative side. I certainly don't have Erica's social skills. But I love the land You gave me. Please let the hay be enough this year.

A part of him wanted Jet to see that he made good decisions, too, and that he deserved his half of the ranch. But the other part of him felt it was stupid, really, to crave his brother's approval.

Turning the swather to the very edge of the field, he hesitated before dropping the blades.

The knee-high grass seemed to wave like the sea, but he knew if he climbed down now and looked at it close up, it would be thin on the ground.

Blaine took a deep breath and steered the machine forward.

Here goes nothing.

"TIME TO GO." Sienna stood in the doorway to Blaine's spare room, watching Lily hold two squirming puppies. Kevin had brought in a dining room chair at some point and was reading the newspaper. She had a feeling that from here on out, she'd be arguing with Lily about going to the candle shop every weekday afternoon. Her niece was obsessed with the puppies.

"Aww, do I have to?" Lily's big hazel eyes pleaded with her. "Look, Aunt Sienna, all of the puppies except Sushi can actually get up on all fours now. What if he can't walk like the rest of them?"

Kevin looked over the paper. "Sushi will be walking within a day, Lil. Don't worry about him."

"But how do you know?"

He gave her an indulgent smile. "I grew up on this ranch. Been watching animals my whole life. When you have as much experience as I do, you just know about these things."

Lily narrowed her eyes in a skeptical glance.

"Tell you what." He folded the paper and set it on his lap. "I'll text you the instant he can hold his weight on those front legs. I'll even video it. Deal?"

Her lips twitched in disappointment, but finally she nodded. "Deal."

"Off you go." He waved to them with a smile. "The puppies will be here when you get back."

Sienna moved aside for Lily to leave ahead of her. "Do you need anything from the cabin before we head over?"

"No."

Outside, Lily stomped to Sienna's vehicle and got into the passenger seat, jerking her seat belt over her lap and buckling it with an attitude.

Sienna was never sure how to handle these situations. Should she lecture Lily about not taking her disappointment out on her? Or should she ignore it, chalking it up to normal thirteen-year-old behavior?

She got in, started the car and headed to the candle shop. Given the fact Lily was living in a new place while her parents' marriage was still in limbo, Sienna was willing to give her some grace. Plus, she'd been very helpful not just with the puppies, but with Clara, too. A lecture wouldn't be appropriate.

The baby had been active in her tummy ever since lunch, and she thought of the upcoming prenatal appointment she'd scheduled with the local family practice in Sunrise Bend. *Someday, about thirteen years from now, you and I might be having this same type of car ride. You'll be all mad at me for dragging you away from something fun, and I'll be wondering if I should say something about it then, too.*

She smiled as the prairie rolled by. Off in the distance she could see a couple of riders on horseback approaching a herd of cattle. Probably Connor and Bryce. Her nephew had been in great spirits ever since Friday night. He'd hit it off with Kaylee's friends, especially her best friend, Lydia. And when Blaine and Jim had asked him to help out extra hours this week, he'd jumped at the chance.

She couldn't have asked for a better experience here when it came to him. She loved seeing him blossom, and it helped that Becca had been in a good mood for the past few days as well. When Sienna called her after the bonfire Friday night, Becca hadn't wanted to talk because Aaron had showed up with a pizza. What a relief that had been.

Maybe her sister and Aaron really would work things out. And Connor and Lily could have their family back together before school started in the fall. Wouldn't that be something?

Sienna parked in front of the candle shop and turned to Lily, who was still wearing an icy expression.

"You ready?" She gave her niece a smile.

The girl grunted.

She hoped Lily wouldn't be like this in front of the Mayer women. It would be embarrassing. Maybe she *should* say something about being rude...

Lily was already out the door and halfway to the shop by the time Sienna figured out what she wanted to say. She sighed. If Lily continued to be disrespectful, she'd speak to her then.

Her phone rang and, recognizing her divorce attorney's number, she answered it. "Hello?"

"How are you, Sienna? Is this a good time?"

Her blood froze in her veins. She tried to prepare herself for the words she didn't want to hear.

"I'm fine, and, yes, I can talk now."

"I just got off the phone with Troy's attorney. They've drafted a petition to terminate his parental rights as soon as the baby is born."

"Can he legally do that?" She hadn't researched it. She'd been too afraid of what she'd find out.

"In some circumstances, yes. Usually, the other parent files the petition and the court decides. When a parent tries to voluntarily waive their rights, it's more difficult."

A feather of relief eased her tension.

"Troy's case is unusual, though, because he's attached a doctor's diagnosis of a borderline personality disorder. Given the mental-illness angle, there is a good chance the court will decide in his favor."

She'd been right all along. Troy had a personality disorder.

Inhaling sharply, she didn't know what to think. Didn't know what to feel.

The few times she'd brought up the possibility to Troy, he'd coldly shut her down, implying she was a monster for even suggesting it.

He must really hate her and the baby to go to these lengths.

"My question is would you support this? It would help his case if you want his parental rights taken away, too. If you're worried about the baby's safety at all, this is the time to make a decision."

She wanted to end the call and toss the phone as far away as possible. Instead, she steadied herself by placing her hand on the hood of the vehicle.

"I don't know. I don't think he'd ever physically harm our baby." But emotionally?

"It's a lot to take in. I'll email you the documents his lawyer gave me. Look them over. Think about what's best for you and the baby. I'm here if you have any questions."

"Thank you. I will."

She expected him to say goodbye, but he paused. "Do you think he's doing this to get out of paying child support?"

"No." She thrust her fingers through her hair. "I mean, yeah, he doesn't want to pay child support, but it's deeper than that."

"If this is going to hurt you financially, we can fight it." The sound of paper rustling came through the line. "When you've made a decision, let me know what you want to do."

"Wait." Her thick brain was starting to loosen up. "If I agree I don't want him having parental rights, is that the end of it?"

"No. There would still be a court date and a hearing."

"And if I do nothing?"

"It will be up to him to prove he should be allowed no rights."

She asked a few more questions before they ended the call. As she stared at the phone in her hand, a hollowness spread in her chest.

Troy really did have a mental-health issue. She hadn't been imagining it.

But would he harm their child?

She couldn't imagine him being violent. He'd never laid a hand on her. But his wild mood swings, his unpredictability, his manipulative words—they'd taken a toll on her. She'd never known what she was getting on the few week-ends each month he was in town. It would be asking a lot from a child to understand it, too.

Maybe it would be easier this way.

Sienna forced her feet forward. She wouldn't have to deal with him or worry he'd confuse their child with his extreme mood swings and odd decision-making. He was bound to let down their child.

Was *easy* the best solution, though?

Inside the showroom, Sienna paused to get her bearings. Lily was beaming and holding Clara on her hip.

"And how are you today?" Lily tweaked Clara's nose. The toddler giggled. "Are we going to bake some cake?" She set her on her feet and took her by the hand over to the play kitchen near Holly's desk.

At least Lily had gotten into a good mood.

"Sienna." Julie peeked her head through the door leading to the workshop area. "I'm trying a new scent. Want to learn how to make it?"

"I'd love to." Anything to take her mind off her ex.

She hurried to the back and soaked in the workshop. Julie and Reagan made all the candles back here. Sienna enjoyed putting the orders together with their careful packaging method. Crinkled strips of heavy paper in various colors nestled the products in special boxes with dividers. It satisfied the precision-oriented part of her, the one that dotted every *i* and crossed every *t* when preparing the grants for the college.

Ever since arriving, she'd been hoping to actually learn how to make the candles, too. It looked like today was her chance. Something good to follow something bad.

The workshop held rows of metal industrial shelving and carefully planned workspaces, wax melters and supplies. It was a far cry from her office at the college. A laptop, file organizer and stacks of manila folders took up most of her desk there. She did have a window with a nice view of the campus, though.

"Have a seat. Are you feeling okay? How's the baby?" Julie patted the stool next to her. Sienna realized they were alone.

"Where's Reagan?"

"She's taking a long lunch. Meeting Hannah to go over bridesmaid things for the wedding."

"That sounds fun." Sienna liked Reagan. Was drawn to her, really. Blaine's sister had a gentle spirit.

"I hope so." Her eyebrows drew together. "I don't know about her lately. I hope being in this wedding sparks her to get out more."

"Well, she's going to the rodeo with me and Blaine and his friends on Friday."

"Is she?" Julie perked up. "She didn't tell me."

"Yes, and Kaylee's friends are coming, too. They promised to show Connor and Lily the best food trucks." Sienna rubbed her baby bump as Julie got up and took various items off the shelf behind them.

"Do me a favor." She set wax melts and two fragrance tubes on the worktable. "If you see a cute cowboy, get his number for her."

Sienna snorted out a laugh. Blaine's mom sat

back down and thumbed through a binder until coming to the page marked *Soy*.

"Reagan and I used to wing it when we first started making candles, but we could never quite capture the exact scent twice. She insisted we write every measurement down, along with detailed instructions."

"Like a cookbook." Sienna leaned over to read the page. It was full of measurements in columns and rows for various scents and sizes of the candles. She had to admit, she was impressed that Reagan had put all these detailed charts together.

"Exactly." Julie walked her through the process, and while they made a batch, Sienna's mind drifted to Troy only a few times.

"Now we let them cool." Julie began tidying the workspace.

"And tomorrow I'll be packaging them and sending them out."

"Some of them." Her eyes twinkled. "The rest will get stored for future orders. And Reagan will keep coming up with new scent combinations. That girl can't turn it off. Sometimes I shake my head and think there's no way it will smell good, but she usually makes winners. She's talented."

"And creative." Sienna glanced Julie's way and gave her a smile. "But so are you."

"Aww, thanks. I do love making candles. I think a big part of it is being here with you girls. Keeps me young."

Sienna's phone chimed and she checked it. Lily had texted Can you come out here?

"Uh-oh. Lily needs me. I hope nothing's wrong." Sienna stood and returned to the show-room, where she zoomed over to Lily. "What's going on?"

"Sushi's walking! Mr. Mayer sent me a video. You have to see it!" Lily sidled up next to Sienna. A video of the puppies began playing. Their little cries were too cute. And then the camera panned to Sushi, who, sure enough, pushed himself to stand and hobbled a few steps before collapsing.

"Can we go back? I want to see it for myself."

"I'm afraid not." Sienna hated letting her down. "We have work to do, but we can stop by as soon as we finish up here."

Lily crossed her arms over her chest, her face in a pout. "Mom would let me."

Sienna was taken aback. It wasn't like Lily to compare her to her mom.

"Your mom's not here, and I am. We made

a commitment to work here in the afternoons. And we honor our commitments. The Mayers have been very generous to allow us to stay with them. We don't even have to cook our suppers, because Mr. Mayer does it for us. Helping out with the candles is the least we can do." She normally wouldn't be this stern with Lily, but the combination of the girl's earlier attitude combined with the phone call about Troy must have short-circuited her patience.

"I don't want to help with the candles. I want to help with the puppies."

"Lily—"

"Never mind." She spun on her heel and stalked over to the corner, where two accent chairs flanked a small table. Staring at her phone, she slumped in one of the chairs.

That went well.

Sienna tried to calm her frayed nerves. For the first time she could remember, she resented the position she was in. Disciplining Lily was Becca's job. And this whole parental-rights thing was what Troy wanted, not her. Why did she have to make all the tough decisions?

God, I'm having a hard time here. I don't think I'm strong enough. And I don't know if I want to be anymore.

THE SUN WAS lower in the sky than he anticipated when he called it quits for the day. Blaine
surveyed the dead pasture with its giant rolls
of baled hay. He'd managed to mow the entire
thing at a whopping six miles per hour while
only breaking one of the swather's blades. He
would have preferred breaking none of them,
but hey, after climbing under and into the cut-
ter head, he'd only lost a minor chunk of skin
on his pinkie while replacing the blade. Not
bad, all things considered.

Jim had shown up this afternoon on the
tractor pulling the rake. While Jim combined
the rows of mowed grass—it had been sparse
enough to combine three rows at a time—
Blaine had driven to one of his primary hay
pastures and cut the grass there. Then he'd returned to the dead pasture with the baler.

"Stupid rocks." He kicked at the parched dirt
now fully visible without the tall grass hiding
it. One of the stones had clogged the baler earlier, and he'd wasted precious time unwedging
it. He supposed he should be glad it hadn't bent
any of the teeth.

The harvest could have been better. How
many times over the past nine months had he

dreamed about seeing roll after roll of prime hay in this pasture?

There might not be as many rolls as he wanted, but what was there was good. It would help feed the herd all winter.

Blaine took off his cowboy hat and wiped his brow with a handkerchief. If the rest of the week was forecasted to be this hot, he'd better get the remaining hay cut ASAP. He couldn't afford it drying out and getting too brittle to mow. He needed every single one of those bales.

It was going to be a long, hard week. And if he didn't get all the hay in by Friday afternoon, he might have to skip the rodeo. This land was too important.

Sienna would still enjoy herself. She'd be with his friends. She'd have Connor and Lily and Reagan.

You were the one who suggested giving the kids a fun summer. The rodeo's part of it.

So what? They didn't need him to have a good time.

And Reagan won't go if you don't take her. You're really going to let her down, too?

At the sour taste in his mouth, he shifted his

jaw and stared off in the distance. A small herd of pronghorn was grazing. Beautiful, graceful creatures. He always loved to see them take off and run.

Isn't that what you're doing? Running from your responsibility?

No, the ranch was his responsibility. Everything else came second.

He could practically hear his mom's voice: *People are more important than cows, dear.* How many times had she said that to their father over the years? Too many to count.

Slapping the hat back on his head, he climbed into the baler and started it up. As he drove to the ranch, he wrestled with his priorities.

Maybe he was worrying for nothing. He might be able to finish haying by Friday.

Come on, you know waiting until Monday won't make that big of a difference.

Was this about the hay or being with Sienna? Why was he so worked up about going to the rodeo, anyhow?

It wasn't a big deal. He'd been to a million of them. He'd buy too much greasy food, share some laughs with his friends and call it a night.

But this time it wouldn't only be his friends. It

would be their wives, their girlfriends. It would be all the teens. And his sister. And Sienna.

Life was easier when it was just him and the guys.

should be concerned, their emotions. He had
he'd figured Julie had to feel... And honestly,
Blaine wasn't sure where to even begin to hand
this.

CHAPTER SEVEN

A THRILL RIPPLED through Sienna as she climbed
out of Blaine's truck Friday night in the parking lot. She joined him, Reagan and Connor
at the back of the truck. Lily had begged to
stay home with the puppies, and since Julie and
Kevin would be there, Sienna had reluctantly
agreed. Personally, she wanted Lily to get out
and enjoy what summer had to offer, but it had
been one argument after another all week, and
she was plain worn out from working around
Lily's obsession with the pups.

Ever since the bonfire at Mac's, Sienna had
been looking forward to tonight to spend more
time with all of Blaine's supportive friends.
They helped take her mind off the other stuff
going on—Becca's ups and downs, Troy's diagnosis, the conversation with her lawyer and
the fact she was having a baby soon and wasn't
remotely prepared for it. Which reminded her,

she needed to call Erica tomorrow to find out how her doctor's appointment had gone this afternoon. They talked every few days and texted more often.

"Hey, Connor!"

Sienna turned to see who was calling her nephew. His cheeks were flushed as he waved to Kaylee and her friend Lydia. A few other teens were joking around behind them.

"Is it okay if I go with them, Aunt Sienna?"

"Of course. Have fun. Oh, wait—" She fished in her small cross-body purse for her wallet. "I've got some money for you."

"That's okay. I got paid today." He hitched his chin to Blaine in thanks.

Her nephew. A paid employee on the ranch. Her heart swelled with pride for him.

"Well, keep your phone on and watch for my texts." She was sure there were a million things they should go over before he left. "And come find us if anything is…well, if you need me. We'll be walking around and sitting and…" An odd flutter in her chest kept her from forming a complete sentence. She wasn't used to having Connor go off with almost-strangers. The teens all seemed nice, but she didn't know them. Was she making a mistake?

"Thanks! I will." He tapped the pocket of his jeans, where he kept his phone. "I'll catch up with you later." Then he loped off toward the group.

Sienna didn't take her eyes off him until he caught up with the other teens.

She was worrying over nothing. Her sixteen-year-old nephew was plenty old enough to hang out with what seemed to be a nice group of teenagers without her getting all overprotective.

Still...she craned her neck to catch a glimpse of him. Their backs were to her as they headed toward the entrance.

"Well, should we try to find everyone?" Blaine, who usually seemed so calm, had a nervous air about him tonight.

Reagan let out a resigned sigh. "I guess."

Surprised, Sienna studied her. She'd been under the impression Reagan was looking forward to the evening. She looked super cute in a lavender sundress with cowboy boots and a cowboy hat. Her long brown hair trailed down her back.

Sienna felt positively dowdy standing next to the slender beauty. She had worn a sundress, too, mainly because her maternity shorts tended to get tight around the thighs. But cute cowboy boots and cowboy hat? Nope. Her cushiony sandals and hair half pulled back would have to do.

She entwined her arm through Reagan's. "Your mom told me if I see a cute cowboy I have to give him your number."

"She did not." Her eyes widened in horror. Then she gave the ultimate eye roll.

Sienna laughed. "She did. I told her I'd keep an eye out for one."

"You do not want to date one of those players, Reagan." Blaine straightened—he had his intimidating big brother look on. Sienna would have chuckled if she didn't find it so endearing. She couldn't remember a time anyone had been overprotective of her.

"Like I would, Blaine." Reagan sounded exasperated. "I'm just here for the fries."

He narrowed his eyes at her, then, seemingly satisfied, looked around. "Ahh, there they are."

Mac and Bridget were holding hands and laughing at something. Sienna didn't see Sawyer and Tess yet. They were the only other couple attending. Randy and Hannah had a fishing trip planned up in Montana, and Jet and Holly had driven to Utah to see Holly's cousin.

"Where's Sawyer?" Blaine asked after everyone greeted each other with hugs.

Bridget sobered, looking at Mac, who addressed everyone. "Ken collapsed this afternoon. They don't know what's going on, so they're driving him to the hospital."

Reagan gasped, putting her hand over her mouth. Sienna remembered Tess telling Bridget her father wasn't doing very well. They hadn't spoken about it at the bonfire, but from what she'd pieced together he had lung cancer and had been in and out of treatment and remission for the past couple of years.

"Makes me wish the satellite cancer center was up and running now." Mac shook his head. "Sure would make it easier on them."

"What satellite cancer center?" Sienna asked. The group began moving in the direction of the entrance.

"I'm working with Hannah's brother—David Carr, a doctor in town—to build a small cancer clinic in Sunrise Bend. We've gotten two neighboring towns on board with sharing a team of traveling oncologists. David and I hired a management firm to oversee and manage the project."

"That's amazing." She could imagine the

possibilities of having a rotating group of doctors. She was familiar with Dr. Carr, since she'd
set up her prenatal appointments at his practice.
"Are you building the clinic or renovating an
existing space?"

"Renovating," Mac said. They joined the line
of people waiting to get in. "We talked to the
city council about having the clinic right downtown in one of my empty buildings. They voted
on it and agreed."

"Well, if you need help finding grants for
equipment and services, let me know. There
are tons of them out there if you know where
to look."

"Really?" He brightened. "That's good to
know. I will. Thanks."

The line moved quickly, and soon Blaine had
paid for both her and Reagan. Sienna tried to
pay her own way, but he insisted.

Inside the fairgrounds, a line of food trucks
were to the left, while covered bleachers were
up ahead where the events would take place.
Picnic tables and happy people were every-
where. The air smelled like cotton candy, horses
and French fries. An odd combination…but not
a bad one.

As Blaine strode purposefully to the truck

marked French Fries, Sienna chuckled, glancing at Reagan. "He took your need for fries seriously, huh?"

Reagan smiled, making her even prettier than usual. "Believe it or not, Blaine hears everything, and he takes it to heart. That's why I love him."

She could see why Reagan loved him—it would be easy for Sienna to love him, too. A man who heard everything? Took it to heart? And actually acted on it?

Unheard of in her world.

They got in line with him. All around the park, lights blinked on overhead, adding to the festive atmosphere.

"What are you hungry for, Sienna?" Blaine asked as the line inched forward.

"I think your sister has the right idea. I'm getting an order of fries. And I would love one of those iced lemonades." She shouldn't be staring into his blue eyes, and she really shouldn't be noticing the spark in them when she mentioned the lemonade.

"Oh, I want an iced lemonade, too." Reagan nodded cheerfully.

"Why don't I get the lemonades while you two get the fries?" He angled his thumb in the direction of the lemonade stand.

"Sounds good." Reagan raised her hands near her chest and clapped twice, then turned to Sienna after Blaine was gone. "Maybe Mom's right. I should just find a cute cowboy and get it over with. I'm always torn. Sometimes I want a guy exactly like my brothers, which is idiotic. Jet's overbearing, and Blaine couldn't read between the lines if a cow was mooing in the middle of them. Then I look around Sunrise Bend and...ugh, I can't see a future with any of the men there. I'll never find a boyfriend or get married at this point."

Sienna had to make a concerted effort not to show her surprise. She'd never heard Reagan even mention guys or dating or marriage until now.

"Well, if you do find a guy like your brothers, snatch him up." She stepped forward as the line progressed. "I ended up with someone like neither of them, and I regret it."

She'd probably always regret it.

Troy had not been a good husband. He wouldn't make a good father. So why was she reluctant to help him waive his rights? Shouldn't she be dashing off a letter to her lawyer pronto? It would guarantee she'd never have to deal with her ex again. No texts, no calls, no custody, no child support.

She didn't know why she was hesitant, but she was.

"What was he like?" Reagan asked gently. "I'm sorry. Maybe you don't want to talk about him…"

"No, it's fine." She waved as if it was nothing. Maybe it was. She didn't miss Troy. But she did miss her vision of the future with him.

Not that it would have been anything like what she'd imagined. She'd pictured him being home more, devoted to their child, a true husband and father.

A fantasy. Pure and simple. Her ex wasn't capable of any of that.

Maybe she should call her lawyer. Agree to his petition.

"Troy knows the right thing to say, but he never means it. Or maybe he means it for a minute. I don't know. I couldn't say. But he's up and down, hot and cold, thrilled to be with you one minute, running away the next. We had an entire relationship of weekends."

"A relationship of weekends? What does that mean?" Reagan turned to the window, where an older woman with a long, white ponytail asked for her order. "Three large fries, please."

"I've got this." Sienna dug out her wallet again and handed the lady some cash. "He drove trucks for a living. He was only home for a few weekends each month."

"Oh. I don't think I'd like that." She scrunched her nose, twisting her lips in sympathy.

"It's sad, Reagan, but after a while I preferred it." Admitting it out loud brought a spark of shame, but at least she was being honest.

"You don't miss him, then?"

"No. I miss who I thought he was."

"No chance of reconciliation?"

Sienna shuddered, shaking her head firmly. "No. It's over. Forever. I will never take him back."

"Here you go." Blaine suddenly reappeared, handing Sienna a large lemonade. She flushed. How much of that had he heard?

"Thanks." She didn't meet his eyes. Did he think less of her for refusing to consider reconciling with Troy?

Maybe he hadn't overheard. But if he had? She wasn't giving elaborate explanations about her dysfunctional marriage at the rodeo.

"We got you a large fry, too." Reagan tore the paper off her straw.

"Great. I'm starving. Baling hay all week has been brutal."

"But you're finished now, right?" Sienna asked, thankful for the change of subject.

The ponytail lady handed them the fries, and they all turned to look for Mac and Bridget.

"Not quite," Blaine said. "We'll have everything done by early next week if it goes okay. I've already had to replace two parts. Thought I'd have to drag out Grandpa's ancient sickle mower for a minute there, but Jim and I got the swather back in action yesterday."

Sienna popped a hot fry in her mouth. *Salty, greasy—oh, my. So good.*

They spotted Mac and Bridget up ahead. Sienna gripped her lemonade in one hand and pressed the cup of fries in the crook of her arm in order to keep snacking as they walked.

"Holly said Jet was a positive bear yesterday." Reagan nibbled on a long, floppy French fry. "He thought he'd end up with more hay than he did. He was all mumbly and grouchy, and she told him to go ride around the ranch because she couldn't take his bad mood anymore."

"He didn't tell me any of that." Blaine frowned. "He acted like he'd baled the usual amount."

"Duh, of course, he did." His sister gave him an exasperated look. "You know how he is when it comes to the ranch."

He wore a confused expression. Reagan glanced up at him. "Jet never wants anyone worrying, and he takes it personal when anything goes wrong. So even if things aren't great, he pretends they are."

Sienna's stomach dropped at the description of Blaine's brother. She could see herself in those words, too. She didn't want Becca worrying about Connor or Lily. She didn't want Connor or Lily worrying about their parents. She certainly didn't want anyone worrying about her.

Even if things weren't great, Sienna pretended they were to protect everyone else.

"That's stupid." Blaine blew out a breath. "I flat-out told him I'm about a quarter shy of what I'd hoped to bale."

"That's because you're you," Reagan stated in a matter-of-fact tone.

His forehead furrowed, and Reagan must have thought that ended the conversation, because she moved on to ask Bridget what she got. Nachos, from the looks of it.

"I'm sorry you didn't end up with as much hay as you wanted." Sienna stared up at him. He was so solid. So handsome. So clearly bothered by the lack of hay...or by his brother. She couldn't tell. Maybe both.

"It's alright. I figured I wouldn't. I knew by the end of May when it hadn't rained, the harvest would be smaller than expected. I just didn't want to admit it."

"Nothing you can do about the weather." She nudged his arm with her elbow.

The corner of his mouth kicked up into a half-hearted smile. "I guess you're right."

The five of them meandered over to the stands and climbed the bleachers until they found a spot near the center about halfway up. Sienna set down her lemonade and tore into the fries with abandon. The events had already started, and she didn't bother to pay attention to the barrel racing in the arena. Her lower back had taken to aching in the evenings, and the bleachers weren't ideal, but at least she was sitting.

Blaine sat on one side of her, and Reagan on the other. Mac and Bridget were on Blaine's other side. As the events continued, Sienna and Reagan pointed out the horses they liked. She teased Blaine's sister about some of the cowboys, and Reagan would shake her head and grimace. All in all, it was a lot of fun.

Her phone vibrated and Becca's name appeared. On cue, her nerves went into overdrive. She never knew what she was going to get when Becca called.

"Hey, Bec."

"Where is Connor?" Becca's voice was shrill. "I've been trying to call him, and he's not answering. Did something happen?"

"He's fine." At least, she hoped he was. It wasn't like him to ignore his mother's calls. "We're at the rodeo. He probably didn't hear it ring."

"Oh, well put him on for me."

"I can't." Dread pooled in her stomach. She knew her sister well enough by now to know what was coming.

"Why not?"

"He's walking around with his new friends."

"Who are these friends? Why would you let him go off with strangers?"

"Calm down—"

"Don't tell me to calm down. I can't believe you. This is my son we're talking about."

She did not want to have an argument here. "I'll find him and have him call you."

"If he's not on the phone with me in five minutes, I'll drive up there myself."

Her jaw ached she was clenching it so tightly. "There's no need—"

"I can't even with you right now. Five minutes." And the line went dead.

Blaine was watching her. "Is everything okay?"

A million thoughts crowded through her mind. *Had* she been reckless? Was Becca right that she shouldn't have let him go off with a bunch of kids she didn't know? Hadn't she thought the same thing herself?

She hefted herself up, wincing as she placed her hand on her lower back. "I need to find Connor. Becca's worried."

"I'll help." He immediately stood, taking her elbow to steady her.

"Want me to come, too?" Reagan asked.

"No, you stay," Sienna said. "This shouldn't take long."

She and Blaine made their way down the

bleachers and out of the stands. "I'm going to text him."

"I can have Mac text Kaylee, too. I should have thought of that a few minutes ago."

"It's okay." She texted Connor. Where are you? Your mom is worried.

What if something had happened with him and the group? Had he gotten separated from them? Was he in trouble?

In her heart, she knew he was enjoying himself. Couldn't he be a regular teenager for once? He probably didn't answer Becca's call because he didn't want his mom to spoil the evening.

A text came back immediately from him. Sorry. We were looking at the horses in the stables.

Relief flooded her swiftly, a welcome sensation from the earlier dread. It's okay. Can you call her? Like right now?

She stretched her neck from side to side as she waited for a reply. Yeah.

"He's calling her." She spun to Blaine, not realizing how close he was. He reached out, taking hold of her raised forearms before she landed in his chest. "Oof... I'm sorry."

"Don't be." His voice was husky, his skin warm. Those strong hands loosened their grip, caressing her arms as they slid away. His touch surprised her in the best possible way. But it threw her off balance, too.

It would be so easy to rely on Blaine. But it wouldn't be fair to either of them.

She backed up quickly, directing her attention to her phone. "Let me ask him to text me after he calls her."

His eyes glimmered with appreciation, and she had to look away again.

No, no, no. Blaine Mayer was off-limits.

He tempted her to want things she couldn't have.

A husband, a father for her baby, a steady man who would actually treat her like she was important to him.

She had a life in Casper to return to in a month. She couldn't afford fantasies at this point in her life. They'd only hurt her. And she'd been hurt enough.

BLAINE COULD BARELY concentrate in church on Sunday morning. He'd opted for the early service while everyone else in his family, along with Sienna and the kids, had committed to the late service. He was glad to be alone. He needed some space to process a few things.

What Reagan had said so nonchalantly at the rodeo Friday night had been gnawing at him, but all day yesterday he'd been busy trying to finish up the hay, so he'd pushed it from his mind.

When she'd told him about Jet being upset about his own hay output, why had he been so surprised? Logically, Blaine knew his brother was up against the same weather conditions as the rest of the county. Yet, when Jet didn't say anything about baling less than usual, Blaine had assumed he'd baled more than him. And Reagan had practically rolled her eyes when she'd said, "That's because you're you." What had she meant by that?

He'd never been good at reading between the lines. He just assumed when the people closest to him said something, they were telling him the truth. If they left something out, he wasn't aware of it. Not that everyone was transparent. He wasn't stupid.

Maybe Jet hadn't intended to mislead him. Reagan's assessment about their brother not wanting anyone to worry rang true. Jet always put up a brave front. Even when things weren't as fine as he made them seem.

But surely, he understood he didn't have to hide anything from Blaine.

He didn't need to be protected. He was a grown man. And besides, they were more than brothers. They were best friends.

The congregation rose to pray. He joined them, trying to follow along and failing spectacularly. His mind was jumbled. All his life he'd been two steps behind his big brother. And all his life he'd tried to keep up but couldn't.

He turned his attention to the service folder for the responsive reading. When it was over, everyone sat, and the pastor began the sermon.

"We sure could use some rain," the pastor said. "I've been hearing those words for a few months now. If we had a show of hands, I'm sure every one of yours would be in the air if you've heard or said them, too."

A chuckle rippled through the pews.

"We sure could use some rain." His voice softened as he shook his head. "Drought in Wyoming is nothing new. And there is still time for it to turn around. A couple of rainfalls could make a world of difference for our neighbors. It would green up the grazing land, water our gardens, replenish the reservoirs."

Blaine found himself nodding. The pastor was speaking his language.

"But what if we don't get a couple of rainfalls? What if we don't get any rain?"

His stomach twisted. He might have to consider selling off some of the herd, and he wasn't prepared to make those decisions.

"Is God any less faithful? When we go through rough patches or complete devastation, does it mean God no longer loves us?"

Blaine couldn't help thinking of Cody. The day his brother drove away in fury. The texts and calls Cody had ignored. The day they'd found out he'd been killed in a head-on collision. The afternoon Jet had brought Holly and Clara to the ranch, when none of them had known Cody had even been married, let alone had a child. And the hardest one of all—when they'd learned his brother had pretended they didn't exist.

"...spiritual drought is worse than a physical one. Isaiah, chapter forty-three, verses eighteen and nineteen states 'Remember ye not the former things, neither consider the things of old. Behold, I will do a new thing—now it shall spring forth, shall ye not know it? I will even make a way in the wilderness, and rivers in the desert.' Now before you get excited about rivers in the desert, the context of these verses is important. The Israelites had turned away from God…"

Blaine balled his hands into fists, squeezing until his fingernails dug into his palms.

He hadn't turned away from God. But his brother was dead.

He'd prayed for rain. But the harvest was sparse.

He'd been trying to fight his feelings for Sienna. But they were still there.

As the pastor continued to speak, Blaine's mind wandered to the tail end of Sienna's conversation with Reagan at the rodeo that he'd have to have been deaf not to hear. She'd been adamant she would never take back her ex-husband. That it was over. Forever.

His heart squeezed, wringing out like a dishrag.

Forever was a long time to cut someone you once loved out of your life.

He should know. His brother had cut him out in a split second and never looked back.

Everyone was rising once more. Blaine lurched to his feet. So much for listening to the sermon.

Lord, I'm sorry. I came here to worship, and all I did was fret and think about things I don't need to be thinking about.

The rest of the service passed quickly, and he quietly sang along to the final worship song before everyone was dismissed. Blaine kept the small talk with people light as he made his way to the front entrance and out the door. He descended the concrete porch steps, catching up to Austin, who had AJ on his hip and a baby blue diaper bag over his shoulder.

"Hey, man, how's it going?" Blaine fell into step next to him. "And how's our little buddy doing?"

"Good." The lines in Austin's face said otherwise. "We're good, aren't we, AJ?"

The boy had celebrated his first birthday a few months ago. Now he buried his face in Austin's shoulder.

"Actually, Blaine, I'm not good." They continued slowly walking toward the parking lot. "Did you get your hay in?"

"Yeah." He ground his teeth together. It was still a sore subject. Probably would be until next spring.

"Me, too. I… Well, I came up pretty short." Austin pressed the button to unlock his truck.

A beeping sound came from halfway up one of the rows of parking spaces. The sun was already hot, and the lack of a breeze was stifling.

"Tell me about it." Blaine was glad he wasn't the only one, but he didn't want to wish it on his friends, either.

"What the pastor said back there got me to thinking."

Which part? Again, Blaine felt foolish for not listening better.

"About God doing a new thing. What if this new thing is bad?"

They reached Austin's truck, and he opened the back door, setting AJ into his car seat. The boy protested, and Austin made quick work of buckling him in, kissing his forehead and shutting the door, then turning back to Blaine.

"I don't think that's what you were supposed to get out of it." But what did he know?

"Yeah, you're right." He shook his head, looking flushed. "Forget it."

"No, wait. What were you thinking?"

"Just that life's been changing nonstop for a year, and frankly, I can deal with most of it. But this drought…"

"Yeah, I know." Blaine felt it, too. "I don't know about you, but I'm going to pray for rain."

"I was thinking the same." Austin gave him a slight smile. "Do you think God will listen?"

"He always listens. He just doesn't always answer the way we want."

"That's what I'm afraid of."

"We'll get through it." Blaine rested his hand on Austin's shoulder. "We always do."

"You're right." They stood there for a moment until Austin broke the silence. "You still have any of those puppies left?"

"I do." Blaine hadn't put any effort into trying to find homes for them. He'd better start spreading the word about the pups soon, or he'd be stuck with six Aussies come August. "I have six to choose from."

"I'm tempted to have you pick me out a male."

"Tricolor or blue merle?"

"If AJ was older, I'd want a blue merle." He shrugged. "I could use another good herding dog, but I think taking care of a puppy and AJ would be beyond me at this point."

"I might continue to breed Tiara. Haven't made up my mind."

"You'll have no trouble finding homes for them if you do." Austin opened the driver's side door. "Are you going to the Fourth of July festival?"

"Of course." He'd have to talk to Sienna about bringing Connor and Lily. The festival was just over a week away. The puppies would be old enough to leave for a few hours if his dad didn't want to watch them.

"Good. I'll see you then."

Blaine waved goodbye and made his way to his truck. The summer was passing quickly. Only a little more than a month before Sienna and the kids would return to Casper.

He frowned, not liking the thought. He'd been enjoying having them around. Connor had effortlessly gotten into the rhythm of ranch life, and Lily had been indispensable with the puppies.

And then there was Sienna.

Independent, but not afraid to ask for his help. Generous, but not a pushover.

And alone during what should be a special time in her life. She deserved a partner. But he didn't think she wanted one. And he didn't want to be the next guy she cut out of her life forever.

So he might as well make peace with the fact she'd be gone soon. It wasn't like he had any choice in the matter.

CHAPTER EIGHT

IF HER STOMACH got any bigger, she'd be a danger to society.

Independence Day had arrived hot and sunny. Sienna waited for Blaine to come around to the passenger side of his truck to help her down. Connor and Lily were already standing near the truck bed in the large parking lot behind the feed store in downtown Sunrise Bend. Blaine offered her his hand, and a rush of appreciation filled her as he gently helped her step to the ground.

The sounds of a band warming up and distant laughter from the carnival, along with the delicious smells of barbecue and funnel cakes, filled the air. She had a feeling she'd be eating her way around the Fourth of July festival with Blaine. She glanced at him. Steady as ever. What she wouldn't give for some of that steadiness herself.

The longer she stayed in Sunrise Bend, the more she dreaded returning to Casper with its responsibilities and problems. But mostly she dreaded it because he wouldn't be there.

"I see Lydia and Kaylee," Connor said, pointing. "Come on, Lil, let's go."

"Make sure you check your phones, guys!" Sienna called. They were already jogging away. "And pick up if your mom calls."

Connor looked over his shoulder, gave her a thumbs-up and yelled, "We will!"

"Can't get away from us fast enough, can they?" Blaine gaped as Connor and Lily weaved through families to get to their friends.

"No, they can't." Sienna had worn a long sundress with sandals. Beads of sweat were already forming at the base of her neck. "It's going to be a hot one."

They slowly walked across the parking lot. Their destination was Main Street, where the food trucks and vendors had set up in the middle of the blocked-off road.

"Connor seems better today," Blaine said.

"Yeah, I'm glad." Becca had called Connor two days ago and unloaded about how Aaron criticized her in couples' therapy. Sienna had heard the entire call because she'd been sitting on the porch's rocking chair near the open window, where Connor had been sitting on the couch next to Ollie.

He'd been quiet and gloomy all day yesterday.

She wasn't sure how to handle the situation. This was his mother—her sister—whom they both loved very much. Sienna had told him on more than one occasion that he didn't have to listen to every complaint. He could set limits and still love his mom. But had she gotten through to him?

"Lily doesn't get her calls?" Blaine took her by the elbow, protecting her from a group of fast-moving adolescents, as they headed down the side street.

"Becca calls Lily, but they talk about normal stuff, like the puppies," she said. "Thank you, by the way, for assuring her you're going to find the puppies homes. I think it will be easier for her to leave them if she knows they each have a new family lined up."

"Yeah, well, I thought she was going to start crying when I mentioned selling Sushi. That little guy means the world to her."

"I know. It's going to be hard when we leave." In more ways than one. Sienna pointed up ahead. "Come on, let's go find your mom and sister's table." Mayer Canyon Candles had sponsored a booth, and Reagan had made special red–white–and–blue striped candles for the occasion.

They made it to Main Street and strolled past a variety of vendors selling handmade leather goods, collectibles, homemade jams and other items. Soon, they spotted Reagan. They waited until the line of customers dwindled before chatting with her for a while and asking if she needed anything. She declined, pointing to a box of donuts Hannah had dropped off earlier. After several minutes, Sienna sensed Blaine getting antsy next to her. They waved goodbye and turned in the direction of the food.

"I'm starving," Blaine said. "Let's grab a bite to eat."

"You read my mind."

"Why don't we go to the community center? They serve up a full meal, and we can sit under their tent, get out of the heat."

"That sounds amazing." She was glad he wasn't rushing. His long legs would have outpaced her even when she wasn't pregnant, and every week she got bigger and slower.

Up ahead, she spotted Lily laughing with

Kaylee near the shaved-ice truck. Connor and Bryce, whom she recognized from the ranch, were joking around next to them with Lydia and a few other boys and girls. Sienna smiled and waved at Lily, who waved back.

The sight of them enjoying themselves satisfied her in a way she couldn't describe. This was why she'd come here. She nudged Blaine and pointed to the group of teens. "You were right. This will be a summer to remember."

He turned his attention to where she pointed. "It's not hard when school's out, they can spend time with friends and the weather's good."

"True." They continued their slow stroll to the community center. "Thank you for bringing me here. I'm sure you have better things to do."

"I don't. I'd rather be with you."

Her cheeks grew warm. "That's the nicest thing anyone's said to me in a long time."

"I hope you don't mean that."

Sadly, she did. Between her sister's tunnel vision about Aaron and her own preoccupation about Connor and Lily, Sienna had grown used to feeling like the happiness of her loved ones rested on her shoulders. So to think someone wanted to be around her when she was plagued with worries was pleasant to hear, and she found herself wanting to open up to Blaine, to share more about her life.

"My ex-husband, Troy—" she kept her chin high "—wasn't around much. I got used to seeing him only a weekend here or a weekend there, and I'm afraid I grew independent."

"You say that like it's a bad thing."

They reached the community center's lawn, where a large white tent had been set up. A line formed at a table in front of the entrance. They reached the end and stood behind a middle-aged couple.

"I don't know. If I had needed Troy more or if he had been around more…" She swallowed, unsure why it bothered her to talk about it. "If I had been less independent, maybe things would have been different…"

"Why wasn't he around?"

"His job. He drove long-distance for a trucking company."

"Then he didn't stay away because of you." Blaine stared ahead. "He didn't know how blessed he was. If he did, he would have been around more, wouldn't have let you go."

Her heartbeat fluttered as her breath caught.

Did Blaine have any idea how much her parched heart was soaking up his words?

"I don't know if he was capable. He had issues." She didn't want to pull a Becca and bad-mouth her ex, but she also wanted Blaine to know the truth. "One minute he would be so icy cold I'm surprised I didn't get frostbite. An hour later, he was bouncing with excitement, wanting to spend time with me. It was confusing."

"Why would he do that?"

They were next in line. She shuffled forward. "After our wedding, I suspected he had a personality disorder of some sort. He got so angry when I brought it up, though, I didn't make that mistake again. Anyway, he recently confirmed it."

"Is that why you broke up?"

"No." She glanced up at him. She couldn't tell him here. Not this close to the other people waiting to pay.

Blaine took out his wallet, and Sienna handed him a twenty. He shook his head as if he'd never seen or heard of such a thing as her paying for her own meal. Then he placed his hand at the small of her back to urge her forward.

His simple touch loosened the grip she had on keeping her failed marriage in the past, where it belonged. She'd tell him the rest before she lost her nerve. The beverage station was deserted at the moment, so she wandered to the table where ice-cold pitchers of water, lemonade and iced tea were placed. Blaine stayed by her side. When she was sure they were alone, she faced him.

"Troy left me the day I told him I was pregnant." She watched his face for his reaction. Disbelief mingled with anger. "He told me it was over. He was filing for divorce and he wanted nothing—and I mean nothing—to do with our unborn child."

"What?" he hissed. "Why?"

She shrugged, reaching for the metal pitcher of lemonade. Beads of water dotted the side of it. "I hoped he was going through one of his hot-and-cold phases. What I didn't know was he had a girlfriend. A much older girlfriend. I'm not proud to admit that fact didn't shock me as much as him telling me he wanted to legally waive his parental rights."

Blaine tensed as he drew himself to his full height. "Did he?" His voice was razor-sharp and low. "Waive them?"

"He's trying to." As each day passed, she became more confused about what to do. What

would be best for the baby? What would be best
for her? And…what would be best for Troy? She
didn't know at this point. "I feel bad saying this,
but in some ways having him out of the picture
for good would make my life easier."

Glass of lemonade in hand, she turned, her
belly bumping a pitcher of water in the process.
Blaine reached out and steadied it.

"Let's eat before I knock over the entire
table." She injected levity in her tone. Opening up about the less savory parts of her past
was difficult. "I didn't mean to dump all this
on you."

He didn't respond, just plucked the lemonade from her hand and set it on a nearby table,
where there were several seats open. "You sit.
I'll get us food."

For once, she didn't argue. She let him take
the lead and hoped he wasn't put off by what
she'd told him.

As BLAINE LOADED two paper plates with shred-
ded pork sandwiches, mac and cheese, coleslaw
and cornbread, he tried to wrap his head around
what Sienna had just told him.

Her ex had cheated on her? With an older
woman? And didn't want to claim his own child?

He nodded his thanks to the workers refilling the warming trays of food and returned to the table with plastic silverware packets tucked into his pocket and both hands holding their plates. He set down one plate in front of Sienna, put the other at his spot across from her and slid one of the silverware packets her way before taking a seat.

"Oh, wow, this looks yummy." She took a bite of the mac and cheese.

He let his food sit there a moment as he watched her intently. No one else was sharing their table, but he kept his voice low just in case.

"Explain this waiving-parental-rights thing." He had to know more. Normally, he'd let the subject drop, but it felt too important.

She finished her bite, patted the napkin to her lips and set it back down. "It means what it sounds like. He would have no rights or obligations regarding the baby."

"No custody?"

"Correct."

"What about child support?"

She shook her head.

He slumped back in his seat, stunned. "I didn't know that was a thing."

"I didn't, either." Her voice was so soft, he

almost couldn't hear her. "It's irrevocable. If the court agrees to it, he can't change his mind."

"Good."

"For me, maybe. But what about the baby?" The look she gave him was heavy. "I never wanted my child to not have a father, you know?"

"Some father. On the road all the time and dating a nursing-home patient." The words were out before he thought them through. He winced, unable to bring himself to see her re-action. He wasn't trying to hurt her.

At the odd, strangled sound coming from her throat, he glanced up. She had her hand over her mouth and appeared to be…laughing? No, that couldn't be.

But her face grew red as she tried to stifle the laugh, then she took away her hand and shook her head. Yep, she was laughing. He couldn't prevent his own grin from spreading. He tore off a chunk of cornbread and popped it into his mouth.

"Thanks, Blaine." She sighed, tucking the fork into the coleslaw. "I know you're right. And to be honest, any relationship Troy would have with our child would be unpredictable. I don't really want that for my baby, either—a

lifetime of broken promises. I'm under no illusions about my ex. He'll lavish you with attention one minute and miss your birthday two
days later. It was hard enough dealing with it
as his wife. I can't imagine a child trying to
navigate it."

Blaine kept his mouth shut, or he'd release
the string of unkind words sitting on the tip of
his tongue. Sienna had enough to deal with. He
took a big bite of his pork sandwich.

"I keep wanting the baby to have some sem-
blance of a normal life—what other kids have,
you know?" Her elbow was resting on the table,
white plastic fork dangling from her fingers.
"But it puts me in a tough spot. My lawyer
needs to know if I'll support Troy's petition.
He finally went to the doctor and was officially diagnosed with a personality disorder, so
the courts might allow him to waive his rights.
But if I support his petition, it will increase his
chances of them ruling in his favor."

He tried to put himself in her shoes, but he
couldn't. It seemed like her life would be less
of a hassle without her ex-husband in it. But
what did he know?

"It would be tough explaining his absence,"
she said. "I mean, how do you tell your own

kid their father cut himself out of their life on purpose? I've been down a similar road, and it hurts. It hurts so much."

Blaine stopped chewing, the bite of food tasting like cardboard all of a sudden. He knew what it was like to be cut out of someone's life on purpose, too. And he still hadn't recovered.

"Who cut you out of their life?" He resumed chewing and watched her. He didn't know much about her past, other than she'd come to live with her grandmother back in high school, and after the grandma died, Sienna had moved to Casper.

"I'm sure we've talked enough about me." She averted her gaze. "What about you? Obviously, you're single. I hope you had better taste in women than I did in Troy."

She wanted to know about his dating life? He lunged for his glass of water, taking a gulp, since not a single thought on how to reply came into his head.

"It's been a while since I've dated anyone." The truth was the easiest to say. "Mom and Holly want that to change. They're always talking about how I should call this girl or that one. None of them are my type." He shouldn't have admitted all that.

"What is your type?" Her big green eyes were clear, open, inviting. It would be the simplest thing in the world to reach across the table and take her hand in his. *You. You're my type.*

"Not who they're talking about," he said gruffly. "I've got a ranch to run, anyhow."

"You can't run a ranch and have a girlfriend?"

No, he couldn't. "I don't think so."

"Look at Sawyer and Tess. And Jet and Holly. And Mac and Bridget." She took another bite of her sandwich.

Thinking of his friends getting picked off one by one by the ladies made him grimace. They'd all found real love. Lasting love.

He didn't know if it was possible for him.

And the only one who tempted him to find out was sitting across from him, seven months pregnant with no plans to stay.

THE FIREWORKS WERE set to begin in fifteen minutes. Sienna was lounging in a camping chair with Tess on one side and Reagan on the other. Holly and Bridget were on the other side of Tess, and Hannah chatted with Cassie—Austin's nanny for AJ—on a quilt spread out in front of the chairs. The half moon was already shining brightly above them as the constellations blinked on, one star at a time. Today had been amazing. And challenging, exciting, nerve-wracking and eye-opening.

Something had shifted within her. Something she didn't want to dwell on.

It was too scary to contemplate.

She looked around for Connor. He was watching the fireworks with his friends nearby. Even from here, she could tell he was enjoying himself as he joked around with them. Lily had returned to the ranch with Julie and Kevin earlier. Her niece had had a fun time, too, but in her words, she needed to get back to the puppies.

"So, Reagan, I noticed how Brad Sanders was eyeing you earlier." Tess bent forward to talk to Reagan with Sienna between them. "I hope he asked you out."

Reagan stiffened. "He did not. And I don't want him to."

Tess laughed mischievously. "I think you'd have a good time. And don't even try to say he isn't cute."

Reagan leaned closer to Sienna, keeping her voice low. "He dated all of my friends in high school. Every one of them. I would never go out with him."

Sienna stifled a laugh.

Holly, perking up at the talk of Reagan dating, scooted her chair closer to Tess's to hear better. "What about Tim Evans?"

Reagan glared at her. "Holly, I love you like a sister. I'm glad Jet married you. But if I ever hear you mention Tim Evans to me as a potential date again, I'm disowning you."

Holly rolled her eyes, shaking her head. Again, Sienna laughed. Who knew Reagan could be this assertive when it came to dating?

"What's wrong with Tim?" Holly asked, unfazed by her speech.

"What's right with him?"

"He owns a successful business."

"He's a mortician. I don't see myself living in a funeral home."

Holly's face fell. "But—"

"No." Reagan leaned in to Sienna again. "I'm this close to inventing a boyfriend, just to get everyone off my back."

"Blaine said something similar earlier." Sienna's gaze zoomed to where he and his buddies were standing, not too far from the ladies, talking, laughing and waiting for the fireworks.

"Yeah, well, no one's harassing him now that you're here." She reached down for her bottle of water, and Sienna was thankful for the darkness. Did they think she and Blaine could be a couple? For real?

Her heart flipped at the thought. It had been what she'd been fighting for days—this feeling, this longing for the real thing.

Blaine was the real thing.

Maybe it was the fact he was a cowboy, devoted to the land and the animals on it. Or maybe it was their history—the easy companionship and fun they'd had in high school. His handsome face, strong arms and beautiful blue eyes were all factors, too. But she wasn't one to be swayed by looks.

No, it was his personality, his way of taking life as it came, his solidness—those were the things that captured her heart and wouldn't let her go.

She was falling for Blaine Mayer.

And she couldn't stop it.

In a few short weeks, she and the kids would pack up and leave. She'd have her baby. Resume her job at the college. Be available for Connor, Lily and Becca, whenever they needed her.

She'd lost her father, her mother, her grandmother. She wouldn't lose the rest of her family, too.

Why was she thinking about it now, anyhow? She was surrounded by new friends, enjoying a gorgeous summer night. This wasn't the place to be reflecting on life.

She needed a distraction. Badly.

"What does your ideal boyfriend look like?" Sienna asked Reagan.

"I don't care what he looks like. He'd just better be able to handle me."

Handle her? Gentle, creative, sweet Reagan? What guy wouldn't be able to? She was like a dream come true.

"In what way?" Sienna asked.

"I don't put up with cheating."

"I don't, either."

"I have to work nights and weekends sometimes when we're busy, so he has to understand the business is important to me."

"Sounds reasonable. I think most guys would understand."

"I'd want my parents to like him. And he, them."

"Your parents are easy to love." Sienna tried to suppress the regret that she'd never known Troy's parents. He wouldn't speak of his mom and had no contact with his father.

"A guy who's honest, too."

"That goes without saying," Sienna said. "And I think he should be cute. You deserve a gorgeous guy."

Reagan chuckled and squeezed her arm. "Thanks, Sienna. I needed that."

A popping sound had them all gazing up at the sky. The first fireworks display exploded in white streamers. It was followed by starbursts of green and ribbons of red and blue.

"Are you doing okay?" Blaine said near her ear.

She startled, turning her head, surprised to see him crouching behind her, his eyes watching her intently.

"I'm great. Aren't the fireworks pretty?"

He didn't respond, but she could feel his warm breath near her cheek. It tempted her to lean back and let her cheek touch his. And that thought had her picturing pressing her lips to his.

Stop it!

She fanned herself, then realized she looked idiotic and clasped her hands around the arms of the chair.

"Are you too hot? I can take you home if you'd like." There was that breath on her cheek again. Didn't the man understand how attracted she was to him? How much she was starting to need him?

"I'm not hot. I want to stay."

"I'm right here if you need me." He shifted to one knee, staying close to her chair. Impulsively, she grabbed his hand and squeezed it. He gave her a surprised glance.

But he didn't take his hand away.

Instead, he entwined his fingers with hers. Her gaze remained trained on the sky, but she didn't register any more fireworks.

Because Blaine Mayer was holding her hand. And it was the most romantic thing she'd ever experienced.

Tomorrow, she'd talk herself out of these feelings. But tonight, she'd hold his hand under a sky popping with fireworks. And she'd tuck away the memory to cherish for years to come.

CHAPTER NINE

"ALRIGHT, CONNOR, LET'S go over the game plan." On Friday Blaine, Jim and Connor stood outside one of the corrals. The bulls had an air of excitement about them. Blaine was convinced they always knew when they were about to be pastured with the cows. "Today is kind of like the beginning of the year for the ranch."

"What do you mean?" Connor turned off the UTV and stood next to it, waiting for further instruction.

"The cycle starts all over again," Jim said. He'd driven the four-wheeler over. "The bulls join the cows, and soon we'll have a herd of pregnant cows again."

"We need to be cautious," Blaine said. "When feeling threatened, cows run. But bulls? They want to fight. So we're going to rely on the older bulls to help the younger ones see the trailer as nonthreatening." He checked the hitch where the trailer was attached to the truck. Everything appeared to be ready. "I'll back the trailer to the gate, and Jim will take the four-wheeler to steer them through the series of corrals. Your job is to open and close the gates. As soon as you open one, climb up on the fence. I don't want you getting hurt. I'll be behind the bulls with a long paddle to keep them moving. Let's hope none of them get cold feet about getting in the trailer."

"Will they all fit?" Connor asked. Jim gunned the four-wheeler and drove along the fence to the gate of the large corral, where the bulls were milling about.

"No. We'll be taking more than one load. I'm glad the weather is perfect. I would have waited until next week if it was too hot or windy, or even too cold. They get ornery easily."

"What else should I do?"

"Keep an eye out for us. If one of the bulls is getting close, holler."

"Okay."

"Go ahead and drive over there." He pointed to the smallest corral. "Once I back the trailer to the gate, I'll need your help getting it lined up."

He nodded and started the UTV. Blaine

climbed into the truck for the short drive. Ever since the fireworks, he'd been busy moving the bales of hay to winter storage. He'd still had too much time to think about Sienna, though, and everything he'd learned about her.

What she'd told him about her ex-husband had curdled his stomach. She deserved better than that.

And what she'd said about wanting her baby to have a father? He hadn't been able to stop thinking about it. He tried not to let his mind wander to kids or having a family. Mainly because he'd never really wanted to get married.

But Sienna had him questioning himself.

If the impossible happened and somehow they ended up together...could he be a father to someone else's child? Could he be a father period?

Checking his mirrors, he backed up the trailer, then rolled down his window.

"How much room do I have?" he yelled to Connor, who was standing near the gate. Connor used his hands to show him the distance. Blaine nodded. "Do I need to go to the right or left?"

He pointed to the left. Soon, the trailer was flush against the wooden gate. Blaine cut the engine and got out of the truck, striding over to Connor.

"You can slide it open." While Connor took care of the gate, Blaine got on his two-way radio and told Jim they were almost ready. Then he and Connor drove the UTV back to the big corral.

Blaine understood Sienna's devotion to Connor and Lily. They were good kids, and Blaine wanted the best for them, too. He and Connor had discussed his home life on several occasions as they'd ridden out to check cattle. It sounded like his mom wanted to stay married to his dad, but Connor was worried his dad didn't feel the same. Blaine had nodded and muttered something about relationships being complicated, but what else could he say? He didn't have much experience in the matter.

He felt awkward in those situations. Like with Sienna. She'd shared deeply personal things about her marriage and ex-husband, and he hadn't reassured her. He'd just blurted out exactly what was on his mind. Although, he had to admit, Sienna had been amused. And she was the one who'd reached for his hand at the fireworks. Hadn't pulled away, either.

Was he reading too much into it?

The first bulls were approaching the gate as Connor straddled the fence nearby. On the four-wheeler, Jim blocked most of the bulls from retreating, but one escaped, and being the expert he was, Jim wheeled back around and herded it with the rest of them.

"Okay, Connor, go ahead and shut it!" Blaine yelled when they were all through. "Then hustle to the next gate and do the same thing."

They continued moving the bulls until the trailer was full. Then Blaine drove Connor and Jim several miles away to where the cows were pastured, stopping the truck at a distance from the herd.

"Why did you park so far away?" Connor asked, getting out of the truck. They all went to the back of the trailer.

"It's better to let them come together naturally." Jim shifted his cowboy hat back as he squinted to the herd. "Don't want any of 'em fighting."

"Stay back." Blaine waved for Connor to keep his distance while he opened the trailer door. The bulls meandered out and seemed to know exactly where to go, grazing as they went. The three of them watched for a while, and Blaine sighed in relief as the bulls mingled with the cows. So far, the day had gone according to plan.

"Looks like there won't be trouble." Jim reached for the passenger door. "Let's get the rest of 'em taken care of."

"Blaine?" Connor asked from the back seat as they drove back.

"Yeah?"

"Have you decided if you're keeping Tiara and Ollie? You know, to continue breeding them?"

He cringed. He'd been avoiding thinking about the subject. Tiara was healthy. And Ollie had proven his worth as a herding dog time and again since arriving. But without Lily around to help with the puppies, could Blaine continue breeding them? Sure, his dad helped a lot, but Lily did many of the tasks Blaine would have to do with future litters. Like weighing them, watching over them, making sure they all met their milestones. She even groomed Tiara every day.

Lily was passionate about puppy care. And Blaine was passionate about the ranch.

"I don't know yet, Connor."

"Oh." He sounded disappointed. "What will happen to them if you don't keep them?"

"Laura would find another breeder. She won't separate them."

"Ollie's happy here."

Blaine looked at him in the rearview. His chin was tucked. It was obvious the kid had bonded with Ollie. Lily had told him the dog slept at the foot of Connor's bed each night.

It was going to be hard on all of them—the dogs included—when Sienna and the teens left. At least they still had some things to look forward to before they returned to Casper. Tomorrow the four of them were riding out to one of his favorite spots on the ranch and having a picnic. The kids wanted to take out the four-wheelers, and he'd told Sienna he'd take her in his truck, since it would be more comfortable.

"I promise you I will not make the decision lightly," Blaine said, meeting his eyes in the mirror. "The dogs are important. I want what's best for them. And if I can't give them what's best for them, I'll make sure they go to someone who can."

He wasn't sure he could give anyone what was best for them.

Wouldn't Sienna be better off near her family? Wouldn't her child be better off having a father in its life? Wouldn't the dogs be better off with someone passionate about breeding them? Someone who could give them the care and devotion Lily did?

He was stretched thin as it was. It wouldn't be smart to stretch himself even thinner. The people and animals depending on him deserved better than that.

SIENNA DRANK IN the view as Blaine kept his truck at a distance behind Connor and Lily, both on four-wheelers, on their way to the picnic spot the next day. Wyoming was truly wide-open country. To the left, mountains created a jagged edge where they met the sky. To the right, pastures revealed cattle either grazing or lying down. They looked like lumps of black-and-brown from her position. A slender blue ribbon of a creek that hadn't completely dried up came into view.

The truck handled the terrain with ease. Both windows were open, allowing a breeze to flow through the cab.

She and Blaine hadn't spoken much since the festival. And they'd only said a few words today. The silence wasn't awkward, though. It never was with him. It had been a full week since the fireworks, and she was glad to be out of her normal routine. A picnic miles away from civilization under a big blue sky was exactly what she needed.

"Connor said you got all the bulls out to pasture with the cows yesterday." Sienna had enjoyed hearing her nephew explain the process last night while Lily attempted to sketch Sushi from memory.

"We did. He was a big help." Blaine glanced over at her with a grin. "Did he tell you about the young bull we introduced to the heifers?"

"No." She shifted to watch him. The corners of his eyes crinkled. He seemed younger, happier when he talked about the bulls. "What happened?"

"Well, Jim and I thought the bull wasn't quite ready for the herd, so we figured the heifers would help get him used to the idea. Let's just say the ladies were really interested in him, and the poor fellow wasn't sure what to make of it. He turned around to flee, and they ganged up on him, sniffing him all the way. It was pretty funny."

She chuckled. "I'm sure. Do you think he'll get used to them?"

"He already has. I checked on him this morning. He looked content."

"Well, good." Her phone vibrated. Becca's name appeared. She ignored it. They'd spoken for an hour last night, mostly about Aaron possibly moving back in. Sienna hoped he would. She wanted them to be a family again. "Have you been able to find the puppies homes? Lily's worried about what will happen to them."

He winced. "Not yet. I've been in contact with the two people Ralph promised. Now that the bulls are taken care of and the hay is in, I can focus more on finding the puppies homes. You do know Lily's never going to be okay with Sushi being sold, right?"

"I know."

They kept following the kids, and Sienna checked her phone once more. Becca had texted her. Troy stopped by earlier. Thought you'd want to know. Call me when you get a minute.

The bottom dropped out of her stomach. She didn't want Troy bothering her sister or giving Becca some sob story about how heartless she was.

"What's wrong? You look like you're in pain." Blaine frowned.

"No, nothing like that. It's my ex. He stopped over at my sister's place."

"I thought he was out of the picture."

"Like I said before, he's hot and cold, either clinging or distant." The thought hit her that maybe he'd gone to Becca's to convince her to pressure Sienna into supporting him waiving his parental rights. "I hate to do this, but would you mind if I call her back really quick?"

"Go ahead."

She pressed Becca's number. It rang until it went to voice mail. "Hey, it's me. Call me back when you get this. I'm sorry Troy bothered you."

"Has she been okay lately?" Blaine asked. "Connor's been in a good mood."

"Yeah, she has." Sienna placed her hand on her belly. "I talked to her yesterday. She thinks Aaron will be moving back in soon."

"That's good news."

"Yes, it is. If it really happens."

"Why wouldn't it?"

How could she explain? Her childhood had been splintered. Becca's had, too. And the wounds from it affected everything. It was hard for them to trust other people's words. Maybe if he had some background, he'd understand.

"You know my brother drowned when I was four, right?"

His shocked face told her he hadn't known.

Why would he, though? She hadn't felt comfortable talking about it until she was an adult.

"It devastated our family. Becca was closer to him than I was. She's eight years older than me and was three years older than Dan. I feel like everyone blamed each other and also themselves when it happened. Dan was a decent swimmer, so no one noticed when he swam farther out than he should have. We were at a reservoir. They think he got a cramp and couldn't make his way back. There were a lot of people there that day. Becca had been allowed to bring a friend. Normally she would have been swimming with Dan, but she and her friend were too cool to be seen with him—her words, not mine."

"I'm sorry, Sienna."

"I am, too. I remember when it happened. I'd been whining. Mom was mad at me. Dad had his eyes closed and was stretched out on a blanket. Becca and her friend wouldn't let me near them."

"And no one saw your brother struggling."

She shook her head. "My dad walked out on us two months later. I haven't seen him since. Mom fell apart. She kept a roof over our head, but she was never the same. She left right before

I was supposed to start high school. That's why I came here to live with Grammy. Becca and Aaron had been stationed overseas at the time. When they returned, I moved in with them. I haven't seen my mother in years."

"Wait. Back up. Your mom left you? You were a freshman when you moved here. I remember."

"I do, too." She couldn't help but smile. The instant she stepped foot in Sunrise Bend, she'd fallen in love with it. "When I realized Mom wasn't coming back, I called Becca, Becca called our grandmother and it was settled. I'd stay with her until Becca, Aaron and baby Connor returned to the states."

"I can see why you're close to your sister."

"Yeah. She's always looked out for me. We had each other when we didn't have anyone else. Still do."

"That's how it is with my family, too." He veered to the left to follow the kids. "We're always here for each other."

"I know. I think it's amazing. It's been—" she hesitated, unsure of how to say what was on her heart "—eye-opening for me in some ways. This is how a family is supposed to work. No matter how hard Becca and I try to give

Connor and Lily—and soon, my baby—a family they can count on, it's always in the backs of our minds it could fall apart. That someone will just walk away."

"I know what you mean." He stared ahead.

"You do?" She couldn't imagine he had any idea what she meant, not after she'd spent these wonderful weeks with his loving mom, his dad, who was more than willing to drop anything for his family at a moment's notice, his sisters and brother—they were tight. None of them were walking away from this family. Why would they?

"Did Erica ever mention our little brother, Cody, to you?"

She knew Cody had died in a car accident a few years ago, and Holly had been married to him at the time. Then Holly and Clara had moved here, where she'd promptly fallen in love with Jet. "I know the basics, but she doesn't talk about him."

"When he was a teenager, he made some poor choices. Got in with the wrong crowd." His jaw clenched. "Long story short, a few years after he graduated, his actions were affecting us all. We had to put a horse down because of him, and a lot of stuff was said. By all of us."

She scrunched her nose, dreading hearing the rest.

"He took off. Cut us out of his life." The tension seemed to drain from him, leaving resignation in its wake. "You know Holly was married to him, right?"

"Yes. And Clara is his baby."

"Yeah, well, none of us knew he'd gotten married. And Holly didn't even know he had a family. He told her he was an only child. An orphan."

"Oh, Blaine. I'm so, so sorry." Sienna reached over and placed her hand on his bicep. It flexed beneath her fingers. She withdrew her hand. "He died before you two could make things right."

He nodded, then gave her an anguished glance. "I tried. I called him. Texted him. He never answered. And part of it was my fault."

"Why do you say that?"

"I could have stopped him from hanging out with those guys when he was younger. I could have—"

"No, you couldn't have." She shook her head rapidly before shifting to study him. "We make our own choices. Don't blame yourself."

He flicked a closed–off glance her way. "You don't understand."

"I do understand." Boy, did she. How many times over the years had she watched each member of her family grapple with guilt and blame over her brother's death? "I used to think I could have saved my brother, too."

"That's different."

"Maybe. But I carried it for a long time. If only I hadn't been whining, my mom would have seen him. That sort of thing. I think my sister still thinks it was her fault. It's probably why she struggles with anxiety and can't see straight when it comes to Aaron. Both of my parents blamed themselves. It was in their every move, every silence. I think we all have an alternate version of what should have happened that day at the reservoir—if only we'd done things differently."

He didn't respond.

"What would you have done differently?" She asked it quietly, holding her breath to see if he would answer.

Seconds stretched in silence, until finally he glanced her way. "I wouldn't have kept his secrets. I would have told my dad the day it all started. Then Cody would have stayed away from those guys, he would have had a good life—here, with us."

Sienna closed her eyes briefly. *Oh, Blaine.* She wanted to comfort him. Wanted to share some hard truths with him. But she could feel the mood, and after years of dealing with her sister, her nephew, her niece and, yes, even her ex-husband, she'd learned when to keep her mouth shut.

Instead, she did the only thing she could. She prayed.

Oh, merciful Lord, please heal Blaine's wounds from his brother's death. Help him release the guilt he holds, and show him the truth. That he's loved by You. That he's forgiven.

"Blaine?"

"Hmm?" It looked like he was battling powerful emotions.

"Have you ever asked God to forgive you? You know, for keeping Cody's secrets?"

Pressing his lips together, he nodded.

"Then let the guilt go. You're forgiven."

He didn't say another word, and a few minutes later, Connor and Lily parked their four-wheelers near a dry creek bed along a line of trees. Blaine parked, too, and as Sienna reached for the door handle, he placed his hand on her arm.

"Wait."

She blinked, watching him.

"Thank you." So much tension, so much emotion, trembled in the words. "I needed to hear that."

"We can't change the past." She covered his hand with her own. "But we can do things differently in the future."

WE CAN'T CHANGE the past. An hour later, Blaine still couldn't get her words out of his head. They'd eaten the sandwiches, potato salad, chips and cookies Sienna had packed, and now Connor and Lily were helping clean everything up. Lily was chattering about how fun it was riding out here but she missed the puppies. Sienna stood off to the side with her hands against her lower back as she attempted to stretch.

He couldn't tear his gaze away. She was beautiful. Loose waves of red hair were pulled back into a ponytail, and her dress revealed her toned arms and baby bump. She looked over her shoulder at him and offered a soft smile. It slammed him in the chest.

He felt it all the way to his core.

All the questions about him and marriage and

being a father melted away. He could see himself with her, gladly raising her baby as his own.

Too bad it would never work.

His priority was the ranch. Her priorities were her sister, nephew and niece.

He was manual labor. She was intellectual.

He lived in Sunrise Bend. She lived in Casper.

He was never anyone's first choice. She was his first choice and had been since he'd met her.

"Blaine?" Connor was in front of him. "Would it be alright if Lily and I headed back now? I know the way. I want to show her where we saw the prairie dogs."

"It's fine with me, but you'll have to ask your aunt."

Sienna's smile broadened. "Go ahead. Be careful, though. Don't go too fast."

Blaine wanted to chuckle. Four-wheelers were meant to go fast, and these were teenagers they were talking about. He glanced at Lily, and a wave of protectiveness came over him. Maybe Sienna was right to caution them. He'd hate to see either of them hurt.

"We won't." Lily grabbed her helmet as Connor quickly shut the lid on the cooler and carried it to the bed of the truck. Then they started the four-wheelers, revved them a few times and took off toward the sloping land in the distance.

"Want to follow them?" Blaine lifted the quilt and carefully folded it before tucking it under his arm.

"We can give them a head start."

Good, because he needed to talk to her privately. Normally, he would keep his thoughts to himself. But having her only a few feet away and it being just the two of them loosened his tongue.

"Sienna, do you ever miss living here?"

"All the time." She turned back to him. A breeze tickled stray hair around her face. "I loved living here."

Hope spread through him. If she loved living here once, maybe she'd be interested in living here again.

"It's been—" he tried to find the right words "—great having you back." *Great? Try amazing, life-changing.* He wasn't good at this.

"I've enjoyed it, too." Her eyes glowed in appreciation, making him bolder.

"Back in high school, I had a thing for you."

"You did?"

She had to have known, hadn't she? He nodded. "I did."

"I didn't realize…" Her eyebrows drew together as she tilted her head. "You were easy to be with. There was no drama. I could just be me."

Was that a good thing? The way she was looking at him made him think it was. He closed the short distance between them.

"I might still have a thing for you." His skin prickled. What if she rejected him?

"I might have one for you, too."

Hope ran rampant through his veins. He caressed her shoulders, running his hands down her biceps to her hands. Then he slid his hands around her waist. Her stomach prevented him from getting too close. It reminded him that she was carrying a precious baby inside her.

Blaine had spent his entire life caring for newborn animals, helping them grow, keeping them safe, protecting their mothers. They were his responsibility and he considered it a privilege.

"Where do you live, Sienna?" He leaned in closer, wanting to hear every detail of her life. "A house? Apartment?"

She looked surprised, but she melted in his arms. "Apartment. We sold the house after the divorce."

"What's it like?"

"I don't know." She smiled up at him, gently biting the corner of her bottom lip. "I just kind of live there. I didn't have the heart to do much with it. I do know one thing that's missing, though—a cat. My ex was allergic, but I always wanted a kitty to spoil."

"A cat, huh? Is that the only thing?" He was so close his lips were almost touching hers. With one hand on her lower back, he caressed her cheek with the back of his index finger.

He heard her sharp intake of breath and knew he was affecting her as much as she was him.

Slowly, he lowered his mouth to hers. The kiss was everything he'd imagined. The feel of her in his arms—so soft—brought out the protector in him. The one that had ached to be hers since he'd first met her.

He pressed her closer, and his pulse raced as her hands crept behind his neck and she kissed him back. Having her in his arms felt right. He couldn't imagine not having her in them forever.

Slowly, they broke away, and her shimmering gaze locked with his as she placed her hand against his cheek.

"You make me feel cherished."

"That's how you're supposed to feel." He continued holding her. "You're special, Sienna."

Her eyelashes dipped. Had he said the wrong thing?

"Come on. We'd better catch up with the kids." She took his hand and led him toward the truck. He opened the passenger door for her and lifted her by the waist into the seat. Her cheeks flushed, and he almost leaned in to kiss her again.

Instead, he shut the door and jogged around to the driver's side.

Did he dare hope that a future with Sienna might not be as out of the question as he'd thought?

CHAPTER TEN

A FUTURE WITH Blaine was out of the question. He was temptation wrapped in chaps and a cowboy hat, and it was all Sienna could do not to cry as she thought about returning to Casper for good in less than a week.

It had been two weeks since the picnic.

Two weeks since her knees turned to jelly at Blaine's kiss.

Two weeks of magnetic glances, of suppers together, of playing with the puppies and talking about the little stuff. Favorite movies, the best flavor of ice cream—mint chocolate chip, of course—how they got through boring winter nights. She loved to read cozy mysteries and watch cooking shows in the winter. He liked watching football.

Two weeks of helping Blaine find homes for all the puppies, except for Sushi. Two weeks of Connor hanging out with his new friends—

bonfires, ice-cream runs and all the fun she and Blaine had hoped he'd have.

Two weeks of learning the ins and outs of candle making, as Reagan and Julie taught her more each day. She found it challenging, invigorating.

At least it was a gorgeous Saturday. Sienna sat in the rocking chair on the cabin's porch, waiting for Mac to pick up Connor and Lily so they could ride horses with Kaylee and her friends at his ranch. Blaine's friends were incredibly thoughtful. They treated her and her niece and nephew as if they were family. What she wouldn't give to be part of their group permanently.

How was she going to leave all this?

Even Becca and Aaron seemed on the verge of reuniting for good. The hope in Becca's voice every night when she talked to her filled Sienna with joy. Maybe her sister would get back to the loving mom she'd been before their marriage began unraveling.

Sienna sighed. Where did that leave her, though?

Troy had texted her a few days ago to tell her she was being selfish. Ironic, coming from him. She'd called him back, but he hadn't answered. She still couldn't make up her mind on what to do about his upcoming court petition, and since he wouldn't be filing it until after the baby was born, she wasn't in a rush to decide.

The reality of the baby coming soon was getting harder to ignore, though. She'd had a routine prenatal checkup last week. Everything looked good. When she returned to Casper, she'd start having weekly appointments. It didn't seem possible the baby would be arriving so soon.

Mac's truck rolled up, stopping in front of the cabin. She pressed her hands into the arms of the rocking chair and hefted herself to a standing position.

Opening the cabin door, she called, "Connor, Lily—Mac and Kaylee are here."

Lily, wearing her new cowboy boots they'd purchased last week, raced out in shorts and a T-shirt, her hair in a French braid. Connor took a little longer, but when he appeared, Sienna couldn't help but smile. Her nephew was growing up. His black T-shirt no longer hung limp on his frame. He'd developed muscles from all the ranch work. He had on jeans, cowboy boots and a cowboy hat. He looked the part of a ranch hand, that was for sure.

"Okay, guys, remember what we talked about." She followed them down the porch steps.

"Don't worry. I'll text you when I get there, Aunt Sienna." Lily waved goodbye.

"I'll make sure Lil's safe," Connor said. "She's ridden before, but I have more experience."

"I know you will. And answer the phone if your mom calls." They nodded, waved and loaded into the truck. Soon it was disappearing in a cloud of dust.

Leaving her alone.

One thing she hadn't missed in the weeks she'd spent here was being alone.

Come Thursday, she'd be on her own in Casper again. Alone in her apartment. Alone at night. Alone until her baby was born. Sure, Becca and the kids lived nearby, but it wasn't the same.

Sienna trudged up the steps and reclaimed the rocking chair. She'd never minded being alone. But lately… She glanced at Blaine's house. She craved his companionship. Liked being around him. He made her feel like she was the only woman in the world. She loved it, really.

Sighing, she closed her eyes.

There was no future for them. They lived hours apart. And she had to get used to that reality.

"Hey, did they ditch you?"

Her eyes opened at the sound of Blaine's voice, and her lips curved upward. "Yes."

"What do you say we head into town for some ice cream?" He arched his eyebrows, propping his boot on the bottom porch step. Those blue eyes drew her in, making her want things she had no right wanting.

"Make it an iced decaf coffee from Brewed Awakening, and I'm in."

He grinned. "Done."

The drive into town did nothing to ease the tightening in her chest at having to leave in a few days. Even Blaine's chatter about grazing the cattle on the far edges of his property didn't cheer her up, and normally she loved hearing him talk about the ranch.

After parking, they went into the coffee shop and exchanged chitchat with Joe, Bridget's elderly employee, for a few minutes before ordering iced coffees and muffins. Then they took their drinks to the table near the front window.

Her mind flashed back to the day she arrived and stumbled onto this place. All the snapshots in her head of her and the baby rushed back.

New pictures clicked by, one by one, and this time, they all included Blaine.

Him holding the baby. Pushing a stroller next to her. Carrying her toddler inside.

She pulled back her shoulders, taking a deep breath.

"Is everything okay?" He frowned, dunking his straw into his drink.

"Yeah." She tried to reassure him with a smile.

"The kids are fine at Mac's. I'd trust him with my life." He reached over and covered her hand.

"That's not it." She blinked rapidly. "It's going to be hard to leave all this."

His gaze sharpened. "Then don't."

"I have to."

She wasn't sure if his silence reassured her or made it worse. He seemed to be grappling with something.

"Why don't I skip tomorrow night?" His eyes seared into hers. The guys were all meeting tomorrow night at Randy's to go over what needed to be done for Randy and Hannah's wedding. Apparently, they were grilling fresh trout. No women were allowed. "He'll understand."

"No, that wouldn't be right." Sienna wouldn't

take that from him. "He's your best friend. You need to be there."

This conversation suddenly felt heavy. Too heavy.

"Becca shared some good news with me last night." There. It was easier to talk about her sister. "It sounds like Aaron is moving back in before the kids return. I want that for them."

He averted his eyes. "Yeah, I do, too."

"It will be nice to get back to my weekly coffee dates with Erica." She ignored the way her throat tightened. Erica had driven to the ranch last weekend, and Sienna had enjoyed catching up with her about all the drama back in Casper. They'd swapped tales of pregnancy woes, the most recent being the fact Sienna could no longer see her toes when she stood.

"Sounds like you miss Casper." A muscle in his cheek flexed.

Did she? She stared out the window at the pretty purple and pink flowers in window boxes across the street. "I suppose I miss what it was. It won't be the same when I go back."

"What do you mean?" He looked puzzled.

"Oh, you know. Things like taking Connor and Lily to my house for a movie and a sleepover so Becca and Aaron could have date night. We did that a lot when the kids were little. I know all the Disney cartoons by heart. But they're older now. They don't need a babysitter. Things have changed."

He smiled.

She shifted the ice with her straw. "I'll have to figure out how to manage the baby and working. There's a day care nearby, but it makes me nervous. Don't get me wrong, I like my job. It gets repetitive sometimes and I get frustrated when we aren't awarded the grants we apply for, but my coworkers are nice and the hours are good."

"What else?"

"Nothing, I guess." She shrugged. "Everything else will be the same. My apartment, the café where I buy soup and salad every Wednesday, coffee dates with your sister, going to my church." Instead of cheering her up, the thoughts of returning to her routine gave her a case of the blues. "You've lived here your entire life, haven't you?"

He nodded.

"What would you miss if you moved away?"

"Me, move?" he scoffed. "Not happening."

"Well, I know that." She refrained from shaking her head. "Hypothetically speaking."

His eyebrows dipped into a *V.* "Well... I'd miss everything, I guess. My family and friends, for sure. I'd miss saddling up Boots and riding to all the hidden places on my ranch where no one would ever think to go. There are a few spots in the spring with the prettiest wildflowers. I like big, open spaces. No crowds. No one around at all for miles. It would be tough to give all that up."

Yes, it would be tough. She returned her attention to her coffee. She couldn't picture him in a city. He belonged on the prairie, in his house on the ranch. Near his family. Near his friends. Doing what he did best—taking care of what was his.

So why did she have the most irrational desire that *she* could be his? Was that why she asked him the question? Hoping he'd express even a hint of dissatisfaction with his life? A longing to experience life somewhere else? Somewhere like Casper?

Foolish thinking. He would never give up his ranch, and she'd never ask him to. It was a part of him. Something he couldn't and wouldn't turn his back on.

Just like Becca and the kids were part of her.

She couldn't and wouldn't turn her back on them, either.

And that left them both exactly where they were. Together for a few more days. And then this romance would be over.

"SOMETHING WRONG?" RANDY, holding a can of soda, strolled over to Blaine the following evening. Ned came over as well, then sprawled out on the lawn to lick his paws.

All the guys had arrived an hour ago. Jet and Mac were grilling the trout, Sawyer and Austin were discussing the dry conditions, and Blaine was doing what he did best. Standing there silently, taking it all in.

"What?" Blaine asked, startled. "Nothing's wrong."

Everything was wrong.

Sienna was leaving Thursday, only four days from now—not that he was counting—and she'd made it clear yesterday at the coffee shop she was going back to Casper. For her, there were no other alternatives.

When she'd mentioned it being hard to leave, hope had flared so bright, it blinded his good sense, only to be snuffed out as the conversation progressed. And then she'd asked what he'd miss if he ever moved away from Sunrise Bend.

He'd never once considered leaving.

And just talking about it yesterday confirmed he wasn't going anywhere. Sunrise Bend was his home. The ranch was more than a job—it was his life.

"Are you sure?" Randy asked. "You're not mad at me for not keeping my end of the bargain, are you?"

"What are you talking about?" Blaine sifted through his brain to try to figure out what Randy was referring to. Nope. Nothing.

"I always said I wasn't getting married." A corner of his mouth quirked up as his eyes twinkled. "And look at me. On the verge of forever with Hannah."

"Oh, that." Blaine grinned. "Of course I'm mad at you. We were all going to be bachelors. And now it's down to me and your brother— your much smarter brother, I might add."

"I don't know. Snatching up Hannah seemed pretty smart to me."

"Yeah, I don't blame you." Blaine playfully punched Randy's upper arm. "She's perfect for you, man."

"I can't wait until the wedding's over."

"The planning getting to you?"

"You can't imagine. Miss Patty has been waiting for this moment for years. Years. I mean, I love Hannah's mom. And it's nice to know she loves me, too. But she and Hannah are poring over things I just don't care about. Like give me a catalog of fishing lures and I'll spend hours on it. But place settings and cake flavors?" He shook his head as if disgusted. "I can't do it much longer."

"You won't have to. In a few short weeks, the wedding will be over. You two can go on your honeymoon, and get started on your new life together."

"Thanks, man." Randy blew out a loud breath. "I needed to hear that."

"Can I ask you a question? A personal one?" Blaine hesitated before continuing. "How did you know Hannah was the one?"

Randy got a faraway look in his eyes. "The exact moment? I don't know. It kind of crept up on me. But when she made me keep Ned overnight before she knew about my heart condition, I realized how perceptive and caring she was. And I couldn't imagine not having her with me or, worse, watching someone else fall in love with her. I was scared, though, and I didn't act on it."

"What made you act?"

"Passing out in the store before Sawyer's wedding rehearsal. Kind of forced me to tell her the truth. And all of you, too. I spent the sorriest night of my life that night trying to convince myself I couldn't have her, that it wasn't fair to her."

Blaine didn't speak. He'd never heard Randy talk like this. He hadn't known he'd gone through all this.

"But the big lug over there talked sense into me." Randy chuckled, gesturing to Austin, who gave them a wary glance. "Made me see I was being dumb."

"That's what brothers are for." Jet came over and put his arm around Blaine's neck, ruffling his hair. "Right, Blaine?"

"If you say so."

The other guys joined them.

"What are big brothers for?" Austin asked.

"Telling us we're being idiots about women." Randy grinned.

"Ahh." Austin nodded. "I couldn't let you turn your back on Hannah. You two were meant for each other."

Blaine wanted to back up a step, to get out of this circle of teasing and truths, but he stayed where he was.

Randy hitched his chin to Mac. "How did you know Bridget was the one?"

"Easy. She was getting the coffee shop ready to open, and she and I discussed hiring Kaylee part-time. I offered her a discount on rent if she'd hire Kaylee, and do you know what she said to me?"

They all shook their heads.

"To keep my discount. She said other things, too. Put it this way, boys, she was not impressed by me. At all." He lifted one shoulder in a shrug. "And that, my friends, got my attention. But it wasn't until I spent time with her that I realized how much I needed her. She's direct, kind and, well, pretty blunt."

"I could have told you that." Sawyer lifted his hands as if to say *duh*. Bridget and Sawyer had been friends for years in New York City, and Sawyer still referred to her as being like a sister to him.

"What about you and Holly, Jet?" Randy asked.

Jet flushed, scratching the toe of his athletic

shoe over the ground. "I don't know. It was really complicated. And I fought it. Hard."

Blaine tilted his head to watch his brother more carefully. Last year when Holly moved to the ranch, they'd talked about her, but Jet had been closed off about his feelings. Blaine had picked up on the fact that Jet liked her and had encouraged him to not let her get away.

"Complicated?" Austin teased in a nonthreatening way. "She was your dead brother's wife. And she had his baby. I'd say it was complicated."

Jet chuckled, shaking his head. "Yeah, well, what can I say? I do everything the hard way."

They all joined in laughing. Then, for some weird reason, all eyes turned to him.

"So Sienna..." Mac arched his eyebrows. "What's going on there?"

"Nothing," Blaine snapped. "She and the kids are leaving Thursday."

He didn't miss the sly glances they all exchanged. It irritated him.

"Are you hung up on the idea of her having a baby?" Austin asked.

"No." He wasn't, either.

"Well, if you don't think you could raise another man's child..." Austin's voice trailed off. "Your brother's doing a good job."

"That's not an issue." He widened his stance, crossing his arms over his chest.

"She seems into you," Jet said. Then he frowned. "But what do I know?"

He inhaled sharply, wanting to tell all of these idiots to mind their own business.

"Look, I'm not getting married," Blaine said. "You all can have your weddings and what-nots, but at the end of the day, it's just going to be me and my ranch." He tightened his jaw, hating the words because they were no longer true. He didn't mean them the way he used to.

He wanted Sienna on the ranch with him.

Wanted the wedding and the whatnot.

Wanted it all.

"Come on, guys." Jet made the settle-down motion with his hands. "Sienna's only a few months out from a divorce, and she's having a baby. She's probably not ready to think about dating."

Exactly. Disappointment plunged deep within him, though. Jet had spoken the truth, so why was Blaine still thinking about forever?

"Uh, Mac, is the trout on fire?" Jet pointed to the grill.

"Oh, no!" He jogged over to it, flames rising, the rest of the guys joining him.

"Hey, don't listen to those guys." Jet came up to stand next to Blaine. "If you want to stay single, it's fine by me."

He probably should appreciate his brother's words, but they rubbed him the wrong way. He didn't want to stay single. But he didn't want to hash it all out here, either. Or anywhere, really.

Why couldn't relationships be easy? Why couldn't he just tell Sienna how he felt about her? And why couldn't she jump in his arms and tell him she felt the same?

He wanted her to stay. What did Casper have that he didn't?

Connor and Lily. And Becca. And her job.

Right.

Austin's phone rang, and as he answered it, Blaine turned his attention back to Jet. "I don't know what I want."

"Really?" Jet looked surprised. "You?"

"What's that supposed to mean?"

"I don't know." He shrugged. "It's just that you're steady. You seem to know what's right for you. I can always count on you. I didn't realize you were having second thoughts about staying single. Does Sienna feel the same?"

Blaine often felt like the less competent brother when he was around Jet. To hear his brother say he could always count on him meant a lot.

"I don't know, and it doesn't matter. Her life's in Casper."

Austin's voice rang out loudly. "I've got to go. Cassie's grandfather is in the hospital. I'm meeting her and her mom there." He pointed to Randy. "The babysitter has AJ until nine. If I'm not back by then, will you go over there and watch him for me?"

"Of course, man." Randy gave Austin a quick hug. "Tell Cassie we're praying."

"I will." He took long strides to the side of the house, then disappeared.

"Alright, who's ready to talk about the bachelor party?" Mac asked.

"Me." Blaine raised his hand. Anything to get his mind off Sienna.

"Sienna, can I talk to you a minute?"

Sienna looked up from her desk Monday afternoon as she was putting the final touches on a package. Julie was standing nearby.

Holly had taken a sniffly Clara home at lunch and was taking the rest of the day off. Reagan was in the back making more candles. And Lily was spending her remaining afternoons at Blaine's, watching the puppies with his dad. Sienna wasn't fighting her on the issue anymore. It didn't matter in the grand scheme of things.

"Of course." Sienna wiped her hands down the sides of her shorts and gave Julie her full attention.

"We sure have enjoyed having you and the kids—although I'm sure they wouldn't want to hear me call them kids—here this summer." Her warm smile sparked Sienna's emotions, bringing the sting of tears to the backs of her eyes. She was really struggling with the thought of leaving this generous family.

"We've enjoyed it, too." Sienna attempted to smile. "You made us feel very welcome."

"That's partly what I wanted to talk to you about."

A twinge of worry made Sienna pause. She sounded way too serious.

Julie dragged over a nearby chair to face Sienna, then took a seat. "That's better. My feet and my back ache this time of the day."

"Mine, too." Boy, did she know it.

"I know you have your own life back in Casper. A good job, family. Friends, my daughter included. I'm thankful you and Erica have each other. So forgive me for asking this, but I'd hate for you to leave without me even trying."

Sienna drew her eyebrows together, confused.

"Would you consider working with us permanently?"

She blinked repeatedly, not expecting those words to come out of Julie's mouth.

"Um…" How could she possibly respond? Julie was right. In Casper, she did have a life, a job, a family. She enjoyed her weekly coffee dates with Erica.

But Casper didn't have Blaine.

"I can see I surprised you." Julie took off her glasses and rubbed the lenses with a tissue. "Don't worry about answering right away. I know how close you are to your sister and Connor and Lily. I get it, hon, I do. But you took to the candle-making process so quickly. Reagan and I have a hard time keeping up with the demand. You're a natural at it. And we like working with you. In fact, we'd like to see a whole lot more of you."

They wanted her around.

They thought she was good at making candles.

They liked her.

After too many years of worrying about everyone else's happiness, it was as jolting as a jug of ice water poured over her head to have someone thinking about her happiness for a change.

But, as nice as the offer was, there was no way she could accept. The reasons tapped out, rapid-fire.

She needed to be near Becca and the kids.

She was about to have a baby.

She wouldn't be able to work for a few months once it was born.

Oh, and then there was the itty-bitty problem of Julie's son.

Blaine tempted her to stay. Even more than the charm of Sunrise Bend, the joy of working with these kind, fun women. She wanted to be near him. Didn't want this romance to end.

"If things were different—" she swallowed, trying to find the right words "—I would seriously consider it."

Hope lit Julie's face. "We'd pay you a good salary. And we can offer benefits, thanks to Tess's research. She's more than a bookkeeper, let me tell you."

"Yes, I know." She didn't want to hurt Julie's feelings, but she couldn't let the woman think for a minute she could stay. "But like you said, I have my sister to consider."

"I understand." Julie tried to hide her disappointment as she nodded. "I had to try, though. You're like family. In fact, I was hoping for a while there you might become family."

Her back stiffened. "What do you mean?"

"Well, with you and Blaine getting along so well."

She didn't know what to say, so she remained silent.

"Blaine is—" Julie paused, glancing at her hands before returning her attention to Sienna "—not the easiest to read if you don't know him well."

She'd always found him easy to read. Like a large-print book with a light shining on it.

"Oh, I know my son looks like he's taking life in stride. But there are depths to him he doesn't talk about. He keeps things close to his heart."

Sienna supposed it was true. But didn't most people?

"But I know my Blaine." She pushed her glasses up the bridge of her nose. "And I know you're good for him. Just like I know he's good for you."

She opened her mouth to protest, but Julie held out her hand. "Before you say anything, hear me out. Maybe the timing's wrong. I know divorce is worse than a death in some ways, and it takes time to process. Then there's the baby. I can't begin to imagine what you're going through."

Sienna held her breath as her throat tightened. Her divorce had been like a death. But it hadn't been sudden or shocking. She'd felt it coming, had known their marriage was sinking for a long time.

The end had still been painful, though.

"Whether you know it or not, my son needed you and Connor and Lily this summer." Julie's tenderness was going to make her cry.

"We had fun with the puppies."

"It was more than the puppies. You helped him loosen up. He's had tunnel vision when it comes to the ranch, especially the hay and that pasture. I told him he can't control the weather—only God can—but it went in one ear and out the other. If you hadn't been around, he would still be beating himself up over it. Instead, he's been out and about this summer with you and the kids. It's done him a world of good. He's almost back to himself."

Back to himself. Yeah, she could see that. "He mentioned Cody."

"Good." She nodded. "He doesn't open up about him. Keeps the hurt all jammed down inside." Julie clasped her hands. "I think we all blamed ourselves for Cody cutting us out of his life. I know I did. The worst was not knowing he'd gotten married until after he died. Those regrets are always there, even as life goes on. His father and I didn't handle Cody right, didn't know how to stop him from self-destructing when he was in high school. I'm sure each of us, including Blaine, has a list of things we would have done differently."

Sienna knew it to be true. When her dad walked out, it had crushed her and Becca and their mother. And years later when her mom left without so much as a goodbye, Sienna had been crushed all over again, but this time she hadn't been all that surprised.

People left. With no warning. No explanation.

The people she'd needed, the ones she'd depended on, had abandoned her. Maybe that was why she'd never allowed herself to depend on Troy too much. Maybe she'd chosen a husband who wouldn't be around. It had been easier that way.

"Anyway, enough with the depressing talk. Thank you for bringing my boy's cheerful nature back." Julie patted her hand. "I've missed it."

"I don't think I'm the one to thank."

"Oh, you are. You two were friends long ago, and look at you now. Friends again. Forgive a meddling mom for hoping it could be more. I want you to know you are always welcome here."

"You're not meddling, but thank you." The tears she'd been holding back were knocking at the door. The Mayer family had treated her like one of their own. What she wouldn't give to have them in her life permanently.

But Blaine wasn't hers. This ranch wasn't Casper. And she wasn't taking risks with love.

The people she'd needed might have walked away from her, but she would never abandon Becca, Connor or Lily. She'd be by their sides, whatever the cost.

CHAPTER ELEVEN

HE'D LET HIS brother walk out of his life. Could he really let Sienna walk out, too?

Blaine brushed Boots after checking cattle Wednesday morning. Everything on the ranch was going smoothly. The bulls were happy to be with the cows. He and Jim were negotiating with suppliers to buy additional feed for the winter. And he'd been checking off his never-ending hot list item by item each day. He was even close to making a decision about keeping Tiara and Ollie. But all he could think about was the beautiful redhead who'd stolen his heart as a teen and held it in her hands as an adult.

She and the kids were leaving tomorrow around noon. Yesterday had been her final day working at the candle shop.

Why was it so hard to think about her leaving?

He set aside the brush and began picking the

horse's hooves. A few stones were dislodged from the front left. He expertly made his way around to the other hooves.

Blaine had spent every evening with Sienna this week. They'd held hands on the bench swing in his backyard and watched the stars come out while Connor and Lily played with the puppies. They'd talked about their fears and their dreams, tiptoeing around their feelings for each other, but those feelings had been there, shimmering between them.

He hadn't told her he didn't want her to go. Hadn't admitted she'd be taking his heart with him.

This ranch wouldn't be the same without her. Would he still love it the way he did before she'd arrived? Or would it feel empty? Meaningless?

Was he emotionally prepared to find out?

Connor strode through the stables with Ollie trotting by his side. Good, a distraction.

"What's up, Connor?"

"I was wondering about something." The kid had on his worried face, and Blaine hadn't seen it in a few weeks. He hoped this didn't involve Connor's mother.

"Yeah?" He guided Boots toward the paddock leading to the pasture where he kept the horses. Connor and Ollie fell in beside him.

"Have you decided if you're keeping Tiara and Ollie yet?"

"I want to." He squinted at the horses grazing in the distance. "I'm not sure how I'll make it work by myself, though. Your sister really helped me out all summer."

"I've been thinking. If you kept the dogs, you could hire someone like Lily when they have puppies. You know, like hiring a babysitter. For the first couple of weeks at least."

"That's not a bad idea." It grew on him as he considered it. "Especially in the summer. I'm not sure about the rest of the year with school and all."

"Well, how often do you need to breed them? If they had one litter each summer, would it be enough?"

They came to the gate, and Blaine opened it, patting the horse's neck before letting him loose. The sunny day would get hot later, but for now it was peaceful and mild. Then he closed the gate again and turned to Connor.

"Now that you mention it, I don't see a problem with breeding once a year. I'll run it by Laura. See what she thinks."

Blaine wanted to keep the dogs. As soon as the puppies went to their new homes two weeks from now, he planned on bringing Tiara around the ranch more, too. To only breed them once a year would take a lot of the worries off his mind.

"So you'll keep Ollie?" Connor's eyes lit with hope.

"If Laura agrees to one litter a year? Yes."

He nodded eagerly and let out a loud sigh in relief.

"You love Ollie, don't you?" Blaine gestured for him to join him as he walked down the lane toward the equipment shed.

Connor nodded. "He's a good dog."

"He is." Blaine paused, shifting to face him. "I have to keep him and Tiara together. You know that, right?"

"I wouldn't want them separated."

"I talked to your aunt about this, and I don't want to get your hopes up, but if your mom and dad don't mind, I'd like for you and your sister to have Sushi."

"Really?" His eyes popped. "Lily is going to flip. That would be awesome."

"Yeah, well, don't tell her yet. I don't want her disappointed if your parents say no."

"Could we take him with us when we go home tomorrow?" Connor asked.

"No, he's not ready to leave his mama yet. I can drive him down in a week or two."

"You'd do that?"

"Yeah." Heat climbed his neck. Was he using the puppy as an excuse to see Sienna again? Maybe. Maybe not. He wanted the kids to have the pup.

"Is your sister up?"

"She was eating a bowl of cereal before I came out here."

"Would you do me a favor and bring her to my ranch office? I have something for each of you."

Connor gave him a quizzical look, nodded and jogged away. Blaine lengthened his strides and went into the pole barn, where his office was located. Inside the office, he opened the bottom drawer of his desk and pulled out the envelopes he'd prepared.

Both kids had helped him out all summer. He'd paid Connor an hourly wage each week, and he'd given Sienna money every Friday to give to Lily for watching the pups. But he wanted to give them something more—a bonus for making his work easy these past two months.

A few minutes later, the teens arrived, rosy-cheeked and short of breath. They sat on the folding chairs opposite his desk. He leaned his forearms on it.

"You both stepped up and helped me out this summer big-time," Blaine said. Connor and Lily exchanged confused glances. He continued. "Connor, you took to ranching like a pro. With you and Bryce taking care of the chores, Jim and I were able to get the hay cut and baled before it dried out too much. That can be the difference between the cattle having enough to eat in the winter or not. I needed you, and you came through for me."

"I liked being out there, Blaine."

He smiled at him, then turned his attention to Lily. "And Lily, without your help, I don't know how I would have taken care of the puppies. You have the touch with animals."

He tapped both envelopes on the desk then handed one to Lily and the other to Connor. "This is a bonus. For all your help. I appreciate it. Don't open it here. You'll just embarrass me."

"Thank you." Lily's eyes shimmered and she stood and gave Blaine a quick hug. "Thanks for letting me help with the puppies. I'll never forget it."

"Yeah, thanks." Connor nodded, his smile shy. "I won't forget all you taught me about the ranch, either."

"You're welcome. Now go on and enjoy your day." He waved them off, grinning to himself as they whispered to each other all the way outside.

He sat there for a long time, his thoughts turning to his friends, how each of them had taken a chance on love. Could he do the same?

Sienna liked him. It was obvious. But love? He didn't know if she loved him.

Well, she didn't have to love him yet.

If she'd consider staying here in Sunrise Bend, they could explore their feelings more. Maybe she'd learn to love him. All he had to do was ask her to stay.

SIENNA'S SPIRITS FADED that afternoon as she placed her neatly folded clothes into a suitcase. This was it. The last hurrah. Their final full day here.

Connor and Lily had burst into the cabin earlier all excited about the cash bonus Blaine had given each of them. And an hour later, Julie had picked them up and taken them to the candle shop, where she'd planned a surprise going-away party for them with their new friends. Teens only—well, except for Julie and Kevin, who were in charge of the food and would be chaperoning the event.

Sienna had already cleaned out the fridge, packed most of the snacks in a bin and thrown another load of towels into the washing machine. Tomorrow would be hard enough without having to do all the chores.

The closer her old life got, the bleaker it looked. She'd fallen hard for Blaine. And there was nothing she could do about it except leave. And hope her feelings for the cowboy would fade in time.

The buzz of her phone distracted her from packing. When she saw her sister's name, she immediately answered.

"Hey, Becca. What's going on?"

"Can you bring Connor and Lily home early?" Her sobs made her speech choppy, hard to understand. "Aaron left, and I don't think he's coming back."

Sienna stood there stunned as Becca cried.

"I tried everything, Sienna, I really did. I thought we were going to make it. But this morning he accused me of emotionally blackmailing him. I don't even know what that means." The crying commenced again, although it wasn't as raw this time. "He said I act like a martyr to punish him. I told him he's ridiculous. He slammed out of here."

Rubbing one eyebrow with her free hand, Sienna didn't even know where to start.

"I don't think he's coming back." The words were eerily quiet.

Danger signals blared in her mind as Sienna padded down the hall to the kitchen.

"You two have argued before," she said gently. "And you've spent the past two months together trying, Becca. He'll be back." When her sister didn't respond, her hands grew cold.

Sienna could handle crying. She could handle endless repetition of the same old complaints. But this—this silent pain—she recognized. Her mom had shut down the exact same way in the days before she walked out of her life for good. "Bec?"

"Just come home," she whispered. "I can't do this anymore."

Sienna didn't want to leave this afternoon. It was bad enough having to go tomorrow. And what would the kids say? They'd be upset. Lily was already struggling with leaving the puppies, and Connor had mentioned one final horseback ride tomorrow morning with Bryce.

But her sister's dead silence filled her with anxiety. Closing her eyes, she swayed slightly, trying to figure out what was best for everyone. She didn't know the severity of the situation.

Leaving today would mean losing out on her last night with Blaine. She couldn't do it.

"It's going to be okay, Becca." She gripped the phone tightly, doubting herself. "We'll be home tomorrow afternoon, and I'll stop and pick us up a pizza on the way in."

"No!" Her voice was haggard, sharp.

"It's only one night." Was she being selfish?

"Forget it." The words came out softly, despondently, like a vapor.

The call ended so abruptly, Sienna could only stare at the phone in her hand. After setting it on the counter, she pressed her fingers to her temples. Becca scared her when she was like this. Angry Becca, she could handle. But despondent Becca?

Sienna had lived with two despondent people who'd vanished from her life. What if her sister took off like their parents had? Would

Sienna, Connor and Lily be returning to an empty house? With no sign of their mother?

She couldn't stand the thought of Connor and Lily being confused and hopeless and heartbroken.

The phone rang again, and she snatched it up. "Becca?"

"No, it's me." At the sound of Troy's voice, she recoiled. "I did what you wanted. Saw a doctor. Guess I really am a mental case. Hope you're happy."

His speech was stilted, odd. She'd dealt with this mood before, but for the life of her, she didn't know how to deal with it now.

"Anyhow, you got what you wanted. Now give me what I want."

She was aware of her sharp intake of breath as her chest tightened uncomfortably.

"I spoke with my lawyer," she said. "Regardless of what you think, I'm not happy that you suffer from a personality disorder, Troy. I wouldn't wish that on anyone."

"Then file the petition to have my rights waived. If you're the one who files it, I'll have a better chance of winning."

"It's so extreme. What if you change your

mind a few years from now? You can't go back. You know that, right?"

"So is this about child support? We both know I'm not cut out to be a dad."

"It's not about child support." She pinched the bridge of her nose. "I don't want you doing something permanent you'll regret later."

"I won't regret it. I meant what I said. I want nothing to do with the kid. Nothing."

There was no sense arguing with him. It would go nowhere. But her heart still pounded.

If he wanted to cut all ties and all responsibilities, that was his decision, not hers. "I'm not filing the petition. If you want to, that's your choice. I certainly won't fight it. But I'm not helping you do this, either. Don't put this on me."

All the tension and worry from the past months spilled over as the line went dead. She widened her eyes at the phone in her hand.

She didn't have the time or mental space to think about Troy at the moment. Becca needed her. She was certain of it, and that meant her plans for leaving tomorrow were getting moved up to this afternoon.

Sienna would never forgive herself if she

waited until tomorrow and came home to an empty house and her sister gone.

She pressed Becca's number and waited as it rang.

And rang. And rang.

She left a quick voice mail for her to call her back. Then she texted her, asking if she was okay.

No response.

She hurried to her bedroom and shoved all the remaining clothes from the dresser into her suitcases. Packed her makeup and toiletries.

And called Becca again.

No answer.

Dread churned inside her.

She was driving back as soon as the kids returned.

She couldn't live with herself if she didn't.

CHAPTER TWELVE

AT THE SOUND of a vehicle rumbling past the front of the house, Blaine hauled himself to a standing position in the spare room, keeping one of the puppies in the crook of his arm as he absentmindedly petted it. Connor and Lily must be back from the party his mom had put together.

The hours were speeding by too quickly. He hated the thought of Sienna leaving tomorrow.

That's why all afternoon, he'd been trying to figure out what to say to her tonight after supper. He needed to talk to her. Needed to ask her the hard question, the one she most likely would be saying no to.

But there was a chance she'd say yes. He had to at least try.

He was going to ask her to stay.

Mom already told him she'd asked Sienna to stay in Sunrise Bend and work for them. Sure, she'd declined, but if she changed her mind, she'd have a job here. And she could continue living in the cabin. A job and a place to live—two problems solved.

But he wasn't stupid. She didn't need a job or a place to live. She needed to be near Connor and Lily and her sister. She'd said it time and again.

Still...he had to try. This was his life, too, and he wasn't imagining their connection. Maybe, just maybe, he'd be enough for her to stay.

It wasn't like she'd never see her loved ones again. In fact, she could go to Casper anytime she wanted. He'd drive her himself if need be. He would never rip her from her family.

Blaine set down the puppy and watched affectionately as it toddled off to Tiara. The roly-poly fluffballs had been fun to play with these past few weeks. He'd called Laura earlier, and she'd agreed one litter a year was reasonable and probably good for Tiara as well. As of today, the dogs were officially his.

A knock on the door made him jump. He slipped out of the room and strode down the hall to answer it.

Sienna was standing on his doorstep. Her eyes

glimmered with worry and something else...
Something he couldn't put his finger on.

"What's wrong?" He took her by the hand
and led her inside. They made it to the living
room before she turned to him. He waited for
her to speak, but the silence grew, along with
a sense of foreboding.

She bit her lower lip. "I feel terrible about
this, but we're taking off early."

He looked into her worried green eyes, not
sure he'd heard her correctly. "Come again?"

"Becca called. She wants us back tonight."

Just like that? He stiffened. "And you're
going."

She nodded.

"Sienna, she'll be okay for one night." He
wasn't sure how to handle this. How could he
ask her to stay now? He didn't want to have the
conversation with her upset like this.

"I don't think so," she said quietly.

"Wait until tomorrow to leave. It won't even
be twenty-four hours."

"I know, but..."

Was she wavering? He plunged ahead, antsy
about the timing, but what else could he do?
Let her leave without saying everything in
his heart?

He'd done that with Cody. And he'd never seen his brother again.

"I was going to talk to you tonight, but while I have you alone…" He caressed her upper arms, but her tense muscles didn't relax. "I understand if you have to take the kids back to Casper. And I realize you have a lot going on there. But this summer—it's been incredible."

"It has been." Her eyes grew watery, and her voice was little more than a whisper.

"Honestly, I don't want it to end. Being with you, spending all this time with you, talking to you—I haven't been able to open up like this to a woman. Ever."

She gulped.

"I'm glad you're back in my life." He wished she would give him an indication—anything, really—that she wanted to hear what he was saying. "I had feelings for you in high school, and then you were gone. Now you're here, and my feelings never really went away."

She turned her head to the side, looking away from him.

"I get that this is bad timing with you being pregnant. And I know you have to return to Casper for the moment, but I want you to consider moving here. You can live in the cabin.

You can work with Mom and Reagan and Holly. I don't want what we have to end. We get along great. We're both mature, older now. We could date, keep getting to know each other until you're ready. I could see us together...forever."

A tear slipped out and dripped down her cheek as she looked up at him.

"Don't cry." He swiped away the tear with his thumb. "I don't want to make you cry."

A tender sob ripped from her throat, and she pressed her lips together, shaking her head.

"In my fantasies," she said, her voice wobbly, "I'd live in the cabin and work with your family, and you and I would date and get closer and be together forever." She attempted a smile, but it went horribly wrong. "But that's all it is, Blaine, a fantasy."

"It doesn't have to be." He drew her closer.

"I'm having a baby, Blaine." She took a step back, waving both hands to indicate her stomach. "And I can't think straight. Not with Becca and... I'm just so worried I can barely breathe. When I said I need to get back to Casper, I meant it. Something's wrong with my sister."

"Okay, it's okay." He'd wanted a different response, but she was worked up. "I understand.

Take Connor and Lily home and help your sister. In a few days, you can come back and we can figure it out."

"You know I can't do that." Her eyebrows twisted as she frowned. "It's not that simple. I mean, Connor and Lily are a big part of my life. Ever since Grammy died, I've lived within a few miles of them. I'm like their second mom."

You know I can't do that. The words he wanted to say froze in his throat. He did know she couldn't. She'd been adamant about it from day one.

She shook her head, blowing out a breath and blinking at his chest. "Aaron left again, and what he said really hurt my sister. So I can't just drop the kids off with a 'see ya' when I know she's distraught. I can't do it. The worst thing is I don't even know if she'll be there."

He was confused. Sienna was leaving early and she didn't even know if her sister would be home? A twinge of anger stirred. "Then why are you going?"

"*Because* I don't know if she'll be there." She stared at him like, *don't you get it?* No, he didn't get it. Should he?

"Where would she be? How will you find her?" He took a small step to the side, raking his hand through his hair. "Why not stick around here until you know she's home?"

"You don't understand."

"You're right. I don't." It wouldn't be the first time, either. Why couldn't he be better at figuring out the things between the lines? He inched closer. The only words he still needed to say wouldn't be silenced. "I love you. I want to have a relationship with you. I can see us married, rocking on the backyard swing together for years to come. I want it all, and I know this is bad timing, but I don't see any other time we can have this discussion. I'm not trying to rush you. I just need you to know how I feel about you."

More tears sprouted from the corners of her eyes, and she covered her face with her hands. He groaned and pulled her into his arms, caressing her back, whispering *shh* in her hair.

He loved her. He wanted her here. And his heart was crumbling to dust because he didn't know how to convince her.

If he didn't convince her, she'd be gone. And his life would never be the same.

SIENNA DREW BACK, wishing she could stay wrapped in those strong arms forever. "I can't stay, Blaine. My family is in Casper. Your life is here. I wish it was different, but it isn't."

"I'm not asking you to give up your family. We have technology. You can FaceTime them every day. I'll drive you to Casper every weekend if you want."

She stared into his clear blue eyes and could see the honesty shining through. He really would drive her to Casper every weekend if she asked him to.

But she needed to be within walking distance of Becca and the kids. Just like she'd been for most of her life. Four hours away was too far if something went wrong.

Anger at Aaron shot through her. Why couldn't he have stayed and fought for his marriage? Then she wouldn't be so terrified of going back and finding no trace of her sister.

Did all men walk away when the going got tough?

"You *are* asking me to give them up." She rubbed her forearms, hardening her heart. "FaceTime doesn't cut it for me. I want to go to their school events. I like bringing them donuts on a random Friday morning. And there's the unexpected stuff, like what if Lily needs a ride home from band practice? Who will be there to pick her up?"

The way his jaw shifted warned her she was crossing lines she shouldn't.

"Her mother?" he said. "Her father?"

"Yeah, well, they haven't been all that reliable lately." Frustration mounted. He didn't get it. She was the one the kids relied on. She was the one they called.

"Okay, so a friend's parent could give her a ride. And Connor has his license. He could pick her up."

"That isn't the point."

"Then what is?"

"You're saying all the things that tempt me, Blaine. I enjoy working with your mother and Reagan and Holly. I've always loved Sunrise Bend. I like your friends. Like your church. Like this ranch. I like you. But everything you mentioned is on your terms."

"What do you mean?" His face scrunched in confusion.

"What would you be giving up?" she asked. "It never crossed your mind to leave your family behind. To leave this ranch and move down to Casper to be with me."

"What would I do there?" To his credit, he seemed curious, not mad. "All I know is ranching."

"I'm not asking you to move, Blaine. That's

not what I'm getting at." Her shoulders fell. She felt tired. Drained.

"Then what are you getting at? Tell me what to do. Tell me what you want me to say." His voice rose in anguish, and she covered her ears, overcome by a sense of everything falling apart.

"First Troy, now this." She let out a strangled cry.

Blaine's arms were around her once more. His gaze probed her face. "What happened?"

"He called me earlier. He wants me to be the one to file the petition for him to waive his parental rights. And he thought I'd be gloating over his diagnosis. It's like he never knew me at all. Why would I ever be happy to learn someone I cared about has a serious illness? And I'm dumbfounded he expects me to be involved in this. Doesn't he get that I'm the one who loses either way? Just like now."

As soon as the speech left her mouth, she covered her lips, horrified by everything festering inside her.

Blaine's arms fell down to his sides. His silence crushed her.

She took a few jagged breaths until her heart rate slowed to normal.

"I love you, Sienna." His words flowed slowly and sweetly, like honey drizzling from a spoon.

"I love you, too, but it's not enough."

"Yes, it is. I love you."

"Then let me go." Her heart broke as she said what needed saying. "I can't give you what you need. What you deserve. I can't move here and live happily ever after."

He stared at her for a long moment, then asked, "Why not?"

"Because I'm the glue holding it together in Casper. I would be a nervous wreck here. Love doesn't conquer everything. My feelings for you won't change reality."

Blaine was offering her everything. But what good would it be if it meant leaving behind her precious loved ones?

She brushed past him to leave. She couldn't stay any longer. She needed to get the kids to pack their stuff. They'd hit the road as soon as they said goodbye to the rest of Blaine's family.

Everyone she cared about expected her to make these big, life-changing decisions.

She didn't have the energy to make them anymore. She just needed to get back to her ordinary life. Or what was left of it.

CHAPTER THIRTEEN

"IF YOUR PARENTS agree you can have him, I'll drive Sushi to you in a few weeks." Blaine hugged Lily, then Connor, and cast a sideways glance at Sienna. They had said their good-byes to everyone fifteen minutes ago and driven straight back to the cabin to load her vehicle. While Blaine and Connor stacked everything in the back of the SUV, Lily had gone back to his house to kiss the puppies goodbye. When she returned, she still had Sushi in her arms.

"Thank you so much. I know Mom and Dad will let us keep him," Lily said with tears in her eyes, hugging Sushi one last time. She kissed the puppy's forehead. "'Bye for now, sweet baby." She handed the pup back to Blaine. "Will you text me pictures of him?"

"I sure will." He adjusted the squirming dog in his arms, and the little guy calmed right down.

"Send pictures of Ollie, too, for me." Connor looked torn.

"I'll do that." He nodded to each of them. "Anytime you want to visit, the door's open."

"Alright, we'd better hit the road." Sienna held up her keychain. Blaine sprang into action, opening the driver's side door for her. She got settled in her seat and looked up at him.

He didn't want to meet her gaze. Didn't want to see the rejection there.

Did she feel even the smallest fraction of what he felt for her? She'd said she loved him, but she couldn't mean it, not if she was leaving. He kept hoping she'd pull him aside and tell him she'd thought it over and decided to come back after returning the kids to her sister.

But his love wasn't enough for her. She didn't believe love conquered all.

Could have fooled him.

Before he did something stupid, like get on his knees and beg her to reconsider, he tapped his knuckles twice on the top of the vehicle.

"Take care now." He pulled down the tip of his cowboy hat to her and couldn't resist one last look at her pretty face. It was drawn, sad. Maybe she had regrets. He didn't know.

"You, too." Then she closed her door, held her hand up in goodbye and drove away.

As the vehicle grew smaller in the distance, so did his heart.

The timing had been wrong.

Maybe he should have opened up about his feelings sooner. Maybe he hadn't offered her what she really wanted. What *did* she really want?

He kicked at the gravel and took the puppy, now asleep, back to the house. Tried to clear his mind as he climbed the porch steps and let himself inside. After returning Sushi to Tiara and the other puppies, Blaine got a caged-in feeling and headed out to the pole barn.

Keep busy. Don't think about her.

He'd bury himself in what he knew. The ranch.

But as he pushed the button for the pole barn's overhead door to open, his mind was filled with their earlier conversation.

She'd accused him of wanting her on his terms. Of not giving anything up. And then she'd mentioned her ex—like Blaine could ever be compared to that guy.

A stack of boxes near the wall caught his attention. Spare parts for the tractors. He hefted one up and carried it to the back storage room, where he'd built shelves the previous winter. After shoving it on an empty shelf, he returned to move the other boxes.

She was wrong. He wasn't only thinking of himself. He was thinking of her, too. Sunrise Bend did have a lot to offer.

He frowned, wiping his forehead with the back of his hand. Maybe he *had* been selfish.

She liked her job in Casper. Her sister and the kids were her life. She felt responsible for them and wanted to be there. How could he fault her for that? He couldn't.

Memories of all the things she'd mentioned about her family trickled in. How her brother drowned and it had devastated all of them. Then her father left—more like disappeared—and no one was the same. And later her mom took off, too.

Sienna and Becca only had each other. Well, except for Aaron, who might well be out of the picture, too, at this point.

Maybe he hadn't fully understood her situation.

He hefted another box in his arms and carried it to the back room. If their places had been switched and Blaine knew Jet was struggling with something, wouldn't he drop everything to help his brother?

Bad comparison. Jet never struggled with anything he couldn't handle. Blaine wouldn't need to drop everything.

But Cody... Cody had been different.

In the back room, he set the heavy box on the floor, no longer caring if it made it onto a shelf.

What if it was Cody who needed him?

Regret shot through his torso. Blaine had always worried about the kid. He'd been a risk-taker. Bored. Easily lured into trouble. And even when Blaine and Jet told him to knock it off, he'd always fallen back into his bad habits. It had been so frustrating. And he'd been helpless to do anything about it.

That had been the worst part of Cody leaving and refusing to answer his calls and texts—he'd had no way of knowing if his brother was okay or not.

Sienna was in a similar position with her sister, and even more, she was like a second mom to those kids.

No wonder she'd left. No wonder she hadn't considered returning.

After being abandoned by her dad, her mom and even her ex-husband, she probably couldn't handle the idea of her sister being out of her life, too.

Shaken, he dropped his face into his hands. Where did that leave him?

He couldn't move to Casper. His skills involved raising cattle and growing hay, and that was about it. Plus, this ranch was his. He was a third-generation rancher, and he couldn't imagine walking away from it.

But could he imagine a future without Sienna?

Any future without her looked gray and miserable, as sparse and brittle as the dead pasture had been last year.

The clunk of footsteps had him straightening. Jet was standing in the doorway. "I thought I'd find you back here."

"Oh, yeah?" He wiped his palms on his jeans and brushed past Jet on his way out of the room. "What do you need?"

"I don't need anything." Jet followed him to the open bay, filled with light.

"Then why are you here?" Blaine uncapped a dry-erase marker and pretended to read the list on the whiteboard.

"Just making sure you're okay."

"I'm fine." Blaine glanced over his shoulder at him. "Why wouldn't I be?"

"Oh, I don't know. Maybe because the woman you love just drove away."

He stilled. How did his brother know all that? Slowly, he turned to face him. A younger Blaine would have denied his love, but he didn't see the point now.

"What do you do?" He shrugged. "That's life for you."

Jet widened his eyes, trailing his finger down the side of the whiteboard. "That's your response? You're just going to let her go?"

"Yep." He eyed the other boxes, tempted to haul them to the back room to get away from his brother.

"Really?"

"What do you want me to say, Jet? Did you come over to gloat? I messed it up with Sienna, the same as I messed it up with the dead pasture and about a million other things over the years. Are you happy?"

"What are you talking about?" Jet looked genuinely perplexed. "You didn't mess up the dead pasture. The drought did that. To be honest, I was surprised you got as much yield as you did out of it. You were smart to plant the wheatgrass."

Normally, his praise would have put a bounce in Blaine's step for days, but it didn't matter now. Nothing did.

"Yeah, well, I'd be shocked if I have enough hay to feed my cattle this winter." He bent to pick up another box and thought better of it. He might as well have the full conversation with Jet now. Then he could move on and get back to his life. His lonely, empty life.

"Does Sienna know you love her?" Jet asked quietly.

Blaine nodded.

"And she still left?"

He nodded again.

"Did you say something stupid?"

"Probably. I mean, I didn't think I did, but now I'm not so sure." Blaine headed toward the office and gestured for Jet to follow him. Inside, they both sprawled out on chairs.

"Why don't you run it by me?" Jet asked. "I won't judge. You know how much I messed up with Holly."

That brought a brief smile to Blaine's face.

"Sienna's close with her sister—Connor and Lily's mother. In fact, she's kind of a second mom to the kids. She's worried because Aaron—their father—took off. It had been looking like they'd resolved their marriage issues."

"Ouch." Jet leaned back. "So she left early for Becca's sake."

"Yeah."

"See? That's good."

"It's not good." Blaine ran his tongue across his teeth. "Her ex is hassling her. Doesn't want anything to do with the baby. Apparently, he called her today. I didn't know this before I asked her to stay."

"But you did ask her to stay?"

He nodded, his throat painfully tight.

"What else?"

Blaine gave him the short version of the conversation. "The worst thing about it is she's right. I'm asking her to give up everything, while I give up nothing."

"You're also offering a lot of things she doesn't have." Jet leaned forward. Neither spoke for a while. "Now what?"

"I don't know."

"If you love her and want to be with her, we'll figure out something with the ranch. We can join the two herds together again, or we can hire a manager. Maybe in time, she'll come around to living here."

"You'd be willing to do that? After all the trouble I gave you about splitting it up last year?"

"Of course, Blaine. You're not just my brother. You're my best friend. I want to see you happy."

The words healed the part of him that had felt like a runner-up to Jet most of his life. Reagan was right. They were different people. Blaine was who he was, and it was time to stop feeling like he didn't measure up.

"Thanks, Jet. You're my best friend, too."

"So go after her."

"That's the thing. I love Sienna, but I don't know if I could be happy in Casper. I only know ranching. And I don't want to leave it. It fulfills me, you know?"

"I do know." Jet stood. "You don't have to make any decisions tonight. Give it time. It will work out."

Blaine rose, too, and they made their way through the pole barn to the driveway, where Jet had parked.

"If you need me, I'm here." Jet pulled him in for a half hug. Blaine returned it.

"Thanks, man."

He stood there for a while after Jet drove away. Was his brother right? Would it work out?

He didn't know. Sienna hadn't exactly been overwhelmed by his declaration of love. And she'd flat-out refused to even consider pursuing a relationship with him.

The one thing he did know, however, was that she'd move mountains to help her sister, but she wouldn't consider staying a few extra hours to be with him.

He didn't want to be anyone's afterthought. He didn't want to be a distant second or third or fourth in her life.

He was done being the runner-up.

And that meant this fantasy of spending his life with Sienna had to end. He'd only be crushed if he held on to hope any longer.

AFTER THE FIRST hour on the road, the urgency to make sure Becca was okay began to subside. And each mile of lonely highway brought new insights into her conversation with Blaine.

She was driving away from the most incredible man she'd ever met. A life with him would mean a life of happiness. The love she'd never dreamed possible waited for her in Sunrise Bend, and she'd turned him down.

Leaving her family and life in Casper was too big a risk.

Connor hadn't said much on the ride so far. He'd been staring out the passenger window. And Lily had been quiet in the back seat, too. Neither of them had put up a fight when she'd told them they needed to leave early, which had surprised her. Sienna felt bad for ending their time on the ranch prematurely, even if it was only by a day.

In time, they'd all get back into their routines. She'd get the nursery ready and start putting a game plan together for after the baby was born. School would start back up at the end of August. The kids would talk Becca into keeping Sushi, Sienna had no doubt. They'd have the puppy to keep them busy, and she'd have the baby.

"Aunt Sienna?" Lily asked from the back seat.

"Yes?" She smiled at her in the rearview mirror.

"I went to Blaine's earlier to check on the puppies."

"I'm sure he appreciated it."

She kept her eyes downcast. "I knocked, but no one came, and then I heard voices, so I let myself in."

A fearful sensation set her nerves on edge. "Oh?"

"I stopped in the hall when I heard you and Blaine talking. I didn't mean to eavesdrop, but…"

Sienna gripped the steering wheel, wondering how much her niece had heard.

"I told Conner, and we think you should be with Blaine. He's the greatest guy, Aunt Sienna." Her hazel eyes brightened. "We know you love Sunrise Bend. Everyone's so nice, and you love making the candles."

Sienna glanced at Connor. He'd shifted to face her fully.

"Lil's right. The ranch is awesome, and Blaine's a good guy. He'd make you happy."

She swallowed the emotions their words evoked. "You two make me happy. Your mom makes me happy."

Connor looked back at Lily.

"We're getting older," Lily said. "We can deal with Mom. If she gets sad, we'll hug her and be there for her."

"And you're always telling me it's not my job to worry about her problems," Connor said. "I can set limits and still love her. She has the counselor now. She can call him if she's upset."

So Connor *had* been listening to her all these months.

"She can always call me, too." Sienna gave

him a tender smile. "It won't be easy, you know. Sometimes it's hard setting limits when it's your mom."

"I know." He shrugged. "The thing is, though, no matter how long I listen to her talk about Dad or listen to her cry, it's never enough. I used to think it helped her when I listened. But now I'm not so sure. Nothing really changes, you know? It's the same thing the next night."

His words were a jolt of truth to her heart.

Nothing did really change. Being there unconditionally for her sister never made much of a difference. No matter how much she sacrificed to be there for Becca, it wasn't enough.

Is that how I feel? Like I'm sacrificing for her?

She'd always told herself she was there for Becca because she loved her. But right now— driving back early—it didn't feel like love. It felt like fear. She was scared Becca would fall apart without her. But her sister had been falling apart for months.

Becca was a wonderful sister, a good mom. She was just going through a rough patch.

"We think you should go back to Blaine after you take us home," Lily said. "We know you like him. You're all smiley and holding hands all the time. He's perfect for you."

He was perfect for her.

But she wasn't perfect for him.

Sienna had left the one person who accepted her, asked nothing from her except for her presence.

He simply wanted to be with her, liked being near her.

He was the one man who loved her unconditionally.

Yeah, for now.

If Sienna took a chance and moved to Sunrise Bend, she had no guarantees Blaine wouldn't wake up one day and realize he'd made a mistake, that he didn't want to be with her. Just like her parents had. Just like Troy had.

No matter what Connor and Lily said, they needed her around. Becca did, too. And she wasn't about to let them go. Even if it meant losing the man who'd captured her heart.

BLAINE STOOD IN front of his bedroom window late that night watching the stars in the black sky. Even in the darkness, he could make out Grandpa's swing. He turned away. All he could see was Sienna's smiling face as she sat there with him night after night.

And now she was gone.

He padded down the hall and peeked in on the puppies. He'd brought Ollie in to sleep with Tiara and the pups, and they'd all curled up together, sleeping peacefully. Together at last.

He doubted he'd get any shut-eye tonight. Continuing to the kitchen, he wrestled with his thoughts. Anger began to build.

God, why did You bring her here, just to take her away? Why did You even let me get close to her? It would have been better if she had stayed a distant memory. Then I wouldn't be going through this.

He entered the kitchen and whipped open the fridge. Bending to scan the contents, he shook his head and slammed the door shut. He wasn't hungry. Wasn't thirsty.

He was mad.

Mad at himself for bungling the conversation with her earlier.

Mad at her for not responding the way he wanted.

Mad at Jet for even suggesting he leave the ranch.

Mad at God for allowing this to happen.

Blaine pivoted and stalked over to the couch.

He sat, then leaned his head back on the cushion so he could stare at the ceiling.

Did he matter at all to Sienna? Had she given him the slightest thought since driving away?

He'd been tempted to call her tonight when he knew she would be back in Casper. He'd wanted to find out if her sister was okay and to hear her voice.

But he'd decided against it. He'd said his part. She'd said hers. End of story.

Wiping his hands down his cheeks, he shook his head. He didn't matter to her. Not the way she mattered to him.

He must not have mattered much to Cody, either. Had his brother even looked at the handful of texts he'd sent? Listened to the voice mail he'd left?

Did Blaine really matter to anyone in the grand scheme of things?

Jet was right. The ranches could be rejoined. A manager could be hired. If Blaine decided to move a million miles away, his family would wish him well and their lives would go on as usual.

No one needed him.

Like a popped water balloon, all the anger he'd been holding spilled out. He sat there clenching and unclenching his fists. He'd always taken life as it came. Hadn't questioned much. Knew his place. Knew what to do in most circumstances.

But right here, right now, felt like a crossroads. And he recognized he had a choice.

Bitterness or acceptance.

God, forgive me. I'm like an angry bull knocking my horns against a fence to tear it down. You've answered so many of my prayers over the years. I just wanted You to answer this one, too. I love her. I love that redhead. She's smart and calm and fun. Easy to be with. I've never felt so full of life as when I'm with her.

He let all the good memories wash over him. Soon the anger, the bitterness shifted to something more painful. To loss. To regret.

Lord, I want it my way. I don't like giving her up. But I have to. I know it worked out with Jet and Holly, but I'm not my brother. Never have been. And Sienna left because her family is more important to her than me.

Was he wrong? Maybe she was scared of losing them.

He knew that fear well.

It was time to be completely honest with himself about Cody. He'd been clinging to his final memories of his brother—bad memories—but in the months after he left the ranch, Cody had gotten his life together. Holly had said so. She also believed he would have reconciled with them all eventually. According to Holly, Cody had been happy.

So why was he still holding on to this guilt?

Sienna had told him to let it go, that he'd been forgiven. The scripture the pastor had spoken about earlier this summer came back.

Remember ye not the former things, neither consider the things of old. Behold, I will do a new thing—now it shall spring forth, shall ye not know it? I will even make a way in the wilderness, and rivers in the desert.

He was ready to make peace with Cody's death. God was in the business of making ways in the wilderness and rivers in the desert.

God, I convinced myself I was to blame for Cody's problems. But I wasn't. We all have free will. Sienna does. Her sister does, too, although Sienna might not like it. Would You get through to her? Help her see she isn't responsible for her sister's, Connor's or Lily's happiness?

Blaine clasped his hands behind his head. Better times with Cody trickled back to him, ones he'd forgotten. Of riding around the ranch on horseback, of stopping at the candy store in town after church on Sunday, of Christmas mornings and all kinds of things he hadn't thought about in years.

He wasn't sure what he was going to do about Sienna, but he knew one thing. Jet was right. Time would work this out. And he'd be okay.

Sienna knocked again on their front door as Connor fumbled to find his key. A sense of dread brewed in her gut. They hadn't stopped along the way, and the night sky held an ominous breeze.

Was her sister home? Or had she taken off? Like Dad? Like Mom?

Please, God, don't do that to Connor and Lily. Please let her be home.

"Got it." Connor held up the key with a lopsided grin and moved to insert it in the lock at the exact moment the door opened.

Becca was standing in the foyer, looking surprised, and Aaron was next to her with his arm around her shoulders.

"What are you doing back? I thought you were coming home tomorrow." Becca opened her arms wide to hug the kids, and they moved inside, hugging both parents as Sienna squeezed into the foyer and shut the door behind her.

"When you called earlier, I was worried." Sienna couldn't keep the edge out of her tone. She'd packed everything in a hurry, said their goodbyes in a rush and practically peeled out of Blaine's life to get here. And what did she find? Becca had been here with Aaron all along?

"I texted you more than once." Sienna took out her phone and pointed to it. "Didn't you get my messages?"

"Oh, no. Sorry." Becca flushed, looking up at Aaron. "We, ah, had a long talk."

He squeezed her shoulders. "I'm back. For good. And I can't wait to make up for lost time."

"Mom—Mom, guess what?" Lily clasped her hands near her chest and started bouncing up and down. "Blaine is letting us keep one of the puppies. Sushi! He was the runt of the litter, the one I told you about. I took care of him every day. He's bringing him here in two weeks!"

"A puppy?" Becca shot Sienna a questioning glance. "I don't know about that."

Aaron had pulled Connor into a hug. "I think a puppy is a great idea, Bec."

"You do?" Her face lit up. "Well, if you two promise to take care of him, feed him, fill his water bowl, walk him, then I guess we'll take him. He's your responsibility, though."

"We will!" Connor and Lily said in unison. They met each other's eyes and laughed.

"Come on, you can tell me all about your summer while we unload your stuff." Aaron opened the door, and they turned and went outside, leaving her alone with Becca.

The happy family reunion was everything Sienna wanted for the kids and her sister, but she couldn't help feeling betrayed. She motioned for Becca to join her in the kitchen.

"After your call, I couldn't help but think the worst." Sienna leaned against the counter. "I didn't know what I was going to find when I got here. I didn't even know if you'd be here."

"Where would I go?" Becca frowned.

"I don't know. But it wouldn't be the first time I walked into an empty house."

"I'm not Dad. I'm not Mom." Her chin rose. "That's what you're getting at, right?"

"I didn't say you were." But, yeah, she was getting at that.

"Look, Sienna, I know I've got issues, but abandoning my family isn't one of them. I really don't appreciate you implying I would do that."

The need to defend herself rose up.

"Aaron and I made some decisions today," Becca said. "We're continuing to go to counseling until the counselor thinks it's no longer necessary. And I'm going to see someone else—a therapist—to work through things regarding Dan and our parents."

Sienna clamped her mouth shut, frowning. All of that sounded good, but she couldn't let go of the anger pressing inside her.

Becca reached over and placed her hand on Sienna's shoulder. "You might want to see a professional about Dan and our parents, too."

"Me?" Why would Becca think she needed therapy?

"We dealt with our childhood traumas in different ways." Her sad smile was full of love. "I know I've been too clingy and emotional. And maybe you've had to step into the role of being a parent too many times." Becca held up her hands, palms out in defense. "That's on me. I'm going to work on it."

Sienna kept her spine rigid as the words spun circles around her mind. The anger subsided as she recognized the truth in her sister's words.

"I think you're right, Becca." In some ways it was a relief to hear her sister's honesty. But she also felt duped. Like she'd gotten sucked into her sister's drama for so long…and it hadn't been necessary.

She'd been blaming Becca for her need to live in Casper, to stay close to the kids, but was it even true?

"I'm glad you and Aaron are working things out." She choked down the sadness. "But I'm not going to pretend I'm not upset we left the ranch early for nothing. You should have called me."

Connor and Lily entered the room, cheerfully chatting with their father. Sienna had to face facts. The kids were right—they were getting older. And from the looks of it, their family would work through any issues that came up.

But where did that leave her?

Alone. They didn't need her. They all had each other.

Too hurt to stay any longer, Sienna turned to go.

"Wait, Sienna." Becca sighed. "I didn't mean to upset you. I haven't even thanked you for everything. For taking the kids this summer. For giving Aaron and I the space to work on our marriage. I couldn't have done this without you. How can I ever repay you?"

Becca hugged her tightly, and some of the tension eased.

"We're sisters. That's what we're here for." Sienna attempted to smile. It was true, too. They'd always had each other's backs. "I'm going to take off. I'm pretty tired."

"Are you sure?" she asked. "Why don't you stay a while?"

Sienna shook her head. "I don't think so."

After hugging everyone goodbye, Sienna drove the short distance to her apartment, rolled her suitcase to the entrance, unlocked the front door and went inside. It smelled stale. She flicked the lights on. A standard two-bedroom, it was clean, beige and tidy. It felt sterile. Lonely.

She kicked off her shoes. Leaving the suitcase in the living room, she padded straight to the bedroom, pulled back the covers and climbed into her bed. Only then did the tears begin to fall.

She'd left Blaine and Sunrise Bend and the candle shop and her friends behind. She'd left them to make sure Becca was okay.

And Becca was okay.

Better than okay.

It was what she'd wanted. But now she was questioning everything.

Her sister had been through life crises more than once, and she'd never walked out on the kids. She'd never vanished like their mom and dad had. Becca was a lot of things—emotional, prone to anxiety, even self-centered at times—but she wasn't like their parents.

Had Sienna been projecting her fears of being abandoned on her sister?

She burrowed deeper into the covers.

Blaine's face—his handsome, hurt, devastated face—had etched itself into her mind. He'd told her he loved her. Given her an alternative to her life here. And what had she done?

She'd accused him of not giving anything up. And it wasn't even the reason she'd left.

Sienna had trust issues that would fill a quarry. She hadn't trusted her sister to do right by Connor and Lily. She hadn't trusted Aaron to stick around for his family. She hadn't even trusted Connor and Lily to be able to handle their parents' problems.

But most of all she hadn't trusted herself.

Lord, what's wrong with me? I never really loved Troy. That's why when he left me, I didn't fall apart like Becca did. Blaine's everything I want. And I'm scared. I'm so scared. Help me!

Sitting up, she grabbed the Bible from her nightstand. With the flip of the switch, the lamp glowed, and she turned to the back of the Bible for the subject index. Trailing her finger down, she stopped on the section marked Trust.

She paged through and found the first five passages, but they weren't what she was looking for. The sixth one, though, watered her parched soul.

O taste and see that the Lord is good: blessed is the man that trusteth in him.

The Lord was good. She closed the Bible. She had only to look at what happened this evening to taste and see His goodness.

Becca and Aaron had reunited. They still had a bumpy journey ahead, but they were committed to each other. If God could work on Becca's heart to take the scary leap of seeing a therapist and continuing to go to couples' counseling with Aaron, surely God could help Sienna trust that He had good things in store for her as well.

Lord, please forgive me for thinking the worst earlier about my sister. I didn't realize how much my parents' actions affected me. I didn't realize how much I haven't trusted anyone to stick around.

The pain and emotional turmoil of the past day eased. Her eyelids drooped as exhaustion overtook her. She needed to make things right with Blaine. She just didn't know how.

CHAPTER FOURTEEN

BLAINE WOKE THE next morning with a throbbing headache. The puppies were whining in the spare room. He swung his legs over the side of the bed, wiped his hands down his cheeks and let out a loud sigh. The three hours of sleep had not helped him. Sienna was still gone.

He made his way down the hall to the spare room, then petted Tiara and Ollie, filled their water bowls and allowed the two adult dogs out of the room. They trotted straight to the sliding door leading to the backyard. After he let them out, he stared at the beautiful landscape with low hills in the distance and cattle moving out of his view. Pastel pinks and purples colored the sky. The sun was waking up, and he had decisions to make.

Blaine would be willing to give up the ranch and move to Casper, but not under these circumstances. Sienna had made it clear her family came first. If he moved to be near her, he would be accepting the position of being the runner-up in her life.

He wasn't willing to stay in the shadows when it came to love. His friends had shown him the importance of mutual love and respect.

But just because Sienna couldn't put him first now didn't mean she couldn't later. And if her feelings did change—if she could love him wholeheartedly to the point he wasn't second-best—well, then he might be willing to move to Casper to be with her.

It would be hard. But it would be worth it.

The dogs chased each other outside for a few minutes. Then they stopped several feet apart. Ollie's ears perked as he let out two barks. Tiara bent her front legs, then took off with Ollie chasing her. They finally slowed, sniffing each other affectionately before playing again.

It looked like they were in no hurry to come back inside, so he retreated to the kitchen and prepped the coffeemaker. Once it was filled, he pressed the on button and returned to his spot in front of the sliding door. The dogs were panting as they lay near each other on the lawn. They looked like they didn't have a care in the world.

That's how it was with Sienna. When he was with her, it felt like they were in sync. Like he didn't have a care in the world. Until yesterday.

As the coffeemaker sputtered, he thought about his options.

He could give Sienna space.

He could call her to see how she was doing.

Or could he try to forget about her and move on with his life.

No. He couldn't forget her. She was impossible to forget.

He had another option. He could do things the old-fashioned way. He could court her.

Staring unseeing out toward the hills, he mulled over the concept. It might work. He could go down there on weekends...for as long as it took. Maybe it would prove to her he'd never abandon her.

The way they'd left things felt jagged and raw. What if he drove down there today? He'd tell her what was on his mind. Assure her he'd be at her apartment every Saturday to prove not all men walked away when the going got tough.

It was the only idea that made sense at this point.

The coffeemaker beeped as the dogs trotted toward the sliding door. Blaine let them in, petting both before pouring himself a cup of coffee.

He and Sienna could make their relationship work. He was sure of it. Sienna just didn't know it yet.

SIENNA WOKE TO the sound of cartoons blasting through the paper-thin walls. One eye struggled to open. Then the other. Her body felt as heavy as solid iron. The baby's arms and legs rolled around in her tummy, and she groaned, smiling.

"I see you're awake, too. It won't be long before you'll be begging to watch cartoons like the neighbors." She hauled herself out of bed and made the mistake of glancing at the mirror. Splotchy face. Hair a disaster. Shaking her head, she forced herself to look away.

After showering, she debated whether she should unpack her car first or head to a drive-through for breakfast. Either way she had to figure out what to do about Blaine soon.

She couldn't leave things the way they were now.

The man likely had no idea how deep her feelings were for him. And she hated that she'd given him the impression he wasn't important to her.

He was important. Very important.

Someone knocked on the door. She went to the entrance, figuring it was Becca, and looked through the peephole.

Erica? What was she doing here?

Sienna unlocked the door and ushered her inside. Erica held two iced coffees and a white bag Sienna recognized from her favorite coffee shop.

"Mom told me you came back early, and I thought I'd surprise you." Erica set the coffees and bag on the nearby table and gave Sienna a warm hug. "How are you?"

"Better now that you're here." She smiled and pointed to the coffees. "Which one is mine?"

"They're both decaf iced mochas. Oh, and I brought donuts. I figured half a dozen should get us through catching up. And, boy, do we have some catching up to do."

As Sienna took her iced coffee along with a glazed donut to the couch, she was grateful for Erica's friendship. They'd gotten each other through some difficult times all year, and it was time for her to be honest with her friend.

As soon as Erica had settled into the comfy

chair kitty-corner to her, Sienna took a deep breath. "I'm in love with Blaine."

Closing her eyes, she waited for laughter or condemnation, but when neither came, she opened them one at a time. Erica simply took another bite of a chocolate cake donut and nodded.

"You're perfect for him. And he's perfect for you."

"I'm sorry I didn't tell you earlier."

She waved her off. "Don't be. I know it's complicated. You're dealing with Troy and the baby and your sister, not to mention working for my mom, who probably would drop to her knees in tears of joy at the thought of you and Blaine getting married. No—no need to apologize."

She fought back tears. Erica got her in a way few people did.

"And listen, I'm all for it. Blaine will never— and I mean never—let you down." Erica set the rest of her donut on a napkin as a pained expression crossed her face.

"What is it?" Sienna asked. "What's wrong? Is it the baby?"

"No." A wisp of a smile crossed her lips as she massaged her belly. "I was just thinking about Blaine and how I wish Jamie was a little more like him."

She didn't know what to say. Erica's husband had been on the road more and more, checking on their businesses. And he tended to get distracted easily—the few times she'd met him, he'd been more interested in looking at his phone than enjoying a dinner out.

"Does Blaine know?" Erica asked, tilting her head. "He's not the best at picking up on things."

Tears threatened as she thought of yesterday. She willed them away, holding her breath until she was reasonably sure she could talk without breaking down.

"I don't think he knows how much I care about him."

"That's probably for the best. I don't know if you could convince him to get serious with you, anyhow. He's not getting married. He's said it so many times, I couldn't begin to count. Oh, I'm sorry, that sounds harsh. I didn't mean to—"

"No, no, it's fine." Sienna let out a soft laugh. "Actually, he was the one who told me he loved me. Yesterday. He wants me to move there, work at the candle shop. And date."

"And date?" Erica tried on the concept and seemed to like it, judging by her eager nod. "You know what this means, don't you?"

She shook her head.

"You've cracked the shell around the nut that is my stubborn, wonderful brother. Where all of us have tried, you're the only one to succeed. He must really be into you."

She could feel the heat rising to her cheeks. "Well, I'm pretty into him."

"Yet, here you are."

"Yeah, yesterday was pretty bad." She told Erica about getting Becca's call and how worried she'd been. Then they discussed Troy's phone call. And finally, Sienna gave her the briefest of recaps on how she and Blaine had left things. "I don't know what to do. I love him, and I hurt him, and I don't think he'll ever believe I could put him first at this point. I said a lot of things I'm not sure I even believe anymore."

Erica made a production out of wiping the crumbs off her hands. Then she gripped the sides of the chair and stood up.

"You're going to tell him. Everything. He can take it. If anyone in my family can take the whole truth, it's Blaine. In fact, he needs it from you. Tell him everything you just told me."

"What if he doesn't believe me?"

"Give him time."

"What if I'm not ready? I mean, I've been here for my sister and the kids for so long, I'd feel like I'm abandoning them."

Erica closed the distance between them and took her hands in hers. Sienna rose to stand, still holding her hands.

"Whatever happens with Becca and Aaron and the kids, you'll be there for them. You will always be there for them. Whether you're in Sunrise Bend or here in Casper. Don't worry about that. You love them. Blaine will understand as long as he knows he's first in your life."

Sienna pressed her lips together to keep her emotions under wraps and nodded. "I know you're right, but I worry...what if I can't put him first? What if I mess up and run off to Becca again when he needs me?"

"No one is perfect. Just do your best. Trust me, he will mess up, too. And you'll forgive him."

The biggest worry of all still lingered way back in the deepest recesses of her heart. She'd never allowed it to take form, but it was there. Had been there for most of her life.

"What if something happens and I shut down

like my parents did?" she whispered. "What if I walk away from him and all we have? It's better to leave things the way they are now. I couldn't bear to think of him in that kind of pain."

Erica hugged her again. "Oh, Sienna, is that why you're worried?" She backed up, keeping her hands on Sienna's shoulders, and looked into her eyes. "You don't have it in you. You're strong when everyone around you crumbles. You take the waves head-on instead of sprinting in the other direction. You don't have to ever worry about walking away. You couldn't if you tried."

The tears came then, and she let Erica hold her as she cried for the little girl who'd lost her brother and her father all in the same year. And she cried for the teenager whose life had been upended when her mom walked away. She cried for her time in Sunrise Bend being cut short in high school. And she cried for the adult woman who'd married a man she didn't love because she hadn't been able to trust the real thing.

When all her tears had been shed, she excused herself and washed her face before returning to the living room.

"What are you going to do now?" Erica asked.

"I think I need to go back. Talk to Blaine

face-to-face." She hadn't allowed herself to seriously consider what he'd offered. Until now.
And she wanted it. Oh, how she wanted it!

"Good plan. Are you thinking today?"

"Yes. I need to do it before I lose my nerve."
Would he welcome her, though? Or had she
hurt him so badly he wanted nothing to do with
her? "Should I call him and let him know?"

Erica grimaced. "He's probably out looking
at cows."

"True. Plus, he might tell me not to bother."

They sat in silence. Then a knock on the
door made them both jump. Sienna placed her
hand over her heart. "Oh, that scared me. I'll
be right back."

She went to the door and didn't bother checking the peephole this time. When she opened
it, her jaw dropped to the floor.

Blaine!

She soaked him in, from his cowboy hat and
shimmering blue eyes to his T-shirt, jeans and
cowboy boots. He held a huge bouquet of red
roses. She practically swooned.

He stepped forward, wrapping his arm around
her waist. "Whoa, there. Are you okay?"

"Wonderful," she said breathlessly as she
smiled up at him.

"Ahem."

They both looked toward the living room, where Erica was standing with both hands on her hips. Her big grin lightened the mood.

"Blaine, you are now officially the smartest brother in our family." She sailed over to him, bopped the brim of his cowboy hat and winked at Sienna. "I trust you two will figure things out."

Then she left, and the door clicked shut behind her.

"You're here." Sienna's pulse was racing faster than a rabbit being chased by a dog. "I was trying to figure out when and how to go back to the ranch. I never should have left like that."

He led her to the couch, where they both took a seat, shifting to face each other.

"I couldn't leave things the way we did." He took off his hat and set it on the end table. "I pushed you, I rushed you. Don't get me wrong, I meant everything I said, but you were right when you told me I wouldn't be giving anything up, and you would. I never really thought about how much you'd be giving up."

She pressed her hand to his cheek. "That's where you're wrong, Blaine. I'd been so focused on Becca and the kids that I didn't think about what I wanted. What I needed."

"What do you want? What do you need?"
You, Blaine. Only you.

BLAINE PREPARED HIS heart for pain. Yesterday, he'd been somewhat certain she loved him and would want to stay and have a life with him. But now? He had no clue.

"When I got to Becca's house last night, Aaron was there with her. And she acted surprised I would even think to return early."

"I guess that means they're okay?"

She nodded. "I think so. I mean, they're both taking the necessary steps to make their marriage work. But that's not my point."

He looked into her pleading green eyes and hoped she wasn't going to let him down again. Not when he'd gotten this far.

"I realized I was wrong to leave the way I did. I was afraid I'd get there and she'd be gone. I couldn't stand thinking of Connor and Lily going through what I'd been through with my parents. But I'd forgotten that Becca had been through the same thing. And I underestimated her. I underestimated them all."

He clenched his hands, thinking about how her childhood had affected her. No wonder she wanted to be close to her sister and the kids.

"Erica helped me see things more clearly."

When Erica was involved, he got nervous. She saw too much and said exactly what was on her mind.

"I've been afraid of losing the people I love." She ducked her chin, then met his gaze. "I couldn't deal with what you said yesterday because it scared me. And I didn't tell you all the things you need to know because I didn't believe they were possible for me."

Hope rose in his chest.

"I love you, Blaine. And last night when I walked into this empty apartment, I realized I'd made the wrong choice. I chose to cling to my sister and the kids, but they don't need me to hover around them. They want me to be happy, too."

He couldn't think of a thing to say. He waited for her to continue.

"The only time I've been truly happy is when I'm with you. I feel bad, Blaine, because I take from you more than I give. I needed you all summer. You were the one who made sure the kids had fun. You were the one who accepted me—divorced, pregnant and all. I don't deserve you, Blaine Mayer, but I sure do love you."

He crushed her in his arms, then whispered in her hair, "I love you, too. Oh, I love you."

Then he eased back and stared into her eyes, tucking her hair behind her ear.

"You have it all wrong, Sienna. You think of others before yourself. You put your life on hold for two months because you knew your family needed it. Connor and Lily needed the ranch, and their parents needed the time and space to work things out. And, frankly, when I think of how accommodating you've been with your ex, well, I'm humbled."

She smiled. "You think I should support him waiving his rights, don't you?"

"I think you know what's right for you and the baby. I admire the fact you're worried he'll regret it, even knowing having him around will only complicate things more. I will support you no matter what you decide. But I'm getting ahead of myself."

"What do you mean?" Her eyebrows drew together as she tilted her head.

"Look, I know you're having a baby—" he gave a pointed look at her bulging bump "—and asking you to move so far away from your sister this close to the baby coming was dumb of me. I want to be together, but I'm fine doing it on your terms. I'll drive down here on weekends and we can date. And if in time you think you'd be willing to move up by me, I'll pack your apartment myself if need be. But if you decide here is where you need to stay, I'm willing to move."

Her stunned expression made him pause.

"You okay?"

She nodded.

"But I've got to be honest, and I expect you to be honest right back." He shifted his jaw and hoped for the answer he wanted to hear. "I won't be second-best, Sienna. I will never ask you to give up your family, but I need to be first in your life if we're going to have a real go at this. I want it all—love, commitment. I've been around good marriages. My parents, my brother, my friends are all committed to their spouses. And I know I'm jumping the gun talking marriage, but for us to have something real, I need to know we're on the same page."

"We're on the same page." She nodded, smiling through shining eyes. "I'm sorry I made you feel that way, Blaine. I was wrong, and I know it. So, yes, you will be number one in my life. And I know now that you wouldn't ask me to ignore my family. There will be times Becca calls crying, and I will be taking those calls. And if Lily or Connor have an emergency, I'll be there for them. But you will always be first in my life."

"Does this mean we're going to try dating?" He couldn't stop staring at her lips. "I'll come every week."

"No, I don't think so."

His heart fell. Had he been reading her all wrong?

"My heart's always been in Sunrise Bend. It's time for me to be there permanently."

He needed to make sure he understood. "Okay, forgive me for being slow, but does this mean we'll be dating?"

She leaned forward, wrapping her arms around his neck, pressing her forehead to his.

"Oh, we're way past dating, Blaine Mayer."

The only reply he could think of was to claim her lips with his. And as he kissed her, he knew how blessed he was.

Sienna was his, and he couldn't wait to bring her home.

CHAPTER FIFTEEN

TWO WEEKS LATER Sienna gave the counter a final wipe, then placed her hand on her aching lower back. Becca, Aaron and the kids would be here any minute to pick up Sushi, and she couldn't wait to see them. She walked onto the cabin's front porch, smiling at the blue sky. Blaine had stopped by twenty minutes ago, giving her a kiss before jogging down the lane to his house to shower off the smell of cattle before they arrived. How she loved that man.

The day Blaine had shown up at her apartment was still etched in her brain. After working things out, they'd called Erica to come back over and celebrated by going out to lunch. Then Sienna had taken him to Becca's house and introduced him to her and Aaron. The kids had been thrilled to see him.

The next day Blaine had helped her pack up the essentials of her apartment, and they'd driven separately back to the ranch. When she'd pulled up to the cabin, her heart had practically leaped for joy.

She was home.

And last weekend, they'd celebrated at Randy and Hannah's wedding with all of Blaine's friends.

"Hey, there, beautiful!" Blaine yelled, sauntering her way. If her belly wasn't so ginormous, she'd run to him and jump in his arms. But she'd have to be content waddling his way. He caught up to her and instantly pulled her close. The baby chose that moment to kick, and he grinned before kissing her.

"Hoo." She fanned herself when they broke away.

"Looks like you've got a feisty one in there." Keeping his arm around her waist, he led her back to the porch. "Sit down. Rest."

She smiled. She heard those words ten times a day from him, Julie, Reagan, Holly—and even little Clara had told her to "west" this week. They'd all welcomed her back, and Julie had shed a few tears of joy. Sienna would always treasure the moment.

A vehicle approached.

"They're here." Blaine stood wide-legged on

the top step of the porch, staring at the drive. "Lily's going to be disappointed the other puppies all went to their homes already."

"Any disappointment will vanish as soon as Sushi is back in her arms."

"True."

The SUV stopped in front of the cabin, and her family poured out. Aaron went straight to Blaine, shaking his hand, while Becca held her arms out as she climbed the steps to Sienna. They hugged for a long time.

"Looks like this one's coming soon, huh, sis?" Becca stared at her baby bump.

"Any minute." She rubbed her belly. "I'm not sure how I feel about it."

"You're going to be a great mom. Are you sure you don't want me to be your birthing partner?"

"It's too far. I'll be okay. Julie was ecstatic when I asked her. She's been through it five times."

Becca pressed the side of her head to Sienna's. A surge of love for her sister made her smile. Becca had been seeing the therapist, and Sienna had been talking to Blaine's pastor about her own issues from the past. Their relationship felt safer than it had in a long time.

"Aunt Sienna!" Lily hugged her, barely getting her arms around the baby bump. "I miss you."

"I miss you, too." She gently caressed Lily's hair. "I'm glad you're here now."

"Me, too. I can't wait to bring Sushi home."

"Hey, Connor, I see your best friend found you." She nodded to Ollie, who'd raced over as soon as they'd gotten out of the vehicle.

"I missed this guy." Connor laughed, scratching behind both of Ollie's ears.

"Come on in." Sienna gave Becca and Aaron the tour of the cabin, and then they all went over to Blaine's, where Tiara and Sushi were sitting in the hallway waiting.

"Oh, there you are!" Lily ran to Sushi and dropped to her knees. She took the pup in her arms and hugged him, kissing the top of his furry head. "You're coming home with us today."

Blaine crouched beside her. "I'm glad this guy's going to the best home. Remember how you worried he wouldn't make it those first days?"

She nodded, her eyes glistening. Then she shifted to put her arms around Blaine's neck and gave him a quick hug.

"Thank you, Blaine. This was the best summer of my life."

Becca and Aaron reached for each other's hands, exchanging a loving look.

"Yes, we want to thank you, too," Becca said to Blaine as he rose. His face was flaming. "Thank you for all you did for these two this summer."

He nodded, and Sienna moved to his side. He put his arm around her shoulders.

"Maybe Connor and Lily could come next summer, too," Sienna said.

Blaine shot her a quick glance. Then a smile spread across his face. "Why didn't I think of that?"

"Do you mean it?" Connor asked, his eyes full of hope.

"Yes." Blaine nodded. "Absolutely."

"Can Tiara have puppies again when I come?" Lily asked, holding Sushi, who was licking her chin.

"I hope so." Blaine chuckled. "I'll need your help."

Sienna leaned her head against his shoulder. She couldn't have imagined in June that she'd be living in Sunrise Bend full-time and hosting her happily married sister, her brother-in-law and the kids for the day. Oh, and inviting them to spend the summer with her next year.

Here, with Blaine and his family, anything felt possible. Just as it had in high school.

She'd found her home in Sunrise Bend. And she couldn't wait to see what was in store next.

ONE WEEK LATER, Blaine paced the hospital hall. What was taking so long? Surely, she should have had the baby by now?

His mom came out of Sienna's room. "Blaine, honey, Sienna's asking for you. It's a girl!"

He raced into the room to see Sienna's radiant face as she held her precious bundle wrapped in a blanket near her chest. Blaine moved to stand next to her, staring in awe at the tiny baby.

"Look at her little fingernails, Blaine." Sienna stared up at him then, and he got choked up.

"She's beautiful. Just like her mother." He grazed the baby's hand with a feather-light touch. "What are you going to name her?"

"Madeline." She smiled. "I always liked that name."

"Well, Madeline, welcome to the world."

He gave Sienna the softest kiss on the lips he could manage, and they stared, smiling, at the baby for what felt like hours.

When the nurse came to move her and the baby to another room, Blaine assured Sienna he'd meet her there as soon as he let the family know the room number.

With a sense of awe and pride, he strode down the hall to where his family was waiting. His dad gave him a hug, then Jet and Holly congratulated him, and Reagan carried Clara over. He took his adorable niece in his arms. "Are you ready to meet your cousin?"

"Yay!" She clapped her little hands.

"Let's hope she's ready for a brother or sister, too," Holly murmured.

"What?" his mom yelled. She must have supersonic hearing—he was convinced of it. "Are you...? Is this...? Are you...?"

"Mom, we're having a baby." Jet gave Mom a deadpan stare. "We found out a few hours ago."

"Oh, praise Jesus!"

Blaine pulled Jet into a hug. "Congratulations, man."

"You, too, brother." Jet clapped his hand on his shoulder. "You're going to make a great daddy...when you finally propose. Don't you think it's time?"

"Soon." Blaine grinned. As usual, Jet was right, and this time it didn't bother him at all.

Just then Becca, Aaron, Connor and Lily rushed into the lobby. "We got here as soon as we could. Are we too late?"

"It's a girl," Blaine announced. "Mama and daughter are fine."

And he'd make sure they were fine for the rest of their lives. He couldn't wait to make Sienna and Madeline his. To cherish and protect them forever.

EPILOGUE

WOMEN STILL MADE him nervous. And pregnant women? Yeah, they terrified him. Thankfully, Sienna had taken to motherhood like a champ. Blaine loved being with her. Every day. And that's why he was ready to take the plunge and ask her to marry him.

Every morning, he stopped by at 5:00 a.m. to feed the baby, and every morning when he held Madeline in his arms, he wanted her and Sienna to be officially his, so he could be with them all the time. A month old already, the baby was the cutest thing he'd ever seen. She had Sienna's eyes. He loved those green eyes.

Her ex, Troy, had been granted a fast track to successfully waive his parental rights. Sienna had found out last week, and she'd made her peace with it. Blaine planned on officially adopting Madeline as soon as they were married. She just had to say yes.

He opened the oven a crack. Yep. He was ready.

Flowers on the table. Lasagna and garlic bread in the oven. His dad had made the lasagna earlier and told him to bake it for forty-five minutes. Dad was a phenomenal cook, so Blaine wasn't worried about the meal.

He patted his pocket. Box was there. Ring was secured.

He was good to go.

His heartbeat was pounding as he exhaled.

Last Friday, Blaine had made the mistake of telling the guys he was asking Sienna to marry him tonight. They'd thrown out the dumbest ideas he'd ever heard.

Sawyer said he should bake the ring into a puppy treat since she'd helped with the puppies. Blaine had hung his head in disgust. And Randy had, once again, thrown out the old fishing-rod-and-lure idea, although as a fisherman himself, Randy hadn't even used it on Hannah. Mac was no better. He'd suggested, "You should have Bridget put it in one of those frozen coffees Sienna likes so much."

To which Blaine had replied, "What if she chokes on it?" That had shut him up.

And Jet—his own brother—had told him to just let Mom and Reagan plan it. Uh, no.

So here he was, shaking like a leaf, waiting for her to arrive.

He'd ask her in his own way.

At the sound of her knock, he straightened his shoulders and went to the front door with Tiara and Ollie trailing behind him.

She had on a long, flowy shirt and black pants. Her hair waved around her shoulders. He pulled her inside and kissed her thoroughly.

"It was so sweet of your mom to watch the baby. She insisted we needed a proper date. But I told her we eat supper together every night, anyhow." She kept her arms around his waist. He could stay like this forever.

"My mom's always right. Don't try to fight it."

She laughed. "I won't."

He kissed her again.

"I feel like I've been in another universe lately. Feed the baby, change the baby, wipe the spit-up off my shirt, feed the baby again. It's a nice change to feel normal even if it's only for an hour." She lavished attention on both dogs before straightening.

"You're doing a great job. I don't know how you do it every day." He took her hand and led her down the hallway to the kitchen table, where he'd set two place settings, lit a candle and placed two dozen pink roses. "Those are for you."

"Oh!" She placed her hand over her heart. "This is so romantic."

"It should be. You deserve a little romance." He held the chair out for her to sit, and once she did, he closed his eyes and said a silent prayer. *Lord, give me the right words to let her know how much I love her.*

"The more I spend time with you and the baby, the more I want the three of us living in the same house. It's no secret I love you. And I want to share it all—the feedings, the spit-up, the everyday moments that make up a life. I know you need a cat, and we'll get a kitten whenever you want." He took out the jewelry box and got down on one knee, then he opened the box. "Sienna, will you marry me?"

"Yes, Blaine, of course, I'll marry you." Tears glistened in her eyes as she allowed him to slide the diamond ring on her finger. "How could I not if you're willing to share spit-up and get me a kitten? It has to be fluffy."

"Done." He chuckled, then kissed her.

"Do you want a big wedding like Randy and Hannah's?" Her eyebrows drew together slightly.

"I want whatever you want."

"So a smallish affair?"

"The smaller, the better." He grinned. "All I care about is that you say 'I do.'"

"I do."

"Then that's all I'll ever need. You're everything to me."

"Oh, Blaine…"

He kissed her again. She was his. He couldn't be happier.

★ ★ ★ ★ ★

Rescuing Her Ranch
Lisa Jordan

MILLS & BOON

Heart, home and faith have always been important to **Lisa Jordan**, so writing stories with those elements comes naturally. Happily married for over thirty years to her real-life hero, she and her husband have two grown sons, and they are embracing their new season of grandparenting. Lisa enjoys quality time with her family, reading good books and being creative with friends. Learn more about her and her writing by visiting www.lisajordanbooks.com.

Visit the Author Profile page at millsandboon.com.au.

Trust in the Lord with all thine heart;
and lean not unto thine own understanding.
In all thy ways acknowledge him,
and he shall direct thy paths.
—*Proverbs* 3:5–6

Dedication

For Jeanette and Gabe Walter—
you're NF warriors and such blessings to so many!
May your stories bless others
and change their lives.

Acknowledgments

Lord, may my words glorify You.

My family—Patrick, Scott, Mitchell,
Sarah and Bridget. I love you forever.

Thanks to Jeanne Takenaka and Alena Tauriainen
for brainstorming, texting and calling
when I was feeling overwhelmed by this story.
Thanks to Dana R. Lynn and Christy Miller for
being wonderful sounding boards. Thanks to my
Novel Academy morning sprint crew for daily
prayers and encouragement as I wrote this story.

Thanks to Jeanette Walter, Jen Tezbir,
Dalyn Weller and Jeanne Takenaka for your
willingness to answer my research questions.
Any mistakes are mine.

Thanks to Cynthia Ruchti, my inspiring agent,
and Melissa Endlich, my exceptional editor,
for continually encouraging and inspiring me to
grow as a writer. So thankful you're on my team.
And to the Love Inspired team who works hard
to bring my books to print.

CHAPTER ONE

MACEY WAS BACK where she started.

But this time, instead of standing on Cole Crawford's porch with tears streaking her makeup while blasting him for the humiliation he caused her, she was offering her help.

Only because Everly, her baby sister, had begged her.

Otherwise, she'd still be ignoring Cole like she'd been doing for the past decade.

With her career—and quite possibly her reputation—ruined, Macey returned home. Disgrace drove her out of Denver where she'd been a nanny for the Crane family for the past six years—since graduating college with her degree in early childhood education.

Maybe she should've waited until morning to leave the city instead of driving through the mountains, going thirty miles an hour while the blizzard howled and swirled around her.

But she couldn't stay a minute longer. Her broken heart pined for the security of home where no one could take advantage of her.

With her car loaded down with nearly everything she owned and nowhere else to go, failure and shame chased her all the way back to Stone River, the cattle ranch nestled in the valley of the San Juan Mountains in southwestern Colorado that had been in her family for three generations.

Now, with an icy wind sliding down her back, Macey scuffed her boots on the snow-covered welcome mat. She glanced over her shoulder and nearly sprinted back to her still-warm car parked in front of Cole's stone-face condo.

But she couldn't do that. She'd given her word.

If she wasn't jobless and slightly desperate at the moment, she wouldn't have given in to Everly's pleading.

Tightening the hold on her tote bag, she drew in a steadying breath, released it slowly, then pressed the doorbell.

The oak door trimmed in white opened, and Macey forced her jaws to stay closed.

The tall, lanky kid with braces from her

childhood had grown into a broad-shouldered man who filled the doorway with his presence. Worn jeans did little to disguise his muscular legs. His hoodie stretched over his broad shoulders as he held a little girl with blond curls in his arms. His square jaw sported a darkened shadow that couldn't conceal the dimple in his left cheek. His dirty-blond hair had darkened to a rich brown. About the only thing unchanged were his eyes. They were still as blue as the Colorado sky.

"Cole?"

A smile stretched across his face, revealing even white teeth. He stepped back and opened the door wider. "Macey Stone. Hey. Come in."

She moved into the foyer, and he closed the door behind her. The heated interior warmed her cold cheeks as she breathed in the scent of freshly brewed coffee in the air.

He shifted the little girl, who had the same blue eyes as her daddy, to his other arm. "I have to admit, I was a bit surprised when Everly called first thing this morning to say she couldn't care for Lexi but that you agreed to fill in for her. I didn't know you'd returned to Aspen Ridge."

Macey tugged off her gloves and stuffed them

in her pockets. "It was a last-minute decision. Did she tell you why she couldn't come?"

He nodded, his jaw tight. "Yes, and I hope the interview goes well."

"If Ev's offered the long-term substitute job at Aspen Ridge Elementary, that will get her foot in the door for a full-time position next year."

"While I'm happy for her, it also means I may be looking for a new caregiver for my Lexi Lou." He blew kisses on the child's neck, causing her to giggle.

Lexi cupped Cole's face. "Daddy, you're so silly. I'm not Lexi Lou. I'm Lexi Jane."

Cole thunked the heel of his hand against his forehead. "Oh, that's right. My mistake."

The little girl giggled again, her eyes never leaving Macey.

"Everly said you were a nanny in Denver."

"Yes, I was. For nearly six years." A rush of tears pooled in Macey's eyes, and she forced them back. She wasn't about to have an emotional breakdown in front of Cole and his daughter.

"Was? You're not any longer?"

"No. Things ended suddenly last night." She rubbed her arms to erase the feel of Mr. Crane's tightening hold on her skin.

He frowned. "So if things ended last night, then that means you must've driven through the mountains in the blizzard to get home. We're like five hours from Denver. When did you sleep?"

"It was about seven hours, since visibility wasn't all that great. I arrived at the ranch around four this morning and managed to get three solid hours of sleep before Everly woke me up."

"You must've wanted to get home pretty quickly."

"You have no idea." Not ready to talk about what drove her out of Denver and away from the three children she loved like her own, Macey pressed a smile in place. She turned to Lexi and held out her hand. "Hi, Lexi Jane. My name is Macey, and I'm Everly's sister."

The little girl's eyes widened as she scrambled out of her father's arms. She stood in front of Macey. "You got my name right." Then she turned to Cole, small hands on her hips. "See, Daddy, she knows my name. Maybe she can teach you."

Cole shot them a lopsided grin. "That's not a bad idea."

Macey crouched in front of Lexi. "Everly has

an appointment today. Do you mind if I stay with you while your daddy goes to work?"

Lexi leaned against Cole's legs as her bottom lip popped out. "But Everly and I were going to make cookies today. Chocolate chip. Daddy's favorite."

"Well, Everly remembered and gave me the ingredients to make cookies with you." Macey pulled a package of chocolate chips from her oversize shoulder tote and showed it to Lexi. "See?"

Lexi danced in a circle and jumped up and down. Then she reached for Macey's hand and waved to Cole. "Bye, Daddy. You can go to work now. Macey and I are gonna bake cookies."

Cole laughed, a sound that rattled Macey's locked memory bank. "Well, that was easier than I thought."

"Cookies work wonders."

"Not just the cookies." He studied her a moment, then gripped the back of his neck. "Listen, Mace, I know we haven't talked in a while—"

"A while? It's been ten years." She held up a hand. "To be honest, I don't have the energy to rehash the past right now."

A muscle jumped in the side of his jaw, and he gave her a single nod. "Fair enough."

He opened a door and grabbed a hanger. "Give me your coat and I'll hang it up for you."

She shrugged out of her red wool coat, unwrapped her knitted gray cashmere scarf and handed both to him. "Thanks."

After hanging her coat in the closet, he waved her into the house. "Come in, and I'll share Lexi's routine with you."

She toed off her winter boots, lining them up in the corner by the closet, then followed him into a large open room painted off-white. She dug her socked toes into the tan carpeting. "Nice place."

Morning sunlight poured through floor-to-ceiling windows that offered a gorgeous view of the river snaking through Aspen Ridge, the small ranching community, into the base of the San Juan Mountains.

A dark leather couch with matching recliner had been angled in front of the large flat-screen TV. Lexi's table and chairs, playhouse and toy box sat in the corner next to a child-sized purple recliner and overflowing bookshelf.

A professional portrait of Cole holding Lexi as an infant hung on the wall next to the TV.

No other pictures, plants, throw pillows, knick-knacks or homey touches adorned the room. Nothing feminine or any evidence of a wife. And the place was spotless.

Cole grabbed a notebook off the coffee table in front of the couch. "This is what Everly and I use to share information about Lexi. She lets me know how Lexi's day has gone, and I communicate about her nights." He flipped it open. "Here's her daily routine. She does better with a schedule. I'm not sure how much Everly's told you about Lexi…"

"To be honest, very little. She takes confidentiality seriously. All I knew was she was caring for a little girl with a medical condition. Until this morning, I didn't know she was your child."

"And you still came." Cole eyed the little girl sitting on the couch with a book next to a stuffed pony. "Lexi has neurofibromatosis. Or NF1 for short. Basically, benign tumors form on nerve tissue in her body. And each case is different. For Lexi, though, it's affecting her hearing, which is also affecting her learning."

"She's so happy and upbeat."

"She is. For the most part. Like any kid, she has her moments."

Macey glanced at Cole's left hand and found it bare. "Everly mentioned you're no longer married."

He shook his head and gripped the back of his neck. "My ex and I were married only a couple of months when she became pregnant. She didn't want kids right away, and we fought about it. She left us the day after Lexi was born. She signed away her parental rights, and I was served with divorce papers the day after I brought Lexi home from the hospital. So, we've been on our own from the very beginning."

"I'm so sorry. That must've been tough." Her instinct was to wrap her arms around him, but she stayed where she was.

Even though the decade-old anger had faded, she and Cole weren't exactly friends anymore.

He lifted a shoulder. "It is what it is. I can't change the past. I'm just doing what I can to be the best father she deserves. I'll do whatever it takes to give her what she needs."

Her phone vibrated in her back pocket. She pulled it out and saw Everly's picture on her screen. "Excuse me a second." She turned away from Cole and Lexi. "Hello?"

"Mace, I got it! Mrs. Penley hired me for the

long-term sub job." Everly squealed so loudly that Macey had to pull the phone away from her ear.

"Ev, that's great. Congratulations." Macey forced joy into her voice, but her stomach burned, just knowing what Everly planned to ask her.

"Thanks. I know it's a lot to ask and you just got home, but I don't suppose you'd consider caring for Lexi until Cole can find someone more permanent. She's a super sweet kid, and I really hate to leave him in a lurch, but I really want to take this job. Say yes, please?"

Even though Cole had taken Lexi into the kitchen, she was sure he could hear her side of the conversation.

"Can we talk about this later? Preferably after I've had more sleep and time for my brain cells to kick in."

Everly remained silent for a moment. "Well, Mrs. Penley asked if I could start tomorrow. I need to handle some paperwork and take a tour of the school."

Macey swallowed a sigh. "Ev, I haven't even taken care of Lexi yet. I don't even know if we'll get along."

"That's silly, and you know it. Of course, she's going to like you. Everyone does."

Not everyone.

"Please, Macey, I wouldn't ask if this weren't so important. We're talking about my teaching future. You know how hard I've worked for this." The pleading in her sister's voice tugged at Macey.

What could she say? Macey would've re-aligned the planets for Everly if she'd been asked. Her baby sister had to overcome a lot of obstacles in her twenty-two years, and Macey didn't want to stand in the way of her dream. But to see Cole on a daily basis…was she up for that?

She glanced at the single father brushing his daughter's hair into a ponytail while Lexi stood on a stool at the counter, and her heart softened. "Okay, yeah, fine. I'll talk to Cole and see what he thinks. But you owe me. Big time."

Everly squealed again. "Yes! Anything you want. Thankyouthankyouthankyou."

Before she could respond, the line went silent in her ear. Macey tossed her phone from hand to hand, then walked into the kitchen.

With her hair pulled back, Lexi now spread peanut butter on a slice of bread. "Look, Macey, I'm making Daddy's lunch."

"You're doing a great job." She turned to Cole. "Not sure how much you heard."

Holding a jar of homemade jam, he closed the fridge, then leaned against the counter. "Enough to know I'm losing your sister as my daughter's caregiver."

Macey nodded, dropped her gaze to her darkened screen, then looked back at Cole. "She asked if I'd be willing to fill in until you could find someone more permanent."

He straightened, and his eyebrows lifted. "Oh, really? How do you feel about that?"

Macey pocketed her phone, then shrugged. "Lexi doesn't know me. We may not be a good fit."

Cole shot her a half smile. "I've known your family nearly all my life. Your brothers are my closest friends. Plus, I trust your sister. If she believes you can do this, then I do too. Besides, Lex is pretty easygoing. She gets along with most everyone."

Pressing her back against the sink, Macey ran a thumb and forefinger over her gritty eyes. "I've been home only a few hours, and my plate is filling already."

Cole touched her elbow. "Hey, what's going on?"

"Bear called yesterday. Dad passed out in the pasture after lunch, and Bear found him facedown in the snow. They called 911 and rushed him to the hospital. The doctors are running tests, and they suspect pneumonia. Mom spent most of the night by his side. When I came downstairs this morning, I found her at the table with this overwhelmed look on her face. She's been planning the annual Stone River Sweetheart Ball. But now with Dad sick, she's stressed about getting everything done on time. Since I'll be home for a while, she asked if I'd consider taking over."

Macey didn't share about the flashbacks she had to the humiliating prom she'd planned in painstaking detail only be left as the laughing-stock in the community.

"Wow, Mace. I had no idea. I'm sorry to hear about your dad. The Sweetheart Ball is such a great fundraiser." He dragged a hand over his face. "Listen, don't worry about Lexi. I'll come up with a different solution. Maybe my cousin Piper can help me out."

Macey should've felt relief at being freed from caring for Lexi, but the tightness in Cole's jaw and the deepening lines around his mouth made her think finding someone to care for his daughter was going to be harder than she imagined. Her shoulders sagged as she shook her head. "No, don't do that. I'll take care of her until you can find a permanent provider for her."

Cole's head jerked up and his eyes brightened. "You have no idea what that means to me. Without much of a family to fall back on, I wasn't quite sure what I was going to do. But if you're sure…"

She nodded, but the voice in her head urged her to grab her coat and run back to her car. But after what had happened last night, she wasn't sure about anything right now, especially on such little sleep.

Cole slid the sandwich Lexi made into a plastic baggie and dropped it in his lunch box. Then he gripped the edge of the counter. "After Mom died suddenly of that heart defect when I was a freshman, your family's charity event has always been important to me." He made a face. "Listen, since you're willing to help me out until I can find a permanent solution for Lexi's care, then the least I can do is give you a hand with organizing the Sweetheart Ball."

She waved away his words. "You don't have to do that. You have more than enough to keep you busy."

"I want to."

"I don't know, Cole."

He reached for her hand. "Listen, Macey. I was a jerk at our prom, and I've regretted screwing up our friendship for the past ten years. I'm so sorry I stood by while Celeste humiliated you. I cared more about being accepted than standing up for my best friend. Let me prove I'm not that same punk, and you can trust me again."

Macey rubbed a hand across her forehead and over her tired eyes. She smothered a yawn, then nodded. "Okay, let's talk more when you get home. What time should I expect you?"

"Probably around five. If something changes, I'll let you know. Will that be a problem?"

Macey shook her head.

He glanced at his watch and headed to the living room. "I'm already late, and my uncle's going to be furious. We'll talk more tonight. Thank you, Macey. I mean it."

As he headed out the door, Macey allowed his words to linger between them. She wanted to lean into them, to know he'd be there for her. But their years of friendship had been destroyed by a single humiliating act that brought her shame when his voice could have changed everything.

Even though she wanted nothing more than

to return to the safety of Stone River, Macey remained in Cole's living room, determined to prove she wasn't a failure. After all, no matter how she felt about Cole, his sweet daughter didn't need to suffer.

Mom's words from earlier drifted into her head—maybe God brought her home for a reason.

While she tried to determine her purpose for the future, she'd guard her heart because the last thing she needed was to fall for Cole again, only to have him break it once more.

COLE HAD BEEN given a second chance for redemption, and he wasn't about to waste it. He still couldn't believe Macey Stone was back in town and she'd offered to care for his daughter.

He certainly didn't deserve her kindness, especially after the way he'd treated her all those years ago. Only an idiot would've let a friend like her storm out of his life.

Now he'd make amends for the humiliating prom fiasco and rekindle their friendship.

Truth was, he missed her. He hadn't realized how much until he opened his door and found her standing on his snow-covered porch.

Even though he was a regular visitor at Stone

River Ranch, Macey had always managed to sneak away while visiting her family before he could see her.

Time hadn't diminished her beauty. If anything, it enhanced it. Her chestnut-brown hair still fell in light waves around her shoulders. And those expressive brown eyes couldn't hide her emotions.

Thumbing through his emails on his phone, Cole opened the door to the mobile office at the Riverside Condos construction site and ducked inside to escape the cold biting at his neck.

"About time you showed up."

Cole's head jerked up and his gut tightened. Wallace Crawford, his uncle and his boss, sat at Cole's desk with his booted feet on the over-size desk calendar.

"Yeah, sorry about that. I had a last-minute childcare issue." Cole set his insulated travel mug on the L-shaped desk and dropped his lunch made by Lexi in the mini fridge tucked under the microwave.

Wallace pushed to his feet and grabbed his black cowboy hat off the coatrack behind Cole's desk chair. "Don't get too comfortable. We have a meeting."

"A meeting with whom?" Cole pulled out his phone and tapped on his calendar app but didn't find anything scheduled.

"Aspen Ridge City Council."

"For what?"

"I've been talking with Mayor Cobb about building a strip mall, and he thinks it will be a good boost to the local economy."

Cole frowned. "A strip mall? Where?"

"Off the highway exit that leads into town."

Cole turned to the framed map of Aspen Ridge hanging above the drafting table. He tapped the exit Wallace referenced. "But that's Stone River Ranch property."

Wallace grinned, looking more like a wolf hunting prey. "Exactly. The city council sent out a letter of intent. They offered to purchase a portion of the property."

"Which part?"

"Old Man Stone's crumbling homestead on the southwestern section of the ranch."

"South Bend?" The southern portion of the ranch the Stones referred to as South Bend where Deacon Stone's parents had lived until their unexpected death ten years ago. "Deacon refused to sell their land when you made an offer after his parents had been killed by that drunk driver."

Wallace lifted a shoulder. "Yeah, so? I have it on good authority that the Stones are hurting for money. My—I mean, the council's offer could help them stay in the black and it gives me…us the land we need for the project."

"Why that land? And why a strip mall? We're still finishing up the Riverside Condos project. Let me do some research for other parcels that may work better."

"I don't want to look at other properties. The council wants this land. If the Stones refuse to sell, then they can acquire it through eminent domain. And they want you to be project manager."

"The council wants me? Or *you* want me to do your bidding?" Cole gripped the back of his chair and shook his head. "No way. I can't. Barrett and Wyatt Stone are my best friends. Deacon and Nora and Deacon's sister Lynetta helped my mom more times than I can count when she got sick. I can't do that to them. Not to mention, it would be a conflict of interest."

Wallace hooked his thumbs around his belt loops, his fingers framing his decades-old rodeo belt buckle. "Let's sweeten the pot a little, shall we? After your mother's heart gave out, I took you in. Remember the college education I paid for? And that condo where you live? And let's not forget about the medical insurance you need for that little brat of yours. Specialists and those fancy hearing aids don't come cheap. So I'd say you owe me. Pay me back by getting the Stones to sell. Or look for another job…and a new place to live. The choice is yours." Cole clenched his jaw and fought back the words blistering his tongue.

Some choice.

Family meant nothing to Wallace. Something Cole learned years ago when family services had forced him to live with his last surviving adult relative.

Wallace had Cole backed into a corner and by the smirk on his face, he knew it.

Since graduating college six years ago, Cole worked for his uncle, saving as much as possible so he could reimburse him and be released from the debt hanging over his head.

Not that the guy even needed the money, but Cole didn't want to owe anyone.

"And just so you don't think I'm lacking a heart—get them to sign and you can be the new CEO of my Durango area office. I need someone with smarts to oversee the operations there so I can spend more time on my ranch in Montana. You'll receive a raise, better benefits and I may even throw in a company car."

Coming from anyone else, Cole would've jumped at the opportunity being offered. But with his uncle, everything came with a price. Question was—could Cole pay it and still live with himself?

If it weren't for Lexi, Cole would've walked out the door at that very moment without hesitation. But he'd do anything to provide his daughter with the best care possible, even if it meant selling his soul to someone like his uncle.

Cole scrubbed a hand over his face. "I'll do what I can to get the Stones to sell, but no promises. And we do this by the book."

His uncle clapped him on the back. "You're such a Boy Scout. Stick with me, son, and you'll see how business is really done."

Before Cole could respond he wasn't Wallace's son, nor did he want to do business the way his uncle did, Wallace stalked out of the trailer.

Grabbing his mug, Cole followed behind, feeling like a jerk. If he talked to Bear and Wyatt and told them about Wallace's land scheme, maybe they'd be little more understanding.

He wouldn't be surprised, though, if they shut him out the way Macey had. And rightly so.

Somehow, he needed to find a way to make this work without hurting those he cared about.

CHAPTER TWO

MACEY WANTED NOTHING more than a hot meal and a pillow for her head.

If today was anything to go by, caring for Lexi would be a dream job. She'd been surprised when Cole arrived home earlier than the five o'clock time she'd been told to expect, but even though she'd enjoyed her time with his daughter, she didn't mind a shorter day.

Fatigue settled in her bones like a long-term guest. She hadn't gone without sleep like that since cramming for finals in college. Not even the nights she paced the nursery when little Jaxson Crane screamed due to colic while his mother slept peacefully.

She wondered how Jayden, Jenna and Jaxson were doing without her.

When her defenses were down throughout the day, the three charges had crept into her

thoughts. What had Tricia and Derek told their
children about Macey's sudden departure?

If only she could've said goodbye. Maybe it
wouldn't have hurt so much.

Doubtful.

Nothing could erase the betrayal that buried her trust.

Shutting her eyes couldn't drown out Tricia screaming at her when she discovered her
husband in the living room…and in Macey's
arms. She'd refused to listen to Macey's cries
of innocence as she was ordered to pack and
leave, especially when Derek claimed Macey
had thrown herself at him.

Never again would she allow anyone to take
advantage of her.

For now she was safe. No one would hurt her
while she was surrounded by her family.

Pulling in the driveway, Macey shut off the
engine and exited the warmth of her car. She
headed for the timber-and-stone ranch house,
looking forward to climbing the stairs and falling into bed, even if it wasn't even dark yet.

Behind her, a deep woof coupled with a low
growl startled her. She jumped and whirled
around.

Dakota, or Kota for short, her brother's English shepherd bounded up the steps and sniffed around her boots. His tail wagged as he looked up at her. Macey dropped to her knees, snow and cold seeping into her jeans. She flung her arms around the aging dog. "Hey, Kota. How's it going, boy?"

Kota sniffed Macey, his tail picking up speed. He licked Macey's cheek. She laughed and tried to catch herself so she didn't fall backward.

"Hey, there. No one's home. Can I help you with something?"

At the sound of the deep voice, Macey pushed to her feet and turned. With one hand cupping Kota's head, she jangled the keys still in her gloved hand. "Good thing I have a key."

Barrett, nicknamed Bear by the family, her fraternal twin brother, younger by two minutes, stood on the sidewalk with a coiled rope in his gloved hands. Brown eyes like hers lit up as a smile transformed his stern features. "Hey, Mace. Wyatt mentioned you were back. Sorry I wasn't around this morning to welcome you home."

"Hey, Bear." She lifted a hand and smiled. "No worries. You were busy."

His breath visible in the freezing temperature, he pushed up the brim of his dusty chocolate–colored cowboy hat to reveal more of his tanned face.

Macey pressed a hip against one of the wooden posts of the covered front porch. "Mom's at the hospital, I take it?"

He shook his head. "Actually, Norman Fowler's office."

Straightening, Macey frowned. "Grandma and Grandpa's attorney? Why?"

Bear rubbed the back of his gloved hand across his forehead. "There's been a…development with the ranch."

"What sort of development?"

"After you and Everly left, we received a letter of intent. Supposedly the Aspen Ridge City Council wants to purchase a portion of the land to build a strip mall." Lines bracketing her brother's mouth deepened.

"A strip mall? Why? What part of the ranch?"

"South Bend."

Macey's shoulders sagged as she rested an elbow against the post and cupped her head. "Grandma and Grandpa's property? You can't be serious."

"As a heart attack." He dropped the rope on the porch. "If we don't agree and sign, then they will claim condemnation and take possession. They plan to tear it all down."

"How can they do that?"

"Through eminent domain. With South Bend being closest to town and the highway, they feel it will drive traffic into Aspen Ridge and help the economy. Or so they claim."

"But…" Macey shook her head. The rest of her words remained unspoken. Growing up, she'd taken many horseback rides across the pastures of the original homestead and visited the waterfalls as her grandfather taught her how to use his camera. She'd always said South Bend was her favorite place on earth. Even though nothing was in writing, Grandpa had said it would be hers one day.

Was that not meant to be?

Bear lifted his hat and dragged his hand through his dark brown hair, which was in need of a cut. "After receiving the letter, Mom called Fowler's office and set up an appointment."

"She went alone?" Macey tried to keep the accusatory tone out of her voice, but Bear's raised eyebrow showed she hadn't quite succeeded.

Shaking his head, he laughed. "Like Mom needs any one of us to protect her. The woman's fierce, especially when anyone messes with the family. She wanted to get some facts before she talked to Dad. Besides, Wyatt's with her."

Macey gave Kota a final pat, then closed her fingers around her keys once more. "I'm going to Fowler's office to see what's going on. There has to be a way to protect what's ours."

As she headed down the steps and brushed past him, he caught her elbow. "Hey."

"What?"

His eyes crinkled in the corners as his lips lifted into a half smile. "I'm glad you're home. You look good."

A flash of tears warmed her eyes. Blinking rapidly, she smiled through the haze, then pulled him in for an impulsive hug, breathing in the long-familiar scents of hay, horses and Colorado fresh air. "Thanks, Bear. You look good too. I'm sorry you lost your appeal with the rodeo association."

He stepped back and lifted a shoulder. "It is what it is. Until that mess is settled, there's not much I can do but work the ranch."

But she didn't miss the shadow that passed over his eyes and spoke louder than his words.

As much as she hurt for him and could relate to the false accusations, she had faith he'd work it out. He always did.

She climbed back into her car, then steered around the horseshoe drive lined with tall aspens blanketed with snow, their leafless branches scratching the late afternoon sky puffed with clouds.

Snow drifted against the posts of the fenced pastures. In a few months, lavender and white columbines and vibrant red Alpine paintbrushes would color the grass. Sunshine reflected off the acres of white pastures, pristine and untouched by cattle or wildlife.

The Stone River Ranch arched sign threw a shadow over the hood of the car as she drove through the gate. The ranch house shrunk in her rearview.

As she headed south toward Aspen Ridge, smoky gray mountains crowned with white snowcaps provided a majestic backdrop for the small ranching community that had been settled over two hundred years ago by her ancestors.

Her fingers tightened on the steering wheel as she turned into town, passing the brown-and-white Welcome to Aspen Ridge sign.

Netta's Diner, which had belonged to her grandparents and now her aunt, sat on the corner of Pine Avenue and Main. With its cheery yellow siding, and matching rockers dusted with snow lining the covered wooden porch, the place invited guests to step inside for a home-style meal.

Macey parked in front of the attorney's office across the street from the diner, then stamped the snow and slush off her boots on the rug in front of the door. She hurried inside, the warm office smelling of cinnamon and coffee, and offering relief from the single digit January temperature, despite the late afternoon sunshine.

Allison Brewster, one of Macey's friends from high school and Mr. Fowler's granddaughter, sat at the reception desk. She looked up with a ready smile on her face, then her blue eyes widened. Squealing, she raced around the desk, her arms flailing in the air. "Macey, your mom mentioned you'd come back home. I planned to give you a call after work."

Macey hugged her friend, then looked down at Allison's oversize sweater stretched over her rounded stomach. "How are you feeling? How's this little one doing?"

Allison smiled and cradled her belly. "We're both healthy and strong. No morning sickness. Apparently, third time's a charm."

At twenty-eight, Macey wasn't even close to being married, let alone pregnant with her third child. But Allison had been more than happy to settle in Aspen Ridge after marrying her high school sweetheart.

Allison jerked her head toward the closed door to the right of her desk. "I'm assuming you're here to be with your family?"

Macey tightened her hand on her oversize purse. "I was hoping to join them, if possible."

"Sure, I don't see why not." She moved to the door and tapped before sticking her head inside. "Excuse me, but there's someone else to join your meeting."

Macey stepped into the office filled with heavy, wooden furniture and books on the floor-to-ceiling bookcases. The room smelled of paper, lemon oil and a faint lingering scent of the pipe tobacco that Mr. Fowler favored when no one was around.

Macey's mother turned in her chair and waved her into the office. She patted the empty seat next to hers. "Macey, come in. We're just about to get started."

She sat and a strong arm slid around her shoulders. Macey looked into the blue eyes of her younger brother, Wyatt. He grinned, looking so much like their dad. "Hey, sis."

He'd been a lanky teen, but six years in the Marine Corps filled out his shoulders. Even

though he had been discharged two years ago
after his wife died in childbirth, his hair was
still cut to military regulation.

She gave him a one-armed side hug, the side
of her head brushing against his blue-and-black
plaid flannel shirt. "Hey, baby brother. It's so
great to see again. Bear said you guys were here.
I came to see what was going on."

Mr. Fowler cleared his throat. Dressed in a
dark blue suit, his balding white hair neatly
trimmed, he stood behind his desk, fingertips
pressed against the polished wood. His eyebrows lifted, wrinkling his forehead. "Ms.
Stone, it's been a while. You look well."

Macey lifted her chin and gave the man a
nod. "Thank you, Mr. Fowler. As do you."

Behind her, the hardwood floor creaked, and
Macey turned. Her eyes widened. "Cole? What
are *you* doing here?"

Instead of wearing jeans and the olive-col-
ored hoodie from that morning, Cole was now
dressed in a light gray suit that fit him well,
polished black cowboy boots and a red-pat-
terned tie.

He pocketed his hands as his lips thinned.
"I'm the project manager, working with the city

council and Crawford Developments, overseeing this process."

"Crawford Developments as in the company your uncle owns?" At his nod, Macey glanced between her mother, brother and Cole. "What process are you referring to?"

Mr. Fowler cleared his throat and tugged on the sleeves of his suit jacket. "Maybe we should return to our conversation and fill Macey in on the details."

Macey's stomach tightened again.

Mr. Fowler explained the letter of intent from the city council outlining their desire to buy the southern portion of the ranch to build a strip mall.

Even though Bear had warned her, Macey still felt her face paling as she turned to her mother and Wyatt. "Please tell me this is some sort of joke. You're not going to allow this, are you?"

Wyatt reached for Macey's fisted hands. "Mace, we may not have a choice."

"Of course, we have a choice. They can't just take our property."

Mr. Fowler cleared his throat once again, the sound grating on Macey's fatigued nerves. "Macey, are you aware of eminent domain?"

She lifted a shoulder. "Bear mentioned it, but I don't understand the details."

"If your family chooses not to sell, then the local government is claiming eminent domain to access your family's property for the strip mall. They will purchase the land at a fair market value."

"But what does that mean, exactly?"

"The local government has the power to take private land for public use. In this case, the Aspen Ridge City Council will be working with Crawford Developments. They are willing to pursue partial taking, meaning they don't want the whole ranch—just a portion of property from your family. Both parties have the right to obtain their own appraisals of the property in question. Once those appraisals have been exchanged, we'll enter negotiations. If the two parties can't reach an agreement, then the city council will send out a final offer. If your family refuses that offer, then the local government will go through the courts to take the property. Your family will still receive just compensation."

Macey's eyes darted between her family, Cole and Mr. Fowler. "But that property has been in our family for over two hundred years. And now we're supposed to sit back and say yes?" Without waiting for an answer, she turned to her mother. "What did Dad say about this?"

"He doesn't know yet." Mom picked up the pen on the table in front of her and twisted it between her fingers. "Once we have all the facts, I'll talk to your father."

Wyatt stood and rounded the table, putting his large hands on her shoulders. "Macey, Dad's not doing so well right now."

Macey swiveled in her seat and looked up at him. Her fingers tightened on the back of the chair. "I thought he had pneumonia. You mean it could be more than that?"

He nodded, lines deepening in his forehead. "They're still trying to find the cause of his high fever, but now his organs are shutting down."

"Shutting down? Why didn't you say something sooner? We should be at the hospital, not at the attorney's office trying to protect our property." She cradled her forehead, then lifted her chin and directed her attention to Cole. "Does your uncle know my father is in the hospital and unable to fight this? Or was that part of his plan? And did you know about this when I agreed to care for your daughter?"

Cole's jaw tightened as he held up a hand. "Macey, I know what this looks like, but I promise you—I did not know about this when you offered to care for Lexi. This is business. The city council isn't trying to take your family's entire ranch. They're offering to buy a small portion. And your family will be paid fair market value for it."

"So I've heard about three times now. But you know what? To you, it may be business, but to me—" she waved a finger between her mother, her brother and herself "—to us, it's personal. And we will do whatever we can to prevent you, your uncle, the city council, or anyone else from taking what is ours."

Head pounding and eyes gritty, Macey wanted nothing more than to find a bed and a pillow, but she couldn't rest right now. They needed to come up with a plan. To rally together and protect what was theirs.

Still feeling the sting from being unfairly terminated, Macey wasn't about to let someone else take advantage of any of them, even if it meant losing another job.

How was he going to get out of this mess and still meet Lexi's needs?

Somehow, Cole needed to convince the Stone family to sell their property to the council.

Not only would the strip mall offer more jobs and economic opportunities to Aspen Ridge, but the success of the sale would enable Cole to provide better opportunities for his daughter. With the incentives Wallace dangled in front of him, Cole needed to do whatever it took to ensure his daughter received the best care possible.

Then money wouldn't be a constant issue.

No way would he allow history to repeat itself.

Growing up as the only child of a widowed, overworked single mother who'd preached they were responsible for themselves and charity wasn't an option, Cole had fought hard to make his own way in the world. The last thing he wanted was for Lexi to know the gnaw of hunger in her belly or the shame of seeing her toes sticking out of worn shoes.

His cell phone buzzed with an incoming text. He reached for it and read the words from his cousin Piper: On our way up.

Cole glanced at his smart watch. How was it six o'clock already?

When Cole learned about the Stones' meeting with Norman Fowler, he'd left work early and asked Piper to care for Lexi until his meeting with the Stones was over.

He'd been naive to think Macey wouldn't have shown up at Fowler's office. The Stones stuck together. Like a real family should.

Her accusations from earlier still echoed in his head, but he needed to put that out of his mind. At least for now.

Even though he could work for another three hours, Cole forced himself to shut down his laptop. The rest would have to wait until tomorrow. He needed to go home and spend the evening with Lexi. If he had time and a shred of mental energy, maybe he'd do more work after tucking her into bed.

His office door opened as he slipped his laptop and the rest of his paperwork in his backpack.

"Daddy!" His daughter flew across the room and into his arms. "I missed you."

"I missed you too, peanut." He wrapped her in a hug and planted a kiss on top of her curly blond head.

She cupped his cheeks and stared at him with those bright blue eyes inherited from her mother. "Can we get pancakes now?"

"Sure thing. Let me gather my stuff, and

we'll get out of here." With her gathered in his arms, Cole pocketed his phone, then flung the strap of his backpack over his shoulder, knocking his worn Colorado Rockies ball cap off the corner of his desk that his dad had bought him after they'd gone to a baseball game together. Cole put it back where it belonged. Assured his work area was spotless, he turned to his cousin who waited patiently near the door.

"Thanks for keeping her, Piper. I appreciate the last-minute fill-in while I attended that meeting."

"Hey, when you own your business, you can make your own hours." She linked her arm through his. "Even though Macey's helping you out, you need to make time to find a full-time nanny or consider enrolling Lexi in a preschool program now that she's four."

"She's on the list for Stepping Stones Learning Center's fall program."

"Good. You can pay me by taking Avery and me to dinner."

He admired his cousin's drive. Pregnant at seventeen and forced out on her own, Piper had cleaned houses to support herself. Once she turned eighteen, she and Ryland Healy had gotten married and welcomed their daughter,

Avery, a week later. After Ry's tragic death, Piper put herself through college, earning her degree in business administration, while still running her housecleaning business, The Clean Bee, and caring for her daughter.

Now her thriving business had a handful of employees, and she was the most sought-after housecleaning and organizational business in the area.

How could Cole not admire her spunk and tenacity?

"Sounds good. Let's eat at the diner. Lexi loves Lynetta's pancakes."

"Sure thing. I need to pick up Avery from dance class, then we'll meet you there."

They stepped outside, and Cole sucked in a breath as the brisk winds pinched their cheeks. He drew Lexi closer to his chest and hurried to his truck parked behind the office. He put Lexi down, then transferred Lexi's car seat from Piper's car into his. He set his backpack on the floor, locked the door and pocketed his keys. Cole reached for Lexi's hand. "Come on, squirt. Let's go grab a booth at Netta's where it's warm."

They crossed the street. Cole opened the door of the diner and followed his daughter inside. The warmth of the room reheated their cheeks as he inhaled the scents of burgers and fries hanging in the air. Dishes clattering in the kitchen behind the breakfast counter competed with the conversations buzzing in the full dining room.

They slid into a red booth near the front. He set his phone facedown on the table, then pulled Lexi's coloring book and crayons from her backpack. He shrugged out of his wool overcoat and helped Lexi out of her pink puffy jacket and matching hat.

The door opened again, and Cole looked up, expecting to see Piper and Avery. Instead, Macey Stone stepped inside.

She rubbed her mittened hands together. A gray knitted hat covered her dark hair and a matching scarf wound around her neck. Her red wool coat parted, giving a hint of a light blue sweater she wore.

Her gaze connected with his, and the light in her eyes dimmed.

Lynetta Spencer, the diner owner and Macey's aunt, rounded the counter with outstretched arms. She engulfed Macey in a tight hug. "Girl, it is so good to see you. When your mama said you were back home for good, I about fell off my stool."

"Hey, Aunt Lynetta. It's so great to see you." As Macey stepped out of her embrace, she shifted her eyes to Cole's, then muttered something to her aunt.

Lynetta raised an eyebrow and fisted a hand on her rounded hip as she seared him with a look. Then she headed to his table. An apron covered her full figure. Her dark hair, the same shade as Macey's, was twisted on top of her head in some sort of messy bun held in place by a yellow pencil.

Great. Would he need to find a new place to eat?

Lynetta cupped Lexi's cheek. "Hey, darlin'."

Lexi leaned into her touch, then held up her coloring book. "Hi, Miss Netta. Like my picture?"

Lynetta dropped on the bench next to her and slid an arm around his daughter's shoulders. "Sugar, that's the prettiest purple turtle I've ever seen."

Lexi tore it out and handed it to her. "Here, you can have it."

"Aww, thanks, precious. I'll hang it up behind the counter." She slid out from behind the table and stood. She pressed a gentle hand on Cole's shoulder, giving it a light squeeze. One eyebrow lifted, but her eyes softened. "I understand business, but that's my parents' property up for grabs. Your mom was like a sister to me, which makes you family too. I don't want to see anyone get hurt. Got it?"

Cole looked up at the woman who had been his mother's best friend since elementary school. The same woman who promised to look after Cole if anything should happen to her.

"Yes, ma'am. That wasn't my intention."

"My daddy's nice. He won't hurt nobody." Then Lexi's eyes lit up as she stood on the red vinyl bench and pointed. "Look, Daddy, there's Macey." She waved, her voice raising. "Hi, Macey."

All eyes in the diner turned to them, including Macey's. The reddened color of her face matched the round stools lining the counter. She smiled tightly and gave a little wave.

Lexi scrambled under the table and raced over to her, flinging her arms around Macey's legs. "Wanna sit with us?"

Without responding, Macey lifted Lexi in her arms and returned the hug. Then she set her down and took her hand, returning her to where Cole sat.

Lynetta eyed them. "Have you two kept in touch over the years?"

Cole scoffed. "Not exactly. Everly was offered a long-term subbing position at the elementary school, so Macey agreed to care for Lexi until I can find a more permanent solution."

Lynetta slid an arm around Macey's shoulder. "That's my girl. Always thinking of others. She's the best nanny a family could want."

"Lexi's been talking about her all afternoon, so I believe it."

Macey jerked her head toward the street. "Can I talk to you for a minute?"

Cole shifted his gaze to Lexi. Lynetta slid into the booth and picked up a crayon. "You two go. I'll keep an eye on this little one for a moment."

Cole hesitated. "If you're sure…"

Lynetta waved them way. "Go. Talk. The sooner you do, the better it'll be. For everyone."

He didn't know about that. But he followed Macey outside and stood on the sidewalk near the window so he could keep an eye on his daughter. He shoved his bare hands in his pockets to keep them warm. "What did you want to talk about?"

Macey rewrapped her scarf around her neck. "I want to know what you think you're doing."

He lifted a shoulder. "I'm planning to eat dinner with Lexi, my cousin Piper, and her daughter Avery."

Macey gave him an exasperated look. "I'm not talking about now. I'm talking about earlier in Fowler's office. What was that all about?"

Cole scrubbed a hand over his face. How many times were they going to rehash this? "We explained everything in Fowler's office. What else would you like to know?"

"Why my family's property? Why not property on the other side of town or even in a different area? Aspen Ridge isn't big enough for a strip mall."

"The property in question is near the highway and closest to Aspen Ridge. It makes more sense since it would bring more traffic into the community. Your family will be paid a fair market value."

"I'm so tired of hearing that phrase. You can't put a price on history. That section of the land was the original homestead when my great-great-grandparents settled the town. After Mom and Dad got married, my grandparents moved back to South Bend and restored the original house. Besides, all the traffic and noise from the strip mall will disturb the cattle. And Stone River cuts through our property. How will the construction affect the waterway? What about contaminants ruining the soil?"

"All of those issues will be addressed. We won't do anything to jeopardize the water supply, soil, or even the cattle. Besides, from the research I've done, it looks like your family could use the money."

Macey's eyes narrowed. "What does that mean?"

"Instead of talking to me, maybe you need to be talking to your family. There's more to this whole situation than you know. I understand wanting to protect family. I will do anything for my daughter. Crawford Developments will do everything to protect your family's property."

"If only I could believe you." She looked over his shoulder, a shadow filming her eyes.

Cole's fingers tightened into fists in his pockets. "Listen, Mace, I know you have trust issues when it comes to me, but I promise I didn't know about any of this when you agreed to care for Lexi. Talk to your family and see what they want to do. This wasn't my choice, but it's my job. Like you, I have plenty at stake as well."

"What? A promotion with a corner office view?"

Cole ground his jaw. "A promotion, yes. But a corner office means nothing to me. I care more about the medical benefits for my daughter." He paused a moment, then ran a hand over his face. "What does this mean for us? Caring for Lexi, I mean. And me helping you with the Sweetheart Ball."

Pocketing her hands, she sighed, white puffs of air punctuating her frustration. "I need the money and your little girl shouldn't suffer. Plus I don't have time to do all of the organizing on my own. But won't those be conflicts of interest for you now that you're overseeing this project?"

"I can separate business from my personal life." Even as he spoke the words, they didn't ring true to his own ears. Yeah, the next few months were going to be a challenge, but it wasn't anything he couldn't handle.

"But it's all personal. Don't you see that? I want what's best for my family and you want what's best for your daughter. Somehow, there needs to be a compromise." Without another word, she walked away.

The Macey Stone he knew growing up was more like the Macey who was so kind and patient with Lexi, not this angry person who was acting colder than the January air.

But could he really blame her? Honestly, he'd probably feel the same way.

Even though he'd said it wasn't personal, it was. For all of them. Somehow, he had to work it out for everyone's best interest.

Whatever that may be.

CHAPTER THREE

IF MACEY COULDN'T get her family to join the fight with her, then why was she wasting her own time and energy? Somehow, they needed to come together as a united front.

Especially for Mom's sake.

Her mother sat in the same seat at the end of the rectangular dining room table for as long as Macey could remember. Her shoulder-length caramel-blond hair with streaks of gray around her temples had been pulled back into a clip, with a few wisps framing her face. Macey didn't like the deepening lines etching her mother's forehead, the brackets pinching her mouth, or the way she pushed her food around her plate.

Macey schooled her tone and tempered her anger as her gaze volleyed between her two brothers sitting across the table from her. "You guys don't get it. Saving the ranch needs to be our highest priority."

Bear threw his head back and laughed, the sound bouncing off the exposed beams. Raising his eyebrow, he pushed his empty plate away. His chair creaked as he leaned back and folded his arms over his chest. "*We* don't get it?" He wagged a finger between Wyatt and himself. "The two guys who have been working the ranch daily while you've been five hours away?"

She tried not to let his words get under her skin. Forcing a smile, she said to her brother, "I've been away doing my job."

He leaned forward, resting his arms on the table, and seared her with a glare. "Exactly. But you haven't been here on a daily basis, so you don't have any idea of what's happening. The least we can do is hear them out before rejecting their offer. Like Fowler said—they don't want the whole ranch. Just a portion of it."

"And a strip mall could help the town's economy." Wyatt wiped his daughter's face and handed her a plastic cup of milk.

"*Et tu*, Wyatt?"

Her younger brother held up his hands. "Hey, I'm not being a traitor. I'm simply looking at all sides."

"The letterhead may have the city council address, but now that we know they're using

Crawford Developments, this has Wallace Crawford written all over it. He tried to buy South Bend once already, but Dad refused to sell. And for good reason. We need to keep what is ours."

"Ours? If you feel so strongly about the ranch, then why'd you run away the first chance you got?"

"I wouldn't exactly call going to college and getting a job running away." Macey wasn't about to rehash the past mortification that caused her to leave Aspen Ridge, but that didn't prevent the sting of her brother's words.

Macey's eyes darted between Mia, Wyatt's two-year-old daughter, and Tanner, her sister Mallory's five-year-old son sitting between Mom and Everly, who watched the grown-ups with wide eyes.

Mom cleared her throat. "Instead of arguing over dinner, we need to put it in God's hands and let Him work out the details."

Realizing she wasn't going to change her brother's mind, Macey swallowed her fighting words along with the last bite of her pot roast. She set her fork next to her plate and looked at him. "You're right, Bear. I haven't been around, but that doesn't mean I don't love the ranch or shouldn't know what's going on. Now that I'm home, I'll pull my weight around here and do what I can to help save the ranch."

"Even if saving it means letting go of a piece of it?" His tone gentled.

Was she willing to do that?

"Yes, even if saving it means letting go of a piece of it. I'm meeting with Cole soon, who's helping me with the Sweetheart Ball, so I'll get started on the dishes." She slid back her chair and carried her plate to the kitchen. She ran water in the sink and added a squirt of dish soap.

"We have a dishwasher, you know? No need to wash them by hand." Everly set her plate on the counter.

"I don't mind. Gives me time to think." Macey submerged her hands beneath the bubbles, allowing the heated water to warm her chilled fingers.

Standing behind Macey, Everly wrapped her arms around her sister's waist and pressed her cheek against Macey's back. "Thanks for helping me out with Lexi."

"You were right—she is a doll. We had fun baking cookies. Thanks for remembering about that. Otherwise, I would have had a very disappointed little girl on my hands. Are you ready for tomorrow?"

"As ready as I'll ever be, I guess. I'm sure it'll be a bit different than student teaching." Six years younger than Macey, Everly, with her lighter hair and blue eyes like their mom, looked more like a high schooler than an educator.

Mom carried in the plate of leftover pot roast and set it on the stove. She pressed her back against the counter and kneaded her temples.

"You okay, Mom?"

She lifted her head and gave them a tight smile. "Yes, just a little headache starting. I'll be fine."

"As soon as Macey and I finish the dishes, I'll drive you to the hospital so you can see Dad for a bit before bed." Everly turned to Macey. "You wanna go too, Mace? Dad'll be thrilled to see you."

Macey's hands stilled on the plate she was washing. "Thanks, but Cole's coming by to work on plans for the Sweetheart Ball with me. Give Dad my love though and let him know I'll come and visit soon."

Mom pushed away from the stove and reached for a dish towel. "Are you sure you have time to work on the ball, honey? I can cancel it or push it out further into the year, if need be."

As eager as she was to jump on that offer, the look on Mom's face had Macey swallowing her protest. Of course, she couldn't cancel. It wasn't that Macey didn't want to plan it. The thought of working with Cole still twisted her stomach in knots.

But she didn't want to burden her mother with stressing about her too.

Macey forced a smile into place. "Nope, it's not a problem, Mom. I've got it handled."

Mom slid an arm around her shoulders. "Thanks. I'm so glad I could count on you."

After cleaning the kitchen, Macey headed up the polished oak stairs to the room she'd shared with her sisters for the first eighteen years of her life and retrieved her laptop.

Family photos lined the tongue-and-groove paneled stairwell, showcasing the changes and additions to the family over the years, particularly the grandchildren.

With Mallory still in the navy and stationed on a carrier somewhere in the Pacific Ocean, her son Tanner lived at the ranch until her deployment ended in six months.

A knock sounded on the door. Macey hurried downstairs. She took a quick second to run a hand over her hair. Maybe she should've changed out of her jeans and sweatshirt she'd worn to help with barn chores before sitting down to dinner.

Knock it off.

She opened the door and cringed at the way Cole's presence sent her heart tripping over her ribs. "Cole. Hi, come in."

He stepped into the kitchen, stripped his black knit cap off his head, then smoothed down his hair.

Macey waved a hand to the table. "Have a seat. Want coffee or anything?"

He held up a hand as he pulled out a chair. "No, thanks. I'm good. I have only an hour or so before I have to pick up Lexi from Piper's."

"You could've brought her with you, you know."

"She wanted to hang out with Piper. Even though they're second cousins, Piper's kind of like the only mother figure in Lexi's life right now."

"I remember Piper from school being very sweet and friendly to everyone. She and Bear used to be close until they had a falling out after her husband was killed."

"Ryland's death was tough all around."

"He was Bear's best friend. My brother hasn't been the same since that night. But you didn't come here to talk about the past." Macey lifted the cover of her laptop and opened the file her mother had sent with plans from previous years. "The ball's been held at the barn on South Bend for as long as I can remember. After my grandparents passed, my parents decided to continue the tradition." Then she stopped and glanced at Cole. "If this sale goes through, then this may be the last Sweetheart Ball on our family's property."

Cole shifted in his chair. "Then let's make the most of it to create a lasting memory."

"I don't want to create a lasting memory. I want to hold on to what's ours. But like Mom said over dinner—we need to put it in God's hands and let Him work out the details." Macey returned to the open document on her screen. "Aunt Lynetta and Uncle Pete will do the catering. I'm sure it will be a similar menu as in years past—an assortment of hors d'oeuvres, mixed green salad, a choice of filet mignon or roasted chicken, seasoned baby potatoes, vegetable medley and a dessert table. Tickets need to be purchased in advance to attend. They're on sale at the diner, and we'll sell them during WinterFest too. Mom said there was a problem with the posters, so they're being reprinted. Then they'll need to be hung up around town."

"Sounds like the bulk of the details are in place. Other than hanging posters and selling tickets, what do we need to do?"

"Market the event, contact local businesses for prize donations, set up the barn at the homestead, decorate, show up and pray everything goes off without a hitch."

Cole grinned and snapped his fingers. "Piece of cake. You'll handle this like a pro. You're a natural organizer, which is why you were on the prom committee for three years in a row."

Macey held up a hand. "Can we not mention prom? Like ever again?"

"Sure, not a problem. Consider it stricken from my vocabulary."

Macey drummed her fingers on the table next to her laptop and bit her bottom lip. "How would you feel about me caring for Lexi here at the ranch? If I'm going to make the ball happen in less than a month, then I can't be tied to your condo all day. Plus she can play with Tanner and Mia here."

"As long as Lexi's in your very capable hands,

I'm fine with you caring for her here. You're doing me a huge favor so I'll do whatever it takes to make things easier for you."

"Then stop the land sale from happening." The words tipped off the edge of her tongue before she had time to filter her thoughts.

"I really wish I could, Mace. The last thing I want is to bring you more pain."

She promised her family to listen to the offer and consider all sides. But was she truly willing to let it go even if that's what the family deemed was best?

Hopefully it wouldn't come to that.

Maybe having the Sweetheart Ball would show the community the value of the property over having a strip mall that could endanger small businesses in town.

If Cole could find another suitable property like the parcel at Stone River Ranch, then maybe he could make his uncle happy and still salvage his relationship with the family who had been a huge part of his childhood.

Problem was, that strip of land *seemed* perfect for what Wallace wanted to build.

A strip mall could be an asset to the small

ranching community, provided they attracted the right retailers.

But Cole really hated the idea of ruining the integrity of Aspen Ridge's small town feel by bringing in chain stores.

The town was straight out of a movie, which was why he'd stayed to raise his daughter after his ex-wife abandoned them.

Sure, a few chain restaurants would offer more variety, but they wouldn't have the same personal touch as Netta's Diner. However, Aspen Ridge's city council was serious about wanting to grow and offer sustainable jobs for the community. Would retailers even be willing to come to a town of less than four thousand residents?

Cole scrubbed a hand over his weary face.

After working on the ball with Macey, he'd spent the remainder of his Friday working past midnight. Then Wallace had called before six this morning, asking if Cole planned to work that day. Needing to keep his uncle happy, he agreed to half a day and asked Piper once again for help.

He'd dropped a teary-eyed Lexi off at his cousin's house at seven this morning and had been staring at the computer since seven thirty.

He rubbed his burning eyes. With a sigh, he hit print, and the file of properties he compiled spit out from the printer.

He hadn't wanted to spend Saturday in the office, but if he could get his uncle to change his mind, then it would be worth the short time away from his daughter.

After pocketing his phone, he grabbed the pages and crossed the hall to Wallace's office.

His uncle, dressed in stiff Wranglers, a blue-and-white plaid pearl-snapped long-sleeved shirt and his worn cowboy boots, leaned back in his black leather executive chair and held the receiver of the office landline to his ear.

Deep lines etched the man's weathered face, and his graying hair made him look like an Old West cowboy instead of the founder of a million-dollar corporation.

Cole rapped his knuckles against the open solid wood door. Wallace looked up and waved him in with two fingers.

Not wanting to eavesdrop on the call, Cole moved to the large window that offered a breathtaking snowcapped mountain view of the San Juan National Forest. With his office on the third floor of the building he owned, Wallace could look over Main Street to watch the daily activity of the business district. He liked to keep his finger on the pulse of what was happening in town.

The phone receiver rattled into its cradle and Wallace let out a whoop, causing Cole's heart to slam against his ribs. "Wylie's Western Wear just agreed to sit down with the council and discuss being one of the anchor stores in the strip mall. Great news, isn't it, son?"

He wasn't Wallace's son.

The man was nothing like Cole's father, who had been killed on a job site when Cole was six, but he kept his mouth shut. After all, he still owed his uncle.

Cole clenched his jaw and turned, his fingers tightening on the sheaf of papers. "I was reviewing different properties around Aspen Ridge and surrounding communities. Maybe one of them would be a—"

"Why?" Wallace cut in, raising his right eyebrow—the man's tell for annoyance.

"Excuse me?"

"Why are you researching other properties? I want the Stone River Ranch property."

"I understand that, but one of these others would offer many of the same benefits and we wouldn't need to go after the Stones' land."

Wallace rounded his desk and walked toward Cole in slow, measured steps obviously meant to intimidate. Then he rested a heavy hand on Cole's shoulder, squeezing tighter than necessary. "Son, I don't pay you to second-guess me. If you're getting soft, I'll bring in someone who can close the deal. Is that what you want?"

Heat scorched Cole's neck, but he schooled his expression with a tight smile and shook off his uncle's hand. He lifted his chin and met the man's gaze. "No, sir."

Wallace grinned, reminding Cole again of a wolf watching his prey. "Good. Glad we understand each other. Now get with Fowler so the public notice can be posted. The quicker we act, the sooner we can be ready to break ground when the weather warms."

Wallace's phone buzzed. He moved to his desk and pressed the intercom. "What is it, Bernice?"

"Macey Stone is here to see you."

The man sighed. "Send her in."

Cole headed for the door, but Wallace blocked his path. "You might as well stay and hear what she has to say. Just be sure to tuck that bleeding heart away. Remember, this is business."

Macey appeared in the doorway, wearing

jeans, and a white sweater under the red wool jacket she'd worn yesterday.

Wallace strode to the door with his hand outstretched. "Ms. Stone, come in and have a seat. What can I do for you?"

Macey ignored his hand and the invitation. Remaining in the doorway, she seared both of them with a fiery look. "You can stop the process of stealing my family's property."

Wallace laughed, but his eyes sparked. "Ms. Stone, you and I both know I'm not stealing anything. The city council is offering your family fair market value for a few acres. You will have plenty of land for your cattle. With your daddy laid up and Barrett licking his wounds over his fallen rodeo career, I hear the money will help keep your family's little ranch afloat a while longer."

"*Little* ranch? Our family has nearly a thousand acres."

"And my ranch in Montana has five thousand."

"Why are you doing this?"

He waved a hand toward Cole. "As I'm sure my property manager has explained, it's an opportunity to grow the economy. I'm merely working with the city council on this for the good people of Aspen Ridge."

"Right. You're telling me you have nothing to gain? You've always put yourself first and others second, Mr. Crawford. We'll fight you every step of the way."

"I'm sure you'll be a worthy adversary, young lady. But just be sure you're doing what's best for your family. The longer this drags out, the less generous I... I mean, the city council may be."

"Is that a threat?"

"No threat. Simply stating I always get what I want."

"We'll see about that." She turned and strode out of Wallace's office, slamming the door behind her.

Wallace growled low in his throat, then reached for his Broncos coffee mug.

For a moment, Cole expected him to hurl it against the wall. Wouldn't be the first time.

Wallace drained the cup, then pierced Cole with a sharp look. "I don't care how you do it, but get them to sign. Otherwise, you'll find yourself out of a job. I'm sure you don't want that, especially with that expensive specialist your daughter needs that your insurance doesn't cover."

He flung the door open and marched down the hall, barking an order at Bernice.

Cole dragged a hand over his face, then returned to his office. He fed the lists of other properties through the shredder, feeling every bit sliced and diced as those bits of paper.

Somehow, he needed to show the Stones what a gain this could be instead of a loss.

Because Cole needed to keep this job for the sake of his daughter. Even if it meant working for a man like Wallace Crawford.

CHAPTER FOUR

MACEY WASN'T ACTUALLY going behind her family's back. She simply wanted a second opinion.

But after the previous night's dinner conversation, she didn't expect them to be very receptive of her idea. She just didn't understand why they weren't as on fire to save the ranch. Especially after her impromptu meeting with the despicable Wallace Crawford.

How could Cole work for a man like that? Even if he was an uncle. What hold did that jerk have over him?

As Macey rounded the corner, her eyes drifted to the way the sun glazed the San Juan Mountains in the background of Main Street. Clouds crowned the peaks jutting against the brilliant blue sky. The aspens and frosted pines of the national forest and the silvery river flowing through the base eased the tightness in her chest.

There truly was no place like home.

"Hey, Macey. I heard you were back in town. Long time no see."

Macey whirled in the direction of the male voice and came face-to-face with Aaron Brewster, Allison's brother-in-law and one of her closest friends all through school. Just the person she'd come to see.

She hugged him and let out one of those little squeals she really disliked hearing from other people. "Aaron! It's so good to see you."

He wrapped his arms around her so tightly he lifted her off her feet. "I stopped by Cody and Allison's this morning, and Allison said you'd returned home. Why didn't you tell me you were coming?"

"It was a last-minute decision. Since I've been home, things have been busy."

Aaron's brows scrunched together behind his dark-rimmed glasses. Aaron wore faded jeans and a navy sweater beneath his yellow ski jacket. A light wind tugged at his short curly hair. "Everything okay?"

"Well, that's kind of why I'm here. I called

your house, and Jacie said you were working this morning. Do you have a minute?"

Aaron looked at his watch. "I have about fifteen, then I have to meet a client."

"Honestly, I was a little surprised to learn you were open on a Saturday."

He shrugged. "I work until noon for those who can't come into the office during the week."

"Aaron Brewster—always caring for others. Mind if I just tell you quickly what I need?"

"What? And miss out on these billable minutes?" He laughed, a sound that Macey really missed. They'd had such good times together.

"Before I dive into my problem, how are Jacie and your little one doing?"

"Jacie's great." He nodded across the street. "She finally got the bridal shop up and running. Our little guy, Liam, turns two next month."

"I saw the storefront yesterday when I came into town. Between you and your brother, you're keeping your parents stocked with grandchildren."

"Cody and Allison have a head start on Jacie and me, but we're pretty happy." He glanced at his watch again. "So how can I help?"

"The ranch is in trouble."

He frowned. "How so?"

"The Aspen Ridge City Council sent my parents a letter of intent. They want to buy a portion of the ranch to create a strip mall. But I think Wallace Crawford is actually the brains behind this deal. And if we don't sell, they're claiming condemnation and going through the eminent domain process."

"Why does Aspen Ridge need a strip mall?"

"Exactly my question. My mom, Wyatt and I met with Mr. Fowler yesterday, but my impression was he was more for the council and Crawford than my family's interests, even though he's been our attorney since my grandparents were alive."

"What does your dad think about this?"

Macey shifted her feet and tightened her hold on her tote bag. "He doesn't know yet. Dad's in the hospital with possible pneumonia. Mom's waiting for more information before telling him."

"Not the homecoming you were hoping for, huh?"

"Not exactly. But that's a conversation for another day. I don't want to keep you from your appointment, but would you mind looking over the papers if I drop them off on Monday?"

"Not at all." Aaron pressed a quick kiss against her cheek. "Great seeing you, Mace. Let's catch up when I have more time."

"Sure thing. Thanks. And give Jacie my love."

With a renewed sense of hope, Macey slid her bag onto her shoulder and headed across the street to the diner.

As she reached for the door, it swung open. She jumped back to avoid getting smacked in the forehead as a child raced out onto the sidewalk.

"Lexi, wait for me."

Macey recognized that deep voice.

Cole barreled through the open door and snagged Lexi around the waist.

"I was right here, Daddy. I wasn't going anywhere." Laughing, Lexi patted her chest.

"You are not allowed outside without me, and you know it. No arguments." He swung her in his arms.

"Sorry, Daddy." She rested her head on his shoulder.

He tightened his arms around her. "I forgive

you, sweetheart. I just don't want anything to happen to my favorite Lexi."

"You're silly. I'm your only Lexi." The child's face lit up as she laughed. Lexi cupped her hands around Cole's clean-shaven face and rubbed her nose against his. Then her eyes connected with Macey's, and she waved. "Hi, Macey."

Cole turned, but his smile wasn't close to the sunshine his daughter exuded. He set Lexi down and held on to her hand.

Macey crouched in front of her. "Hey, Lexi. How's it going?"

"Netta made me sprinkle pancakes. Now Daddy's taking me to look at puppies. Wanna come?"

Macey snuck a glance at Cole. A muscle on the side of his jaw jumped as he lifted a shoulder. "I've never been a dog owner, so if you want to join us, I'd appreciate your input."

Macey turned her focus back to Lexi. "What kind of puppy are you going to get?"

Lexi lifted her hands and scrunched her face. "I don't know. Daddy says it needs to be little. Our 'partment is too small for Clifford the Big Red Dog." She cocked her head. "Does Clifford live at the shelter?"

Smiling, Macey shook her head. "I believe

he still lives on Birdwell Island with Emily Elizabeth."

Lexi's eyes widened. "You know about Clifford?"

"Yep. My grandma used to read Clifford books to me when I was your age."

"I don't have a grandma."

Macey cupped the child's cheek and ran her thumb over the baby-soft skin. Then she shifted her attention to Cole. "Are you going to the shelter on Elk Avenue?"

"Yes, my mother worked there part-time when I was a kid, so I know Ray and Irene Douglas well."

"I remember. They're also my brother's in-laws. You may see Wyatt there. He helps them from time to time." Macey glanced at the diner, then looked back at Lexi. "I need to meet with Lynetta about the catering menu for the ball, but I can do that afterward. If you're sure... I don't want to intrude on your time with your daughter."

"It's all good." Cole pulled his keys out of his front pocket. "I'm parked across the street. You're welcome to join us." Then he touched her forearm as they headed for the crosswalk.

"For what it's worth, I'm sorry for my uncle's attitude earlier. To him, this is just business."

"He'll destroy our family's legacy if this sale goes through. A family that helped you when your mom became sick, remember?" The crosswalk light flashed green. Lexi skipped ahead with Cole only a few steps behind her.

Once they reached the sidewalk, Cole pressed a button on his key fob and unlocked his truck. He helped Lexi into her car seat, then held the door for Macey. As she passed him, his lips thinned. "I love your family very much, and you know it. The last thing I want is to hurt them. But I need this job and benefits for Lexi's sake. If this deal goes through, then he'll pay for treatments from one of the top pediatric audiologists in the state to help her. I'll always put my daughter's needs first. Even if it means making difficult business decisions relating to those I care about."

Macey pulled herself into the truck cab, then reached for the door. Despite her mounting frustration, she softened her tone. "He's a bully who's using you to do his dirty work. Surely there are other options. Can't you talk to him?"

Cole laughed, a hollow sound to Macey's

ears, and shook his head. "I am one of the last people Wallace will listen to. He made that clear this morning when I tried to show him other properties just before you came in."

"Maybe you need to find a different job." Macey eyed Cole, noting the tender way his expression softened as he glanced back at Lexi.

"If only it were that simple." His words, a mix of sadness and resignation, slid out in a breathy whisper. He closed the door, rounded the front of the truck and slid into the driver's seat.

"Who's this specialist your uncle's dangling in front of you?"

"Some college buddy of Wallace's."

"So, he's purposefully withholding information until you do his bidding. So not fair. The man's a jerk." Macey softened her tone. None of this was Cole's fault, so she needed to back off and stop taking her frustrations out on him. "You're in a tough spot, Cole, and I'm sorry about that. I understand your need to do what's best for Lexi, but I need to do what's best for my family."

Bear's question from the other night echoed in her head. Despite her answer to him, would she be at peace if they had to give up the land she loved so much?

Hopefully, it wouldn't come to that.

No matter how much Cole wanted to convince Macey he truly had her family's best interests at heart, he had to put the land sale out of his mind and focus on his promise to look at puppies with Lexi.

When she'd invited Macey to join him, he wanted to veto the idea, but one look at Lexi's eager face had him swallowing his words.

Pulling into the parking lot of the Aspen Ridge Animal Shelter felt like coming home. Sitting on several acres at the end of Elk Avenue, the animal shelter was an extension of Ray and Irene Douglas's small farm. Their white sided two-story house with black shutters and a covered front porch sat to the left of the animal shelter, its front facing the driveway. A sidewalk connected the house to a large red barn edged against a grove of pines. Three blanketed horses stood in the fenced pasture near the barn.

The shelter building had been painted the same red as the barn, with the black trim matching the house. Two leafless dwarf apple trees sat on either side of the building. A row of frosted shrubs lined the front. A plaster black Lab yard ornament holding a welcome sign sat next to a wrought-iron bench. The gravel semi-circle driveway had been blacktopped since his mother worked part-time as a kennel attendant.

Cole's mother always parked behind the building next to the other employees' vehicles, and they entered through the back door. Cole promised himself someday he'd park out front and go in the main door.

Today was that day.

Cole opened the passenger-side door, helped Macey down, then released Lexi from her car seat. Lexi took each of their hands as they walked through the door and were greeted by dogs barking and pawing at their glass-enclosed kennels.

Twirling in a circle, Lexi squealed and clapped her hands. "I'm so excited, Daddy."

He knelt in front of her. "I'm glad, but remember, we may not be able to take a doggy home today. We're just looking."

"I know. I'm still excited."

A woman with silver-streaked hair pulled back into a knot at the base of her head looked up. Wearing jeans, and a purple sweatshirt with the shelter logo in the upper left corner, she smiled as she rounded the corner of a chest high counter with her arms extended. Her eyebrow raised as she noticed Macey standing next to him. "Hey, Cole. It's so good to see you."

"Hey, Mrs. D. You look great." Walking into her embrace, he pressed a kiss against her soft cheek and breathed in the powdery scent he'd associated with her for so many years.

"Oh, you sweet talker, you." Then she reached for Macey. "Wyatt said you were back home. It's good to see you again, Macey. So, you two are together now?"

Macey threw up her hands and shook her head. "Oh, no. No, not at all. I'm caring for Lexi right now."

Cole sighed. Yeah, there was no way Macey would ever trust him enough to be friends, let alone anything more.

Mrs. Douglas crouched in front of Lexi. "How are you doing, Lexi?"

"I'm fine. Daddy said we could look at doggies today." Lexi leaned against Cole's legs and looked up at him.

Irene toyed with a curl that had escaped Lexi's ponytail, then trailed her finger down his daughter's cheek. She glanced up at Cole.

"She looks so much like your mother. Janie would be so proud of you, you know?"

Nodding, Cole swallowed against the sudden tightness in his throat. "Mom would've loved her."

"Yes, she would have. I miss her. She was well loved and would do anything for anyone."

"That was my mom." An ache pinched his chest as he nodded again.

Mrs. Douglas straightened and clasped her hands in front of her, her eyes darting between Cole and Macey. "I tried to hire her away from the diner to work for me full-time, but Janie loved her customers. At least I got her in the afternoons for a couple of hours. My heart broke when she passed away."

Cole's vision started to cloud up and he blinked back tears. He hadn't expected this visit to be so emotional.

Yes, his mom would've been thrilled with Lexi. But how would she have felt about Cole's role in trying to acquire the Stone land?

"So, do you have a particular breed you're interested in? Or a particular dog? Have you checked out our website? Filled out an application?" Mrs. Douglas waved a hand toward the glass-walled kennels that allowed visitors to see dogs napping on their beds, chewing on toys, or pawing to be freed.

"No, I guess I didn't come very prepared." Cole glanced at Macey who knelt in front of the glass-walled kennels where a fluffy black-and-white dog lay on a dog cot and watched them.

Mrs. D. dismissed his words with a wave of her hand. "No worries. Right now, we have six dogs ready for their forever homes. If you give me an idea of what you're looking for, then I can help you find the right match."

"We're living in a condo until I can find the right house with a good-sized yard, so the dog needs to be small, calm and definitely kid friendly."

Mrs. Douglas steepled her fingers, touching them to her chin, then smiled. "I think I have just the dog for you, but she won't be ready for adoption for another week. Follow me."

Cole gestured for Macey to walk ahead of him, then set his hand at the small of her back as she stayed in line with him. They passed the enclosed kennels as memories flooded him.

While his mother had worked, Cole loved sitting in the play yard with the dogs tumbling over him. They didn't care what kind of clothes he wore or the brand of shoes on his feet. They just wanted love and attention…and a place to call home. He would've been a great dog owner. But no matter how many times he had pleaded, his mother never gave in to his request for an animal.

Looking back now, they couldn't have afforded it. Despite all of her efforts and the two jobs she held, they'd barely had enough to support the two of them.

Mrs. Douglas guided them to an office across the hall from the kennels. "Have a seat in here, and I'll bring Polly to see you."

Macey sat on a brown microfiber love seat. Because it was the only seat in the office, Cole sat next to her, his shoulder brushing against hers. He hugged the arm to give her more room and pulled Lexi onto his lap. A calico cat walked into the room and rubbed its head on Cole's legs.

Lexi gasped. "Look, Daddy. It's a kitty."

She jumped off his lap and wrapped her arms around the cat.

Macey scooted off the love seat and sat next to her. "Lexi, you have to be careful. You don't know if that kitty likes hugs."

At that moment Mrs. Douglas entered the room holding a purple leash connected to a small black-and-white dog with wavy hair. "Not to worry. Hawthorne loves everyone."

She brought the dog closer to them. Its little nose sniffed Lexi. "And this cutie is Polly. She's a schnoodle."

"Schnoodle? What's that?" Cole leaned forward and ran his fingers over Hawthorne's fur.

"A miniature poodle and a miniature schnauzer mix. She was surrendered to us recently when her owner moved into assisted living and could no longer care for her. Polly is about six years old, apartment friendly and she loves small children. Her previous owner had a large family with several small grandchildren. Unfortunately, none of them were able to take the sweet girl. She's been with us for a couple of weeks, and our vet hasn't released her for adoption just yet. But she will be ready in a week for a new home."

Hawthorne left Cole and wound his way around Mrs. Douglas's legs. Still holding on to Polly's leash, she scooped up the cat and placed him on the tower in the corner.

Cole moved to the floor next to Lexi and waited for the dog to approach them again. "Hey, Polly. How are you doing?"

The dog's ears perked, and she cocked her head at the sound of her name.

Mrs. Douglas opened a container on the desk in the corner and grabbed a handful of tiny dog treats. She gave a few to Macey, then handed the rest to Cole. "See if she'll take these treats, one at a time, out of your hand."

Cole placed a treat on his palm. Polly took a few tentative steps, licked her lips and took the treat.

Mrs. Douglas crouched and petted the dog's head. "Good girl, Polly." She looked at Lexi. "Would you like to try feeding her?"

Eyes wide, Lexi nodded. Then she looked at Cole. "Can I, Daddy?"

"Sure. Just do what I did. Put the treat in your hand and hold it flat for Polly to take."

Lexi did as instructed, then giggled as Polly ate the treat. Lexi rubbed her hand on her shirt. "Her tongue tickles."

"Yes, it does."

They played with Polly for another fifteen minutes, allowing Lexi and Polly to get used to each other.

"I think we've found a match." Cole pulled his phone out of his pocket and snapped a picture of his daughter petting Polly. "What's the next step?"

"We'll fill out some paperwork. Usually, we suggest a trial stay to make sure the dog is the right fit for your family. Then, you can decide if you'd like to make her a permanent addition to your household."

"What do you think, honey?"

Lexi petted the dog curled in her lap. "Polly needs us, Daddy."

His daughter's tender heart never ceased to amaze him. He pushed to his feet. "Okay, then. Let's fill out some paperwork. The week we wait for her to be released will give me time to get food and supplies for her."

"Sounds good."

Cole turned to Macey. "Would you mind staying here with Lexi and Polly while I fill out the paperwork?"

Smiling, Macey ran a hand over Polly's fur. "Not at all. We're good here."

"Thanks." He knelt in front of Lexi. "Hey, squirt, stay here with Macey and I'll be right back. I need to sign papers so Polly can come live with us."

"Okay, Daddy." She didn't take her eyes or hands off the dog in her lap.

As he followed Irene back to the front counter, the back door opened.

Wyatt Stone walked in, carrying a large bag of dog food. "Hey, Mama D. I stopped by the feed store, and Drake donated another bag of food."

"Thanks, hon. Put it in the prep room, and I'll call Drake later and thank him."

Wyatt disappeared around the corner, then returned a moment later. He crossed the room, hand extended. "Hey, Cole. How you doing, man?"

Cole hesitated a moment, a little surprised by Wyatt's pleasant attitude. He shifted away from the counter and shook his hand. "Good. And you?"

"Can't complain." Wyatt glanced around. "No Lexi?"

Cole jerked his head toward the office. "Actually, she's in the other room with Macey and our new schnoodle, Polly."

"Macey, huh?" Wyatt grinned.

Shrugging, Cole ignored his friend's implication. "Lexi invited her."

"And no one can say no to Lexi, am I right?"

"One of my greatest struggles."

Wyatt gave him an understanding nod. "Oh,

I hear you. I'm there myself with Mia. Thank God for my family. Hey, listen—I gotta get back to the ranch, but the offer to join my single fathers support group is still open. Or give me a call any time with questions or concerns. I don't have all the answers, but the group has men from all walks of life. They've been a great support system."

"Thanks, I appreciate it." Cole looked over his shoulder as Macey and Lexi walked hand in hand into the reception area with Lexi holding Polly's leash. "We're doing fine, just the two of us."

But even as he spoke, his words sounded hollow. His daughter needed more than what he could offer. She needed a woman's touch.

Someone like Macey.

But that wasn't going to happen. Especially with this land sale building a wall between them.

Wyatt crouched and petted Polly. "Hey, Polly. Looks like you found a new home."

Lexi's eyes widened as she knelt beside him. "You know Polly?"

"Sure. Polly and I became buddies after I took her for a couple of walks." Wyatt straightened, then glanced between Macey and Cole.

"Why don't you stop out at the ranch? I'm sure Lexi would enjoy seeing the horses."

"Horses? Really?" Lexi scrambled to her feet, nearly rolling Polly onto the floor. "Can I ride one, Daddy?"

Cole shot Wyatt a "Thanks, pal" look, then turned back to his daughter. "I don't know, Lexi."

"Why not?" She pointed to Wyatt. "That man said I could. I heard him."

"I believe he said you could see them." Cole's gaze shifted between Wyatt and Macey, whose tight smile signaled she was less than impressed with her brother's suggestion. "Wouldn't it be a conflict of interest, considering I'm working for my uncle?"

Wyatt lifted a shoulder. "Doesn't have to be. You grew up with us, man. You've been to the ranch more times than I can remember. You've been like family before you ever worked with your uncle."

And that was a part of the problem.

Lexi dropped Polly's leash and grabbed his leg. "Please, Daddy?"

"What do you think, Mace?"

She lifted a shoulder. "Wyatt invited you. This is between you guys."

Staring down at Lexi's big blue eyes, Cole felt his resolve slipping. He gripped the back of his neck. "Okay, fine."

Even though Lexi clapped and danced with Polly spinning in circles next to her, Cole didn't share her enthusiasm.

In fact, his clenched gut said it was a very bad idea.

But how could he say no to his daughter?

CHAPTER FIVE

MACEY NEEDED JUST an hour or so by herself.

Time to think and come up with some way to combat Crawford's attempt to gain access to their land.

Once word had spread about the council's desire for the strip mall, many of their friends and neighbors had expressed their outrage and promised to stand with the Stones.

But was it enough?

Because for all who wanted to protect their property, an equal number—or more—were in favor of the strip mall.

Even a week later, Bear still remained a little cool toward her. Macey kept her mouth shut because she didn't want to add to Mom's growing fatigue.

Before her mother left for the hospital this morning, Macey suggested taking her place so she could rest, but Mom had said if she stopped, she was afraid she'd fall apart. She needed to be strong now and could rest later.

But what was that strength costing her? Costing all of them?

So Macey spent the last week doing what she could to help ease her burdens at home, like doing Mom's barn chores, housecleaning and getting dinner on the table. Although sitting at the dining room table still didn't feel right without Dad at the head.

Now she wanted a quick ride before returning to the ranch house to make lunch for everyone.

Since coming back from Denver, she'd been surrounded by people. And she loved it, especially being with her mom again.

When she wasn't caring for Lexi, helping on the ranch, or working on the plans for the ball, she lent a hand at the diner and chatted with customers, getting their views about the proposed strip mall.

A quick getaway by herself would refresh her enough to face the upcoming week.

Morning sunshine warmed her face as she headed to the barn. With temperatures above freezing and the sun shining over melted snow, today seemed like the perfect day to ride and clear her head.

Her worn cowboy boots hugged her feet like old friends, and the hat she dug out of her closet took her back to riding South Bend with Grandpa. Maybe that sudden feeling of nostalgia was why she was so intent on heading out to her grandparents' property. Especially if Crawford got his way and took over the land.

She entered the barn, allowing a few seconds for her eyes to adjust to the changes in light. After breathing in the sweet scent of hay and the rich scent of saddle leather, she exhaled slowly, forcing her shoulders to relax.

Heading to Cheyenne's stall, she slid the door open and stepped inside.

Her quarter horse lifted her head and eyed Macey.

"Hey, Chey. Wanna go for a ride?" She ran a hand over the mare's gleaming chestnut coat and rested her cheek against Cheyenne's neck. Taking the mare by the halter, she led her into the aisle. She cross-tied her by clipping the lead straps to both sides of Cheyenne's halter for her protection as well as Macey's.

After taking the hoof pick out of the grooming basket, Macey moved to Cheyenne's side and ran her hand down the mare's leg. Cheyenne lifted her foot.

Macey removed a couple of small stones from the horse's hoof, then repeated the same process for the other three hooves.

She exchanged the hoof pick for a brush. With a hand on the horse's hip, Macey talked to her in soothing tones as she removed bits of hay and debris from Cheyenne's coat.

Macey tossed the brush into the basket and headed to the tack room. She draped the reins over her arm and lifted her saddle off the rack. She grabbed a pad and carried everything back to the aisle where the horse stood patiently.

Macey set everything on the bench across from Chey's stall. She reached for the saddle pad, settling it on the horse's withers.

A childish giggle followed by low-toned male voices outside the barn caused Cheyenne's ears to twitch. The barn door opened, sweeping in chilly air, and shadows spilled across the floor. Wyatt, Cole and Lexi headed inside.

Even though Wyatt had invited Cole and Lexi to come and see the horses last week while they talked at the animal shelter, Macey was still surprised he'd actually shown up at the ranch.

So much for her quiet retreat to South Bend.

"Hey, Mace. Whatcha doin'?"

She straightened the saddle pad and lifted her head. Wyatt and Cole stood in front of Cheyenne's stall. Wyatt's arms rested on the door as he grinned like an annoying little brother. Macey glanced at him, then lifted an eyebrow at Cole, who wore a buckskin-colored cowboy hat with a black band that shadowed his face.

She forced a casual tone in her voice. "You came."

Before Cole could speak, Wyatt pushed away from the stall and folded his arms over his chest, feet shifting apart, every bit the former marine. "I invited him here, remember? So be nice, sis."

"I'm always nice." She eyed Cole, daring him to challenge her words, then swiveled her attention back to her brother. "What are you guys doing?"

"We're going to take Lexi for a ride." He lifted a chin at Cheyenne. "You riding too?"

Macey lifted the saddle onto Chey's back. "I planned to ride to South Bend and shoot some photos of the waterfalls."

"Glad to hear you're getting back into your photography. Mind if we tag along?"

Macey cocked her head and lowered her voice. "Seriously, Wy?"

He lifted a shoulder and glanced at Cole. "Sure, why not?"

Macey swallowed a sigh. "Don't you think it's a conflict of interest?"

Wyatt shook his head and shoved his hands in his back pockets. "I see it as old friends taking a ride together."

"Apparently, my vision's a bit cloudier than yours." She turned back to the mare and cinched the saddle in place. "Suit yourself. I can't tell you what to do."

"Great. You lead, and we'll follow. That way, you can get the shots you want and I can help Cole with Lexi."

Seeing Cole in worn jeans with a threadbare, navy pullover hoodie that stretched across his chest messed with Macey's concentration. Not to mention the morning scruff on his unshaven chin. Why did he have to look so good, no matter what he wore? Then, he settled his hat back on his head, shadowing his face once more.

Macey's heart thunked against her rib cage. She needed to leave the barn before she did or said something stupid.

Lexi ran up to her and wrapped her arms

around Macey's jean-clad legs. "Hi, Macey. I'm so excited to ride a horsey today."

Looping the reins around her wrist, Macey leaned over and hugged the child, who was dressed in jeans with embroidered butterflies on the thigh and a pink hooded puffy coat. An oversize pink cowboy hat sat on her hair, which framed her face in two lopsided braids. "Hey, sweet girl. It's so good to see you. I like your hat."

Lexi patted its crown. "My Piper let me borrow it. She said cowgirls needs hats. Do you know her?"

Macey nodded as she put herself between the child and Cheyenne's muscular legs. Not that the gentle horse would kick, but with Lexi's sudden movements, it was better to err on the side of caution. "I know your Piper. She's friends with my sisters."

Cole scooped up his daughter. "Lexi, let's leave Macey alone, okay?"

"She's never a bother." Macey's eyes connected with Cole's.

His eyebrow arched as if to ask if he was the one who bothered her.

Needing space between them, Macey closed

the stall door, snatched her camera bag off the post, then led Cheyenne out of the barn.

She squinted against the morning sunshine and lowered the brim of her hat to shield her eyes. Holding on to the saddle horn, she put her left foot in the stirrup and threw her right leg over the horse. The leather squeaked as she settled in her seat. She gathered the reins and gave Cheyenne a gentle nudge with her knee and clicked her tongue. "Come on, girl. Let's get out of the way so these guys can saddle up."

She lifted her face and breathed deeply, allowing the sun's rays to warm her skin against the cool air that cleared her lungs. Guiding Cheyenne toward the gravel road that led away from the ranch, she glanced over her shoulder to find the doorway to the barn empty.

Maybe she could snag a few moments of quiet before they joined her.

As Cheyenne trotted through the open Stone River Ranch gate, Macey glanced over her shoulder once again. This time, Wyatt rode Dante, his black stallion, while Cole followed on Patience, Mom's mare, with Lexi seated in front of him.

A gentle breeze whisked over her heated

cheeks as she guided Cheyenne down the dirt road toward South Bend.

"Go faster, Daddy!" Lexi's giggles competed with Patience's hooves thundering against the road, kicking up melting snow and mud.

The man seemed quite comfortable in a saddle.

Macey pulled up on Cheyenne's reins and tied them loosely around the saddle horn. She removed her camera from her bag and attached the lens, manually focusing the men in her viewfinder. After snapping a few pictures, she zoomed in on the joy lighting up Lexi's darling face.

Then Macey dismounted and snapped a few shots of Cheyenne against the backdrop of the San Juan Mountains.

"Whoa." Wyatt pulled on Dante's reins and brought his black stallion to a stop next to Macey. Cole flanked the other side of her.

"Look, Macey, I'm riding a horsey." Lexi pulled off her hat and waved it, her cheeks pink from the weather and the excitement.

Macey grinned and lifted her camera one more time. "You sure are, sweetheart. Are you having fun?"

The child nodded and leaned back against

Cole. "Daddy said I can take lessons when I turn five." She held up a splayed hand. "Someday I can ride all by myself. He said until then I have to ride with him to stay safe."

"Yes, it's so important to stay safe. I learned how to ride with my daddy too. Just like you're doing." Macey framed Lexi and caught Cole's profile as he leaned down and kissed the top of his daughter's head.

Dismounting, Wyatt nodded toward the path that cut through the trees. "Let's take the trail to the homestead." His eyes volleyed between Macey and Cole, then he nodded to Lexi. "Cole, want to ride Dante? Lexi can stay on Patience, and I'll walk the horse."

A look of apprehension flashed across Cole's face, but at Lexi's high-pitched squeal, he replaced it with a laugh. "I guess we have Lexi's answer."

Wyatt held on to Lexi while Cole dismounted. After instructing Lexi how to hold on to the saddle horn, Wyatt picked up Patience's reins. He led them slowly down the rutted trail through the grove of pines frosted with snow.

Cole put his leg in Dante's stirrup and lifted his other leg over the stallion's back.

Macey mounted Cheyenne again and pulled up next to him. "No Saturday meeting today?"

"Only if the boss wants one."

"Doesn't he care about what you want?"

He lifted a shoulder. "What I want isn't relevant. At least not right now. My number one concern is ensuring Lexi has the best care possible. And if that means appeasing my uncle for now, then I'll meet with him on a Saturday. It's only for an hour or so anyway."

"Care for what? If you don't mind me asking. After you mentioned her medical condition, I did a little research. There's a lot to neurofibromatosis."

"Yes, there is. And each case is different. As I mentioned last week—Lexi's hearing is being affected, and she needs hearing aids. We meet with the pediatric audiologist next month. I have to keep a close eye on her because when she gets sick, it hits her hard and she usually ends up in the hospital. I try to keep her as healthy as possible to avoid that. Plus Wallace isn't as accommodating as he could be when it comes to dealing with Lexi's medical history."

"Why not find another job?"

Cole let out a sigh as his gaze drifted across the pasture. "I owe him."

"What do you mean?"

"After Mom died, Wallace took care of me and paid for my education. In exchange, I work for him."

"Sounds like he's taking advantage of the situation."

"It is what it is. This promotion promises even more money and better benefits for Lexi, so I'm letting him pull my strings."

"That's why you're pushing for my family to sign."

"It's only a portion of the property."

"Maybe so, but it's still our property. My parents shouldn't be bullied into selling. I do see your dilemma, though. What happens if your uncle doesn't get the land for some reason? For you and Lexi, I mean."

Cole lifted his hat and scratched the back of his head. Then he set it back in place. "I don't know. And honestly, I really don't want to find out."

"I'm sorry you have to go through this alone with very little family support. I'm sure you know this already, but there are programs in place to help children like Lexi get the quality care she needs. Then you wouldn't have to rely on this job so much."

"My mother taught me we take care of our own. We don't accept handouts. Call it family pride or whatever, but as long as I can provide the care Lexi needs, then that leaves room in those programs for families who can't afford them any other way. Listen, Mace. I don't expect you to understand. The last thing I want is to cause your family any pain, but I truly have to put my daughter's needs first."

Even at the cost of her family's future.

Wyatt whistled, jerking Macey's attention to the end of the trail where her brother had stopped leading Patience. He turned the horse and led her back to Cole and Macey. His eyes darkened, and lines bracketed his tight mouth.

"What's going on, Wyatt?" Cole dismounted.

"Macey, take everybody back to the ranch, then send Bear out here. We've got trouble."

Dante nickered as if sensing his owner's stress and danced in place. Wyatt pressed a hand against the stallion's neck.

"What kind of trouble?"

"There's a crew on ranch property without our permission. And I'm going to find out what they're doing there." Then his gaze skated to Cole. "It may be a good idea for them not to see you."

Nodding, Cole's jaw tightened as his eyes darted between the trail opening and his daughter.

Even if Macey didn't agree with Cole's choices, the last thing she wanted was for him to lose his job, particularly now that she knew more of his motivations.

But should her family give up without a fight? There was no easy win in this situation.

WALLACE'S HARSH ACCUSATIONS blistered Cole's ears as he ducked his head against the sleet and headed for his truck.

A call from Macey about Lexi not feeling well had him leaving work, which didn't score points with his uncle who was still furious with him.

As he headed back to his condo, he replayed his recent conversation with his uncle. Could he have handled it differently?

Once Wallace had appeared on the job site on Monday morning following Cole's visit to the ranch, Cole questioned him about the Crawford Developments crew being on Stone River property without permission.

Well, that blew up in Cole's face because his

uncle accused him of spying and working with the enemy.

How could he get his uncle to see the Stones weren't the enemy? The man was blinded by his hatred of Deacon Stone and driven to acquire the property by whatever means possible.

Somehow Cole needed to put that conversation out of his head and refocus his attention on his daughter.

Which was one more reason for his uncle to blast him for leaving to care for her.

The man didn't have an ounce of compassion in his narcissistic body.

But Cole didn't care. Lexi had to come first, and if Wallace wanted to fire him…well, it sure would solve a lot of problems.

Except the medical insurance issue.

Even then, he'd make that work.

Somehow.

Macey was right—there were programs in place to help Lexi. Every time Cole started to check them out, though, his mother's words and that long-ago argument resurfaced.

We do not accept charity, Cole Edward Crawford. We will make our own way in the world.

Too bad his mother's way meant working herself to death at a way too young of an age, leaving Cole at his uncle's mercy despite his begging to stay with Lynetta and Pete Spencer. The court deemed a blood relative was more important than one of the heart.

The only brother of Cole's father, Wallace provided everything Cole needed materially. He'd finished his high school years wearing name brand clothes and driving a car that didn't break down every fifty miles. Then he'd paid for Cole's college tuition with the understanding Cole would work for his uncle after graduation and pay him back for what he'd done for him.

A price that cost Cole a lot more than he'd ever expected.

While he tried to be grateful because Wallace had pulled him out of poverty, the man had a heart the size and hardness of a marble.

Gruff may work in the boardroom or on the job site, but not where Lexi was concerned. Especially when she was sick.

Sleet bulleted Cole's windshield as he parked in front of the condo and hurried through the storm to his front door.

He entered the code and stepped inside. Polly barked, jumped off the couch and raced to him.

After their trail ride over the weekend, Mrs.

Douglas had called to say Polly had been released by their vet for adoption.

Still excited from riding a horse, Lexi had been over the moon when he shared the news and begged to pick up Polly that evening.

Even though the little dog had been with them only a couple of days, she seemed to be settling in well.

Kicking off his wet shoes, he scooped her up and hurried into the living room where Lexi lay on her side with her knees pulled to her chest. Dried tear trails streaked her face as her eyes remained closed.

He set Polly on the floor then knelt on one knee and brushed back the hair falling out of her ponytail. "Hey, Lexi Lou. Daddy's here."

With eyes still closed, she smiled and whispered, "I'm not Lexi Lou, I'm Lexi Jane."

"Cole."

Cole looked up and saw Macey standing in the kitchen doorway, holding a dish towel. "Hey, Mace. What's going on?"

"Lexi didn't want to eat her snack this morning. When I touched her forehead, she felt warm, so I took her temp. It was 100.2, and she's complaining that her right ear is hurting.

I brought her back here so she could rest in her own space. That's when I called you."

"I'm glad you did. Thanks for that, by the way. She seemed fine this morning when I dropped her off at the ranch. A little sleepy, but I didn't think too much of it." Guilt gnawed at him as he cupped his daughter's warm cheek. "Have you given her Tylenol or anything?"

A tender look in her eyes, Macey shook her head. "I wanted to wait and see what you'd like to do."

"I'll call her pediatrician and see if I can get Lexi an appointment today."

"Daddy, my ear hurts." Tears leaked out of her tired-looking eyes.

"Show me which one."

She covered her right ear with her small hand.

He kissed her forehead and felt the heat radiating off her skin. "I'll call Dr. Jeanette and see if she can look in your ears today, okay?"

Lexi nodded and rested her head against Cole's hand.

He reached for his phone and hit the pediatrician's office number on his speed dial. When the receptionist answered, he explained the situation and swallowed a sigh of relief when she mentioned a last-minute cancellation. If he could be there in ten minutes, then the pediatrician could see her right away.

Cole relayed the information to Macey. "You can head home, if you want."

"You sure? You won't need to return to work? You paid me for the full day."

"I'll let Wallace know Lexi's sick, and that I'll work from home for the rest of the day."

"Okay. I'm going to swing by the diner and talk to Lynetta about the ball. Let me know if anything changes and you need me to come back."

"Thanks, I will."

Forty minutes later, Cole dashed through the sleet, careful not to slip on the icy black-topped driveway, and buckled Lexi in her car seat. They'd sat in the busy waiting room for nearly thirty minutes, then saw the pediatrician for ten. Now, Lexi's chest shuddered from spent tears after getting her inflamed ears checked.

Double ear infection. And her temperature had risen to 102 degrees. Thankfully, the prescription for an antibiotic had been called in to the pharmacy already.

Cole turned on Lexi's favorite radio station and pulled out of the parking lot. As he headed to the pharmacy, Lexi spoke up from the back seat. "Daddy, I want pancakes."

"Okay, punkin. I'll make you some as soon as we get back home."

"Nooo, Daddy," she wailed, turning her head and crying into her hood. "I want Netta's pancakes."

Normally, Cole did not give in to temper tantrums, but his heart melted at his daughter's sobs. If pancakes would help her to feel better, then he'd do what he could to help. He tapped the voice command on his steering wheel. At the prompt, he said, "Call Netta's Diner."

The phone rang on the speakerphone. "Netta's Diner, how may I help you?"

The voice sounded similar to the diner owner's, but with Lexi's crying in the back seat, he couldn't quite tell for sure. "Lynetta?"

"No, this is Macey. Lynetta's not available."

"Macey, it's Cole. Hey, I need to place a take-out order of pancakes for Lexi."

"Sure, Cole. Anything else?"

"No, just the pancakes. Lynetta knows how she likes them."

"Lynetta stepped out for a few minutes. I'm minding the register until she gets back."

Cole bit back a groan and glanced in the

rearview mirror to see if his daughter had been paying attention to the conversation. "Okay, I'll just take them however they come. I need to swing through the pharmacy drive-through, then I'll be by to pick them up. When I get there, is there any way someone could run them out to me? Lexi has a double ear infection, and I really don't want to take her inside if I don't have to."

"Take her home, and I'll bring the pancakes to you."

"You don't have to do that."

"I planned to return anyway so you could go back to work. Just get Lexi home so she can feel better."

He turned into the pharmacy drive-through lane. "Great. Thanks. You have no idea how much I appreciate it."

"Aunt Lynetta would do the same."

Less than ten minutes later, Cole carried a sleeping Lexi back inside. Polly greeted them at the door again with a bark and a dance to welcome them home.

Ignoring the little dog for a moment, he changed Lexi out of the polka-dot leggings and long-sleeved light purple T-shirt he'd helped her put on that morning and back into the unicorn pajamas she'd tossed on her bed. He got her settled under her favorite mermaid blanket on the couch and turned on the soft classical music station she liked to help her stay asleep. Polly jumped on the couch and licked Lexi's cheek.

Her face scrunched as she pushed the dog away.

Cole scooped up the fur ball, cradled her to his chest, then set Polly on the other end of the couch. This time, she curled against the curve of Lexi's legs bent at the knee.

A quiet knock sounded on the front door, sending Polly off the couch and barking at the door.

He hurried across the room, scooped up the dog again and opened the door. Macey stepped inside, clutching a large take-out bag.

He took the bag from her, set it on the side table inside the door, then reached for his wallet. "What do I owe you?"

Cheeks pink, Macey bit down on her mitten and pulled it off. She waved her hand, dismissing his question. "It's been taken care of."

Cole scowled. "What do you mean?"

"When Aunt Lynetta came back, she made Lexi's pancakes and insisted on adding eggs and juice. Plus a burger and fries for you. Then she said it was on the house."

Cole pulled out a twenty and held it out to Macey. "I appreciate her thoughtfulness, but I can pay my own way."

Macey folded her hand over his, crushing the money between his fingers and palm. "No one said you couldn't. But when someone else wants to do something nice for you, just say thank you.

"Thank you." Heat warmed Cole's neck. "You don't need to stay. I can spend the rest of the afternoon working here."

Macey shifted her feet and looked at him hesitantly. "Aunt Lynetta asked me to check on Lexi and report back to her. So if you don't mind me taking a quick peek…"

"Well, I wouldn't want to get you in trouble with the boss." Grinning, Cole closed the door behind her. He nearly bumped into Macey as he turned around. Her hair brushed against his chin, releasing the floral scent of her shampoo.

He grabbed her arms as her hands flew to his shoulders. His eyes locked with hers as he loosened his hold. "Whoa. Sorry about that. I didn't expect you to be so close."

He certainly didn't mind, though.

Being around Macey almost daily for the past couple of weeks reignited feelings he'd thought long gone.

But they were friends, and that was all they ever could be.

With everything else on his plate, the last thing he needed was to fall for the daughter of his uncle's enemy.

No matter how well she cared for his child and fit into their lives.

CHAPTER SIX

MACEY SHOULD'VE GONE back to the ranch instead of stopping at the diner.

Then she wouldn't have been there when Cole called. And she wouldn't have ended back up at his place. Or nearly in his arms.

Stepping back, she dropped her fingers as if his shoulders had been on fire and shook her hands. "No, it's my fault. I didn't move in far enough."

Trying to distract herself from the lingering feel of Cole's strong hands on her shoulders, Macey picked up Polly and rubbed her cheek over the dog's soft fur. "Polly seems to be settling in well."

"It's been only a couple of days, but she and Lexi adore each other. I hope it wasn't too chaotic this morning with her and Lexi not feeling well." He grabbed the bag and carried it into the kitchen, the scent of grilled meat wafting between them. "Can I get you anything to drink? Coffee? Water? Juice box?"

"I'm good. And no, it wasn't a problem. Polly is a sweetie." Smiling, she held up a hand as she moved silently toward the couch. She returned Polly to her spot behind Lexi's legs. Leaning over Lexi's sleeping form, she ran a finger over the little girl's cheek, feeling the elevated warmth. "Poor thing."

Macey straightened and headed for the kitchen.

Cole removed the cardboard to-go boxes and flipped up the lid. The hot scent of salted fries hit her. To her horror, her stomach growled.

Smirking, Cole nudged the overflowing box toward her. "Maybe you need this more than I do."

"Actually, I had a salad before lending Aunt Lynetta a hand."

He opened the cabinet above the microwave and pulled down a couple of plates. "Want to split the burger?"

Leaning against the counter with one arm pressed against her traitorous stomach, Macey shook her head but snitched a fry. "No, thanks, but I wouldn't say no to a fry or two."

"Take as many as you'd like. I don't need to

eat all of them." Ignoring the plate, he reached for the burger and stood over the sink, biting into the juicy sandwich. "Man, that tastes good. I'd eat at the diner for all my meals if my wallet could afford it."

"While I love Aunt Lynetta and Uncle Pete's food, I don't think my waistline could handle it on a daily basis."

Cole raised an eyebrow. "Like you have anything to worry about."

She dipped her head, but not before heat crawled across her face.

Cole devoured the burger, then wiped his fingers on a paper napkin snatched from the take-out bag. "Guess I was hungrier than I thought." He peered into the living room. "Apparently, Lex needs sleep more than pancakes right now. I really need to get Lynetta's recipe so I don't have to bother you guys every time she wants pancakes. Which would be daily if she had her way. Thank you again for delivering them."

"It wasn't a bother. Really. I was heading back to the ranch, so this was on my way." Macey glanced at the sleeping child, then refocused on Cole. "She's very special. But I don't have to tell you that, do I?"

Cole's eyes drifted to his daughter and he shook his head. "I don't deserve her."

The tenderness in his eyes was nearly Macey's undoing. She shifted her feet and searched for the right words. "You're a great father, Cole. Anyone can see that. I'm sorry your uncle has you over a barrel. We both value family. Unfortunately, we're on opposite sides of this case, trying to protect our own."

Cole's jaw tightened. He dropped his chin to his chest. "I wish I could make my uncle listen to reason. He's so insistent on building this strip mall when he has half a dozen other projects he could be working on. Before you called, I was at the job site for a new apartment complex along the river."

"You mean the Riverwalk Condos…or whatever they're called? Those belong to your uncle?"

"Yes." Cole gathered the take-out container and dropped it in the stainless-steel trash can on the other side of the sink. "I'd rather see him build more affordable housing, but he wants to offer luxury condos to the community. Aspen Ridge is a small ranching town. Not many people could afford the monthly rent, let alone buy one. But my uncle doesn't see that."

"Why do you work for him again?" Then she winced and held up a hand. "Sorry—I really need to mind my own business."

He raked a hand over his face. "Quite honestly, right now, I don't even have the time to look for a different position. I'm too busy juggling Wallace's demands while trying to keep Lexi healthy. I'm not doing too hot of a job doing either right now."

"Hey, don't beat yourself up. Ear infections are a normal part of a child's developing years. I had many ear infections as a kid and needed tubes. The antibiotic will kick in soon, and she'll feel like her perky self tomorrow."

"Lexi's not like other kids."

"I disagree. Lexi's very much like other kids. She's able to have a blessed life. Yes, Lexi *is* special. In spite of her NF1. She's special for who she is. She's kind, caring and so sweet." Macey pushed away from the counter and poked him in the chest. "And you're a major part of that. You're raising such a wonderful little girl. I really admire the stellar job you're doing."

"Thanks, that means a lot." Cole grabbed her finger, then wrapped his hand around hers. He took a step closer and looked at her with such light in his eyes that her breath caught. His eyes dropped to her lips.

She swallowed and slowly pulled her hand out of his warm grip. She took a very necessary step back and pulled in a deep breath to steady the rapid pounding against her ribs. She glanced at Lexi who continued to sleep. "Anybody can see how well you're doing. It's gotta be tough doing it on your own though."

"We manage." His voice sounded hoarse.

She returned her attention back to him. "Wyatt knows a thing or two about being a single parent after losing Linnea in childbirth. Like you, he's been raising Mia on his own since the day she was born. And you both had to grieve your losses while parenting a baby. You should check out his support group."

Cole tucked his hands under his arms. "I'll figure things out one way or another. Just hopefully not at the expense of my daughter."

She rested a hand on his shoulder. "Just know you don't have to go it alone."

Cole's phone suddenly vibrated. He pulled it out of his back pocket, glanced at the screen and sighed deeply. Thumbing over the accept button, he answered. "Yeah, Wallace, what's up?"

Macey couldn't make out his uncle's words,

especially when Cole turned his back to her, but the way his shoulders bunched and how he dragged a hand over the back of his neck, it couldn't be good.

Cole sighed again. "Well, no, it's not life threatening, but she's got a fever and an infection." He paused as the other man's rumble sounded through the line. "Okay, fine. I'll see what I can do, but no promises. Yeah. Yeah. Okay. Understood." He ended the call and gripped the phone.

Was he about to launch it through the window?

"Everything okay?"

Cole ground his jaw and rolled his neck. "Wallace needs me back at the job site. I need to call my cousin and see if she's available to watch Lexi." He tossed the phone on the counter and dragged his fingers through his hair as he stared into the living room.

"You're working in this weather?"

"We're doing interior work." He sighed. "Man, I really hate to wake her to put her back in the car again."

Macey took two steps toward him and touched his back. "I'll stay."

Cole whirled around so quickly she jumped

back. A frown deepened the lines between his eyes. "What?"

"I'll stay with Lexi. Just tell me what time she needs to take her medicine."

Cole lifted his hands. "I don't know when I'll be home. You had her this morning. Plus you have plenty of other things to do. I'll call Piper."

"Piper is just as busy running her business and caring for her own daughter. I planned to spend the full day with her already before we realized she was sick. But if you'd rather take her with you…" Macey lifted a shoulder as she left the rest of her words hanging between them.

Cole heaved a sigh and hung his head. "No, you're right. Thanks. I guess I'm not so great at accepting help."

She lifted an eyebrow. "You think?"

Cole showed Macey the antibiotic and how much to give his daughter. He pocketed his phone and fished out his keys. Then he strode to the living room and brushed a kiss against Lexi's forehead. "I'll be back as quickly as possible. Call if you or Lexi need anything."

Once she closed the door behind him, Macey moved to the recliner. Polly jumped off the couch and into her lap while Lexi continued to sleep soundly.

Sure, she could've used the time to take care of things at the ranch or do more planning for the Sweetheart Ball, but she really felt for the guy who carried the weight of his world on his shoulders.

Clearly, he needed help but was too stubborn to ask.

Her phone buzzed. She pulled it out of her pocket and saw her twin brother's face on the screen. She answered, "Hey, Bear. What's up?"

"I'm headed into town to file a police report. Can you keep an eye on Tanner and Mia so Wyatt can go with me?"

"Police report?" Her eyes skated to Lexi who struggled to sit up again. "What's going on?"

"While out riding the line, I found some fence posts had been pulled up and tossed. Some trees had been chopped and left lying to rot in the snow. The barn at South Bend's been spray-painted." Bear's voice thundered through the phone line.

"Spray-painted?" Macey groaned and cradled her head in her hand. The Sweetheart Ball is in a couple of weeks. Kind of tough to paint over it in the middle of winter. "Does this have anything to do with Crawford's crew Wyatt had seen on Saturday?"

"When we questioned them, they said they were just looking around. Wyatt and I believed them and reminded them to get permission so they didn't get charged with trespassing."

"Then who could have done it?"

The line went silent. Had their call gotten dropped?"

"Mace, Cole Crawford's hat was found behind the barn along with an empty can of spray paint." Bear's voice lowered to the point where she wasn't quite sure she'd heard correctly."

"Cole? No way. He has enough on his plate without sneaking over to cause damage. Besides, Bear, you know Cole wouldn't do anything like that." A chill slid down the back of her neck. Macey had an idea of who was really responsible.

"Now you're defending the guy?"

Macey turned away from the couch and lowered her voice. "Bear, come on. He's one of your best friends. Of course, I'm defending him. You should be too. He wouldn't hurt any of us on purpose."

"He's involved in taking our land, remember?" Her brother's growl reverberated through the phone.

"He's working for his uncle. That's different."

"Whatever. Can you help or not?"

"I can't. I'm caring for Lexi right now. Where's Mom?"

"She's at the diner, helping Aunt Lynetta. One of the servers called in sick."

"That's right—I was there earlier until Cole needed help again with Lexi."

"All right. I'll see if Ev's home from school. Maybe she can help." Cole blew out a breath. "Listen, it may be best if Cole didn't come around the ranch for a while. Until this thing gets figured out." He hung up before she could protest or even say goodbye.

Macey dropped the phone in her lap and buried her face in her hands.

No matter what happened between her and Cole in the past, she trusted her instincts on this one.

If only she could be in two places at once, but she'd given her word to Cole and couldn't back out. Especially with Lexi being so sick.

Problem was she couldn't shake the betrayal that seeped into her heart from not being able to help her family. Or the way Cole and his daughter were becoming more and more important to her.

She needed to be careful because somebody was going to end up hurt.

"What's wrong, Macey?" Lexi peered behind the curtain of Macey's hair.

She straightened, pushed her hand away from her face and smiled at the little girl standing next to her. Macey pulled the child onto her lap and pressed her lips against Lexi's forehead. Still warm, but not as high as it had been.

"Nothing, sweetheart. How are you feeling?"

Lexi rested her cheek against Macey's chest. "My ear still hurts. But my belly is hungry."

"Would you like some pancakes?"

Lexi sat up and nodded, her feverish eyes bright again.

"Let's warm your food. If you feel up to it, we can play a game or read a story once you're done eating." Lexi scrambled off Macey's lap, then she stood and held her hand out to the little girl.

Lexi took it and they headed into the kitchen. "Okay. Where's Daddy?"

"He's working. That's why I'm here." Macey removed the take-out box from the fridge and retrieved a plate from the cabinet.

"I love you, Macey." Lexi wrapped an arm around Macey's leg.

Blinking back a rush of tears, Macey crouched in front of Lexi and pulled her into her arms. "I love you too, sweet girl."

The more time she spent with Lexi, the less she wanted Cole to find someone more permanent. And her heart would break all over again when she lost another child she loved who wasn't hers.

COLE NEEDED A BREAK, even if it was only for the rest of the evening.

He blew out a breath and rubbed a fist over his sternum, hoping to alleviate the pressure building behind his ribs. With Wallace's attitude getting crankier and his demands increasing, working for him was getting harder.

Knowing Macey would be at his condo when he returned home filled him with more excitement than it should have.

Home.

When was the last time he really considered his condo a home? Sure, he kept it neat and clean for Lexi, but even he could see it lacked a feminine touch.

What would a home be like with her in it?

Don't even go there, man.

He and Macey were just now mending what

he'd broken years ago. He wasn't going to do something stupid and destroy their friendship a second time.

As he unlocked the door, music and laughter greeted him. He pushed the door open quietly.

The coffee table, which was covered with a Chutes and Ladders game, a couple of books and a paper pad with an assortment of markers, had been pushed away from the couch. Upbeat children's music blasted from Macey's cell phone. She held on to Lexi's hands, then twirled her, causing more giggles to erupt from his daughter. Then Macey gathered Lexi into her arms and kissed her on the cheek. Polly jumped and barked at their feet.

"Looks like someone's feeling better." He pressed a shoulder against the door frame.

Both heads jerked up. Lexi pushed out of Macey's arms and raced across the room toward him with Polly at her feet. "Daddy! I missed you."

"I missed you too, peanut." He gathered her close, smelling the scent of her still-damp hair. "You must be feeling better."

Lexi nodded. "Uh-huh. Macey said dance parties always make her feel better, so we tried it. Guess what?"

"What?"

"It did! Macey is so smart." Lexi wriggled out of his arms.

Cole released his daughter, scratched Polly's chin and captured Macey's gaze. "Yes, she is."

Closing the door behind him, he toed off his boots and lined them up next to Macey's. Then he shrugged out of his Carhartt jacket and hung it in the closet next to hers.

Side by side.

Partners. Help mates. What would that be like? With someone like Macey.

No.

With Macey herself.

He ran a hand over his head, smoothing down his hair and moved closer to Macey. "How's it going?"

She shut off her phone and pocketed it. Then she gathered the markers, paper pad and shoved the game pieces into their box. She put everything where it belonged on Lexi's toy shelf. Then she moved the coffee table back in place.

Finally, she straightened and shoved her hands in her front pockets, her arms stiff. She cocked her head, the laughter gone from her eyes. "As you can see, Lexi's feeling a little better. I think it's more from the pain reliever though. She ate her pancakes, took her medicine and had a bath after her fever broke. Then we played a game, read a story, drew pictures and danced to music."

"I'm glad to hear it. Thank you so much. I really appreciate it."

She nodded, then moved past him toward the door. He caught her arm. "Hey, you okay?"

She glanced at his hand and he dropped it. She shook her head. "No, not really."

"What's going on?"

Lexi ran over to her toy shelf and grabbed the paper pad. "Daddy, I drew a picture. Wanna see it?"

"Sure, Lexi Lou." He knelt on one knee in front of her.

She cocked her head and gave him a stern look. "Silly Daddy. I'm Lexi Jane."

He gave a damp curl a little tug. "My mistake."

She pulled out a paper and held it up. "Look. It's you and me and Macey. And I drawed a heart too."

Cole took the picture, his heart twisting. Three stick figures with oversize heads and legs coming out of their necks stood side by side holding very large hands with each other.

"Do you like it?" She bounced on her toes, her eyes wide and eager.

He wrapped an arm around her tiny waist and drew her to him. "I love it. It's the best picture I've ever seen."

"Macey said that too." Lexi threw her arms around his neck, nearly knocking him off balance.

From the corner of his eye, he could see Macey edging closer to the door.

"Hey, squirt. I need to talk to Macey a minute, then we'll put this on the fridge, okay?"

"Okay, Daddy." Lexi dropped the picture on the coffee table, then burrowed under her mermaid blanket. Polly curled up next to her.

He straightened and turned as Macey buttoned her coat and shouldered her tote.

"Hey, what's the rush? I was hoping we could talk for a few minutes. I had an idea for the ball that I wanted to run by you. Why do I sense you're angry at me?"

She crossed her arms, the sweetness she displayed around Lexi dissolved from her face. "Missing anything? A hat perhaps? Maybe some spray paint?"

He cocked his head. "What are you talking about?"

Macey pulled her phone out of her back pocket and pointed it at him. "Bear called and said someone vandalized ranch property. A worn Colorado Rockies hat was found at the scene, along with an empty can of red spray paint."

Cole's eyes widened and he held up his hands. "Mace, I promise you—I had nothing to do with that. But I will look into it and see what I can find out."

He cupped a hand over his eyes. He'd spent so much time at the Riverside Condos job site that he hadn't been in his office much this week. Was his hat still on his desk when he stopped in before he'd headed to the job site? He couldn't remember.

What other surprises were in store for him today?

Her shoulders sagged as she pressed a shoulder against the coat closet door. "That's what I told Bear."

He folded his arms over his chest. "If that's what you thought, then why accuse me?"

Her head lifted, her eyes challenging him. "I didn't accuse—I asked if you were missing anything."

His eyebrow shot up. "Well, your tone and posture are quite accusatory."

"You're right. I'm sorry. It's just this whole

land battle is exhausting." Polly pawed at Macey's leg, and she stooped to pick her up. She buried her face in the dog's neck.

"It doesn't have to be."

Macey set Polly on the floor and stood. Her chin lifted as her eyes scraped across his. "If we give in, you mean?"

Cole nodded, even though he knew it wasn't the right answer.

"If we sell, then what do we do when the next developer wants to take a different piece of our ranch? Little by little, we'll be out of a place to live. We need to stop it from happening from the very beginning."

"Sometimes private land is essential for public domain."

"Sure, when it comes to the health and welfare of the community, but a strip mall? Seriously? That's just Wallace being greedy and going after my dad because of a grudge."

"I wish things were different."

"Me, too. When I was at the diner earlier, I was talking to customers. You may be surprised by how many aren't interested in a strip mall and want to help us to preserve the integrity of the ranch." She pulled her gloves and keys out of one of the pockets. "You should know that Bear and Wyatt filed a police report. Your hat is considered evidence. The police may be stopping by to ask some questions."

Cole dragged a hand over his face. "This is not fair. I'm being used as someone else's scapegoat. You realize that, don't you?"

He wasn't about to take the fall for someone else's crime. But more importantly, he didn't want Macey to think he'd do anything to hurt her family or their property for his personal gain.

With her head lowered, Macey nodded. Then she looked at him again, her eyes shadowed. "There's one more thing."

He could only imagine what that could be. "What?"

"Bear thinks it would be a good idea for you to stay away from the ranch until this thing is settled."

Cole shook his head. "What do *you* think?"

She fiddled with her keys and shrugged. "I don't know. This has me tied in knots. I know you didn't do it, Cole, but I don't trust your uncle at all." She waved a hand over the room. "Maybe it would be a good idea if I cared for Lexi here at your place instead of the ranch."

"Yeah, sure. Whatever. You're always welcome here. You know that. But what about helping with the ball?"

She shrugged again. "Most of the planning is done. It's mostly getting the barn set up and decorated. I'm sure my siblings can lend a hand with that."

Cole held her gaze a moment, then shook his head. "No, I gave you my word, and I'll see it through. I'll help with the setup and all of that. If I need to be escorted onto the property and chaperoned, then so be it. But we are going to finish this together."

"Okay." Macey rested her elbow on the door frame and shoved a hand through her hair. "You mentioned an idea?"

"Oh. Right. I was thinking about another mini fundraiser for the night of the ball. People could buy roses in white, pink, and red, then write notes to their someone special. They will be waiting for them when they arrive. For those who don't receive a rose, I'll buy white ones and write something to encourage them. You may think it's a silly idea, but I got the idea when I drove past the floral shop on my way home."

She smiled for the first time since she became aware of his appearance after returning home. "Actually, I think it's a sweet idea, and I'm not surprised."

"I used to buy my mom a rose every Valentine's Day. I'd ask Lynetta for odd jobs until I had enough money."

Her face softened. "I didn't know that. You loved your mom very much, didn't you?"

He nodded, kicking his socked toe against the carpet. "She was awesome."

"And you're a great dad. Irene Douglas was right—she'd be so proud of you." Macey gave his arm a gentle squeeze, then dropped her hand. She looked over his shoulder, then refocused on him. "How does someone know if they're doing the right thing?"

Even though her question felt rhetorical, he pressed his lips together and lifted a shoulder. "I don't have an answer because I'm wrestling with the same question."

Somehow, he needed to figure out a solution before anyone he cared about got hurt.

CHAPTER SEVEN

According to Lexi, pancakes fixed everything.

While she sat in a booth by the door and ate the sprinkle pancakes with whipped cream Lynetta made especially for her, Macey taped a poster advertising the Sweetheart Ball to the glass door.

"Macey, look at me."

She turned away from the door and grinned. "You silly goose. Who put that whipped cream on your nose?"

"I did." The little girl fell back against the booth and giggled.

Macey slid into the booth next to Lexi, grabbed her napkin and wiped it off. "Whipped cream goes in your tummy, not on your nose."

"Can we make a snowman after breakfast?"

"Yep. As soon as you're finished, we'll head to the park."

"What's going on here?" Aunt Lynetta refilled Macey's cup, then set the pot on the table as she slid onto the bench across from them. "How are you feeling, sugar?"

"I'm all better. Daddy and Macey gave me a annabotic that made my ears stop hurting. Guest what, Netta? We're going to the park to make a snowman." Lexi clapped her hands and shot Aunt Lynetta a beaming smile.

"A snowman? Well, that sounds like fun." Aunt Lynetta glanced at Macey's untouched ham and cheese omelet. "Something wrong with your breakfast, sweetie?"

Macey picked up her fork and toyed with the food. "Not hungry, I guess. Definitely nothing against Uncle Pete's cooking."

"I know you guys are going through a tough time. Keep your chin up, girl."

"It's getting harder, Aunt Lynetta. I'm trying not to let what happened get me down, but you should've seen how angry Bear and Wyatt were after they came home from the police station. We all know C—" She shot a look at Lexi. "We know you-know-who had nothing to do with it, but they have no other leads at this point. But it's just not that." Macey lowered her head.

Aunt Lynetta reached across the table and grabbed Macey's hand. "What else's going on?"

"After the guys returned to the ranch, they met with the appraiser, but the meeting didn't go as planned. Bear and Wyatt had hoped the land was worth more than what the appraiser had said. They talked about getting a second opinion or something like that. Then this morning, I came in from doing barn chores and found Mom upset about Dad still being in the hospital."

"Your mother is one of the strongest people I know, but all of this worrying has got to be weighing on her. On all of you." Aunt Lynetta stood and reached for the coffeepot.

Being short on help at the diner and worrying about her brother and the problems at the ranch, Aunt Lynetta was also showing signs of fatigue with new lines around her mouth and shadows under her eyes.

"I don't know how to fix any of this." Tears pricked her eyes.

Aunt Lynetta cupped her cheek. "Oh, sweet girl, it's not your job to fix it. Your job is to pray and trust God with the outcome."

"Trusting's so much easier when our lives are running smoothly."

"Amen to that, but then we miss out on the blessings of growing closer to Him."

"What if we pray and trust but don't like the outcome?"

"Even if you don't like the outcome, you have to remember God knows best. He works all things together for good for those who love Him."

"Macey, are you sad?" Lexi rested her head against Macey's arm.

She drew her close and gave her a side hug. "How can I be sad when I get to have breakfast with such a wonderful girl like you?"

Aunt Lynetta nodded toward the door. "I'm so glad you're moving forward with the ball. Would've been a shame if it had been canceled, but no one would've blamed your parents."

Running her fingers over the lettering, she said, "It may be the last one held at South Bend, so Cole and I plan to make it special."

"Speaking of that young man, you two are spending a lot of time together."

"We're friends, Aunt Lynetta. Nothing more. I'm caring for Lexi, and he's helping with the ball. Besides, that's all that can be with us. At least until this land issue is resolved." Macey shoved the roll of tape in her bag along with the rest of the posters she'd had picked up from the printer before heading to the diner.

Aunt Lynetta slung an arm around her shoulders. "God's got this. And your family. Nothing that happens is gonna surprise Him."

Macey rested her head on Aunt Lynetta's shoulder. "I admire your faith."

"Girl, that's the same faith you've grown up with." Aunt Lynetta clicked her tongue. "I know your family's faced a bunch of challenges lately, but you're strong. You guys will get through this." She tapped Macey's chest. "Don't allow your feelings to rule what's in here. God hasn't gone anywhere. Maybe you're the one who put the distance between you and Him."

Leave it to her aunt to tell her like it was.

"I need to get set up for lunch and start my pie baking for this weekend's WinterFest. I've got you. You know that, right?" Aunt Lynetta opened her arms.

Macey slid out of the booth, walked into her embrace, and breathed in the familiar scents of coffee and maple syrup. "Yes, I know. I love you. Thanks for always being in my corner."

Her aunt tipped her chin. "That's a pretty big corner. Once you realize you're not standing in it alone, the better off you'll be."

Allowing those words to linger, she grabbed a

to-go box from behind the counter and scraped her untouched omelet into the container.

Lexi finished her milk and wiped her mouth. "I'm done. Can we make a snowman now?"

"Sure, sweetie. Let's get your coat on, then we'll head back to your house to get your snow pants." Macey reached for Lexi's pink jacket and held it out for her.

The little girl jumped up on the bench and shoved her arms in the sleeves.

The bells above the door jangled as it swung open.

Macey turned and swallowed a groan.

Wallace Crawford strode in, a cocky grin on his face. He held a couple of large pieces of torn paper with colors that matched her posters.

"Good morning, Ms. Stone." His eyes narrowed as he tipped his hat.

Macey moved in front of the booth, placing herself between the shark and his great-niece. Her eyes raked over the papers in his hand. "Mr. Crawford. Destroy anyone else's property today?"

He raised an eyebrow, that smug grin back in place. "Whatever are you referring to, little lady?"

"Drop that patronizing tone with me. I'm

not afraid of you. My family's working with the police, and soon, you will be held accountable for your actions."

His gray eyes hardened and glinted like polished steel. He lifted his beefy paw clutching the papers. "You really think a silly ball is going to help people get behind saving your ranch?"

"Maybe they will if you stop tearing down the posters. Feeling threatened?"

He threw his head back and laughed, the sound bouncing off the walls and drawing attention to him still blocking the doorway. "Hardly. Once people see what the city council has designed, they'll be waiting in line to dig up the property to get the project moving even faster. I heard about your bit of bad luck. Maybe your family should accept the council's offer and stop dragging this out so nothing else happens to the ranch you're crusading to save."

"I don't believe in luck. I know you're responsible for the vandalism, and we're going to prove it. And you underestimate this town. They love our family. They believe in community. This strip mall isn't the first big box retailer they've shut down." Macey pressed her fingers against the table and hoped the bravado in her voice didn't betray the skepticism she was beginning to feel in her heart.

"Maybe not, but it sure will be the last. Especially when I offer them more opportunities for shopping and dining beyond this dump." He waved his hand across the diner.

"Wallace Crawford, I heard that." Aunt Lynetta rounded the counter with fire in her eyes. She stared at him with one hand fisted on her hip and the other waving toward the door. "Your money's no good here anymore. Just turn around and get your coffee somewhere else."

"Oh, Lynetta. When the strip mall opens, you're going to be begging me to bring customers back to this dive."

"You can threaten me all you want and have the audacity to pretend you're innocent in destroying my family's property, but the truth will come out. You think a fancy coffee shop will shut down the diner my parents started over fifty years ago? You're welcome to try. In the meantime, get off my property and stay off it."

Wallace shook his head and tossed the torn poster on the floor. "I have more important things to do with my time anyway." He tipped his hat. "Good day, ladies."

The bell above the door clanged as he slammed it on the way out.

Face heated and heart racing, Macey turned her back to the diners who had watched the show. She zipped Lexi's jacket and helped her pull on her mittens. "Sorry about the drama, Aunt Lynetta."

Her aunt squeezed her arm. "Don't allow him to get under your skin."

"Thanks for sticking up for me. I talked tough, but my stomach turned to jelly."

"Oh, girl, you're so much stronger than you think. And you did well not to cower under that man's intimidation."

"Maybe so, but I can't help but wonder what else he has in store for my family. Or even Cole and Lexi."

"That's what galls me the most." Her aunt nodded toward Lexi who picked up Macey's phone. "He's dangling that precious child's health in front of her daddy like a carrot."

"Isn't there something we could do to help them?"

Aunt Lynetta sighed. "Darlin', I've tried. Believe me. But Cole has his mama's blood rushing through his veins. That woman was my best friend, but she was the most stubborn person

I'd ever met. She wouldn't accept a handout if someone glued it to her fingers. Cole's grandparents accused her of being a gold digger when she and Edward had gotten married. After he passed away, she insisted on making her own way and drilled the same into Cole."

"But there are programs that could help Lexi and release Cole from under Wallace's thumb."

"I hear you and appreciate your heart, but Cole has to be the one to accept it. In the meantime, he'll keep allowing Wallace to pull his strings until he gets so tangled that he's ready to cut them himself. And I'll be the first in line to hand him the scissors and give him all the help he needs. He's like the child Pete and I couldn't have."

"I admire what he's doing by caring for Lexi on his own."

Aunt Lynetta raised an eyebrow. "Just how much admiring is going on there?"

Macey rolled her eyes. "Don't even go there. Like I told you—Cole's just a friend. But I do feel for his situation and wish I could do something other than talking my family into accepting Crawford's offer to help him."

"The pancakes you delivered, then caring

for Lexi while he had to go back to work, sure helped."

"That sweet child shouldn't have to suffer because of adult issues. I did what anyone else would have done."

"Not anyone else and you know it." Aunt Lynetta brushed a thumb across Macey's cheekbone. "And from the moment Cole was mentioned, your lovely skin has taken on a rosy glow."

She pushed her aunt's hand away and shook her head. "You're imagining things."

Aunt Lynetta laughed, a sound that warmed Macey from the inside out, even if it was directed at her. "I don't think so, girl, but time will tell. Then I'll be the first to whisper, 'I told you so.'"

Macey pressed a hand to her face, not surprised to feel the warmth. She did not have time to fall for the guy and his adorable daughter. So how could she protect her heart from getting destroyed in the process?

BEING A GROWN man with a daughter, Cole really hated the feeling of being thirteen all over again and being summoned to the principal's office.

Wallace's door slamming and thunderous shouting of Cole's name from across the hall made his stomach clench.

He ended his phone call and grabbed the land appraisal file off the corner of his desk. Blowing out a breath, he stiffened his spine and rapped two knuckles on Wallace's open door. "Ready for our meeting?"

Wallace looked up from his computer screen, a scowl deepening the lines in his weathered face. "What are you talking about?"

"We had a scheduled meeting forty-five minutes ago to review Leland Stebbins's appraisal."

"You sure?"

"You set the meeting yourself."

With his elbow propped on his desk, Wallace ran a hand over his forehead. "Okay, fine. Get in here and shut the door."

Again feeling like a kid in trouble, Cole did as demanded, then sat in one of the chairs across from his uncle's desk. He opened the folder and pulled out the appraisal report.

Wallace reached across the desk, snatched the papers from Cole's hand and skimmed them, then tossed them back across the desk. "I don't like those numbers. We need another appraisal done. This time, go with Vinny Montrose."

"The council voted against using his services and went with Stebbins instead."

"Just do as you're told and call him. The sooner we can get this one done, the quicker we can sit down with the Stones and hash out a price."

Cole swallowed a sigh and stood. "Sure, whatever you want."

"What I want is for you to get that Stone family to accept the offer so we can move forward. Stop cozying up to the daughter and do the job I'm paying you to do."

And there it was.

Somehow his uncle would make this his fault.

"I've done everything I'm supposed to do. Despite what you think, I haven't been dragging my feet on this." Cole reached for the scattered papers and stacked them together before sliding them back into his folder. He started for the door, then turned back to his uncle who'd tuned him out and shifted his focus to the computer. "By the way, you know anything about my missing hat?"

"Hat? What hat? Do I look like your mother?"

"The one that's been sitting on my desk since I started working here. Dad bought it when he took me to a Rockies game."

"It's not my job to keep track of your stuff." Wallace waved him away.

Cole stalked back to his uncle's desk. "My hat came up missing. Then, it was found on Stone River where the property had been vandalized."

Wallace leaned back in his chair and tossed up his hands. "So if you know where your hat is, then why are you asking me about it?"

"*I* haven't been on that section of the property." He jerked a thumb toward his chest. "*I* didn't remove my hat from my desk."

Wallace's eyes glinted as he pushed to his feet. Bracing his fingers on his desk, he leaned forward until he was less than six inches from Cole's face. "What are you accusing me of, son?"

Cole refused to direct his gaze away. His jaw tightened. "First, I'm not your son. Second, I'm simply asking if you know anything about it. Seems strange that my hat would show up at that site without me being there. I won't take the fall for something I didn't do."

"Maybe you need to be more careful with your things." Wallace straightened and folded his hands over his chest.

Cole slapped the folder against his uncle's

desk. "I had nothing to do with that vandalism, and you know it."

"Do I now?"

"Wallace, I am doing my best to move forward with this project, but I will not get caught up in your schemes." He stared at his uncle.

The man was impossible.

Cole dropped his chin to his chest, shook his head and pulled in a breath. "If you're so unhappy with my work performance, then maybe you should start looking for my replacement."

"I've been considering that for a while now. But let me remind you—you owe me. Who took care of you after your mama died? Paid for your fancy private school and college tuition? Who replaced those rags you wore with brand names?" He jerked a thumb to his chest. "You had nothing before me, and don't you forget it."

Cole ground his jaw as he looked at his expensive polished shoes. Then he lifted his head and skated his gaze over his uncle's smug face. "How can I forget it when you continually remind me? But you're wrong. I had everything until my mother died. Then I was left with nothing. I've been repaying my tuition every month since I've started working for you. That

debt is nearly paid. Once that's done, then so
are we."

"Have you forgotten about the little thing
called insurance? How will you care for that
little brat?"

Cole rounded the desk and gripped his hands
into fists to prevent from reaching for his uncle's shirt collar. "Don't you ever talk about my
daughter that way again."

Wallace shoved him back and gripped the
lapels of his own leather sport coat. "I'll talk
about her any way I see fit, and there's nothing you can do about it. So you'd better watch
your tongue and get back to doing your job."

Cole stalked back to his own office and
slammed the door, his adrenaline surging. He
paced in front of his desk, feeling caged in the
windowless room. Then he yanked his phone
out of his back pocket and thumbed through
his contacts until he found Wyatt Stone's information. He tapped on the number and waited
for his childhood friend to pick up.

"Hey, Cole. What's up?" A child cried in the
background.

"Hey, man. You got a minute?"

"Maybe about half that, actually. Mia's having a meltdown at that moment because I won't let her drink from the dog's water dish."

In spite of the rage coiled in his stomach, Cole couldn't hold back a laugh. "Been there with the tantrums, man. Listen, I wondered if we could meet. I need to ask a favor."

"Sure, dude. Not a problem. Care to swing by the cabin?"

"I'll be there in fifteen minutes."

"See you then." The line ended, and for the first time, Cole could breathe.

Fifteen minutes later, he kicked the snow off his boots as he stood on the full-length covered porch and knocked on Wyatt's cabin door. Inside, a dog barked and footsteps raced across the floor.

The door opened. A toddler with red-rimmed eyes and half of her hair in one ponytail while the other half stuck to her face stared at him without saying a word. A black-and-white spotted English setter nosed around the little girl.

Cole dropped to his haunches and held his palm out as the dog sniffed his fingers while directing his attention to the child. "Hey, you must be Mia. Is your daddy home?"

The little girl nodded and ran away, leaving

the door open. The dog barked and chased after her, leaving Cole alone at the door.

He straightened and peered inside. "Wyatt?"

His friend hurried into the large open room with a dish towel over his shoulder and a cup in one hand. "Hey, man. Come in. Sorry about that. I was filling Mia's cup when you arrived."

"You sure this isn't a bad time?" Cole stepped inside and closed the door. He scuffed his feet on the rug in the entryway.

He took in the exposed log walls and the crackling fire warming the room from the stone fireplace that went to the ceiling. A navy and rust braided rug lay in front of a rust-colored couch and matching chair. A large flatscreen mounted on the wall above the mantel. Framed pictures of Wyatt in dress blues with his arms around a dark-haired woman wearing a wedding gown and one of Wyatt holding his daughter hung on either side of the fireplace.

Colorful dishes and plastic food spilled out of the play kitchen set in the corner of the room.

"Cool digs."

"Thanks. Used to be an old foreman cabin, but I've been fixing it up. It's big enough for Mia and me to call home. So, what's up?"

Cole shoved his hands in his trouser pockets.

"I know I have no right asking this, but I need help, and I don't know where else to turn."

Wyatt scooped up a remote, a doll and a book about farm animals off one of the couch cushions, then waved for Cole to sit. "Sure, whatever you need. Have a seat."

Cole sat on the edge of the couch, balanced his elbows on his knees and clasped his hands. "First, I want you to know I had nothing to do with your family's property being destroyed."

Wyatt slumped in the overstuffed chair and rested his right ankle on his left knee. "I didn't think that for a minute."

Cole shared his recent confrontation with his uncle, then dragged a hand over his face. "I think he's dirty, but I can't prove it. You mentioned one of the guys in your single father support group was a private investigator?"

"Yes, Barry Harrelson. He's a retired cop who works with the Stone River PD on an as needed basis."

"Mind giving me his contact info or maybe set up a meeting with him?"

Wyatt pulled out his phone. His thumbs tapped across the screen. Seconds later, Cole's phone vibrated in his pocket. "I sent you his contact information. I'll text him and tell him to expect your call."

"Thanks, man. I appreciate it."

"Sure thing. We single dads need to stick together, right?" Wyatt eyed him. "You okay?"

Cole exhaled. "I'm about to be canned, I think. I've been holding on to this job because of Lexi, but honestly, being out from under Wallace's thumb may be a blessing."

Wyatt leaned forward and clapped a hand on Cole's shoulder. "Whatever you need, I'm here to help you through it. Just ask."

Ask.

So much easier said than done.

CHAPTER EIGHT

WYATT'S WORDS STUCK with Cole as he stood at the checkout at Regals Shoes.

What would it be like to have someone like Wyatt in his corner? Someone who understood the struggles of single parenting? Maybe he should check out that support group after all. He'd worry about that later. Right now he needed to check out and head back to work for a bit.

Yesterday, while getting Lexi ready for her follow-up at the pediatrician, she'd mentioned her shoes pinching her toes.

He'd come in to find Mrs. Regal marking down shoes and adding them to the clearance sale rack. After finding a pair of regular-priced brand-name shoes for Lexi, he'd cleared the clearance sale rack of kids' shoes and carried the boxes to the front register until the display was empty.

Cole understood poverty and sacrifice. Until he had gone to live with Wallace after his mother's death, going without had been the norm.

Getting shoes for his daughter had been his priority, but the great sale on the shoes gave him an opportunity to pay it forward and help some other kid from feeling less than.

"Your mama would be proud of you, young man. Hope you know that." White-haired Mrs. Regal peered over the top of her glasses at him as she directed her scanner gun at another barcode.

"It's for a good cause." He eyed the growing stack of boxes. The total would still be less than the amount he spent on one pair of his own work boots, especially with the deep discounts she had marked.

"And you and your big heart, young man."

The front door opened, and Mrs. Regal looked up from her register. "Hey, Nora." Then her eyes widened. She dropped the scanner gun, rushed around the counter and hurried to the door, her arms outstretched. She wrapped Macey in a hug that nearly knocked the young woman off her feet.

"Macey Stone. Young lady, you are a sight for

this old woman's eyes. I heard you were back in town and hoped you'd stop in sometime."

"Hey, Marla. How are you doing?"

"Sugar, I can't complain. The good Lord watches over and protects me every day." She released Macey and hustled back to the counter. "You two look around and I'll be with you as soon as I'm done ringing up Cole here."

"We just found the most wonderful dresses for the ball, and we're looking for shoes to go with them."

Cole's heart jerked at the sound of Macey's voice. He gripped the counter and tried not to let his eyes linger over the way Macey's hair brushed against her red wool jacket.

He straightened as she headed to the counter, her eyebrows raised as she took in the multiple bulging bags at his feet. "Someone has a shoe weakness."

Then she shot him a grin that nearly dissolved him into a puddle.

Get a grip, man.

Cole smirked and reached for a navy sneaker covered in white daisies. "Not quite my size."

"Lexi's going to be thrilled with so many pairs of shoes."

"I admit to spoiling my daughter, but not like this."

Ms. Marla scanned the final pair of shoes on the counter and read him the total. "Cole, bless his heart, buys up children's shoes and boots when I put them on clearance sale and donates them to the local day care centers and elementary school for kids who can't afford them."

Heat scalded his neck as he pulled out his wallet. "Mrs. Regal, that was our secret, remember?"

The older woman clapped a hand over her mouth, then took his bank card. "I'm sorry, love. It's just such a good thing you're doing.

Macey touched his elbow and looked at him with almost a wonder in her eyes. "That's very sweet, Cole. What a kind and generous thing to do."

He lifted a shoulder and scrawled his name at the bottom of the receipt. "I'm just paying forward what someone had done for me."

"Someone bought shoes for you?"

"Once, when I was ten." That moment still rubbed a raw edge around his heart.

Carrying a box, Mrs. Stone joined Macey. She shot him a wide smile full of kindness. "Hi, Cole. It's good to see you again."

He nodded to her, wondering if she overheard their conversation. "Hey, Mrs. Stone. Good to see you as well. How's Mr. Stone doing?"

"He's being discharged this evening. Macey and I had a few errands to run, then we're going to pick him up. How's that sweet daughter of yours?"

"Lexi's doing well. She's nearly recovered from a double ear infection." He glanced at his watch. "She's spending the night with my cousin and her daughter."

Mrs. Stone slipped her arm around his shoulders and gave him a quick squeeze. "Give her a hug from me. I miss seeing her at the ranch, but I'll see her on Sunday for children's church."

"Will do. She loves listening to your stories. All the way home from church, she rattles on about what Miss Nora taught her. Last week was all about the big fish who swallowed the man who ran away."

Mrs. Stone laughed. "They were really into the Jonah story and the puppets we made. I'm so glad she enjoys it. She's a gem, and we're so thankful to have her. Both of you."

"Thank you." Her words touched him more

than he could say. He lifted three of the bags. "Mrs. Regal, I'll be back in a minute for the rest."

"I can help." Before he could protest, Macey took the remaining two bags off the counter and nodded toward the door. "You lead, and I'll follow."

He walked backward and pushed open the door with his shoulder, then held it while Macey passed, her scent wreathing him.

Out on the sidewalk, he pulled in a lungful of crisp air, then nodded to his truck parked across the street. "I'm over there."

They paused at the corner for the crosswalk signal to change.

"Just when I thought I had you figured out, you surprise me, Cole."

He eyed Macey, then watched the light turn from red to green. "Let's walk. How do I surprise you?"

"I don't know. Stuff like this." She hefted the bags. "Who does that?"

He couldn't see her eyes through her oversize sunglasses, but the way her lips tipped up made him think she wasn't passing judgment. In fact, her words carried a tone of respect.

He lifted a shoulder, wishing they could change the subject. He shifted all the bags to one hand so he could pull out his key fob and unlock the truck. "Someone who doesn't want other kids to be teased about holes in their shoes."

She set the bags on the back seat, then lifted her sunglasses onto her head, holding back her hair. She stuffed her gloved hands in her pockets. "I'm sorry you had to go through that. Kids can be so cruel. When we were younger, my mom told us about this one time she'd gone into Regals. A little boy was so excited to buy a new pair of shoes, but he didn't have enough money, so she paid the balance. She said she'd never seen anyone so excited over a pair of shoes before. She'd remind us of the story when we whined about wanting something we really didn't need."

Cole shoved his bags next to the ones Macey placed in the back. "Yeah, I'm quite familiar with the story."

Macey's eyes widened. "You are?"

He shoved his hands in his front pockets and kicked a clump of salted snow off his tire. "I'm the kid she was talking about."

"Oh." Her single word almost whispered spoke volumes. "I'm sorry if I embarrassed you."

He laughed, but the decades-old humiliation resurfaced, reminding him of where he'd come from and how he needed to be the one to make his way in the world. "We all have our wounds, right?"

"And that's why you donate shoes." Her voice soft and gentle, Macey gripped his upper arm. "You really are amazing, Cole Crawford."

Cole looked at her fingers on his arm and forced his heart to beat steadily against his rib cage. A woman touching him shouldn't create this type of reaction. Was he that hard up for attention?

But Macey wasn't just any woman. The more he was around her, the more he wanted to touch her, pull her close.

But he couldn't.

Not as long as they were on opposing sides— both desperately trying to get what they wanted for their families. Her family who had been nothing but good to him.

"Hey, have the police learned anything else about the vandalism?"

Macey shook her head. "Not that I know of. Bear and Wyatt removed the spray paint and hosed down the barn with the power washer, so it won't be an eyesore for the ball. You still planning to sell tickets with me tomorrow at WinterFest?"

Cole gripped the back of his neck. "Yes. What time do you want me there?"

"Is nine too early? We'll have a table set up in the food hall. It's out of the elements and receives pretty decent traffic with people getting coffee and something to eat."

He shook his head. "No. I was planning to meet Piper around noon anyway."

"Great. Sounds good. I'll see you later. I need to find shoes for the dress I bought." She headed back to the crosswalk. As she walked to the shoe store, Cole longed to chase after her and invite her out to dinner. Or something. Anything so he didn't have to return to the condo by himself.

But he couldn't. Even if the land deal divided them. She came from such a great family. And he…well, he didn't deserve Macey.

And the more he remembered that, the better off he'd be.

MACEY WOULDN'T LET her aunt down.

She couldn't say no when Aunt Lynetta called

with the plea in her voice. Even if it meant Macey tamping down the panic pressing against her ribs.

With WinterFest tomorrow, the last thing Aunt Lynetta needed was an unexpected trip to the ER after slicing her hand while peeling apples.

With her brothers working the ranch, Everly caring for Tanner and Mia and Mom caring for Dad at the ranch house, that left Macey to finish the baking for tomorrow's pie auction.

Aunt Lynetta's pies were legendary in Aspen Ridge. The pie auction raised money each year for the local animal shelter.

Macey could do this.

Although her aunt seldom followed a recipe, her apple pie was the same one Macey's grandma and mom used. And like the other women in her family, she'd memorized it years ago.

Even if Macey hadn't baked a pie since before her grandma had been killed, it had to be like riding a bike, right? Except she didn't have to worry about skinned knees if she failed.

Just her aunt's reputation.

She glanced at the remaining eight pie plates filled with the bottom crusts. She tugged a yellow Netta's Diner apron over her head and secured the ties in front of her. She reached for a paring knife and grabbed one of the washed apples from the deep sink.

For the next fifteen minutes, she peeled, cored and sliced apples while humming along with the country tunes streaming from the local radio station in the background. With the diner closed and the front of house locked, dark and quiet, Macey soaked in the calm.

Outside, snow drifted down in a whisper. The forecast called for two to four inches overnight, which would be great for the dogsled teams, downhill tubing races and general atmosphere for the WinterFest.

Her phone dinged. She rinsed her hands, reached for it, and found a text from Cole on her lock screen: Hey, tried to call Wyatt but got his voice mail. Wondered if your fam had a vet you'd rec.

Macey didn't have time to tap it all out. She touched his name on her screen and waited while the call rang through.

"Hey, Macey. I just texted you."

"Yes, I saw. I'm up to my elbows in peeling apples, so it was easier to talk on speakerphone."

"Apples? What are you doing?"

"Aunt Lynetta cut her hand. Uncle Pete took her to the ER for stitches. She needs pies made for tomorrow, so here I am." She slivered the remaining apple half and slid it off her silicon cutting board into the glass bowl to be mixed with sugar, cinnamon and lemon juice.

"Want a hand?"

Her fingers stilled as her heart jumped. She swallowed and paused a second. "A hand?"

"Sure, I know my way around a paring knife. I used to make pies with my mom all the time."

"Um, sure. Yeah, great. Consider yourself recruited. Come to the back door."

What was she thinking, agreeing to his request?

"Be there in ten."

Macey ended the call, then rummaged through her tote bag and grabbed her small makeup case. She rushed to the restroom and tugged her hair from the sloppy ponytail she'd tied before entering the kitchen. She brushed her hair and twisted it into a tidier messy bun, pulling a few loose hairs around her face. She swiped on mascara, brushed a little powder on her face, then applied a sheer lip gloss.

Then she made a face at herself in the mirror. What was she doing? This wasn't a date.

Far from it.

"Girl, you are ridiculous," she said out loud.

She returned to the kitchen, tossed her case back in her bag and washed her hands.

A quiet knock sounded on the back door. Macey's fingers tightened around the paring knife as her breath caught in her chest.

Knock it off.

Macey hurried down the small hallway past the diner office, storage room and industrial cooler. She pushed open the back door.

Cole bounced on the balls of his feet. He flashed a smile.

A smile that warmed her against the burst of cold that accompanied him as he stepped inside and pulled the door shut against the wind. "Man, it's freezing out there."

"Late January in Colorado tends to be that way."

He flashed her another smile. Snowflakes melted on his head, causing his dark brown hair to glisten in the overhead lights.

Macey took a step forward, then caught herself. Seriously? Did she actually plan to brush the wetness off his hair?

Get a grip!

Macey spun away, giving herself a swift mental kick, and didn't wait to see if he was going to follow.

She returned to the sink and reached for another apple. Cole propped a hip against the industrial prep sink and pushed his sleeves up on his charcoal sweater. "Okay, boss. Put me to work."

Forcing herself not to breathe in the spicy scent of his cologne or body wash or whatever he wore, she nodded toward the knives mounted on the magnetic strip above the prep sink. "There's another paring knife there. I've washed the apples. I'm peeling them into this glass bowl, then I'll make the top crusts and bake them."

"How many pies are left to make?"

"Eight. She made half a dozen triple berry pies, three lemon meringue and three chocolate silk. Then she cut her hand and called me in to finish."

"Piece of cake. Or pie, I guess." He shot her a lopsided half grin that sent her stomach into a spiral.

"Har. Har."

Cole reached for an apple, the back of his hand brushing against her arm.

What was her problem?

She'd been around Cole many times over the past few weeks. So why was she suddenly acting like a high schooler with her first crush?

"Where's Lexi this evening?"

"Piper and Avery took her to a movie. Then, they're having a sleepover."

"Oh, right. You mentioned her spending the night this morning at Regals. Fun for her and a little break for you."

He lifted a shoulder. "It's too quiet without her. I did some work, but then I remembered I needed to make a vet appointment for Polly. I called the one Mrs. Douglas at the shelter had given me, but they're not accepting new patients right now. I tried Wyatt first, then called you."

"He and Bear are working on a busted water line in the barn. Everly's caring for Tanner and Mia. Mom's making sure Dad doesn't overdo it. And I'm here." Then she gave him a sheepish smile as she sprinkled cinnamon over the full bowl of apples. "I guess you didn't need a play-by-play of the Stone family activities. Regardless, that's why Wyatt didn't pick up."

"I like hearing about your family. You're very blessed to have siblings. Being an only child can be lonely at times, especially with no parents around either. Piper's like a sister, but her priorities are Avery and her housecleaning business, as they should be." Cole peeled his apple in one continuous motion without breaking the skin.

Macey did a mental calculation of how much lemon juice to add to the mix, then eyeballed the measuring cup as she poured. "Yes, I can understand that, especially after being away from my family."

"Mind if I ask what brought you back?" Cole stretched out the long peel, then beginning at one end, he curled the peel together. Then he tucked the bottom end under, placed it on his palm and held an apple peel rose out to her. "For you."

"Look at you, Mr. Creativity." Grinning, she wiped her hands on her apron, then took it. "No one's given me an apple rose before."

"My mom showed me how to make them when I was a kid. Everyone needs a talent. I guess that one's mine."

Oh, he had more than one.

"Your mom made the best Dutch apple pie."

"Yes, she did." He nudged her. "And you didn't answer me."

She could've pretended she didn't know what he was talking about, but Cole deserved better than that. She brushed her thumb over the top of the apple rose, then lifted a shoulder. "My employer hit on me, and his wife walked in on us. She fired me on the spot."

"What do you mean he hit on you?" His voice lowered to a growl.

Macey exhaled, turned and pressed her back against the edge of the sink, the apple rose cupped in her hand. "After college, I spent six years nannying for the Crane family. My college roommate was Tricia Crane's niece, and she said her aunt was looking for a nanny. The pay was good, so I accepted."

"Because of me."

Macey slid the apple rose onto the edge of her cutting board, then rinsed her hands. "Maybe at first. I had agreed to go to prom with you because you and your girlfriend had broken up and you said you weren't getting back together with her. Then she knocked my punch cup out of my hand and it flew all over her dress. She claimed I threw punch on her on purpose and threatened her. When the chaperones asked what had happened, you didn't say anything. I was humiliated when they made me leave—the senior prom I'd spent months planning. Looking back on it now, it was ridiculous mean girl drama. But I just wanted to get away."

Cole's knife clattered against the prep counter. He grabbed Macey's hands, his fingers wet and sticky from apple juice. "I'm so sorry, Macey. I wish I could rewind time and stand up for you the way you deserved. I wanted to fit in and ended up losing the one person who always believed in me."

"I forgave you a long time ago, Cole. It's in the past. Going to college and working for the Cranes allowed me time away. I loved Jayden, Jenna and Jaxson. When I met them, Derek and Tricia seemed to be an ideal couple. When they hired me, Jayden was two, and Tricia was pregnant with Jenna. Things were going well until recently."

"When your employer hit on you?"

Macey nodded. Heat crawled across her face as the events of that night flickered through her mind.

"What happened?"

Macey shot a look at Cole. His eyes drifted back to the apple he sliced, but a muscle jumped in the side of his face as his jaws clenched.

"I'd put the kids to bed when Derek returned from a business meeting or something. He'd been drinking. I didn't expect him to return as early as he did. I was reading in the living room. He'd gone upstairs to check on them, which was normal. Then he came back downstairs and sat next to me on the couch. He tried to kiss me. I tried to push him away, but he was stronger than me. Tricia walked in and when she asked what was going on, he said I was the one who had come on to him. She wouldn't listen to me, demanded I pack my things and be out before the children woke up the next morning. I'd never packed so quickly in all my life. I was on the road within two hours, humiliation chasing me all the way back to the ranch."

"I'm so sorry, Macey. It shouldn't have been like that. You didn't press charges, I take it?"

Macey filled her lungs, then blew out a breath. Her vision blurred as that night replayed in her head. "I didn't see the point. Without any witnesses, it was my word against his. Again, I feared no one would believe me."

"You're home now. And safe. No one will take advantage of you like that again."

"You don't know that. I hope to find someone whom I can trust, who will stick up for me when necessary and stand by my side like my parents do for each other. After taking care of other people's children, I'd love to raise a family on South Bend since it was supposed to be mine someday. But now that may not happen."

"I didn't realize it was part of your inheritance."

She nodded, her eyes awash with more tears. "Not technically. Grandpa knew how much I loved it and said it would be mine. No matter how far I go, South Bend will always be my favorite place on the planet. So many wonderful memories of growing up near my grandparents, riding with my grandpa to the waterfalls, learning how to take pictures, baking with my grandma."

"Sounds like the perfect childhood."

"It was. Problem was, I didn't appreciate it like I should have. I wanted more than the fenced-in pastures of Stone River. Then I found out the grass isn't always greener on the other side of the fence. Just a different type of manure was being spread."

Cole laughed, a deep timbre that bounced off the kitchen walls. Then he sobered. "I'm sorry for my role in jeopardizing your dream."

Macey shook her head. "It's not your fault. I still feel like your uncle is doing it to get back at my dad. My parents keep saying if God wants us to keep our land, then He'll make it happen."

Even if that meant ending up with a broken heart.

COLE CERTAINLY DIDN'T mind the unexpected change to his evening. He'd hesitated in texting Macey. Now he was happy he did. Even if peeling apples and the sweet scents of sugar and cinnamon took him back to baking with his mom.

"You got quiet. Regretting your invitation to help?" Macey patted the pie dough into a circle, floured the rolling pin, and rolled it out. She transferred the dough over the filled pie plate, then slid it over to Cole.

"Nah. Just thinking about my mom for a minute."

"You said you and your mom used to bake."

Cole crimped the edges of the dough between his thumbs and forefingers. He cut slits in the crust, then brushed an egg wash across the top. He carried the pie to the oven and slid it on the rack. "One year, we spent an afternoon baking pies as gifts for our neighbors. Everyone wanted to know the secret to Mom's crust because it was always so light and flakey."

"So what was the secret?"

He eyed her and shook his head. "I don't know if I can trust you..."

"Come on... I'm not asking for military secrets." She nudged him as she rinsed a dishcloth in the sink and wiped off the prep counter.

"Well, that's good because I don't have any." He enjoyed laughing together the way they used to. "Actually, my mom added vodka to her dough. She said it kept it moist and from getting tough. Something about it doesn't cause the gluten to form. I don't remember exactly. The only time we had booze in the house was when Mom was baking."

"Sounds like a wonderful memory."

"It was. After we delivered the pies, we created a blanket fort in the living room and watched *Aladdin* on a DVD, which she'd borrowed from the library. For Christmas, she'd given me a knitted hat and scarf that she'd made, which I still have, and bought me a secondhand handheld video game. I loved the time we spent together without her rushing off to another job to help make ends meet."

"Your mom was a hard worker."

"She was. But she was also kind and generous, quick to give up whatever we had for someone else who she felt needed it more."

"I can see where you get it. Especially the shoe thing. Those kids were blessed by your generosity."

Cole gripped the edge of the sink and dropped his gaze to his feet, warm inside his expensive leather boots. "One time when I was around ten or so, we played basketball during gym class. Every time I ran, the ripped sole of my shoe kept slapping against the floor. I tripped and skinned my knee. My gym teacher offered to duct tape my shoe, and the kids in my class laughed at me, calling me Slappy. I hated it. After school, I walked past Regals. They advertised a huge sale. I found these awesome kicks in my size and took them to the counter, so excited not to be teased again. I had two wrinkly five-dollar bills I'd saved from birthday money. I planned to use one five to buy my mom some nice-smelling lotion for her chapped hands. Mrs. Regal wasn't working. Otherwise, I figure those shoes would've been on sale for five bucks. I'll never forget the look of pity from the teenage cashier when she said it wasn't enough. In fact, I didn't have enough money for even the cheapest pair of shoes in the store.

But then a woman paid the difference so I could have those shoes."

"My mom." Macey's words came out more like an exhale.

Cole nodded, remembering every detail of that day scratched into his memory. "I was so excited to have shoes that didn't need to be taped together. I showed my mom, thinking she'd be happy too."

"She wasn't?"

"Not even a little. She was so upset."

"Why's that?"

"She said we were hard workers who didn't need someone else's charity. I hadn't looked at it as charity but more about the kindness of a nice woman. But from that moment on, I felt like a charity case and vowed never to be in a position where I couldn't meet my own needs. My mom went with me and tried to return the shoes, but the young store clerk didn't know who had paid for them. She was insistent on paying back whomever had bought my shoes. My mom had a huge heart, but she also had a misguided sense of pride. I never bought that brand of shoes again."

"I'm so sorry. I can only imagine how you felt. You don't worry about the children feeling like charity cases when you donate shoes to the schools and day care centers?"

Cole shook his head. "No, because the staff puts out a letter letting parents know about the donated shoes. Those who need them can send in a signed form. The shoes are given to the children's parents at pickup or drop-off. That way, the other kids don't know who's being blessed with the shoes."

"Blessed. That's a great way to look at it. But your mom didn't take it as a blessing, I take it."

"No, she looked at it as a handout. I don't know if you know this or not, but my dad's family was very wealthy. Look at my uncle. When my dad started dating my mom, his parents claimed my mom was after my dad for his money. My mother vowed not to take a cent from them. She never applied for government food assistance, heating help, or subsidy for my care. She said if we couldn't earn it and pay for it, then we didn't need it. I guess that's why I stay in my job and don't look into government programs to help my daughter."

"But that's different, Cole. You're certainly not abusing the system. So many of the programs are in place to help children like Lexi get the best care possible, especially when some insurance programs can't meet that gap."

"I understand that, but if I can care for her on my own, then there's room for another child in those programs who can't afford basic needs like medical care. I'm not trying to be obstinate like my mom or even irresponsible. I can afford the wonderful care Lexi receives through her pediatrician without an issue. With the recent changes in her hearing though, she needs expensive hearing aids. I just need to make sure I can provide for her in the way she deserves."

"And that's why this promotion is so important to you."

"I'll be promoted to chief executive officer for the Durango area, which includes a substantial pay raise. That means I can afford the specialists Lexi needs."

"You're a good father. Don't allow your uncle to make you feel otherwise."

The timer on the oven went off. Macey slipped on silicone oven mitts that went to her elbow and pulled the first pie out of the oven. The scents of cinnamon and sugar tinged the air. Once all the pies were on the cooling racks, she removed the mitts and hung them on the peg near the oven.

"Thanks for helping me. You made the evening go by much quicker."

"Is that my cue to leave?" Cole took a step closer and brushed a dust of cinnamon off her cheek with the back of his hand.

Macey's eyes searched his face. She reached for his hand. But instead of pushing it away, she lowered it and kept her fingers wrapped around his. She shook her head. "No. I don't want you to go."

Her admission speared his gut. Then he slid his free hand over her cheek and around the curve of her neck. Standing so close he could see the glints of gold in her brown eyes and count the number of lashes on their lids. He drew her toward him, lowered his head and kissed her.

Macey slid her arms around him.

He could taste apple and sugar on her lips.

A moment later, Cole pulled his mouth away from hers. He pressed his forehead to hers, then dropped a kiss on the tip of her nose. Then he wrapped her in his arms as she rested her cheek against his chest.

She sighed.

For a moment, he focused on the perfect way

she fit into his embrace, the way her arms held him close to her.

She wanted this as much as he did, and that filled him with an emotion he couldn't quite decipher. All he wanted to do was imprint this moment into his memory.

Macey moved out of his arms. She left the room, then returned a moment later with her camera in hand. "I'm going to take a picture of you in that apron and with one of the pies. I know Aunt Lynetta would love to hang it on the wall next to your mom's picture along with her crust recipe."

He stepped forward, gently removed the camera from her hand and set it safely on the counter. Then he pulled her close once again and traced a finger along her jaw. "I told you that was a family secret. How can I buy your silence?"

Her eyes searched his. Then she stood on her tiptoes and kissed him again.

After a few moments, Cole put some necessary distance between them and moved into the dark dining room. Hands in his pockets, he stood in front of the large window and watched the snow fall lightly and drift against the lamppost that cast halos against the blanket of white.

"Cole?"

He turned at her quiet words. Macey stood in the doorway between the kitchen and the server station. The light from the kitchen turned her dark hair to gold. She held her hands in front of her, her fingers twisted together.

"You okay?"

Nodding, he ate up the distance between them in two long strides. He brushed his thumb across her cheekbone and smiled. "I'm more than okay."

She waved back toward the kitchen. "Good. When you left the kitchen, I thought…"

"What?"

"That I'd disappointed you or something."

The vulnerability on Macey's face had him swallowing the laughter at her ludicrous suggestion. "Hardly. More like the opposite. I'd like nothing more than to keep kissing."

Her arms entwined around his neck. "You should listen to your intuition."

"I would love that. More than you know, but it's nearly midnight. I think I should help you clean up and make sure you get home safely. The last thing I want is for someone to get wind of me being here and jump to the wrong conclusions."

She tugged on his apron as a grin lit up her

face. "You just don't want anyone to see you wearing one of Aunt Lynetta's aprons."

He covered her hands with his own. "We're selling tickets tomorrow, but want to go together? I can pick you up. You know, so we can watch our pies take the highest bids."

"Of course. For the sake of the pies, I'd love to go with you, but I'll meet you there. No need to go out of your way."

"I don't mind going out of my way for you, Macey."

"I'll need to be there early to help set up. Text me when you arrive, and we can meet up."

"Great, it's a date."

"I like the sound of that." Macey shot him a coy smile. Then she brushed a light kiss across his lips and stepped back.

He did too.

Finally, his relationship with Macey was heading in the right direction. He'd do whatever it took to prove he was the kind of guy she could trust.

CHAPTER NINE

MAYBE LAST NIGHT had been a mistake.

And that was why Cole had texted before 7:00 a.m. and apologetically bailed on her, saying he'd gotten called into work and would meet her at noon instead.

That's when he planned to meet his cousin and get Lexi. So maybe he didn't want to be alone with Macey again?

Was he regretting last night? What if he changed his mind about showing up at all?

Too many what-ifs and maybes and reliving those kisses had kept her awake until the early morning hours.

She hated the cliché of being weak in the knees, but that's how he made her feel. And she wasn't quite sure what to make of it.

Cole had texted to say he'd be there around noon, and she'd simply have to be patient. The closer the hands on her watch edged toward twelve, her stomach jumped at the thought of seeing him again.

Macey appreciated Cole's mad pie-making skills…and his company, if she was being honest. Much more than she'd expected. Especially the kisses.

Did he regret kissing her?

Maybe he didn't want to get invested in a relationship that couldn't go anywhere.

Or could it?

No, not at all.

Last night had to be a one-time thing.

She was setting herself up for heartache once again.

She needed to put last night out of her mind and enjoy herself. Having arrived at the festival before nine, Macey had stayed busy helping her mother prepare food at the pavilion and sell tickets to the Sweetheart Ball. She enjoyed walking down memory lane with friends and neighbors.

Located in the municipal park where baseball games were held during the summer, Aspen Ridge's annual WinterFest drew in tourists from surrounding areas with promises of a tubing race, an ice-carving contest, sleigh rides, and fireworks to close once the stars made their appearance. Not to mention the hot food available for sale and the traditional pie auction.

A veil of white draped over the mountains allowing the silvery-gray peaks to showcase their depths against the turquoise sky streaked with lingering clouds. Spindly and bare aspens stood among the pines laden with blankets of snow. The river cut through the edge of the park, its icy surface frosted with snow except where swimmers plunged into its frigid depths for the annual polar bear swim that raised money for the high school water sports program.

Although Macey hadn't attended in years, the festival had tripled in size, judging by her family's comments. Festivalgoers trundled from event to event dressed in colorful outerwear, heavy boots, and thick hats and scarves to protect against the single-digit temperature, and snow flurries drifting through the air.

Rounding the enormous three-sided tent someone had pitched for a makeshift barn, Macey watched a little boy dressed in a bright blue-and-red snowsuit petting a wooly lamb in a small pen. He giggled as the small animal licked his hand. Next to him, two little girls held carrots out to a couple of long-eared goats.

The scents of cotton candy and popcorn

drifted from the food pavilion, reminding her of parades and summer fairs. Her stomach rumbled. She hadn't eaten anything since dragging herself out of bed to do chores before the sun had even made an appearance. And then it was a quick cup of coffee and a muffin she'd eaten on the way to the festival.

She headed toward the large pavilion in search of hot coffee, Mom's vegetable beef soup, and maybe a slice of pie. Inside, she pulled off her sunglasses and tucked them in her pocket.

Long wooden tables covered in white plastic and decorated with blue-and-white flower arrangements that would be given away to festivalgoers lined the long room. People filled most of the seats as they sought refuge from the cold or dug into the hot food being served by Mom's church.

Macey passed by the corner table she and Mom had set up showcasing Stone River Ranch and its benefits to the community. People could also purchase tickets to the ball.

Two middle-aged women dressed in white puffy jackets with faux-fur-trimmed hoods stood with their heads together, their backs to everyone else. Despite their hoarse whispers, their words trailed to Macey's ears.

"I don't understand the big deal. Crawford's asking for only a few acres. Surely they can part with some to help the community. They're being selfish, if you ask me."

"You're preaching to the choir, sister. I'd love to be able to shop at more than Regals or Sadie's. I'm tired of driving all the way to Durango to find a decent dress. And ordering online, you don't know what the quality will be. I want to feel something before I buy it."

Macey hesitated a moment before walking up behind the two women. "Hey, ladies. Can I help you with anything? Answer any questions?"

One of the women looked over her shoulder, then her eyes widened behind her round glasses. She nudged her friend. They turned and lifted their chins. "We were talking about the strip mall."

Macey schooled her tone and forced a smile. "So I heard. You know, that land has been in my family for over two hundred years. How would you feel if the government or a developer wanted to buy your house and tear it down to build a road?"

"Well, I don't know. It would have to depend on the price."

"What if the price they offered didn't match what your property was worth? Would you still go for it?"

"Absolutely not."

"I'm sure others may think my family is being selfish, but there are other considerations. The land in question belonged to my grandparents. Also, we need to be concerned with how the strip mall will affect our water system, logistics for moving cattle, and the noise and pollution from the commercial buildings."

"But what about the jobs that it will bring in? And more tourists to Aspen Ridge?"

"What about stores like Regals Shoes, Curly's Hardware and Sadie's Dress Shop? Or even Jacie's Bridal? Those bigger stores could drive these privately owned shops out of business."

"Young lady, I respect your position and all, but I still think it will be a benefit to the community, so I'm all for that."

"Will you still feel that way when your taxes increase?"

"You don't know that's going to happen."

"There are many factors at play by bringing in more commercial businesses. Aspen Ridge has prided itself on having family-owned businesses and creating a community that's safe to raise our children. The more corporate retailers we bring in, the more growth we're going to experience. Growth is good, but do you want to see Aspen Ridge becoming the size of Durango? More and more private properties like my family's and Heath Walker's will be taken from us for the 'good of the community.'"

They shrugged. Realizing she wasn't about to change their minds, Macey flashed them a bright smile. "Hope you ladies have a nice day."

With her appetite gone, Macey left the pavilion.

Was she on the right side of the fight?

Could Crawford's money make a difference at the ranch? She truly wanted to preserve her family's land, but she also wanted what was best for the community.

But no, this wasn't it. She felt it in her bones.

She refused to look at her watch, check her phone for a text from Cole, or scan the crowd to see if he'd arrived. She wasn't going to be that girl who needed a man by her side to enjoy her day.

As she rounded the corner of the makeshift barn, she nearly knocked over a child. She thrust out her hands to steady little arms covered in pink. "Oh, I'm so sorry."

The child pushed up her hat and looked up at her with tearstained reddened cheeks.

Lexi Crawford.

Macey's heart quickened as she crouched in front of the little girl. She ran a thumb over a fresh tear trailing down her rounded cheek. "Lexi, honey, what's wrong?"

"My Piper is lost." Lexi threw herself into Macey's arms and sobbed.

"Piper is lost?" She gathered the child close as she scanned the crowd around the sheep and goats.

Lexi nodded, her watery eyes wide. "I stopped to look at the sheeps. They have fluffy wool. I turned around. Piper was gone. She's lost. I just know it."

"Oh, honey, I'll help you find her. Okay?"

Nodding, Lexi rubbed her eye with a mittened fist and reached for Macey's hand.

Macey gave her a gentle squeeze. She pulled her phone out of her back pocket and tapped on her mother's number. "Hey, Mom. Have you seen Piper Healy around? I have Lexi with me. They became separated."

"No, honey, I haven't. I've been serving food for the last hour or so. Did you check in at the information booth?"

"I'll head that way. Maybe we'll cross paths with her." Macey stowed her phone. "Hey, Lexi, want to walk with me and we'll try to find Piper?"

Lexi nodded.

They walked through the crowds with Lexi gripping her hand.

"Lexi!"

Macey turned. Avery Healy ran toward them. Then she stopped, turned and waved her hand. "Mom, there she is!"

Macey pointed at Piper running toward them. "Look, Lexi. There's Piper. She's not lost, after all."

Lexi released Macey's hand and ran into Piper's outstretched arms. She cradled Lexi against her and looked at Macey over Lexi's shoulder, her eyes shimmering. "Thank you so much. I don't know what happened. One minute she was there, the next minute she was gone."

"You can't wander off like that, young lady." Lexi leaned back and shook her finger at Piper.

Piper smothered a smile and attempted a serious look. "I can't wander off?"

"No, because I was scared. I couldn't find you."

"Oh, honey. I'm so sorry I scared you. I promise not to wander off anymore."

Lexi threw her arms around Piper's neck. "Good. I missed you."

"Oh, baby, I missed you too. You have no idea. How about if we call your daddy and see when he's planning to meet us? He should've been here by now." Piper pushed back the sleeve of her jacket to look at her watch.

"Cole's meeting you around noon, right?" Macey tried to keep her tone casual.

Piper's eyebrow lifted as her lips twitched. "That was the plan. He seemed very excited about attending. Mentioned something about not wanting to miss the pie auction."

Macey's cheeks heated.

Perhaps last night wasn't a mistake after all. She'd simply have to be patient and find out.

THE MORNING HADN'T gone as Cole had planned. But anytime Wallace was involved, that was par for the course.

Having been summoned to the job site first thing this morning, Cole wavered between telling his uncle he had plans and meeting up with Macey at a later time.

Unfortunately, his uncle won out.

Again.

Hopefully, Macey would forgive him, and he could make it up to her.

That idea kept him company as he worked through the tasks that certainly could have waited until Monday.

After last night's pie-making date—was that a date? Maybe not a scheduled one, but it sure felt like one to him. Especially the kissing.

The more he talked with Macey, the less satisfied he was with his uncle constantly barking orders at him like a drill instructor. Please and thank you weren't a part of the man's vocabulary.

Right now, he needed to focus on getting the job done so he could meet Macey. Hopefully, she wouldn't ditch him. But he wouldn't blame her if she did.

Cole grabbed his hard hat and strode from the mobile office parked behind the new condos at the end of town near the river. Head bent against the wind, he entered one of the buildings and found his foreman overseeing a wiring job in one of the unit kitchens, which was nothing more than an open room with visible studs. "Hey, Miller. How's the timeline on this project? Still on track to have the sub-contractor come on Monday to install insulation and drywall?"

The foreman who had at least twenty years on Cole nodded. "Despite being down a man, we're still on track. You can notify Grady and his crew they can begin work on Monday. We'll have this finished today."

Cole clapped him on the back. "Thanks, man. Knew I could count on you."

"Maybe not for much longer though."

"Oh? What's going on?"

Miller pulled off his baseball hat and scratched the back of his balding head. "I planned to stop by the office during my lunch break to talk, but I guess now's as good a time as any. I'm turning in my two weeks' notice."

Cole swallowed the sigh pressing on his chest. "Why's that?"

"I've been offered another job with Heath Walker. After losing his ranch, he started a construction company a few months ago. He's looking for a new foreman. Less pay, but the benefits are better. At this point in my life, I need less stress. Too many long days and not enough time to see my wife and kids is taking its toll. My daughter's getting married soon, and

Crawford's giving me a hard time about taking the day off. Not right, man. Not right at all."

"No, it's not. It'll be tough to see you go. You're the best foreman on my crew."

"Just so you know, it's not you. The guys and me, we like working for you. But when Crawford's on-site, well, let's just say morale goes down." He thumped his hat against his thigh before returning it to his head.

"I hear you, and I'm sorry about that."

"I shouldn't say anything with him being your uncle and all, but he really does need some better people skills."

Cole laughed. "No joke. Listen, if there's anything I can do, let me know. You're good people, Miller, and I'll put in a word if you need me to."

"Thanks. I appreciate it."

Cole headed back to the field office trailer, tossed the clipboard on the desk, then dropped in the chair. He dragged a hand over his face and blew out the pent-up sigh.

The door flung open, and Wallace strode inside, pulling in a blast of cold air and shrinking the small room with his bulk. "Hey, I don't pay you to sit around."

Pushing to his feet, Cole gritted his teeth.

"I just walked back in from the site. Looks like we need to start interviewing a new foreman."

"What's wrong with Miller?"

"He's putting in his two weeks." Cole palmed his empty cup and reached for the nearly empty coffeepot.

Wallace grabbed a clean cup off the shelf above the microwave and mini fridge. He took the pot out of Cole's hand and drained it into his own cup. "He what? No way. We have a job to finish."

Cole looked at the empty pot and shook his head. He flicked off the coffee maker and dropped his cup back on the desk. "The man's exhausted. Too many long hours with not enough time off."

"Cry me a river. The man's gone soft."

"He had a heart attack, Wallace. He came back to work sooner than the doctor wanted him to because you wouldn't stop hassling him."

"Like I said, we have a job to do."

"And it's getting done, but you really need to relax."

Crawford's head swiveled. His eyebrow raised as he took a step closer to Cole. "What'd you say?"

"You heard me." Hands curled at his sides, Cole stood firm, feet apart.

"I don't think so because it sounded like you were being pretty mouthy."

"Listen, I'm not a teenager you can bully into submission. I do my job, and I do it well." He waved a hand toward the condos. "So do they. You're coming down on them hard, but they're doing everything they can to stay on track. Ease up a little and give them some breathing space before they all walk off the job. Then where will you be?"

"I have half a mind to fire them and bring in a new crew who aren't a bunch of crybabies."

"Go for it, but you'd better plan on hiring a new project manager as well because I'll be leading the walk-off."

Wallace scoffed. "Right. Like you'll leave and risk losing your daughter's health insurance."

"You're not the only developer. I can get another job. With better pay and insurance. Plus I won't have to be a pawn in this manipulative game you're playing against the Stones."

Wallace's eyes blazed and he poked a stubby finger into Cole's chest. "Listen to me, boy, you go ahead and try. I'll see to it the only job you can get is at a fast food joint."

Cole lifted a shoulder. "Hey, that's honest work, so don't knock it."

"You owe me, and you know it."

"Actually, I don't."

The lines deepened in Wallace's forehead. "What are you talking about? Who put you through college? Who paid for those fancy duds you wore? Who bought your first car?"

"I bought the car. You just didn't like me having a sliver of independence, so you bought me a newer one. Plus I worked two jobs to help pay for my tuition, so it's not like you wrote a check for the full amount and you know it." Cole glanced at his watch. "I told you I'd work until noon, and it's already after one. I need to pick up Lexi."

"Fine. Whatever. Be at the municipal building first thing Tuesday morning, and leave your bleeding heart at home. We're meeting with the Stones to review the appraisals and to present them our final offer. We'll be celebrating or filing a complaint with the court come lunchtime."

Without saying goodbye, Cole stalked out of the trailer and slammed the door behind him. As he headed for his car, Wallace's words ignited his anger with each step.

He pulled into the lot at the park where WinterFest was being held and looked for Macey's car but didn't see it. He tried not to let its absence get to him. He didn't blame her for leaving. He should've been more considerate and contacted her when he was going to be late.

But he was there now. More than anything, he'd wanted to spend the rest of the day with Macey and Lexi. To walk together. Laugh together. Eat junk food together. And pretend they lived in a different time. Maybe even a different place and they could be a real family.

Cole never expected to be jealous of another man resigning, but part of him longed to be leaving along with Miller. Problem was, he loved his job and managing construction crews.

He loved building houses out of blocks with his dad when he was a kid. They had talked about having a business together someday. But that had never happened.

He wandered into the park, dodging two little boys chasing after each other with snowballs ready to be launched. Their parents huddled together with hands gripping steaming to-go cups.

Someday, he'd make time for a family. Lexi would be a wonderful big sister.

Problem was, every time he imagined a wife and maybe another kid, Macey's face swam into focus.

Yeah, that was a definite problem.

One he'd have to learn how to get over.

"Daddy!"

Cole spun around at the sound of the familiar voice, then knelt one knee in the snow as he opened his arms. Lexi run into his embrace and flung her arms around his neck. "Daddy, guess what? I won a teddy bear!"

"You did? That's amazing. How did you win it?"

"Macey held me while I threw the ball really super hard. I got it in the hole and won a pink teddy bear."

"Where's your bear?"

Lexi turned and pointed to the large tree, void of any leaves. "Over there with Macey."

Cole's heart tripped as he followed his daughter's finger. He missed the moment because he'd given in to his uncle's demands instead of being with his daughter.

Macey sat on a bench with Piper and Avery.

A small pink bear sat on Macey's lap. He pushed to his feet, brushed the snow off his jeans and allowed his daughter to drag him over to the women. Reaching the bench, he nodded and tried to sound nonchalant. "Hey, ladies. How's it going?"

Piper tapped her watch with a gloved finger. "Did you forget how to tell time? I expected you over an hour ago."

Heat crept up his neck. "I know. I'm sorry. Wallace was in a mood. Things took longer than expected. To top it off, we had a disagreement in the office."

She held up a hand. "Say no more. The less I hear about that man, the happier I'll be." She pushed to her feet and looked at Macey. "Thanks for keeping me company, Mace. And helping with Lexi."

"My pleasure." Handing the bear to Lexi, Macey stood and brushed off her backside. Then she looked up at Cole with those warm brown eyes. "Hey, you."

More than anything, Cole longed to pull her into his arms. He glanced over her shoulder as Piper stood up behind Macey. She winked and gave him a thumbs-up. Then Cole refocused his attention on the woman stealing his heart piece by piece. "Hey, yourself."

"I have something for you." Macey pulled a large envelope from her oversize tote bag and handed it to him. "Happy birthday."

Birthday?

His hand froze. Wait, that was today? He'd been so busy lately that he'd forgotten his birthday. But Macey had remembered.

"What's this?" He eyed her, then the envelope.

"Open it and find out." Macey wrapped her arms around her waist.

Cole turned the envelope over and reached inside. He pulled out the glossy 8 x 10 photos she'd taken of Lexi. And him.

He stared at the joy in his daughter's face as Macey had captured Lexi as she laughed.

The oversize cowboy hat she'd worn had overshadowed her eyes, but it did little to diminish the happiness on her face.

The next one showed Lexi sitting solo in the saddle as Wyatt led her down the trail with the mountains tipped in snow in the background.

And the last picture…well, that was like a gut-punch. Lexi leaned against Cole's chest and looked up at him. His arms had been wrapped around her as he dropped a kiss on her forehead.

"That one's my favorite," Macey said quietly.

He looked at her, his vision blurred. And swallowed.

Hard.

Clearing his throat, Cole brushed a thumb over his left cheek. He tapped the photos against his palm. "These are…" His voice cracked. He cleared his throat again. "I mean, thanks. These are so great, Macey. I saw your camera, but I didn't even realize you were taking pictures of her. Of us."

Macey slid a hand in his and gave it a light squeeze. Then she released her hold. "I apologize for not asking permission, but no one else will see these but you."

He lowered his gaze to the pictures once again as he leafed through them, then looked at her. "No, it's fine. Really. I need to get frames for these. Lexi will love them, especially the one of her on the horse. This is one of the best gifts I've ever received. Thank you."

She lifted a shoulder and toed the ground with her boot. "I'm not a pro by any means, but I like playing around with my camera when I have time."

Cole slid a finger under her chin and lifted it. "You have talent. Don't dismiss that."

Her eyes still on his, she smiled. "Are you hungry? Want some lunch? Or maybe some birthday pie?"

As her eyebrow lifted, a spark ignited in his gut at her suggestion. "After peeling all those apples last night, I didn't think I'd want to see another one. But a warm slice of apple pie sounds perfect right now. Especially when I'm joined by my two favorite ladies."

With Lexi holding his left hand, he longed to grab Macey's with his right, but he didn't want to scare her off. Instead, he had to settle for brushing his shoulder against hers.

For now.

The moment they were alone, he planned to pull her into his arms. She'd fit so perfectly there.

She'd fit perfectly into his life as well.

CHAPTER TEN

How HAD EVERYTHING gotten turned around so fast?

Less than a week ago, Macey and Cole had spent Saturday at WinterFest with Lexi, laughing, talking and having the best time.

Now, four days later, they sat on opposing sides of the courtroom.

Macey pressed a hand against her churning stomach as she tried to focus on the judge's words. He smacked his gavel, causing her to jump.

Her eyes skated across the aisle as Cole hung his head. But Wallace high-fived members of the city council.

Macey leaned forward and found Bear with his head in his hands, Wyatt shaking his head, Mom and Dad holding hands and Everly dabbing her eyes.

They had lost.

Despite the family's best efforts of trying to rally the community to get behind preserving the ranch, the judge ruled in favor of the Aspen Ridge City Council—and the strip mall.

Without looking at anyone, especially Cole, Macey stood, walked down the aisle and pushed through the courtroom doors.

She didn't need to see Wallace Crawford gloat.

Standing in the hallway, she rubbed her chilled hands over her arms. Despite standing next to the aging radiator, the heat did little to thaw the numbness in her limbs.

Dressed in a navy skirt with matching jacket, Macey wanted nothing more than to shed the suit for her jeans and a final ride to South Bend before Crawford took possession of the land.

Outside the courtroom, walls painted the color of aged parchment held framed photos of different parts of the county. Was it a coincidence that Macey happened to stand next to the one that showcased South Bend as the original homestead?

She pressed a hand against the dark paneling lining the bottom half of the wall and tapped a toe against the polished floor tile.

The disastrous meeting on Tuesday between

her family and the city council and Wallace Crawford reviewing all of the appraisers' findings ended with her father and Wallace Crawford exchanging heated words. Her father accused Crawford of trying to lowball their family, and he rejected the city council's the final offer. The city council filed a petition in condemnation with the court—most likely at Crawford's urging.

Aaron Brewster had been certain it would have taken several months for the case to come before the judge, but someone pulled strings to get it added to the court docket just two days after the meeting.

And then they lost anyway.

Dad exited the courtroom talking to Aaron, his lips thinned and his jaw clenched. The young attorney's hand tightened on his briefcase. Seeing Macey, he moved to her and touched her elbow. "I'm sorry, Macey."

She lifted a shoulder. "It is what it is. We lost."

"I'll file an appeal."

"Do you think it will do any good?" She tried to keep her tone even.

"I don't know, but I'm going to do everything I can to get the judge to change his mind. We'll take it to state court if we have to."

Tears filled her eyes, but she tried to blink them away as the courtroom doors opened once again and Mom walked out with Bear, Wyatt and Everly. They wandered over to her, heads down and shoulders hunched.

Macey wrapped her arms around her mother. "I'm so sorry, Mom."

"Me, too, sweetheart. Me, too."

Wyatt stood behind Dad, feet apart and his hands clasped behind his back in a perfect military stance. His jaw tightened. Bear ran his fingers along the brim of his hat while he and Dad continued their conversation with Aaron.

Wallace Crawford strutted out of the courtroom with his legal team and members of the city council. Cole trailed behind. His eyes caught Macey's, but she forced herself to look away. He started toward her family, and she turned her shoulder away from him. Maybe he'd take the hint.

The last thing they needed to hear was a bunch of meaningless words. Especially her.

Cole had chosen his side.

And she'd have to live with that.

"Cole. Get a move on it." Wallace Crawford's bellowing voice bounced off the hallway walls.

Cole followed his uncle out the doors.

Somehow, they needed to figure out how to move past this loss. For her, it wasn't just the loss of her grandparents' legacy, but also knowing her relationship with Cole wouldn't be the same again.

She gave herself another swift mental kick for allowing him into her personal circle. For letting her defenses down. She knew better but did it anyway, thinking and hoping for a different resolution.

"Let's head to the diner. Lynetta needs to hear the news from us." Without another word, Dad slipped an arm around Mom's waist and guided her through the lobby and out the door.

Mom rested her head on his shoulder a moment. He whispered something in her ear, and she nodded. He placed a gentle kiss on her forehead.

With everything her parents had gone through, their love continued to grow.

Macey envied that.

Would she have someone who loved and supported her? Someone who stood up for her?

While Cole may be a great father and have

other traits that would make him perfect husband material, they couldn't have a future together as long as he worked for his uncle.

Wyatt cupped the back of Macey's neck. "Come on, sis. Let's ditch this place. It's giving me hives."

Ten minutes later, they gathered at the diner, hands wrapped around white mugs filled with steaming coffee, but no one said anything.

The server took their order, then Dad leaned back in his chair, his eyes weary as lines deepened in his forehead. He looked at each one of them and shook his head. "Well, aren't we a sorry bunch of sad sacks? Are we going to sit here and wallow and let Crawford steal our joy?"

"He's already gaining our land." Bear toyed with his spoon.

"While I don't agree with the man's methods, we do need to abide by the judge's ruling. For now."

"Aaron plans to appeal." Macey stirred cream into her coffee.

Bear scowled. "That could take months."

"Months that we still retain our property."

Dad leaned forward and sipped his coffee. "Listen, we haven't been beaten yet. Sure, this was a curveball, but remember—God's in control. If He wants us to keep our land, then He'll work it out. We need to trust Him. In the meantime, we keep representing the family and standing up for those values that have made us who we are today." He lifted his mug.

Even though Macey didn't have the same perspective, she lifted her mug and clinked it against the others.

Just then, the door flew open, and Lexi ran in. Cole followed her, saw Macey's family sitting at a table near the counter and reached for Lexi. He knelt in front of her and talked too low for Macey to catch his words.

She folded her arms over her chest and shook her head so hard that her braids smacked her in the cheeks. "No, Daddy. I don't wanna go. I want Netta's pancakes."

Cole's face turned the same cherry red as the vinyl on the stools lining the counter. He took his daughter's hand and started to pull her toward the booths lining the wall on the other side of the dining room.

As Lexi turned, she locked eyes with Macey. She pulled her hand out of her father's grasp and raced over to the Stones' table. She tapped a finger against her teeth. "Look, Macey. Piper took me to the dentist. He counted my teeth. No cabities."

"That's so good to hear, sweetie." Macey gathered the child in her arms and buried her face in the little girl's hair, which smelled of baby shampoo. A lump formed in her throat.

"Can I sit with you?" She looked up at Macey with the sweetest smile on her innocent face.

Macey tightened her hold around the child who had wiggled her way into her heart, and tried to find the right words. More than anything she wanted to say yes, but… "Lexi—"

"Lexi, leave Macey and her family alone." Cole strode to their table, his face still red and his jaw tight. "I'm sorry about that."

"But, Daddy, I wanna sit with Macey."

"Not today." He lifted Lexi off Macey's lap and carried the kicking child back out of the diner.

Macey lowered her head and closed her eyes to hold back the tears threatening to fall.

"Hey, you okay?" Everly placed a hand between Macey's shoulder blades.

Opening her eyes, Macey forced a smile and nodded, not quite trusting her voice. She rested her head against her sister's and let out a sigh. Needing some air, Macey stood and reached for her coat. "I'm going to take a walk. Meet you back at the ranch."

She stepped outside and pulled the lapels of her coat closer together as the cold hit her.

"Macey."

She froze and didn't turn at Cole saying her name.

"Can we talk?" The plea in his voice was nearly her undoing.

Without answering, she rounded the corner and headed for the path that snaked along the river. Spying a bench overlooking the water, she brushed off the snow and sat, the cold metal pressing into the backs of her legs.

He sat next to her. Leaning forward, he braced his elbows on his knees and clasped his hands. "I'm sorry. I know this didn't go the way you wanted. I wish I could fix it."

"Where's Lexi?"

"With Everly. I had no right, but I asked her to stay with Lexi so I could talk to you."

The cold seeped through her dress clothes, and Macey stood. Hands shoved deep in her pockets, she finally faced Cole, releasing a brittle laugh. "You're right, Cole. None of this has gone the way we'd hoped. Who wants to have their private property taken away from them?"

He stood and reached for her. She stepped back and nearly lost her footing. Stupid idea to walk a snowy path in heels.

Cole grabbed her arms and drew her close. "None of this has to change what's happening between us."

Her heart slammed against her ribs. She pressed her hands against his chest to prevent him from drawing her into his embrace. "How can you say that? My family is losing part of our property, and you work for the man who was instrumental in taking it. I really wish things were different, Cole. I really do. But we have no future as long as you're working for your uncle. I'm sorry for the lack of notice, but after this week, I feel like I can no longer care for Lexi. The more we're together, the harder it's going to be to say goodbye."

"Goodbye? We live in the same town. We're bound to run into each other."

"I need some space."

"Ugh. I hate that phrase. My ex-wife said the same thing when she walked out of my life."

"I'm not your ex-wife, Cole."

"You're nothing like her. I get that." He shoved his hands in the pockets of his overcoat. "I wish I could say I understand, but I don't."

He took a step toward her and cupped her chin. He looked into her eyes, and she fought to hold his gaze. "I love you, Macey."

Hearing those four words should've sent her running into his arms. Instead, she shook her head, took a step back and held up a hand. "Please don't, Cole."

"Don't what? Feel how I feel? That's not possible." He raked a hand through his hair. "What about the Sweetheart Ball? It's in two days, and I wanted you to come with me as my date."

"I'll finish the final details by myself. But I think it would be best if we attended separately."

"We agreed to see it through to the end."

"The end. How fitting." She laughed, but there was no humor in this situation. Dropping her eyes to her frozen toes, she shook her head. "This will be the last Sweetheart Ball at South Bend. The end of an era." She lifted her head and looked at him again. "And the end of you and me. I'm sorry, Cole, but the answer is no."

The look of anguish that crossed his face nearly had her snatching back her words. But she forced herself to remain quiet. No matter how much it ached to reject his request, Cole couldn't be a part of her life.

Without another word, she headed back to the diner, tears sliding down her cheeks.

She'd give anything to book a tropical vacation somewhere to escape this mess. Perhaps a little distance would heal the ache in her chest.

Who was she kidding?

No amount of miles between them could ease the pain of a broken heart.

COLE HAD NOTHING to celebrate.

While Wallace took this as a great victory, Cole viewed it as a loss. In more ways than one.

Even though he worked for his uncle, he'd been praying for the judge to side with the Stone family. Even if it meant losing the promised promotion.

After seeing the tears in Macey's eyes, Cole felt ashamed. How could he have been a part of taking from the family who'd done nothing but give to him?

Watching Macey walk away had been one of the most painful experiences in his life. Even though he knew they could be good together, he needed to give her time.

Somehow, he needed to make it right.

But how?

"Cole, why aren't you celebrating with us?" Wallace stood in the open doorway of his office.

Cole strode out into the hall, shoving his hands in his front pocket. "You don't need me."

"Of course, I do. Without you, this wouldn't have been possible."

"You wanted me to get them to sign. They didn't sign."

"Semantics. We still got the land. That's the important thing, right?" Wallace turned away when someone from inside his office called his name.

"If you say so," Cole muttered, heading back to his office, closing the door to drown out the sounds from across the hall.

One of the drawbacks of spending so much time on the work sites was he spent only one day a week in his regular office. With court this morning, his work time was shortened. Maybe he could ask Piper to keep Lexi so he could catch up on work. But he'd asked her already to take Lexi to the dentist, and she was caring for her for the rest of the afternoon.

He needed to stop relying on his cousin so much.

Cole needed to hire a nanny.

But did he really want to get in the habit of

spending more and more time at the office? He'd end up like his uncle, who was the last person Cole wanted to emulate.

As he opened his laptop to search for nannies in the area, Cole bumped a picture frame on his desk. He picked up the photo Macey had taken of him and Lexi on the horse the day they'd ridden together at Stone River.

He didn't know much about photography— he could barely take a decent picture of Lexi with his cell phone, but he did know how Macey's pictures made him feel.

The way she captured his daughter's joy and light in her eyes stole his breath. She managed to draw out Lexi's best qualities in a single photo.

She brought out his best qualities as well.

He deleted his search query. He didn't want a nanny.

He wanted Macey. And not only to care for his daughter.

He loved her. Now he needed to find a way to prove how good they could be together.

A knock sounded on his closed door, then it opened.

Bernice, Wallace's secretary, stuck her head

inside, waving a manila envelope. "Hey, Cole. This just came for you."

Cole rounded his desk and took it from her "Thanks, Bernice."

After she left, Cole pulled out the contents and found a letter from Barry Harrelson, Wyatt's private investigator buddy, who Cole had met with to look into his uncle's business dealings, detailing his findings.

Included with a police report were witness statements from a pair of teens who'd been given a couple hundred bucks by his uncle to trash the Stone place. Things didn't look good for his uncle or his business.

If only this information had come yesterday. Then the Stones may have been spared the heartache of going to court. And Macey wouldn't have walked away, taking pieces of his heart with her.

Now that he had these facts, he needed to figure out the best way to handle the situation in order to protect those who mattered most to him.

CHAPTER ELEVEN

MACEY WASN'T SURE she heard correctly.

Maybe it was lack of sleep or the pounding headache from crying into her pillow half the night, but Dad's words must not have registered.

"What do you mean you're not going to appeal?" Tightening her grip on the red scoop she used to drop grain into the feed buckets, Macey tried to keep her voice level, but the tightening in her chest caused a spike in her words.

Once the horses made their way to their stalls, Mom filled their water troughs. Dark circles shadowed her eyes, and her shoulders slumped as she leaned against Patience's stall door.

Head bent, Dad pressed his back against the closed tack room door and tipped up his dusty cowboy hat, revealing weary eyes. Deep lines bracketed his mouth. He coughed into a closed fist, a deep sound rattling from the depths of his barrel chest. "I'm tired, Mace. Your mother's tired. She deserves a vacation, and I want to take her away from this mess for a while."

"Dad, I get that. Both of you are the hardest working people I know and deserve to get away." Macey dropped the scoop in the wheelbarrow and slid an arm around Mom's shoulders, giving her a light squeeze. "But please reconsider accepting the offer. There's still hope with an appeal. And we can retain our property a little longer."

Mom slid a lock of Macey's hair that had fallen out of her ponytail behind her ear. "I know you're upset—"

"Upset is putting it mildly, Mom. South Bend is the core of who we are. Without it, we wouldn't have the rest of Stone River. Selling it feels like we're cutting away our foundation." Tears flushed her eyes. She ducked her head and reached for the broom.

"I'm well aware of what the property means to this family, Macey. Do you think I like this? None of it has sat well with me since we were served with the first notice. But there comes a time when we need to stop fighting."

Macey thrust her hands in the air. "Dad,

there's a difference between fighting and giving up."

"Hey, if you want to think I'm giving up, then that's on you." Dad pushed away from the tack room door. Hands fisted, he glared at her with fire, fatigue…and maybe a little fear in his eyes. "I've spent my whole life on this ranch, and it's gutting me to see it being torn apart. But I have to think about what is best for this family."

Mom stepped between them and placed a hand on his chest. "Deacon, please calm down. You're going to start coughing again. The last thing I want is for you to end up back in the hospital."

"I am calm." His growl betrayed his words.

Mom blew hair out of her face and took the broom from Macey. She swept spilled feed into the dustpan. Always the one to come in to clean up their messes. "There are pros and cons to accepting Wallace Crawford's offer. The money will help with improvements we need done around the ranch. And having a little extra in the bank will help during those lean months when feed prices go up and cattle prices go down."

"So if we have to sell off a little piece of our

acreage for peace of mind, then so be it." Dad wrapped his arm around Mom's shoulders, the two of them facing her. A united front.

She stood alone.

Macey lowered her gaze to the toes of her barn boots, then lifted her head, her voice quiet. "But whose peace of mind, Dad? Do you really want a strip mall in your backyard? Not to mention the traffic and problems we're going to have with driving cattle."

"So we come up with a new driving plan. We adjust." Dad scraped a hand over his face. "Macey, I bleed ranch soil. I was born on this land, and I intend to die here. But in the five plus decades that I've been alive, I've seen how much work it takes to run a spread this size. The two weeks I spent in the hospital opened my eyes to a lot of things, but the greatest was how close I came to losing my life." He slapped a beefy hand against his chest. "While I'm secure in the state of my heart and know where I'll spend eternity, I'm not ready to make your mom a widow just yet. It's time I put her first and start working down her bucket list."

Macey crossed the room and grabbed on to his arm. "You can still do that, Dad. Book

Mom's dream vacation. We'll all chip in and pay for it. After all, it's the least we can do when you two have given us so much."

Dad removed his hat and scratched the back of his head. "We're not taking our kids' money."

She drew in a breath and released it slowly. Schooling her tone, she looked at her father. "Will you take some advice?"

His eyes narrowed. "What's that?"

"Wait until after the Sweetheart Ball to make a decision." Oh, how she hated the pleading in her voice.

He crossed his arms over his chest, then held up a calloused finger. "On one condition."

"Name it."

"The Sweetheart Ball is tomorrow. I'll wait until Monday to announce my final decision to the family. In the meantime, I'll be praying and asking for the Lord's leading. And you have to do the same."

"Absolutely. All I want is what's best for this family." Macey flung her arms around her father's neck. "Thank you, Daddy."

He squeezed her tightly, then drew back, holding on to her elbows. He gave her a stern look, yet compassion flared in his eyes. "Even if what you want isn't what's best for the ranch?"

She considered his words, then nodding slowly. "Yes, on Monday, I'll abide by whatever decision you make. After all, the ranch is in your name, so you and Mom need to make the final decision. I just hope we don't have to watch them destroy what Grandpa and Grandma worked so hard to build."

Her phone vibrated in her back pocket. she took it out and saw Cole's face on the screen. She hesitated a moment, then her thumb hovered over the decline button.

"Talk to him."

"I have nothing to say to him."

"Then just listen."

Heaving a sigh, Macey answered. "Hello?"

"Macey. For a moment, I didn't think you were going to answer."

"For a moment, I wasn't going to."

"I'm glad you did. I need to talk to you. It's important. Will you let me escort you to the ball, then we can talk afterward?"

"I gave you my answer already, Cole. Let's not rehash this. Please."

"I'll ask one more time, and I'll respect your answer, but at least hear me out. Will you please allow me to take you to the ball and then talk afterward?"

Macey closed her eyes. Everything in her wanted to say no, end the call, and not see Cole ever again. But did she truly want to do that? After ten years of not seeing him?

Cole wasn't that teenager looking for acceptance. He was a father who adored his daughter who was put in a tough position through no fault of his own.

Could she truly blame him for that?

If she had been in his shoes, what would she have done?

"Macey?"

"I'm here. I'm thinking."

"Have you decided?"

"Okay."

"Okay…you'll go to the ball with me?"

"Yes, I'll go to the ball with you. Then we can talk. But there's still so much between us."

"Like my job."

"Well, yes, for one."

"Are you saying if I quit my job then you and I have a chance of a future together?"

"I do not want to have this discussion on the phone. Let's talk this weekend."

"I'll pick you up at seven."

"Six. I want to be there early to ensure everything's set up."

"Okay, great. Six o'clock, it is. Thank you, Macey."

She ended the call and clutched her phone in her hand.

Did she make the right choice?

Only time would tell.

IT WAS TOO late to back out. No matter how much she wanted to.

But everyone expected her to show up at the Sweetheart Ball. She'd given her word, and Macey couldn't—wouldn't—let them down.

She'd put a smile in place, show up and pretend to have a great time.

The doorbell rang, and Macey's heart jumped. Taking a final look in the mirror, she smoothed a hand over the front of her strawberry-pink A-line gown with wide straps and beaded bodice. She'd pinned her hair to the side, secured it with rhinestone combs, and curls cascaded over her left shoulder. She tucked her feet into the silver sandals she'd purchased at Regals that made her feel like Cinderella.

Hopefully, when the clock struck twelve, she wouldn't be racing away from the ball.

For the past three days, she'd been agonizing over her talk with Cole and came to the conclusion she couldn't run away because she was hurt or scared. She planned to end this evening on a high note by telling Cole she loved him.

She couldn't deny it any longer.

A light tap sounded on the door, and it opened. Her father stood in the doorway, hands tucked in his black trouser pockets. His silver-streaked hair had been combed neatly, and he looked so handsome in his black suit, white shirt, and bolo tie that used to belong to Grandpa.

He shook his head as a smile crawled across his face. "Macey, you're going to snatch that boy's breath right out of his lungs."

Macey touched one of the sprayed curls resting on her shoulder.

She could only hope.

"He's here, by the way."

"Cole?"

Dad nodded and pressed a shoulder against the door frame. "I still don't know what happened in Denver, and I know things haven't been easy since you've returned, but I'm so glad you're home. Thank you for being here for your mother and the rest of the family."

Tears warmed her eyes, and she forced them back. She didn't need to meet Cole downstairs with streaked makeup. She picked up the hem of her dress and crossed the room. "Thanks, Daddy. I'm so glad too."

He held out his elbow. "Let's not keep your young man waiting any longer."

With her stomach in knots, she took her father's elbow and they descended the steps slowly. As Cole came into view, her own breath caught in her lungs.

He stood in the foyer, a small box in one hand and his gray cowboy hat in the other. He wore a charcoal-gray suit with a tie that was nearly an exact match to the color of her dress, and polished black shoes.

As she stepped off the last step, he set his hat and the box on a nearby chair and reached for her hands, holding her at arm's length. "Wow, Macey. You look...that dress...you're beautiful."

Dad cleared his throat, and Cole dropped her hands as if he'd been stung. He straightened and cleared his throat. "Good evening, sir."

Dad nodded. "Cole."

Macey smothered a smile and retrieved her coat from the closet.

Cole took it and held it while she slipped her

arms in the sleeves. He reached for his hat and handed the box to her. "I got you something."

She opened it and found a white calla lily with a bright pink center resting between two miniature white roses and greenery. She lifted the corsage to her nose. "Thank you, Cole. It's beautiful. I'll have you put it on me once we arrive at the ball, so it doesn't get flattened by my coat."

He rested a hand on the small of her back. "Ready to go?"

Was she?

She reached for her matching clutch and nodded. "I want to ensure everything is set up. I don't want anything to spoil this evening."

Cole guided Macey outside and down the cleared steps. He unlocked a silver SUV, opened the passenger door and helped her inside. He rounded the front and slid behind the wheel.

"Did you trade in your truck?"

"No, this is Piper's. She said you'd have an easier time getting into her car than my truck."

"She's not going?"

Cole started the engine. "No, she hasn't dated since Ryland died and didn't want to attend alone. She's keeping Lexi overnight. They're having a sleepover in the living room."

"Sounds like fun." Macey pressed a hand against her stomach. Why was she so nervous? She'd known Cole most of her life. The ball was set on her family's property. She knew most of the people planning to attend.

But tonight was different.

Cole headed toward South Bend and parked in front of the barn.

Light flakes of snow drifted from the inky black sky as he reached for her hand and escorted her inside.

Her breath caught. She pressed a manicured hand against her throat.

After Everly learned about her walking away from Cole, she took over decorating duties. And Macey didn't protest. She couldn't find the energy to do it on her own. Instead, she'd sent Everly her notes. She and her friends promised to make Macey proud.

And boy, did they.

How they'd manage to transform a very old barn into a fairy-tale setting escaped her. Tiny lights had been strung through yards of tulle and hung from the barn beams over long tables covered in white linens.

LED votive candles flickered at each place setting, sending light over the individual roses placed across the gleaming white plates. Bouquets of miniature pink roses, bright pink Stargazer lilies, white gerbera daisies and greenery lined the tables. The scents of the flowers fragranced the air. A stage had been set up toward the back of the barn along with an area cleared for dancing.

Uncle Pete's servers finished setting the tables and started setting out the hors d'oeuvres.

Behind her, Cole rested his hands on her shoulders. He whispered in her ear, "You did it, Mace. You pulled it off, and the place looks incredible."

She turned around, and his hands slid down her arms until he entwined his fingers with hers. She gave his hands a gentle squeeze. "Actually, Everly did the decorating."

"With your vision. This is everything we discussed, including the single roses."

"Okay, then, *we* did it together." Standing on tiptoe, she pressed a light kiss against his cheek. "Thank you for helping my family with this."

He wrapped his arms around her and held her close for a moment. "I did this for you. I think we make a great team, and I don't want it to end. It could be the beginning of something wonderful."

She longed to stay in his embrace, but it wasn't the time. For now, they needed to focus on hosting a wonderful evening.

Later, they'd talk. And it gave her one more thing to look forward to.

CHAPTER TWELVE

NOTHING WOULD RUIN TONIGHT.

Cole planned to make sure of it.

From the moment he watched Macey walk down the steps at her parents' house, he knew, now more than ever, they were meant to be together.

Not because she looked so incredible in her dress. But it was the look in her eyes that mirrored what he was feeling in his heart.

And he couldn't wait to tell her.

Again.

But this time, he hoped she'd reciprocate those feelings.

For now, he'd mingle, enjoy dinner and stand by Macey's side as they oversaw this event that meant so much to both of them.

Cole filled two cups with punch. Then he came face-to-face with Barrett. "Hey, Bear. Good to see you, man."

Macey's brother stuffed his hands in his pockets and gave Cole a quick nod. "If it weren't for the fact that my grandparents started this annual event, I'd be holed up in my cabin watching a hockey game."

"It's good to dress up and get out every once in a while."

Bear lifted a shoulder. "If you say so. Personally, I prefer solitude over a lot of unnecessary noise." He looked around the room. "Piper didn't come?"

Cole shook his head. "She wasn't sure about getting a sitter for Avery, so she offered to watch Lexi for me."

Bear's jaw tightened. He nodded again.

Even though Cole's excuse sounded flimsy, they both knew the real reason she stayed away.

Barrett Stone.

But that was for the two of them to work out themselves. Cole wasn't about to get into the middle of that fight.

Macey joined them and slid her hand in the crook of her brother's elbow. "You clean up quite nicely, Bear. So, it is possible to wear something other than worn Levi's, your cowboy hat and still survive."

Bear smiled. Just barely. "Believe me, once

dinner is over and Mom and Dad make their speech, I'm out of here. Then the suit can hang in the closet for another year."

"I'm glad you're here now." She gave him a quick hug, then turned to Cole. "Are one of those cups for me?"

Cole handed her one. "Sorry, I got side-tracked."

Moments later, they were joined by Macey's parents. Dressed in a long-sleeved red lacy gown, Mrs. Stone looked gorgeous and gave Cole an idea of how Macey could look in a couple of decades. Mr. Stone couldn't keep his eyes off his wife.

That was the kind of relationship Cole wanted.

"Macey and Cole, you two have done an incredible job. We can't thank you enough for pitching in to make this ball happen."

Macey tucked her arm into Cole's elbow. "I couldn't have done it without Cole's help."

Cole shrugged. "I didn't do much. This is mostly Macey's doing."

She nudged him. "You did more than that and you know it, Mr. Modest. The roses were Cole's idea. And to be honest, they were a huge hit. Plus the bouquets on the tables are in memory of loved ones who lost their fights due to cardiac issues."

Mrs. Stone glanced at her husband who nodded, then she reached for Cole's hand. "We loved your mother. Losing her so young was tragic. Deacon and I have been talking, and we would like to set up a foundation in her name to help women—single mothers, especially—to ensure they have access to quality medical care. With your permission we would like to call it the Jane Crawford Heart to Heart Foundation. We'll meet with our lawyer to set up the proper paperwork. Then we'll send out the information to all of our donors so they can invest too."

Cole blinked through a sudden haze and struggled to swallow past the boulder in his throat. He brushed a thumb under his eye. "Why would you do that? After everything my uncle has done to hurt your family, and my part in trying to acquire your land?"

Mr. Stone shoved a hand in his front pocket. "One doesn't have anything to do with the other. Your mother was an important part of your life and ours. She was a hard worker who deserved more than what she got, but she never complained. All she wanted was to give you the best life. And this is one way that we can honor

her. If you agree, then we will announce it tonight after dinner, son."

Son.

When Mr. Stone said it, Cole felt a sense of
pride, like he was accepted and belonged. Unlike the way it felt when his uncle used it.

Cole nodded and held out his hand. "Yes, absolutely. Thank you, sir. I'm so honored. And
you know my mother would be appalled by
such attention."

They laughed, and Lynetta came up to them,
dressed in a lovely black gown covered in some
sort of silver sparkle. "Hey, guys, what do you
say we find our seats so they can start serving
dinner?"

"Good idea. I was too nervous to eat lunch,
but now I'm famished." Instead of following her
family to their table, Macey tugged on Cole's
hand. "Will you come with me as I say grace?"

"You sure?"

"Yes. More than anything." The way she
looked at him made Cole want to kiss her in
front of everyone but he wouldn't embarrass
her that way, especially not knowing how she
truly felt about him.

Holding on to her hand, Cole guided her to
the stage.

Macy stepped up to the microphone. "Excuse me. If everyone could find their seats, then we'll say grace and get dinner started."

Chairs scraped across the wooden floor as people settled in their places. Once the room quieted, Macey bowed her head and clasped her hands in front of her, "Dear Lord, thank You for the abundant blessings You've given each one of us. Thank You for this time we can gather together and raise money for such a worthy cause. Thank You for the food and all the hands that made this night a success. Be with those who are supporting loved ones with cardiac issues and those who have lost those they've loved. May we always remember and not take our health for granted. May the fellowship be sweet and the donations plenty. Amen."

Amens echoed throughout the barn.

Her words of thanks and gratitude flowed over him, especially the touching way she included the families who struggled with the loss of their loved ones.

He held her chair as she sat with her family, and he took his place between Macey and her aunt.

Lynetta covered his hand and gave it a gentle squeeze. "Your mom would be so proud of you."

Fresh tears washed his eyes, and he blinked them back. He hoped so.

Throughout dinner, Cole tried to pay attention to the conversation and the delicious salmon in front of him, but his focus was shaken by Macey's arm constantly brushing against his sleeve and the fragrance wafting from her hair.

As their meal progressed and their plates cleared, an assortment of desserts was delivered to each of the tables.

Cole chose flourless chocolate cake. He'd just dug his fork into the cake for his first bite when the side door flew open and slammed against the wall.

A sudden draft blew through the room.

Cole looked up from his dessert and his stomach took a nosedive.

His uncle stood in the doorway, feet apart and hands on his hips. "Well, well, well. What have we here?"

The room fell silent as Wallace strode across the floor, his footsteps measured and heavy. Mr. Stone, Bear and Wyatt slid back their chairs and pushed to their feet.

Setting his napkin next to his plate, Cole stood and glanced at Macey. "Excuse me."

He made his way through the guests and reached Wallace. "What are you doing here?"

"It's a public event. I can be here."

"Not without a ticket. And you didn't buy one."

Wallace waved his hands. "Buy one? Why should I when this place is going to be mine soon enough? And you know what my first plan will be? I'm going to tear this eyesore down board by board."

Cole pressed a hand to his uncle's shoulder and turned him toward the door. "You need to leave."

Wallace shrugged off his hand. "Get your hands off me, boy. I'm not going anywhere."

"Yes, you are," Mr. Stone said. "Wallace, this is between you and me. If you want to settle this now, then let's step outside. But you will not ruin this event." He moved next to Cole, his voice steady and quiet.

Wallace framed his fingers around his belt buckle. "Deacon Stone, you think you're better than everyone else, but you're nothing more than a poor rancher trying to hold on to mommy and daddy's legacy."

Jaw tight, Mr. Stone took another step toward Wallace. "As I said, this is between you and me."

Someone touched Cole's sleeve. He turned and found Macey standing next to him. She reached for his hand and gave it a light squeeze.

Noticing Macey, Wallace sneered and pointed the finger at her. "And you. You come home and stir up all kinds of trouble. You say you're fighting for your family. But you're just being selfish. The strip mall would've provided jobs for the community. But you don't care about that. You're nothing more than a spoiled princess who gets whatever she wants."

Macey's cheeks reddened as Wallace's words echoed off the rafters.

Before Cole could say anything, Mr. Stone stepped between them. "Crawford, that's enough. I will not allow you to speak to my daughter like that."

Wallace moved in front of Cole and poked him in the chest. "After everything I've done for you, this is how you betray me?" He circled his finger around the Stones. "For them? You had me investigated. I can't work with people I don't trust. Now I know where your loyalties lie. Once a charity case, always a charity case.

Good riddance. You can try to side with them, but face it, you don't belong."

Bear and Wyatt each grabbed one of Wallace's arms and propelled him toward the door. "It's time for you to say good night, Mr. Crawford."

"This isn't over, Cole. You can count on it," Wallace yelled over his shoulder as the Stone brothers forced him outside.

Hands deep in his pockets and shoulders hunched, Cole dropped his head as Wallace's words echoed through his head. Heat scalded his neck and crawled across his cheeks.

Who was he kidding? He didn't belong here any more than his uncle did. When people talked about tonight, they wouldn't remember all of Macey's hard work. Instead, they'd gossip about his uncle crashing the event and the venomous words he spewed.

"Is it true?"

Cole's head jerked up. Macey stood in front of him, hands clasped and eyes wide and hollow.

"Is what true?"

"Did you have your uncle investigated?"

"Yes."

"When?"

"Soon after the vandalism incident."

"You had doubts about your uncle and you didn't come forward? That kind of information could have halted the proceedings. Or at the very least, it could have given the judge a reason to wait instead of ruling in favor of the city council."

Cole held up a hand. "Macey, let me explain."

She shook her head, her eyes glistening as she bit her lips. "I think you should go."

"Go?" Surely, she didn't mean…

"Yes, go." She folded her arms over her chest. "When your uncle said all those things about me, you didn't say a word in my defense."

A decade-old memory resurfaced, and Cole heaved a sigh. "Macey, it's not like that. Your dad spoke up before I could. Everything happened so quickly. Then your brothers were hauling him to the door. I wasn't going to add to the scene by chasing after them. The investigation was one of the things I wanted to talk to you about after the ball. I just got the reports."

Macey nodded, but the skepticism on her face showed she didn't believe him. "I wish you would have confided in me about your doubts. Something, anything, to give me a little hope.

But you stayed quiet. I truly thought I meant more to you than that." Macey gave him a look that splintered his heart and walked back to the table where her family sat.

A place where he didn't belong.

Pulling his keys from his pocket, Cole moved to the coat rack, grabbed his coat and hat then headed outside into the frigid February night.

The wind stung his face, but the pain was nothing compared to the shredding of his heart.

Wallace was right—he'd always be a charity case who didn't belong. Especially with someone like Macey. Somehow, he needed to figure out how to live without her.

IT WASN'T SUPPOSED to end like this.

Maybe he should've gone home and waited until Monday instead of going straight to the office after leaving Macey behind at the ball. Packing up his things at midnight may not have been the smartest thing to do.

At least, his uncle wouldn't have time to manipulate him into staying. It was better this way.

Still dressed in his suit but with his tie wadded up in his jacket pocket, Cole's head pounded as he shoved the rest of his personal things in his backpack. He placed the framed photo Macey had taken of Lexi on top, careful not to break the glass.

"So that's it then? After everything I've done for you? You're walking away?" Wallace fisted his hands on his hips and glared at Cole from the open doorway.

"Walking away? You just fired me, remember?"

"What was I supposed to do? You had me investigated."

"If you had nothing to hide, then what's the big deal?" Cole zipped his bag closed.

"You should've been man enough to come to me."

"I tried. You wouldn't listen and acted clueless when I asked about my hat. I'm not taking the blame for your dirty work. If you want the Stone River property so badly, then obtain it legally."

"Oh, I have it already. Don't you remember the judge ruling in my favor?"

"Right, then you won't need me anymore." Cole slid the strap of his backpack onto his shoulder, gave his desk another glance to ensure he didn't miss anything. "Don't be surprised if the police show up with questions. The Stones' legal team will be insisting on another appraisal once they get wind of you bribing Montrose. Since their appraiser assessed their land higher than the price you offered anyway... I mean, the council offered, they may have a different opinion about fair market value."

Wallace's eyes narrowed. "You're worthless, you know that?"

Cole tried to shrug off the barb. "So you've said at least three times already. Insulting me won't help your cause, nor does it make me want to keep this job any longer."

"You wouldn't have measured up in that promotion anyway. Glad I saved myself the trouble by letting you walk now. Since the condo was another perk of working for me, consider this your eviction notice since I own that too."

"Perk? I paid rent, so I'm entitled to thirty days' notice."

He waved away Cole's words. "Whatever. You'll never be anything more than the charity case I picked up the day after your mother's funeral."

Cole fisted his hand and forced himself not to punch his uncle's smug face. "I'd rather be a charity case and have my values rather than all the money in the world and do people dirty in business."

"That goes to show how little you know about how business gets done. Everyone gets their hands dirty."

"Not me." He headed for the door. "I suggest backing out of the Stone River deal and leave the property to who it belongs."

"And I suggest you take your opinions elsewhere because no one here is listening."

"I'm sure the sheriff will listen when I talk to him about the two guys you hired to vandalize the Stones' property." Cole pulled out his keys, removed the ones to this office building and the mobile office at the Riverside Condos job site, and tossed them on his former desk.

Wallace scoffed. "No one's going to believe you."

Cole patted his computer bag and smiled. "We'll see about that."

Chuckling, Wallace shook his head. "You hypocrite. You talk about me doing dirty business, but you're doing the same thing by hiring some punk PI."

"I'm doing what's right." With that, Cole exited the office, allowing the door to slam closed behind him.

The weight of his actions slowed his steps as he crossed the parking lot to his truck. He dropped the backpack inside, then climbed in, and gripped the steering wheel as his chest tightened.

How could he provide for his daughter without a job? Or provide her with the quality medical care she deserved? And now he needed to find a new place to live. His savings would cover them for only a couple of months while he searched.

Standing up for what he believed came with a price, and he was about to pay it. He blew out a breath, loosened his grip on the steering wheel and started the engine, trying not to dwell on the fact that his life was falling apart.

CHAPTER THIRTEEN

MACEY SHOULD'VE WOKEN up with a smile on her face, reliving a magical night at the Sweetheart Ball. Except when the clock struck midnight, she was home alone, tossing and turning while replaying her conversation with Cole.

Why had she reacted that way? Why couldn't she just trust him?

With a pounding headache, she forced herself out of bed and dressed quietly in her barn clothes so she didn't wake Everly.

Even though every part of her wanted nothing more than to crawl under the covers, it would've been a waste of time. She'd lain there replaying last night's events over again in her head and calling herself a fool for pushing Cole away.

He didn't deserve to be treated like that by his uncle. Or by her.

Instead of giving him a chance to explain, she insisted he leave because of her own selfishness.

Skipping the kitchen and the coffee her body was begging for, Macey headed for the mudroom and slid her feet into her boots. Then she shrugged on her barn coat and jammed a hat over her ears. Instead of jumping in the truck or grabbing one of the utility vehicles, Macey trudged through the dark, her snow-covered dirt path illuminated only by the glow of the moon. The crisp air pushed away her headache and shook her out of her fatigued haze.

As she pushed open the barn door, she was surprised to see a light on inside. Who else was up this early? Probably Bear. He seldom slept. The horses whinnied.

Macey headed upstairs to where the bales had been stacked and dropped hay through the floor door. Then she returned downstairs, broke it up and dropped hay in each of the stalls. While the horses ate, she prepared the grain specific for each one, carried the buckets to the right stalls and poured it into their feeders. Then she rinsed out their water buckets and refilled them with fresh water.

The door opened, sending shards of daylight

across the barn floor. Mom stepped inside and closed it quickly to keep the cold out.

"You're up early." Cheeks red, she pulled off her hat, peeled off her gloves and stuffed them in her pocket.

"Couldn't sleep so I decided to get a start on chores. When I came in, the light was on but no one was here." Macey walked the line of stalls and peeked inside to make sure each of the horses were eating.

"Maybe Bear's up and about doing something. You know that boy hasn't slept well since his friend was killed."

"He blames himself for Ryland getting on that bull."

"Well, he shouldn't. It was an accident." Mom rounded up the buckets Macey had used and rinsed them with the hose. "Once they're done eating, I'll help you turn them out and we can get their stalls cleaned before church."

"You don't have to do that. I'll handle it. I'm staying home today." Macey grabbed a broom and swept up the leftover hay.

"You okay?"

That was a loaded question.

Macey shrugged. "I didn't sleep well. And to

be honest, I don't want to face people after last night's debacle."

Mom frowned. "What are you talking about? Last night was fantastic. Sure, Wallace's outburst was uncalled for and I was disappointed when Cole left, but everything else was perfect. In fact, I think you should consider taking over the ball from now on."

Macey leaned on her broom. "You can't be serious?"

"Yes, I am." Mom put the buckets back in place and moved the hose out of the way. "You need to reframe your thinking. Last night's ball raised more money than the previous year."

"But people won't remember that. They'll be talking about Wallace's behavior."

"Let them talk, Macey. Have the courage and confidence to be above that." Mom dried her hands on her jeans, then placed them on her hips. "Just why did Cole leave early last night?"

"We had a disagreement."

"About what?" Mom's gentle tone lacked judgment.

"When his uncle said those terrible things, he didn't stand up for me. It felt like prom night all over again. But I'm not that eighteen-year-old girl anymore." Tears warmed Macey's eyes. "In the heat of the moment, though, I cared only about myself and the property. Not his feelings, or the horrible things his uncle said to him. I feel terrible and couldn't sleep because of it."

"So go apologize and make things right."

"It's not that easy."

"It doesn't have to be complicated, honey. Holding on to someone you love is more important than holding on to a piece of property." Mom hooked her elbow around Macey's. "Come on. Let's head back to the house and get breakfast going. Your dad or one of the boys can turn out the horses."

Heads ducked against the wind that howled across the pasture, they hurried down the rutted path and inside the ranch house where the warmth thawed their freezing cheeks.

The scent of fresh coffee lingered in the air.

Macey toed off her boots, hung up her coat and headed to the kitchen. The rest of the family had made it out of bed. Dad had his Bible open on the table while Tanner and Mia sat in their booster seats, eating pancakes and scrambled eggs. Everly, Bear and Wyatt sat at the breakfast bar drinking coffee while scrolling on their phones.

Dad looked up from his reading. "Macey. I expected you to still be asleep after last night."

She grabbed a cup out of the cabinet and filled it with coffee. Then she added creamer and wrapped her hands around the warm ceramic. "I tossed and turned most of the night, so I decided to start chores early. Horses need to be turned out."

Bear drained his cup and pushed back his chair. "I'll do it. I'm heading that way anyway."

He opened the dishwasher, placed his dirty dishes instead, then bumped the door closed with his hip.

The landline rang. His back to the family, Bear grabbed it. "Stone River Ranch. Barrett Stone speaking."

He listened a moment, then turned. His eyes sparked as a smile spread across his face. "You don't say. Well, thanks a lot, man. Yes, I'll let them know. Dad can give you a call tomorrow and set up a time to work out the details."

He returned the handset to the base and let out a low laugh, shaking his head. "Well, it looks like we're gonna have to tighten our belts another notch to get the money we need for improvements around here."

Dad leaned back in his chair. "Why? What's going on?"

Bear nodded toward the phone. "That was Aaron Brewster. He just had an unexpected phone call from Cole, who has proof that his uncle was behind the vandalism and paid off his appraiser to assess the land for less than what it's actually worth. On Monday, Aaron's filing a motion to stop the proceedings. The matter's been turned over to the police department. Aaron's quite sure the land will be staying in the family."

Wyatt thrust his arms in the air and let out a whoop.

Mom rounded the table and Dad hugged her so tightly he lifted her off the floor. "Cole is such a blessing. He trusted his gut and made a difficult choice. Without him, Wallace would continue to get away with his dirty tricks."

Macey stared into her coffee cup through a sheen of tears.

Once again, Dad was right—if God wanted them to keep the land, then He'd work it out. And He used Cole to do it.

Macey needed to make this right. Not because they may be able to retain their land but because—as Mom said—it was more important holding on to someone you loved than a piece of property.

A simple apology and a request for a do-over were necessary to heal this rift between them.

Could she persuade Cole to give her another chance?

IF THIS WASN'T rock bottom, then Cole didn't know just how much harder he could hit.

The anxiety of the day twisted his gut. Somehow, he needed to get the shaking in his fingers to stop.

At least he'd done the right thing calling Aaron. He could've waited until Monday, but it seemed important to let the Stones know as soon as possible.

He stood in front of the sliding doors that overlooked his deck and stared at the river flowing behind the condo. The overhead afternoon sunshine glazed the surface, turning it frosty white. Bundled against the cold, a man, woman and small child walked a dog along the paved walkway parallel to the river.

A family.

He had the perfect child. Now he just needed the perfect wife to complete him.

Macey.

But that was out of the question now.

Every time he thought about her, an ache gripped him, making it tough to breathe.

He moved away from the doors and returned to the kitchen where an open box sat on the counter next to the sink.

He hated packing. Seemed as if half his life was spent putting everything he owned into boxes and storing it until he found his forever home.

When would that happen?

He wasn't about to uproot Lexi every couple of years when the landlord decided to raise the rent and they needed to find a cheaper place to live. It was time to buy a house, but to do that, he needed a job.

A quiet knock sounded on the front door. Macey?

Heart in his throat, Cole hurried to open it.

He found Lynetta on the front porch, holding on to a large bag, and he forced back his disappointment. "Hey, Lynetta. Come on in."

She stepped inside, sat the bag on the floor and unwound her scarf. "You weren't in church this morning. So I wanted to stop by and check on you. How are you doing?"

"I'm fine." The automatic response slipped out before he had time to check his words.

Lynetta cocked her head, raised an eyebrow and gave him a look that said she didn't believe a word he'd said. "Cole."

He stuffed his hands in his pockets and shook his head slowly. Pressure mounted behind his eyes as weight pressed against his chest. His nose burned as his throat thickened. To his horror, tears leaked out and slid down his face, but he didn't have the strength to swipe them away.

Without a word, Lynetta wrapped him in her arms. He buried his face in her neck and wept as a tangle of fear and frustration that he'd been trying to keep knotted unraveled at her simple question. He gently separated himself from her embrace and dragged the back of his hand across his eyes.

"Sorry."

"Oh, honey, you have nothing to apologize for." She cupped his face and brushed her thumbs over his cheeks.

He waved for her to have a seat on the couch. "I didn't mean to break down like that."

"You needed to get it out." She reached for her bag and carried it into the kitchen where she unloaded several takeout boxes. "I made

you a meal. And of course, pancakes for Lexi."
She looked around. "Where is she, by the way?
And Polly."

"They're at Piper's. After last night, I needed
some time alone to think. And make a plan."

Lynetta pressed her back against the sink and
folded her arms over her chest. "A plan? For
what? Talk to me."

Cole rubbed his forehead, hoping to ease
the throbbing behind his eyes. "I lost my job,
which also includes benefits for Lexi. And since
my uncle owns the condo, I need to find a
new place to live. Without an income and an
address, I could lose my daughter." His voice
broke at that last word.

Lynetta moved over to him and cupped her
hands around his face. "Listen to me—you will
not lose your daughter. Before your mama died,
I promised to take care of you, but then your
uncle took you in. For years I carried the guilt
of letting her down. I can help you now though.
Pete and I have money set aside. It's yours. For
whatever you need. Medical bills. Food. Start-
up cost for a new apartment."

*"You'll never be anything more than the charity
case."*

Heat crawled up his neck. He couldn't risk

looking at her, seeing the pity soaking her eyes. Cole moved out of her hands. "No, I won't take your money."

"Why not?"

"My mother taught me we are not charity cases. I need to be able to provide for my daughter on my own."

"For as much as I loved your mother, she was more stubborn than the bulls Pete used to ride. She spent most of her life proving to your father's family that she didn't need any of their money and her attitude went in the wrong direction."

"But it's up to me to make my own way. To carry my own burdens. To take care of my own problems. I can't afford to rely on the help of others. I had to rely on my uncle and he held it against me, saying I owed him. I won't owe anyone else again."

Lynetta tugged on Cole's arm, forcing him to look at her. Her brown eyes shimmered in the dim light and compassion lined her face. "Oh, honey, I am nothing like your uncle. I love you as if you were my own son. And Lexi is like the granddaughter I'll never have. There's nothing I wouldn't do in this world to protect either one of you. I love you guys."

"We love you too."

"Besides, there's a difference between being a charity case and helping someone in need. You say you have to carry your own burdens, but that's where you're wrong. Jesus died on the cross so we could lay our burdens at His feet. Burdens we weren't meant to carry, might I add. Trust God to do what He knows is best for you. And for Lexi."

Cole allowed Lynetta's words to settle into his bones. He rubbed his palms together, then dropped his hands to his side. "I don't even know where to begin. I just want what's best for my daughter."

Lynetta sandwiched his hands between hers. "There are programs in place to help you with Lexi's care. It does not make you a charity case. There's a small apartment above the diner. Our current tenant just closed on his house, and he's moving out this weekend. I'll go through and give it a good scrub, then you and Lexi can live there rent free until you can find another job."

Cole couldn't talk past the lump clogging his throat once again. "I don't know what to say."

"Say thank you." She opened her arms.

He walked into her embrace. "Thank you, Lynetta."

As he buried his face into the curve of her

neck and breathed in the familiar scents of fresh-baked bread and vanilla, the burdens that had been building inside him crumbled.

Maybe by trusting and leaning into God and others, he didn't have to make his own way. Maybe he could finally lower his arms and stop carrying the world on his shoulders.

COLE TAPED THE lid shut and wrote Dishes—Fragile on the box in black permanent marker. Then, he stacked it by the door, grabbed an empty box and headed back to the kitchen.

Inspired after talking with Lynetta, he wanted to get everything packed and be done with the condo, his uncle...all of it.

The doorbell rang in the too-quiet condo. With Lexi napping in her bed, he tried to stay quiet so he didn't disturb her.

He dropped the box by the sink and headed for the door. He opened it to find Wyatt standing on his front porch. "Hey, man. Come in." He stepped aside to let his friend enter. "What's going on?"

He eyed the boxes. "Moving?"

"Yeah, I guess I am." Cole waved a hand toward the couch. "Have a seat. Want some coffee? I haven't packed the mugs or coffee maker yet."

"Sure, sounds good."

He headed to the kitchen and opened the cabinet. Instead of sitting on the couch, Wyatt followed him and leaned against the doorjamb. "Everything okay?"

Cole's fingers tightened around the coffeepot handle. "I'm…hanging in there."

"Anything I can do?" Wyatt took the cup Cole held out to him. "I understand hanging in there."

Instead of refilling his own mug, Cole gripped the edge of the sink. "After the fiasco at the ball, I lost my job. I'm moving above the diner until I can find a job and a house to buy. Trying not to feel like a failure."

The cup clinked against the counter as Wyatt set his coffee down. He moved beside Cole and clapped a hand on his shoulder. "I get it, man. When I lost Linnea and had to take care of Mia on my own, I felt like I was drowning without even being near a body of water."

Cole nodded, not having words to equate to the pressure that had been steadily building behind his rib cage. "How'd you survive?"

"My daughter needed a father. And I needed help. So I left the corps and returned to Stone

River where my family rallied together to lend a hand."

"Yeah, I don't have that option."

"You're wrong. Even though your parents are gone, you do have family. You have Piper. You have Lynetta. You have us."

Cole eyed him. "You guys? Right. I'm sure your family hates me after everything my uncle put them through."

"Again, you're wrong. My family loves you and always will."

"I doubt your sister shares that same sentiment."

"Macey..." Wyatt trailed off, then turned, pressed his back against the counter and folded his arms over his chest. "Well, I think you and my sister need to have a talk. To clear the air once and for all." Wyatt reached into his back pocket and pulled out his wallet. He removed a business card and handed it to Cole. "Also, if it weren't for the guys in my support group, I seriously don't know what I would've done. My family helps to lighten my load, and these guys keep me grounded. They've been there and get what I'm going through. I think they could do the same for you too. Next get-together's tomorrow night at the church. You're welcome to join us."

"I've carried everything so long on my own. I'm not sure I know how to unload onto someone else."

"Dude, I hear you. Losing my wife nearly killed me. We'd been together since ninth grade. My daughter was my saving grace. She gave me purpose, a reason to wake up each day and take that first step. When I returned to the ranch, Aunt Lynetta said to me, 'Wyatt, trusting God requires action. You need to let go of your fears and worries, then lay them at the Father's feet. Then you have to step back and allow Him to do good work, within you and for you. Yes, sometimes that requires pain, but that pain refines our faith. Take that first step.'"

Cole chuckled. "She said essentially the same thing when she dropped by earlier."

"She's a great lady. She said she wasn't meant to have her own babies so she'll take care of those around her. And she does a great job."

"She's been like a mother to me and a grandmother to Lexi."

Wyatt poked Cole's chest. "Let her in, man. Let her help. It blesses her as much as it blesses you."

Cole nodded, his throat tight. "So I'm learning."

Wyatt grinned. "The door's open. You decide if you're going to walk in."

Cole fingered the card and tapped it against his palm. "Thanks, man."

Wyatt glanced at his watch. "Oh, hey, I gotta split. I'm meeting Mom and Dad at Aaron Brewster's office. Thanks for that, by the way. It took guts."

Cole lifted a shoulder. "It was the least I could do after the pain I caused."

"Your uncle. Not you. Remember that. By the way, Macey's at the ranch looking after Tanner and Mia right now."

Cole closed the door behind Wyatt and pulled out his phone. As much as he wanted to call Macey, what could he say? He had nothing to offer her except his heart.

Would it be enough?

CHAPTER FOURTEEN

MACEY COULDN'T DENY it any longer—she missed Cole. And Lexi.

In the short time she'd been back in Aspen Ridge, they managed to become important parts of her life. She hadn't seen them in nearly a week, and a part of her felt incomplete.

She needed to stop being a chicken and apologize.

Now that the storm had passed and the sun brightened the sky on an unseasonably warm day, Macey decided to take Cheyenne out for a ride.

She wavered with texting Cole and asking him to meet her at South Bend.

What if he ignored it? Or worse, said no?

Only one way to find out, and she had to try at least.

She sat on Cheyenne and framed the waterfall through the viewfinder and manually adjusted the focus. She pressed the shutter release button and captured several images of the breaktaking landscape.

Sunshine glazed the frozen ice-blue water surrounded by craggy rocks. Above her, pine branches laden with snow bowed, creating a winter wonderland canopy. Jagged chunks of ice floated where the sun warmed the stream's surface.

Macey nudged Cheyenne forward, then dismounted. She looped horse's reins over a low-hanging branch and edged closer to the stream, balancing on the snowbank.

Stooping low to the ground, she angled her camera to shoot up the waterfall from ground level, hoping to capture the sun's rays kaleidoscoping through the crown of branches.

Cheyenne nickered and raised her head. Macey pushed to her feet and brushed snow off her legs. She turned to see what caused Cheyenne's response.

Her heart slammed against her ribs.

He came.

Raising her camera, she cupped the lens in her left hand as she focused on Cole riding Wyatt's horse, Dante. She snapped several shots of the horse kicking up snow as they drew closer.

How she managed to hold on to her camera, she didn't know. Her heart beat a steady rhythm as her nerves thrummed through her body. He'd either be happy to see her or turn the horse around and race away.

Pulling on Dante's reins, Cole slowed the stallion, then dismounted. He looped the reins around the same branch as Cheyenne's. Dante nuzzled Cheyenne, and Macey snapped a picture of the two.

Cole's dark sunglasses shaded his eyes, so Macey wasn't privy to his expression, but the slight smile on his lips caused her shoulders to relax. Dressed in jeans, boots and a charcoal-colored winter coat, he stuffed a hand in his front pocket as he ambled toward her.

She resisted smoothing down the tangles from the wind dancing through her hair. "Hey. I wasn't so sure you'd come."

"A guy would be foolish to resist."

His rich tones flowed over her, sparking hope in her chest. "If the weather was nicer, I would've suggested a picnic, but I really don't want to sit on the frozen ground." She walked past him and retrieved a thermos and two travel mugs from her backpack, then faced him again. "However, I did bring hot cocoa. Want some?"

"Sure, sounds great." He smiled at her, then turned back to the water. "Beautiful spot."

"It's my happy place."

"I can see why. It's so peaceful. The rushing water is like nature's symphony." Then he laughed sort of under his breath and shook his head. "Man, that sounded cheesy."

"Cheesy or not, I liked it." She pulled off her mittens and shoved them into her pockets.

The cap wouldn't budge. She tucked it under her arm and twisted with all her strength, but the cap wouldn't budget. Leaning against Cheyenne, she lowered her chin and shook her head. "I can't do this. This is ridiculous."

"What is?"

She waved a finger between them. "This. You and me."

"We're ridiculous?"

"Not we. Me. I'm shaking so much I can't even open this stupid thermos."

Cole moved toward her, took the thermos and set it on the ground. Then he sandwiched her chilly fingers between his warm hands. "What's going on, Macey?"

As if this moment couldn't be humiliating enough, tears welled in her eyes and slid down her cheeks before she could even get her emotions in check. "I'm an idiot, that's what's going on. I imagined this romantic moment of drinking hot cocoa at my favorite spot so I could tell you I was so sorry about what happened at the ball and thank you for saving my family's land and try and figure out where we stood with each other. But now I just feel like there's this giant ball of uncertainty in my stomach and maybe coming here was actually a mistake."

Cole traced the trail of tears with the pad of his thumb. "Macey, breathe."

She pulled her hand free, snatched her mitten out of her pocket and pressed it against her eyes. "Sorry. It's been a whirlwind the past couple of days."

"Well, the good news is, I'm here. And I'm not going anywhere. So relax and tell me what's going on."

Pulling in a deep breath, Macey exhaled, emptying her lungs and pushing out the pent-up anxiety that kept her tossing and turning for the past few nights. She wiped her eyes one final time, then pocketed the mitten once again.

Squaring her jaw, she looked at Cole. His blue eyes shimmered with kindness and the gentle way his thumb stroked her knuckles gave her the courage she needed to express what was in her heart. "I like you, Cole. A lot. No, that's not true." She shook her head.

He frowned. "You don't like me?"

She shook her head, then nodded. She was botching this. "No, I mean, I do like you. A lot. I love you, in fact. There, I said it. I love you."

His lips widened slowly until a grin stretched across his face. He moved closer until he grasped her elbows. His face was so close she could see the flecks of navy in his eyes. "I'm so glad to hear you like me. I'm even happier to know you love me. I love you, too, Macey."

She sighed and pressed her forehead against his. "I wasn't sure how you felt since things fell apart during the ball. I'm so sorry for not listening to you. I was being selfish. After the way your uncle treated you, I didn't need to be a jerk too."

"No, I get it. I planned to tell you everything after the ball. I wanted a perfect evening, but my uncle's unexpected entrance ruined it. But now—just so we're clear…"

He came closer and touched his lips to hers. Her arms looped around his neck as she leaned into him.

Her anxiety melted away like the spring thaw. She pulled back and rested her head on his shoulder as his arms tightened around her. Then she looked up at him. "I need to tell you something else."

"What else could be better than hearing that you love me?" He cupped his hand around her cheek.

"Don't get mad, but I talked to Wyatt. He's the one who gave me the courage I needed to reach out to you. He said you were out of work right now. I'm so sorry about that, but I'm glad you're not working for your uncle anymore. He's not good for you. I know he's family, but he takes advantage of you. I also wanted you to know—I never have and I never will consider you a charity case. You're one of the strongest men I know, and I'm so proud of you."

"Thank you, Macey. You have no idea what your words mean to me. And I'm not mad at your brother. I'm glad you contacted me. I planned to reach out to you, but I've been packing. The sooner Lexi and I are out of the condo, the quicker we'll be away from my uncle. I'm learning family isn't just through blood but also through love." The wind picked up, ruffling his hair as his eyes turned serious. "I need to tell you something as well, and it may not be what you want to hear."

Macey's stomach sank. He said he loved her, right? She hadn't imagined that.

Whatever he had to say, they'd get through it. Together.

THE LOOK OF panic on Macey's face had him wishing he could take back his words.

Cole blew out a breath and dragged a hand over his face.

He entwined his fingers through Macey's and gave her hands a gentle squeeze. Then he drew her close and rested his chin on the top of her head. "I meant what I said—I do love you. And I want to see where this goes."

She pulled back. "But?"

"Wyatt invited me to his men's group, and I went last night. Good group of guys. In fact, Heath Walker attends. After losing his ranch, he became a contractor who started his own business. We talked after the meeting, and he invited me to meet him for breakfast. I met with him this morning."

"How'd it go?"

"It went well. We talked about my experience with Crawford Developments, and he offered me the position of being his project manager. He's a small company with a handful of employees, including one of my former foremen. His previous manager just got married and moved away, leaving a hole he needed to fill right away. He's starting a new job of building affordable housing."

Macey's eyes widened as her hands flew to her mouth. "Cole, that's amazing. Congratulations! I'm so excited for you. You'll be doing exactly what you had dreamed."

He nodded, his jaw tight. "Man, I wish we'd talked yesterday instead of now."

"Why's that?"

"He wants me to oversee the rest of his main job in Durango before we begin building the housing here in Aspen Ridge. The time frame is to have it finished within the next four months."

"Are you moving to Durango?"

He lifted a shoulder. "I'm not sure yet. Either I commute nearly an hour or else I find temporary housing in the city."

"How do you feel about that?"

"I don't mind the city. I just don't want to live there. I love Aspen Ridge, and I want to raise Lexi here. But this job sounds amazing. He offers solid benefits—even better than the ones Wallace offered me."

"I see." Macey bit her lip and toed the snow with the tip of her boot. Then she lifted her eyes. "My dad says it's all about trusting God even when we don't know what's going to happen." She paused and waved a finger between them. "You and me. We're going to work. I know it in my heart. We have some details to figure out. To be honest, I'm not so sure what I want to do with the rest of my life. I just know I want you and Lexi to be a part of it. So if we have to do the long-distance thing for a few months, then I'm game if you are. But if you want to commute, I'm more than willing to help care for Lexi."

Cole's shoulders sagged. He reached for Macey's arms and drew her close to him. He rested his forehead against hers. "I'm so glad to hear you say that. I'm not exactly sure what the next few months will hold, but I do know I want you to be a part of them too."

She stood on tiptoes and brushed a kiss across his lips. "I love you."

"I love you too. And nothing will ever change that." He pressed a kiss to her lips. Taking her hands, he knelt in front of her, snow dampening his knee. "I've known you most of my life, Macey. Even though we haven't even gone on a real date yet, I know I want to spend the rest of my life with you." He pulled a rose-colored velvet box out of his front jeans pocket and opened the lid. "Will you marry me?"

Her hand flew to her mouth as her eyes shimmered. She held out shaky fingers as he lifted the sparkling solitaire from the satin bed and slid it onto her finger.

Perfect fit.

But he had no doubts.

Pushing to his feet, he wrapped her in his arms, lifting her off the ground. "Macey Stone, I promise to stand up for you and spend the rest of my life showing you how much I love you."

"I love you, too, Cole…" She leaned back and gripped his biceps. "I promise to be the one you can lean on. I will be the best mom I can to Lexi…and any other children in our future."

"I like the sound of that." Cole brushed a kiss on her lips.

Macey touched the diamond he'd slid on her finger. "This is the most perfect ring. I can't believe you had it with you. Confident much?"

He laughed, took her hands and kissed her knuckles, then gave them a gentle squeeze. "Actually, I didn't buy that ring. It belonged to my mom. Even though my parents' marriage was cut short by my dad's death, they loved each other very much. When my first wife and I decided to get married, I didn't even consider it for her. Didn't seem like the right fit—maybe that should've told me something. But after I saw you walk down the stairs at your parents' house the night of the ball, I knew you were the one to wear my mother's wedding ring."

Macey cupped his cheek. "Thank you. I will cherish it."

"And I will cherish you." Cole drew her back into his embrace and knew exactly where he belonged—in Macey's arms.

EPILOGUE

It wasn't that Macey didn't think this day would ever come, but the fact that she was about to marry Cole was more than a dream come true. No matter how cliché it sounded.

Eight months after driving home in that snowstorm, Macey wore her grandmother's wedding dress, which had been altered and updated, and her mother's veil as she clutched her bouquet of wildflowers in one hand and curled her other into the crook of her father's elbow.

Sunlight glinted off the waterfall splashing into the river behind Cole where he stood looking dashing in his light gray suit with her two brothers.

Dressed in shades of soft green, Everly and Mallory, who was finally stateside and able to take leave, preceded her down the makeshift aisle under the grove of lush green trees in full bloom. Lexi and Mia tossed handfuls of flowers as Tanner trailed behind them, looking very bored.

Her eyes connected with Cole's as she forced herself to take steady steps in time to the music. Surrounded by family and a handful of friends, Macey didn't even try to stop the tears that slid out the corners of her eyes. Once she reached Cole, he thumbed them away, then took her hand in his.

For the next fifteen minutes, she tried to focus on the pastor's words, wanting to remember every one. She recited her vows, promising to love, honor and cherish the man standing in front of her. He did the same, then slid the simple wedding band onto her finger.

"By the power vested in me by the state of Colorado, I now pronounce you husband and wife. Cole, you may kiss your bride."

"About time." Cole grinned, then his eyes darkened as he cradled Macey's face in his warm hands. They kissed and sealed their future together.

Then, he touched his forehead to hers. "I love you, Mrs. Crawford."

"I love you too, Mr. Crawford."

A slight tug on her gown pulled Macey's attention away from the man who had stolen her heart. She looked down at Lexi, who wore a cream-colored dress with a lavender tulle skirt. Macey crouched and twirled her finger around one of the ringlets framing Lexi's face. "You look like a fairy princess, Lexi Jane."

She flung her arms around Macey's neck. "You need to teach Daddy how to say my name. He still doesn't get it right."

Still holding on to her new daughter, Macey laughed and looked up at her husband. She shot him a wink. "My pleasure."

"Macey?"

"Yes, sweetheart?"

"Since you married my daddy, does that make you my new mommy?"

Tears warmed the backs of Macey's eyes as she pushed through the thickening in her throat. "Would you like me to be your new mommy?"

Lexi nodded, her smile lighting up her face. "I would like that so much. My daddy is too big for me to take care of all by myself."

Macey pulled the child into her arms, her heart swelling three times its size. "How about we take care of him together?"

"Good idea. Can I call you Mommy?"

Not trusting her voice, Macey nodded, then

cast a glance at Cole who brushed his thumb and forefinger over his eyes.

"Yay, I love you, Mommy." Lexi threw her arms around Macey's neck.

"I love you too, princess." Holding on to Lexi's hand, she stood and leaned her head against Cole's shoulder. "If it's okay with you, we need to look into filing paperwork so I can adopt Lexi legally."

Cole dropped a kiss on the top of Macey's head. "It's more than okay with me."

Holding hands, Macey's parents walked up to the three of them. Mom kissed her cheek. "I've said it already, but I'll say it again, you are so beautiful, honey."

"Thanks, Mom. And thank you for loaning me your pearls." Macey fingered the strand of pearls draped around her neck.

"Actually, those were not mine."

"Really? Then where did they come from."

"They belonged to your grandma. Your grandpa had given them to her as a wedding gift. She had given them to Lynetta to wear at her wedding, then Lynetta loaned them to me when I married your dad. She told me to hold on to them until one of you girls got married."

"I loved having a little bit of Grandma and

Grandpa with us today. Thank you for allowing us to get married at South Bend."

Dad pulled an envelope from his inside jacket pocket. "Speaking of South Bend—today seems like the best time as any to give this to you."

"What's this?" Her eyes volleyed between them as she took it.

"Open it."

Macey looked at Cole, then slid a manicured nail under the glue flap. She pulled out an official looking letter, scanned it, then gasped. Her hand flew to her mouth. "Are you serious?"

"Absolutely."

Cole frowned. "What's going on?"

Macey handed him the paper, and he read it. "Wow, is this for real?"

Dad chuckled. "You two are a couple of doubters, aren't you?"

"More like overwhelmed."

Dad squeezed her hand lightly. "You've always loved South Bend, so today seemed like the perfect day to give it to you. Take over the old homestead or tear it down and build something new in its place. It's now yours to do as you wish." He lowered his head and whispered in her ear. "Don't worry about your brothers and sisters. They'll get their share in due time."

Tears washed her eyes for like the hundredth time since waking up that morning. "I don't know what to say."

"How about thank you?"

Macey laughed through a blurry haze. "Thank you both. I love you guys. So much."

They pulled her in for a group hug. "We love you too. All three of you." Mom cupped Lexi's face in her hands. "I'm so excited to have another granddaughter."

Bear ambled over to them, hands in his pockets. "Hey, I hate to break up this hugfest, but the photographer needs the bride and groom if we're to get these pictures going."

Lexi ran ahead with Mia and Tanner. Macey and Cole followed them to the archway where they'd exchanged vows moments ago.

The photographer positioned Macey's family around her. As Cole squeezed her hand, she smiled through another sheen of tears.

She had everything she always wanted—a beautiful daughter, a place to call home and a husband who not only rescued her ranch but also rescued her heart.

★ ★ ★ ★ ★

WESTERN

Rugged men looking for love...

Available Next Month

Winning Her Fortune Heatherly Bell
Hometown Reunion Christine Rimmer

....

The Lawman's Surprise Catherine Mann
The Cowboy Next Door Cheryl Harper

....

For The Rancher's Baby Stella Bagwell
His Wyoming Redemption Trish Milburn

....

LOVE INSPIRED

The Bronc Rider's Twins Danica Favorite
Bound By A Secret Jolene Navarro

Larger Print

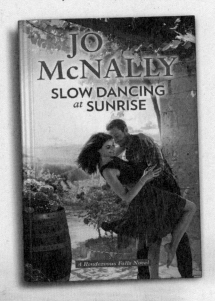

LET'S TALK ABOUT BOOKS!

JOIN THE CONVERSATION

MILLSANDBOON
AUSTRALIA

@MILLSANDBOONAUS

ESCAPE THE EVERY DAY AT
MILLSANDBOON.COM.AU